SOLSTICE

BOOK I OF THE ALESSANDRA LEGACY TRILOGY

K. W. KEITH

For Tufton

ACKNOWLEDGMENTS

To Justin, who didn't realize he'd married an author but graciously shared me with these characters anyway.

To Lee and Shirley, for believing in their little girl even though they can't read her handwriting.

To the RHoSC, ladies who are extensions of my own heart.

To Iesha and her book club of well-read women, who gave me more than the blurb critique I'd asked for.

To Bill, my own personal advisor on PIT maneuvers and one talented photographer.

To Claire, whose unflagging enthusiasm brought light in my darkest hours.

To Lesbollah and Embolism, for squashing every typo and pulling no punches the way only sisters can.

To Melissa, for listening. Daily.

To everyone who's cheered me on and kicked my ass. You know who you are.

And lastly, to Quinn. There aren't words.

solstice \\'sōl-stəs\\

Mid Eng > Old Fr > Latin, *sol* (sun) and *sistere* (to stand still) n. An astronomical event that occurs twice each year when the Sun reaches its highest and lowest annual altitudes in the sky. As seen from Earth, the Sun appears to stop in its path, captured in place for three days, before reversing direction.

CHAPTER ONE

THURSDAY, JULY 23
8:42 A.M.

Lost in thought, Solana Trent tapped on the day's headline with her pencil eraser, the pensive raps falling like rain in the thick silence.

"That hit on John Catello was only the beginning," she said as she battered her article covering the previous day's unresolved shooting. "It just came to my attention that early this morning Anthony Mastriani and Francis Santaglio were also gunned down."

Her declaration hung in the air, which was already warm and dry from the midsummer sun streaming in through her wide office window. "Can you trust your information?" Across her desk, William Donato eyed her over the rim of his coffee cup.

Solana raised her pale green eyes from the paper to her editor-in-chief, detecting the tone of voice that preceded one of his infamous Socratic inquisitions. Noting his cool pokerfaced expression and impassive grey-eyed stare, sharp in contrast to his black hair shocked with white streaks, she understood why so many staffers at the Times found him unsettling. Inscrutable and unrelenting, he demanded concrete answers to question after pointed question, but she enjoyed these analytical volleys that kept her on her toes and fueled her competitive spirit.

"You know I have my sources, Will," she said, prepared for the imminent barrage.

"You've authenticated the intelligence?"

"Through multiple agencies, including the NYPD and the Bureau."

"And why do you believe these homicides are related?"

"Number one, same neighborhood. Mastriani and Santaglio were hit in the Upper East Side, two blocks away from the Catello crime scene. Number two, same time of day. Early morning, estimated between 4:30 and 5:00 a.m. Number three, same weapon. Ballistic fingerprinting suggests a Beretta 92FS 9mm, silenced. Number four, no witnesses - or if there are, no one's talking. Which isn't surprising, given they have the same connection."

"Which is?"

"Number five. They're the head underbosses of the DiStephano crime family."

Donato raised an eyebrow. "*The* head underbosses?"

"Yep. Of the three, Catello was the youngest in tenure, then Mastriani and Santaglio, respectively."

"And let me guess," he ventured. "You aren't satisfied with the theory that this is mob business as usual."

Solana put her pencil down beside the paper with a decisive thwack. "Absolutely not."

Donato nodded, glancing at the pencil she'd laid to rest on her desk. He'd learned to recognize the symbolic meaning of that simple action, a recurring incident every time he cross-examined her. As a rule, he interrogated all of his journalists to help them mold their craft, to make sure they considered all the possibilities before arriving at a final conclusion. He'd discovered that Solana, however, had one of the quickest, most prolific minds he'd ever encountered. She devised, weighed, and discarded numerous theories within minutes - those minutes being the ones in which she unconsciously assaulted the newspaper with her writing implement of choice.

These were the times he needed to question her, to help her direct that rapid-fire thought process and pare down her list of well-considered hypotheses. Whenever that pencil went down he knew she'd formulated her supposition and was about to draw it out for him - and with mob-related cases being her forté, this time he sensed something big.

"So tell me," he said. "What makes you think there's more to this story?"

Solana flipped open one of the numerous dossiers lying across her desk and pivoted it toward Donato so he could see its contents.

"First, think about the targets," she said with solemn fervor, indicating an undated snapshot taken from outside a coffee shop where three men conversed over neglected demitasses of steaming espresso. "Catello, Mastriani, and Santaglio comprised the highest echelon of a crime organization. Like the president of a corporation and his hand-picked C-suite, DiStephano would consider them indispensable. So, for any one of them to turn up dead is surprising alone - that's why Catello's murder yesterday grabbed my attention. But today? *All* of them killed? In order of rank? Within twenty-four hours of each other? It's unheard of. That just doesn't happen.

"Secondly," she continued, snatching another folder, "consider Constantine DiStephano himself." She turned the pages until she reached an eight-by-ten black and white photograph of the distinguished Italian boss as he strode through Central Park, his hair as white as the plume of cigar smoke wafting in his wake.

"He's been the head of his family for thirty-seven years and is most likely considering retirement," she explained. "That means he's been grooming one of these three men as his successor, probably Santaglio, with Mastriani and Catello next in line. Just losing Catello yesterday was a tough blow for him to take, but now that they're all dead? It spells disaster. DiStephano just woke up this morning to find himself without an heir and lacking any others of their capacity in reserve. For all intents and purposes, his empire stands to crumble, and - thirdly - it couldn't have happened at a more interesting time."

"How so?" Donato took another sip of his coffee as she closed the dossier.

"It's no coincidence these three high-profile shootings occurred just in time for tonight's campaign ball for Chandler Kane."

He studied her hard. "That's a bold statement."

"Agreed." Solana sighed and leaned back in her chair, crossing her legs beneath the wide desk. "This is a critical election, Will. Senator Armistead continues to slip in the polls, and the pundits all but confirm Kane is going to oust him. Armistead's pontificating the same tired platform that's gotten him elected and re-elected over the last twenty years, while Kane is fresh blood and has line of sight to the needs of the citizens. He's piqued their interest, especially with the HUD initiatives he's planning for the City. It's an upset for the incumbent and everyone is jockeying for position. New administrations mean new alliances, which in turn require new deals, and I think these murders were deliverables on a contract negotiation. DiStephano wouldn't kill off his own captains. It's possible, of course, but it doesn't make any sense, not where he stands now. My hunch," she said, reaching for another file, "is Mathison's syndicate is behind this."

"You're kidding."

"Think about it," Solana's green eyes sparkled. "For years there's been a turf war between them. When Mathison assumed leadership of his syndicate he was the youngest mob leader in the history of the City, and within two years he's nearly deposed DiStephano from his cushy throne. DiStephano still calls the shots in the gambling, prostitution, and illegal drug arenas, but Mathison's already captured from him the shockingly lucrative strongholds in labor unions, real estate, and construction."

Solana opened the newer, thinner folder on her desk to pick up the small photo she kept neatly paper-clipped to the first page of the file. Rather than pass it over, though, she paused, holding it aloft between her slim fingers to give it a thorough study before sliding it across the desk to her editor-in-chief.

Donato saw the reason for his journalist's hesitation. The little picture made up for its diminutive size by showcasing the persona of its larger-than-life subject, namely the arrestingly handsome Raine Mathison standing beside the open door of a long black limousine. Impeccably dressed in bespoke Armani for some black-tie affair, he'd just stepped out of the car to greet a crowd eager for his attentions yet wisely keeping their distance. The photographer who'd scored this picture wasn't the only one who'd snapped off a shot; other flashbulbs popped brightly in the throng, looking to capture Mathison's powerful air of confident, understated elegance. Donato sensed the boss's potency and influence just by looking through the window of this tiny photo, leaving him to imagine what it must be like to experience the man in person. Solana was right about his age; he appeared to be no older than his early thirties, and –

"Wait a second," he said, snatching the vivid full-color snapshot to get a closer look. Yes. The dark blond waves of his hair contrasted sharply against the black evening sky behind him, and although Mathison wasn't looking directly at the photographer, one could see his eyes were a clear, penetrating blue.

Donato flicked the picture back across her desk to land it on top of the striking man's file. "He's not Italian."

"Perceptive." Solana acknowledged her editor's catch with a sly grin. "Mathison is a Gaelic surname, but rumor has it he's *half* Italian."

"So how did he take over an Italian crime family, then? Wouldn't that raise all hell?"

"Under normal circumstances, yes. But you'd have to understand Nobile Loiacono, the syndicate's former boss. Loiacono never had children, never even got married - he was all business and believed such matters had no place in it. He ran his crime organization like a Fortune 500 company, promoting people based on merit without regard to tenure, rank, or relationship.

"So when Mathison, a business school student, joined the family Loiacono immediately recognized his potential. Intelligent, driven, like-minded, he was a born leader and flew up the ranks as the don's most promising protégé. So when Loiacono vouched for Mathison and selected him as his successor just before he died, it seemed to follow the natural course of business. People trusted Loiacono's judgment, and more importantly, they trusted Mathison, and thus the leadership of the syndicate legitimately passed down to him, despite his contentious genealogy."

"Considering what he's already accomplished, it seems it was a prudent decision on Loiacono's part," Donato observed.

"Turning the labor unions, real estate players, and construction corporations to his side in under two years? It was bound to happen," Solana said. "Mathison's legitimate business is in mergers and acquisitions, which offers his allies plenty of growth and networking opportunity while giving him the ultimate flow-through entity."

She pulled the annual report for Mathison's privately-held corporation from the file, flipped to the balance sheet and income statement, and handed it over to Donato. "Imbrialis Acquisitions posts net earnings in the hundreds of millions, a majority of which is generated by intangibles. It's genius. He began winning labor union allegiances from DiStephano *ab initio*, but the pendulum finally swung to his favor last fall – "

"After Preston's election snafu," Donato finished, a proud smile flashing across his face. As a first-year staffer, Solana's work uncovering that scandal had been commendable by veteran standards, and her exposé had earned her the distinction of being the youngest journalist ever nominated for a Pulitzer. Although she'd ultimately lost out on the Prize, she never let her disappointment hamstring her focus - and that was an accomplishment that impressed him more than the nomination itself. If anything, losing the honor had had the opposite effect on the aspiring reporter: her dedication to the craft burned brighter now than ever before.

"So if memory serves me correctly," Donato recalled, "last year, Everett Preston and Chandler Kane were vying for the republican nomination for this election against Armistead. Preston's platform was a strong one, but Kane's HUD projects were attracting some of the biggest, most influential voting sectors in the City - the labor unions."

Solana nodded. "The battle for union support raged both in public and underground: Preston versus Kane, DiStephano versus Mathison. Preston came to the swift realization he couldn't win without the backing of the unions, while DiStephano still had a significant number of them under his control. Both sensed an opportunity. In exchange for DiStephano's union votes, Preston laundered mob money through his election campaign funds."

"And when you exposed Preston, it left Kane in the clear for the republican candidacy."

"And the unexpected ramification of that?" Solana asked, taking on the questioner's role.

"Mathison wins the rest of the unions."

"Exactly," she smiled. "DiStephano blew it, and the union holdouts realized Mathison knows what he's doing. When the shit hit the fan, Mathison stood only to gain. Which is the number one sign of an intelligent, agile organization - one that's positioned itself in such a way it can take advantage of a fortuitous opportunity at a moment's notice."

"Understood," Donato said. "So how does that fit in with the murders of DiStephano's top henchmen?"

"As people align themselves more closely with Kane as the probable winner of this election, new partnerships will be forming. Carefully, but quickly. Mathison's rapid ascension has not gone unnoticed; I'm sure he's secured several key political alliances already. Furthermore, now that

Mathison controls the labor unions, Kane is going to need him in order to push his HUD proposals through. Many will follow suit, but some may need convincing. *That's where the murders come in.*"

Solana leaned forward in her chair, green eyes aglow. "One of two things is happening here. Either Mathison's killed these guys to further eradicate DiStephano as competition, or he's eliminating embarrassing problems for those politicians he's looking to court before the regime change. I suspect the latter. There's no more fitting time with Kane's campaign ball tonight, and Mathison couldn't have arranged it with more finesse: word on the street is he's actually in Rome this week."

"Perfect alibi," Donato mused. He handed back the annual for Imbrialis and sat silent for a long moment, studying her. He could find no fault in her logic, except for the fact it was one hell of a theory.

But then again, he noted, *following through on theories like this has made her one of the top journalists at the Times by the age of twenty-six.*

"It's possible," he conceded, "but I think you may be reading too much into this."

Solana narrowed her sharp eyes on him as a slow grin became her beautiful features. "But I don't hear you saying I can't look into it."

"You're attending the ball tonight, so I don't see how I can possibly stop you," Donato sighed. "See what you can find out," he said, rising from his chair, "but you know the promises I had to make in order to score these two tickets for us."

"And on such short notice, too," she teased. "Honestly when I asked you for them yesterday I had my doubts, but I have to say, Will, I'm impressed."

"I'm dead serious, Lana," Donato warned. "This is a black-tie, no-press, invitation-only gala, so for Chrissake, be careful and don't piss off anyone important!"

"All right, boss, I got it, I got it!" she laughed. "Now if you're done lecturing me, I need to start drafting my strategy for this evening. Okay?"

He returned her bright, contagious grin. "Okay. I'm in meetings the rest of the damn day, but you come find me if you need anything."

"Roger that," she replied, already writing her outline in longhand on a pad of paper.

Donato made to leave her office, but he no sooner reached the door when one last question appeared in his mind, stopping him in his tracks.

Such an obvious query, too, he wondered. *Why haven't I thought to ask it before now?*

"What is it, Will?" Solana didn't look up from her work, but he could hear the knowing smile in her voice.

"Lana," he said, "how do you know so much about the mob, anyway?"

The sound of hard graphite grinding against note-paper crunched to a halt, and he saw her bite down on her lip to keep that smile from escaping her face.

"Oh, I don't know," she shrugged, raising her eyes to meet his. "Maybe because I'm full-blooded Italian and it interests me?"

Donato stared at her, not appreciating the evasiveness of the comment, yet something in her expression warned him to proceed with caution. "Trent is an Italian name?" he ventured.

"It's a truncation," she stated, then promptly turned her attention back to her notes. "On your way out, Will, would you mind closing the door behind you?"

Donato blinked, feeling rather truncated himself by the abrupt end she'd put to the conversation.

Definitely a story here, he realized as he watched her work, and his editorial mind kicked into gear, already beginning to make suppositions and formulate new questions for her.

But he knew better than to ask them. Any journalist could detect a story, whereas a good journalist respected the delicate process it took to properly uncover it. The profession required a disciplined patience in order to draw out every last detail, and years of experience had taught him when to press a matter and when to let it go - for the time being.

"Sure, Lana," Donato said. "Good luck, then, and I'll see you tonight."

"You bet."

Ꮬ Ꮬ Ꮬ

Solana waited for the sound of the latch clicking home in the strike plate before she flung her pencil down on the desk in frustrated relief.

Jesus. Leaning back in her chair, she closed her eyes and drew a deep, cleansing breath through her nose until her lungs filled to capacity. She held it there for several heartbeats, then let the air out slowly, imagining herself back on her mat during this morning's yoga practice, and after a long moment she felt her calm begin to restore.

Donato had never asked that question before, but she'd known it was only a matter of time until he did. How could he not? Her extensive knowledge in the field of organized crime had landed her within a hair's breadth of the highest honor in the field of journalism, and she knew her boss wondered why it didn't bother her more that she hadn't won the Prize last year.

Her keen eyes flicked to DiStephano's thick file lying like a heavy corpse on the corner of her desk, and she lifted the cover to stare at the photo of the man she'd helped ruin.

For Solana, her work exposing the mob wasn't about the Pulitzer.

It wasn't about the honor of being nominated for one at the tender age of twenty-five.

Nor was it about chasing fame, fortune, or glory.

Sure, that's a nice consequence, she admitted as she closed DiStephano's file, but no. That wasn't what drove her to be the best, the absolute *very* best, at what she did.

It was about settling a score.

An old one, too, aged over twenty years now.

And getting older by the second, Solana thought bitterly. *Unacceptable.*

She took another calming, cathartic breath. She'd chosen this path knowing full-well she'd always have to be at the top of her game, and she'd worked damn hard to get there, giving herself no quarter. Along with the challenge came the many sacrifices that accompanied it, and rather than devote her time to the caprices and wild experiences enjoyed by most young women her age, she lived her life solely for one goal.

She couldn't care less about an accolade.

She wanted to bring down the mob.

It suited her purposes just fine for Donato to think she only had eyes for the Prize. She had her own personal reasons for pursuing these stories - and he didn't need to know them. Regardless of her motivations, the end result would ultimately be the same, and it would be a boon to them both. She'd bring fame, fortune, and glory to the Times, and peace of mind for herself.

All she needed was resolute determination, a sharp pencil, and a long leash from her editor.

It had worked for her with DiStephano - and it would work for her again.

Solana's eyes traveled across her desk, drawn to the absorbing photo of Mathison where it still lay on top of his file after Donato's review. She took it up in her fingers for the second time that morning, appreciating its existence as the only shot she had of him - and most likely the only one she'd ever get. Mathison wasn't big on the press; this was one of the few photos of him that existed in circulation, and she'd only managed to acquire it from one of her informants.

By now she must have studied it dozens of times, but that first glance never failed to take her by surprise. He was power incarnate, and she could see how easily someone might be captivated by that galvanizing charm of his that came across so clearly in just this little picture.

"You're next on my agenda, sir," she warned him out loud. "One slip and you're mine."

CHAPTER TWO

9:27 P.M.

As the black stretch Lincoln cruised down 5th Avenue, Solana looked out across Central Park to its southwestern tip, where the twin glass towers of the Time Warner Center soared with aloof majesty, their glowing white crowns bright against the dark veil of the night sky. There, on the 36th floor of the northern skyscraper, Kane's gala event was already in full swing at the Mandarin Oriental, and her excitement swelled at the sight of her destination gleaming in the distance.

It wasn't the ball itself that enthralled her, but the enticing scent of a story, hidden behind the smiles and handshakes of high society. New York's finest would come out tonight to show their support for Kane and further establish their positions within his platform. If her hunch was right, if Mathison was the link between Kane's campaign and the murders of DiStephano's marshals, the one who called the hits would no doubt be present.

Traffic thickened over 60th to become a tributary of aggressive yellow cabs and swank luxury cars flowing into the tumultuous gorge of Central Park South. The half-mile chasm of West 59th was a roiling torrent of red tail-lights, ubiquitous horns, and glinting chrome rims all the way into Columbus Circle, and Solana appreciated Donato's insistence on sending her to the ball in a limousine from her apartment in the Upper East Side.

Sitting back into the comfortable leather seat, she took advantage of the opportunity to focus her energies, knowing the evening's task would be a challenging one. She'd learned from her previous experience with the DiStephano/Preston debacle that the City's power elite was a heavily guarded class, acutely skilled in protecting their secrets behind the social masks they wore. Open conversation seldom yielded any real insight into their private agendas; it was the non-verbal cues she'd learned to identify that proved infinitely more fruitful. The psychological analysis of an averted look, an unconscious fidget, a dance around a pointed question, an unnatural changing of the subject, or a cagey response often betrayed the information she sought, despite the seasoned attempts to conceal or deny it. She expected another such intoxicating, intellectual game lay in wait for her tonight, and she eagerly anticipated the contest.

After navigating the grid of one-way streets to the hotel's entrance on West 60th, the Lincoln joined the long queue of cars lining the bustling thoroughfare between Broadway and 9th. Antsy, Solana watched from the edge of her seat as she waited her turn to get out of the car, those final seconds of the trip seeming to stretch as long as her limo.

At last, the Towncar glided to a stop beneath the flag

bearing the Mandarin Oriental's trademark fan, and she beamed at the receiving valet who opened her door.

"Good evening, Miss," he said automatically as he offered her his white-gloved hand.

"Thank you, sir." Accepting his help, Solana stepped out of the car onto a vibrant red carpet, and once outside she breathed an energizing lungful of the hot, electric evening air. "Beautiful night, isn't it?"

"Yes, Miss," he answered, perfectly politic.

Solana dropped her voice to a more conspiratorial tone. "Not so much fun, though, for you gents, I bet. You've probably been busting your asses out here tonight."

His professional reserve broke in a genuine smile.

"Nonstop action," he admitted.

"And in this heat, I'm sure it's no picnic."

"Could be better, could be worse," he replied as he personally walked her to the door. "You're attending this evening's fundraiser for Mr. Kane?"

She laughed. "Is it that obvious?"

"Well, the gown helps - he's the only black-tie event on site tonight and you've certainly dressed the part," he grinned. "Have you been to the Mandarin before?"

"I haven't, no."

"Then welcome. Allow me to get this door for you, then follow straight across the lobby to the elevator banks just there. The ballroom is on the 36th floor."

"Sounds easy enough."

"It is. If you get lost on your way there, though, please don't hesitate to ask for me. I'm the only Alex here."

"I see," she smiled her appreciation of his kind attentions. "Thank you, Alex."

"My pleasure, Miss," he nodded, and Solana could tell he meant it. "Enjoy your evening."

Following Alex's directions, she swept across the magnificent lobby and boarded the indicated lift. It whisked her high above the City with astonishing speed, and when the doors opened to the foyer of the pillarless ballroom, she was met with panoramic vistas of the iconic Manhattan skyline towering over the treetops of Central Park.

"Welcome, Miss," said one of the tuxedoed gentlemen manning the broad doors. "Your invitation, please?"

She proudly handed him her envelope. "Of course. Solana Trent, under William Donato."

While she waited for him to check her credentials, Solana caught sight of her reflection in a large mirror and smiled in approval. *Not bad for a country girl*, she grinned.

"Yes, Miss Trent, you're all set. Thank you for coming out to support Mr. Kane this evening."

She winked at him. "Wouldn't miss it," she replied, and at last she entered the warmly lit room.

People who knew her waved their hellos, and while she acknowledged each greeting with a nod in return, she was oblivious to the many stares she received. She knew she was pretty enough, but the truth of the matter was that most people put Solana Trent in the breathtaking category. They found themselves captivated by a young woman who was every bit the scintillating, sophisticated Manhattanite, but possessed of the refined beauty and grace reminiscent of an Italian princess.

She'd swept her thick, dark russet mane of voluminous curls atop her head, drawing attention to her long graceful neck and the delicate sharpness of her petite, striking face. Her lush thicket of dark lashes accentuated the lightness of her mint green eyes, brilliant and glittering over chevron cheekbones colored with anticipation. Her smooth, flawless olive skin had drunk deeply of the summer sun, taking on a becoming warm glow against the elegant black silk evening gown that shimmered in a dark river down her perfect figure. The high neckline of the sultry Valentino followed along her collarbone, then drew over her shoulders to plunge dramatically in a wide V down to the small of her bare back. The fitted dress emphasized her tiny waist and the curves of her backside, where the sumptuous material pleated and dropped behind her in a fishtail hem with a modest train.

She'd chosen a Tiffany Lace necklace to compliment her gown; three rows of diamonds sparkled against her throat, encircled her neck and hung down the length of her nape. Bright white against the tan of her skin, it proudly suspended over the expanse of her back so generously revealed by the flattering cut of the dress. Matching diamond earrings and three-row bracelet completed the ensemble, and the finishing touch was a trace of Tom Ford Black Orchid, her spicy and sensuous signature fragrance. Enchanting and stately, she'd garnered the guests' attention, and it was her objective to observe and meet with as many of them as possible.

The crowded ballroom radiated wall-to-wall exuberance, the air charged with the prospect of victory in November. As she accepted a chilled flute of Cristal from a passing waiter, Solana noted the attendance of prominent socialites and politicians alike. Judges, attorneys, CEOs, powerful influencers fueling the engine of the campaign conversed over cocktails, sparkling in the low light. She paid particular attention to the labor union leaders, AFL-CIO reps, real estate tycoons, zoning officers, registers of deeds, public works directors - all supporters who would play key roles in implementing Kane's HUD initiatives should he take the election.

At the back of the room, she spotted Chandler Kane himself, smiling brightly as he talked with Police Commissioner Andalus and several FDNY chiefs. She sighed, knowing it would take some time before she'd manage to get a word with Kane this evening.

During the one meeting she'd ever had with him she'd discovered that part of his charm as a politician was his genuine interest in people. His conversations were more like in-depth interviews, a chance for him to associate citizens' names with faces and to understand their stories and concerns. This valuable insight enabled him to identify common trends and incorporate them into his proposed plans for the City, and his resulting platform proved he'd heard the *vox populi* loud and clear. Tonight he'd spend his time in similar study of his constituency, and even though it would be difficult, she preferred to catch him alone, perhaps when he moved on as he made his rounds –

"Might it be the dazzling Solana Trent, fashionably late as per usual?"

Game on, she thought as she turned her head to see Alistair Prince taking the last few steps across the floor towards her.

"How little credit you give me, Al," she called back in retort, smiling as the Assistant DA reached for her hand and kissed it in greeting. "You should know by now it's part of my brilliant strategy."

"And what's that?"

"I can never get information out of any of you," she replied, "until you get some champagne *into* you."

Alistair laughed heartily. "Turnabout is fair play."

"How've you been, Al?" Solana thought back to the last time she'd seen him. It had been the end of March, just after the State lost its case against Constantine Di-Stephano. DA Lee had brought him up on money laundering charges in the wake of the election scandal, but still the boss walked, despite the preponderance of evidence against him. As the journalist who'd blown the whistle, she'd worked closely with the DA's office throughout the entire prosecution, and the camaraderie she and Alistair shared was instant.

They'd spent many a late night together in City Hall poring over the evidence she'd uncovered, then swapping war stories over boxes of Chinese takeout. Then, when the State called her as a witness, he'd trained her to weather the opposition's intense cross-examination by role-playing it with her multiple times. The young ADA was relentless, throwing curve-balls, putting words in her mouth, asking leading questions, trying anything to make her stumble. She'd passed every test, but the way he'd broken her was a hilarious, spot-on impression of DiStephano's hawk-nosed attorney that left her breathless with laughter. When she'd told him the tale of how she'd managed to get ahold of Preston's financial records - the *coup de main* had involved a disguise and a meat freezer - it was his turn to sit in stitches.

They'd found laughter together during those trying times... and then shared their sorrows over the jury's devastating verdict.

The cavernous courtroom had been standing room only on that late spring afternoon. Solana could still feel the suffocating press of so many people, still see the flashbulbs reporting like lightning while the envelope passed from the jury box to the bench. She remembered how her heart had lodged itself in her throat when the judge opened the page with the verdict, and then the strength of

Al's hand when he'd reached over the bar separating her in the front row of the gallery from him and the State's team.

Chaos had erupted in the courtroom while the judge read off the same two words for every charge listed against DiStephano, and she'd never forget the look on Al's face when he'd turned to her, his expression the mirror image of her own while the world went to hell around them. Everyone in the house leapt to their feet; most stamped and shouted, others rallied and rejoiced, but they could only sit riveted to their seats, reaching over the banister to each other as the only sane people in a place gone mad.

While DA Lee fed the State's official statement to the clamoring press on the courthouse steps, Al somehow found an alternate way to get them out of there, away from the cornering news hounds and their invasive microphones. Dumbstruck, the voice of the Times and the defender of New York would make no comment on the matter; they only focused on putting as much distance between themselves and the courtroom as possible. They walked together like zombies for endless blocks, hours passing unnoticed, and before they knew it they'd made it all the way to Central Park, just in time for the evening papers to hit the stands on the sidewalk.

When Al spotted the night's edition of the New York Post, he halted in midstride, bringing Solana up short beside him.

Back in the courtroom, some enterprising journalist from Solana's rival paper had snapped a picture worth a thousand words. But the front page wasn't DiStephano or his golden defense team. Instead, it was their faces bent together in soul-crushing defeat, their foreheads touching over their clasped hands across the wooden bar that had separated them.

Finding herself on the other side of the camera lens, the cool impartiality of the reporter's caption catapulted Solana from her numbness. *Assistant DA Alistair Prince and investigative journalist A. Solana Trent react to today's verdict in favor of alleged mobster Constantine DiStephano.*

It made it real. After their countless hours of work, after the stacks of evidence they'd amassed, the system had ultimately failed them.

"I'm sorry, Solana," Al had said, squeezing the hand he'd held since the verdict came down from the bench.

"We did everything right, Al," she'd answered, shaking her head. "I just don't... "

And when she broke down right there on the bustling sidewalk he'd pulled her into his arms, knowing exactly what she couldn't bear to say.

Rattled by the injustice, heartbroken with frustration, angry to the point of tears, they'd found solace in each other that night, seeking truth in the one other person who'd walked each step of that hard, fruitless journey.

Afterwards, the ADA had expressed an interest in cultivating an official relationship, which was a proposition the journalist politely declined. While Solana enjoyed spending time with Al, even though he had so much to offer her, she just didn't have room in her life for him, not with the goals she'd set for herself. The simple fact that DiStephano had walked meant she hadn't worked hard enough, and she couldn't afford to let that happen again. She'd have to redouble her efforts, focus even more on her work, and it wouldn't have been fair to him. She'd told him exactly why she was turning him down, and although he'd accepted her response gracefully, it had made for an amicable, yet definite, parting.

It was good to see him smiling again.

"I've been surprisingly well after your brutal rejection four months ago," Al quipped, his dark eyes twinkling. "For which I suppose I should thank you, otherwise I may not have had the opportunity to develop my relationship with Sarah."

"A princess to your Prince?" Solana grinned.

"Always so clever with your words, Solana," he purred in appreciation of her quick wit. "Yes, we're engaged to be married this Christmas, up in Whistler. But enough about me; tell me about you. Have you met your match, or are you still breaking the heart of every eligible bachelor in Manhattan?"

"Just the eligible bachelors?" she teased. "I must be losing my touch."

"Hardly," Al murmured, remembering full-well just how good her touch had been. "But I have to tell you, Solana, I understand what you were talking about back in March. You were right. If work for you is anything like it is for me, it's amazing I have time for anything else. I'm sure you know we've had several tough wins since the DiStephano disaster, and similarly I believe congratulations are in order for *you*, Ms. Pulitzer Nominee."

Solana smiled her thanks before taking advantage of the change in subject. "It's interesting, isn't it, how the spheres have managed to right themselves after DiStephano's acquittal?"

Al raised an eyebrow. "Waxing Shakespearean may be taking it a step too far. How do you mean?"

He'd taken the bait, and she chose her next words carefully. "Don't you think the recent events concerning DiStephano's interests are the quintessential examples of poetic justice?"

"Ah, I see," her friend grinned, but Solana noticed the

light didn't touch his eyes. After all the time they'd spent together, she knew him well enough to discern a true smile from a forced one. "We didn't get the conviction, but as the saying goes, give them enough rope and they'll hang themselves."

Rather than show her suspicions to the contrary, she decided to follow him down the road that this was simply mob business running its course. "Seems like a perfect opportunity to drag DiStephano back on the stand," she observed. "Do you know if the DA plans on pursuing an indictment?"

"We're building our case again," he offered. "We never stopped, of course, but Lee wants something concrete before we go once more into the breach."

It doesn't get much more concrete than this, dear, Solana thought, but nodded her assent. "I see. If I can help you in any way, please let me know."

Al's dark eyes didn't move from hers as he stepped closer to her.

"I read your piece on Catello this morning and look forward to the sequel on the others tomorrow," he said, lowering his voice. "But if you find anything you *can't* print, Solana, I trust you'll keep me posted?"

"Of course, Al," she told him. "Where would I be without my partner in crime?"

His answering smile glowed soft and warm. "Good."

He looked up then, back toward the center of the room from where he'd ventured in order to meet her, and returned his intense gaze down to hers.

"Come on, Solana," Al said, taking her elbow in his hand. "There are some people I think you should meet."

Something about the urgency in his voice convinced her to follow his lead into the midst of the crowd. As he drew her toward the heart of the grand ballroom, she saw she had a better vantage of Kane, who'd moved on from Commissioner Andalus and the fire chiefs to now field DA Lee's questions. Whomever Al was taking her to meet, their location in the room couldn't be better, but when he slowed his pace and she realized which group they were approaching, she recognized the reason at once. Of all the people here, these were the three who would need to know Kane's position at all times.

"Sarah, darling," Al beamed, "I'd like you to meet Solana Trent."

His new fiancée was Sarah Adriaan, Chandler Kane's campaign manager.

Her two companions were Russ Aio, Kane's press secretary, and Donovan Hawes, Kane's attorney.

The tall, chic blond woman smiled and held out her hand. "So nice to meet you, Ms. Trent."

"Likewise, Ms. Adriaan," Solana replied, joining her in a firm handshake before Al could even open his mouth for the other half of the proper introduction.

Sarah noted Solana's catch and her smile grew broader. "Photographic memory?"

"Part of the job description."

"I can imagine," Sarah said before turning to Aio and Hawes. "Russ, Donovan, this is Solana Trent. And trust me," she added, her respect evident in her voice, "she already knows who you are."

Solana nodded to each man respectively. "Mr. Aio, Mr. Hawes, it's a pleasure."

The two gentlemen returned her pleasantries in spite of their obvious bewilderment.

"Ms. Trent is a journalist for the Times," Al explained. "She – "

"You wrote the exposé on Preston last fall," Aio finished, and his initial surprise gave way to amiable warmth.

Leave it to the press secretary to come up with it first, Solana noted with pride, recognizing the requisite quickness in another member of her field. "Yes, sir."

"Well done indeed," Hawes agreed, and the change in his demeanor was equally marked. "In many respects this campaign owes a lot to you, Ms. Trent."

"I thank you for that," Solana replied, "but the truth will always come out, Mr. Hawes. In this case, I just happened to be the messenger."

Sarah held up her champagne glass in a toast. "Here's to one hell of a message, then."

"Hear, hear." Al seconded the motion, and they all sipped their cocktails in unison.

"So," Aio ventured, passing his empty flute back and forth between his hands, "what stories are you chasing down these days, Ms. Trent?"

"Just one, actually," Solana declared. "As of yesterday morning, the unexpected activity in DiStephano's circle has sparked an interesting, more pressing, investigation that's taken precedence over my other work."

The press secretary seemed to expect her answer. "I bet it would. Compared to last year's fiasco, though, it must be refreshing to pursue such a cut-and-dried case."

Solana hid her surprise at the blatant deflection. "That remains to be seen, but I hope it's as uncomplicated as you say, Mr. Aio."

"Ms. Trent," Hawes interjected. "Have you had the opportunity to meet with Mr. Kane yet this evening?"

Why did he ask that? Just to get us off the subject? If so, why would he put Kane in front of me? Bemused, Solana glanced past the attorney to find his client still quite engaged in animated colloquy with DA Lee. "Actually, no," she informed him. "I haven't."

"Let me see if I can rectify that," Hawes offered. "Even though he's somewhat tied up right now, I'm sure he'd enjoy talking with you."

"I'd take that as a kindness, Mr. Hawes, thank you," she said, and while she watched him take leave of the group she happened to spot Will Donato heading in her direction from the back of the room.

Having caught her gaze, he stopped and beckoned discreetly to her, and she lowered her hand to her side, extending her index finger to let him know she needed a minute. She looked back to watch Hawes approach Kane and Lee, saw the attorney join their lively chat, and from the look of things she expected it would be at least several minutes before any meeting with Kane.

"Al, Ms. Adriaan, Mr. Aio, excuse me for a moment, please," Solana said, and they pardoned her leave as she made her way to her editor.

She gladly accepted the fresh flute of champagne he held out to her when she met him toward the rear of the ballroom.

"Nothing like starting with the high rollers," Donato quipped.

"The stakes are about to get higher. Hawes is attempting to orchestrate a meeting between me and Kane."

"That shouldn't be too difficult; he's already expressed interest in seeing you tonight."

"You've talked with him?"

"When I first arrived I happened to catch him," he explained. "He was making a bee line for Judge Nguyen, who'd only stopped by before catching his red eye to L.A. Kane made his apologies and intends to catch up later, but he remembered you and specifically asked if you were attending this evening."

"Strange, he should *know* - he approved the final guest list."

"Yes, but that doesn't mean you're coming. Schedules change, Lana."

"True." She pursed her lips while she thought for a second. "Did you get a read on him when he asked you? Did anything seem out of the ordinary?"

"Given the brevity of our limited exchange I didn't get much from it, but hopefully you'll have the chance to ascertain that for yourself." Donato glanced over to Hawes where he spoke in close conference with Kane, having managed a word in edgewise. "How's it been going for you so far? Have you been able to discover anything?"

Solana sighed. "Allusions to the DiStephano murders generate rather curious reactions, but other than that I haven't gotten much of anything from anyone."

"Which I'm sure tells you something."

"Or nothing," she frowned, "but the night is still young."

Suddenly, Donato's sharp grey eyes shot over her head. "Yes, it is," he mused, his open expression hardening as he stared at something in the distance behind her. The intensity in his tone made her turn to follow his gaze toward the door of the ballroom - and her pulse quickened when she saw who had captured the attention of her editor, as well as the majority of the room.

Rumor had always been that Raine Mathison was an impressive figure, but now seeing him in the flesh for the first time, Solana found the word too weak to describe him. Watching him show his invitation at the door and graciously nod his thanks to the gentleman who accepted it, she saw that the tiny photograph she kept on h̄ this man utterly failed to convey the presence he comᵢ manded.

He personified the ancient Greek descriptions of Apollo, tall and broad-shouldered, with strong, aristocratic features and a crown of thick, dark blond waves highlighted by the intense summer sun. Although he wore tailored black Gianni Campagna cut perfectly for his well-built muscular frame, his ultimate sartorial asset was his cool, sophisticated confidence that managed to mesmerize her from clear across the ballroom.

An undeniable power emanated from him; it was part of him, in every move, barely held in check as he strode into the room. Many deferred to that sense of dominance, giving the man his space. But then there were those who were drawn to that power, wooed by it, and only seconds passed before half a dozen businessmen were engaging him in conversation as the accomplished, magnetically charismatic CEO of Imbrialis Acquisitions.

"Unbelievable," Solana managed to whisper to Donato next to her. She wasn't sure what she found more shocking - the sudden twist in the evening's event, or her own frighteningly immediate attraction to him.

"Quite the unexpected appearance," her editor concurred.

"And not exactly unwelcome."

"Agreed," he said, also taking note of Mathison's warm reception. "So much for him being in Rome this week."

She couldn't resist. "Schedules change, Will."

"Right." Donato rolled his eyes. "Just keep tabs on him while I see what I can find out."

Solana barely noticed Donato leave her side as she continued to observe Mathison, who'd drawn the audience of several more CEOs interested in the latest activities at his M&A firm. He was evidently a gifted conversationalist; she watched the smiles in the group brighten as he entertained their questions about his newest corporate buy-out or shared tips on successful hostile takeovers and flawlessly executed dawn raids.

But she noticed that whenever he wasn't directly participating in the dialogue, his light blue eyes would scan the room, fix on something in the distance for a split second, then return to the group before him.

He's communicating with someone, she realized with a start, and when she saw him repeat the action she followed the direction of his glance to find the object of his attention. She studied the guests in his line of sight, looking for any telltale sign of who his target might be - and stopped when she saw Police Commissioner Andalus give a barely perceptible nod of respect to him, which she caught Mathison return with equal subtlety.

"That's interesting," she murmured. Was this in recognition of a new alliance? With the *police commissioner?* Or was he looking for someone else and just happened to meet the gaze of Andalus?

Solana trained her eyes on Mathison, waiting for him to search out another guest in attendance. It wasn't long before he did, and she stared, in disbelief, as she watched him receive the same reverent acknowledgments from some of the keenest influencers in the City. Over the next few minutes, he was similarly recognized by judges, labor union leaders, attorneys, and –

"Oh my God," she gasped, watching Alistair Prince give Mathison his token of respect from across the room. Followed by Sarah Adriaan... Donovan Hawes... Russ Aio... DA Lee –

"Where's *Kane?*" she demanded out loud, noticing the candidate no longer stood with Lee or Hawes.

Because now was the time to fucking find him. These silent exchanges were not simply social acknowledgments. Mathison had done it. By turning these prominent individuals to his favor, his organization now occupied the most powerful position in the City's political framework, which meant –

"Ms. Trent," came a pleasant, warm voice from behind her.

Solana whirled to find Chandler Kane arriving to stand beside her, an endearing smile bright across his features. He reached for her hand and she offered it to him out of ingrained habit, still reeling from what she'd just discovered.

"How lovely to see you," Kane said, taking her hand between both of his. "I'm so glad you could make it."

"I'm glad I could be here," she answered truthfully, managing to kick her mind back into gear. "I must admit I'm impressed, Mr. Kane. You have quite the turnout this evening."

Kane looked up to survey the ebullient crowd of his supporters filling the grand ballroom to its capacity. "Yes, things are going quite well," he agreed, still staring out into the packed space. "I couldn't be more pleased with the direction of the campaign."

When Kane hadn't yet turned his attention back down to her, she realized his gaze had locked onto something - and she felt her heart begin to pound. The hairs on the back of her neck prickled when she saw him give a noble nod, and she knew she didn't need to look to see who was on the receiving end of his acknowledgment.

But she did - and got more than she was prepared for.

Raine Mathison no longer focused on Kane. Instead, his calculating ice blue eyes now rested upon *her*, and the intensity of his penetrating stare arrested her right where she stood. Piercing much farther than skin deep, it felt like he could see into her soul, read her every thought, know the darkest desires of her heart. Nothing was sacred. The temperature in the room seemed to skyrocket as his eyes left hers to travel the length of her body, and she felt warm tingles sweep over her skin under his unwavering scrutiny. It was excruciating, as if he were memorizing her detail by detail for future reference, and her own photographic mind responded in kind as the vision of him watching her burned itself into her memory.

God, he's incredible, she wondered, and he must have heard her thoughts over the space between them, because it was at that moment that his beautiful eyes snapped back up to hers, the slightest trace of a knowing grin touching the corner of those oh-so-fucking kissable lips. Although she felt her cheeks burn in response, she lifted her chin and threw him a cool, composed smile, which he returned with a slow, sharp nod before focusing back on the circle of businessmen around him.

Free at last from the fire, Solana drew in a deep breath through her nose, held it for a blissful second, then let it go, hoping Kane wouldn't notice. She looked up to discover him studying her, and she wondered how long he'd been doing so.

"Are you acquainted with Mr. Mathison?" he asked, raising an eyebrow.

"I'm not," she countered. "But I see he's a supporter of the campaign."

Solana watched as a different kind of smile spread across the politician's face, and she knew on sight that she didn't like it. Part satisfaction and part regret, he acted like he had a secret to tell her - only she was the last one to know.

At that moment it became crystal clear to her why Hawes wanted to get her in front of Kane so quickly tonight, and an eerie foreboding filled her as the candidate stepped closer to her, his palms closing tighter over her small hand still held between his.

"Yes, he is," Kane confirmed. "Not only has Imbrialis made a generous donation to the cause, but Mr. Mathison has offered to serve as the campaign's financial advisor."

You've got to be joking, she thought as she looked up into his face. She couldn't believe he'd even dare discuss this so openly with her -

But then, one by one, Solana understood the many reasons why he felt so snug.

First, she couldn't touch him, not with *this*. She'd need something much bigger than the innocuous fact that the CEO of Imbrialis was one of the many volunteers giving his own time and skills to help forward Kane's campaign. She'd have to find out the terms of their deal, because she knew damn well Mathison wasn't donating his legendary financial and business acumen without some kind of *quid pro quo*.

But why would Kane need another advisor? And why would Mathison agree to it?

It's a front, she realized. As she'd told Donato this morning, if Kane won the election, he'd need access to the labor unions to push his HUD proposals through. Those unions were now firmly under Mathison's control, so not only did he need the support of the union members, but he also needed to foster a relationship with their new boss. By inviting Mathison to this event, Kane had sent a clear message to the unions that he was making inroads into securing that partnership, and Mathison, by showing up to Kane's party, proved he was looking to seal the deal.

But the aspiring politician would need an officially-sanctioned, press-kit-approved reason to have an alleged mobster appear in his court tonight. And how easy was that? All Kane had to do was assign Mathison to a management office within the campaign itself, and *voila!*, the kingpin had a reason to be there.

Moreover, by naming Mathison as his financial advisor, Kane had the security of knowing that any meetings and agreements between the two men could be disguised under the banner of Mathison's legitimate business. Meaning Kane would never have to get his hands dirty with the syndicate itself in order to make his campaign promises a reality, while Mathison and his people made money hand over fist.

Solana could just see it now. Every single HUD contract under Kane's administration would be awarded to some person or entity affiliated with Mathison's corporation, with all the labor unions working those contracts under the control of Mathison's syndicate. The cash would keep rolling in for everybody involved in his organization, while Kane looked like a hero who delivered on his commitments to the City.

Last but not least, if Kane had needed any more convincing that Mathison was a safe bet, he'd gotten it tonight when he saw just how favored his new partner was with the powers-that-be in this town. With all the alliances Mathison had formed, from the police commissioner to the goddamn DA, Solana knew the situation was practically ironclad.

And from the look on Kane's face, so did he.

His confidence in his bulletproof position ran strong enough for him to stand here before her with that easy smile, affecting an attitude of solicitous concern while he held her hand with such significance between his... bringing her to the irritating conclusion that he wasn't worried so much about his own situation as he was about *hers*.

He was telling her that she was in over her head on this one, and he couldn't have warned her to back off any more clearly than if he'd said it out loud.

That's all well and good, but if there's a chink in your armor, Kane, I'm going to find it, she vowed as she glanced back over to Mathison, who had taken leave of the CEOs and now made his way to one of the adjoining anterooms.

"Well," Solana said coolly, "I hear he's very good at what he does."

Kane grinned with a smugness that intensified her sense of unease. "He is, Ms. Trent, he is. But so are *you*. Tell me, how are things going for you at the Times these days?" he asked with import, his hands squeezing hers just that slightest bit tighter.

Step lightly, Alessandra. "Well, thank you," she smiled, giving him no more.

"I'm glad to hear that," he said. "I wish you nothing but continued success. Now if you'll please excuse me?"

"By all means."

"It's been wonderful catching up with you." Kane gave her hand one last uncomfortably intimate caress before he finally released it. "Give my regards to Mr. Donato; I'm afraid I haven't had much of a chance to speak with him tonight."

"I will," Solana promised, and when he moved on into the crowd she watched him like a hawk, having already predicted his actions over the next few minutes.

As expected, Kane joined Adriaan, Aio, and Hawes in the center of the room and she observed him patiently, waiting for the inevitable.

While I realize the importance of maintaining appearances, Kane, she advised him after a long moment passed, *you really shouldn't keep him waiting.*

The politician chose that moment to take leave of his assistants and slip out the main door of the ballroom, and Solana went on a hunt for Donato. She had one hell of a lot to tell him.

But first, she needed to wash her hands.

♋ ♋ ♋

Entering the Mandarin's posh MOBar lounge on the 35th floor, Chandler Kane spotted Mathison easily, unmistakable where he stood patiently rotating a rocks glass of The Dalmore on the long bar of polished hammered nickel. The other hand casually in the pocket of his slacks, one black Salvatore Ferragamo resting on the brass foot rail, few men carried themselves with Mathison's kind of prepossessing, nonchalant nobility, and fewer still had hair that glowed golden like his did in the low, amber light.

But only one man could cop his kind of room-dominating attitude, the one that established the baseline energy in any space he occupied depending on his disposition - and tonight he was making people stand up and take notice.

Here in the lounge, Kane perceived the palpable change in Mathison's demeanor at once, noting the difference between the engaging CEO of Imbrialis who'd walked into the ballroom, compared to the taciturn boss now standing alone at the bar. Only moments before, he'd graciously entertained the attentions of the businessmen interested in the happenings at his firm, taking the time to field their questions with wit and finesse. But now he projected quite a different message while he stood there waiting, silently, with an air of dark expectation settled around him like a cloak.

Business was written on the unreadable mask of his strong face, his hard stare etching into his glass of Scotch while he slowly turned it, that motion being the only movement he made. His quiet intensity, his cold stillness was a clear warning to everyone in the room: *Unless I have a matter to settle with you, step the fuck off.*

It was enough to give Kane pause.

Mathison seemed to sense Kane's presence from across the bar like a jaguar catching the scent of a gazelle. His cool eyes snapped up from his drink to assess his quarry, and with a quick motion of his hand indicated that Kane approach him, a slight grin lifting the corner of his lips.

"I apologize for the wait, Raine," Kane said in greeting as they shook hands.

Mathison flashed a rare smile, white against his sun-tanned olive skin. "Your delay is quite understandable, Chandler, given the company you keep."

Kane stared at him blankly, not catching his meaning. "I'm not sure I follow you."

Mathison got the attention of the bartender and held up two fingers, signaling another fine single malt for his companion. When he turned his light eyes back to him, there was a roguish spark in them. "Who was she?"

A second passed before the light dawned, at which point Kane studied him hard. "Is this a trick question?"

"Would I waste our time with so frivolous a thing, Chandler?"

"Most definitely, if it suited your purpose," the candidate said, his keen eyes searching the boss's face for any sign of an ulterior motive but not finding evidence of one.

"You really don't know, do you?" Kane marveled after a long moment.

Mathison set his jaw in a firm line, reining in his irritation. For some reason, he couldn't shake the vision of the bombshell standing with Kane in the ballroom. Something... something was familiar about that bright brunette and it frustrated him that he couldn't fucking place her. So blisteringly hot... such chilling sangfroid... the girl had monopolized his thoughts for the better part of the time he'd spent waiting for Kane, and he'd decided someone that beautiful shouldn't remain nameless in his mental black book.

"No, I don't know," he answered with cross coolness, "and why, pray tell, should I?"

The bartender placed the twin to Mathison's drink down in front of him, and Kane thanked him before taking a draught of the rich golden spirit.

"*That*," he smiled, savoring the taste of his words just as much as the eighteen-year Scotch, "is Solana Trent."

Mathison set his glass down harder than he'd intended, the surprised sound clattering down the length of the bar as the bold block letters of her infamous byline typed across his mind.

A. Solana Trent.

The starling of the New York Times, she was respected, ambitious, fearless; the press hailed her as a modern-day Woodward or Bernstein on account of her exposé on the Preston-DiStephano conspiracy. He most certainly knew of her, and there was no question now as to where he'd seen her before.

That priceless front-page shot of her and Prince taken the day DiStephano walked.

That's why she'd looked so familiar to him, but nothing could have properly prepared him for the sight of the stone cold fox herself.

Recovered from his initial shock, Mathison cleared his throat. "It was my understanding this was a no-press gig."

"True enough, but when the Times called with the request, how could I possibly refuse to admit her in light of the work she's done?"

Mathison considered the matter. He acknowledged the serendipitous contribution her breakthrough story had unwittingly made to both of their careers, but it was proof positive of how sharp she was, how dangerous she could be.

"I suppose refusing her could have raised a flag," he acquiesced. "Do you foresee a problem here, Chandler?"

Kane shook his head. "But with that one, anything is possible."

"Do notify me should the possible happen," he said, putting an end to the subject. "Now, shall we discuss our business at hand?"

Kane's eyes sparkled. "Lay on, Macduff."

Mathison grinned at the apropos reference. "And damn'd be him who first cries, 'Hold, enough.'"

CHAPTER THREE

FRIDAY, JULY 24
4:04 A.M.

The amber face of the digital clock on her nightstand informed Solana she'd been awake for yet another hour, her mind too active to sleep. By now the rosy fingers of dawn had begun to color the ceiling of her high-rise apartment, the first streaks of pink and gold lightening the tenebrous twilight of morning.

Watching the light intensify above her, she contemplated for the hundredth time everything she'd uncovered at Kane's ball. Yes, she'd sensed a conspiracy before she even arrived, but she'd had no idea it was as far-reaching as her observations indicated. Finding out how the hits on Mastriani, Catello, and Santaglio fit in might be the only way to break it.

But that was the thing of it. *Did* they fit in? If so, where? Who stood to gain? Mathison? Kane? Another politician who wanted some insurance before joining the alliance? That could be anyone - the list of potential shot-callers had grown astronomically, just from whom she'd seen covertly acknowledge Mathison last night.

Restless, she threw back the sheets, got out of bed, and rummaged through her dresser. She'd have to pound the pavement for this case. The murder scenes weren't all that far from her apartment, and it was high time she capitalized on that fortuitous opportunity. While the areas would certainly be cordoned off, there was no telling what clues a brisk walk-by might yield.

Even if she came up empty, it would still be time well spent. It was too early for her 6:30 yoga class in SoHo, but she needed to get this frustrated energy out *now*. A good, hard walk would free her mind, and she enjoyed the relative silence of the City during this time of day.

"Yoga will just have to wait," she sighed, throwing on a pair of dark jeans, a fitted black hooded sweatshirt, and her favorite, well-worn pair of running sneakers.

Outside on the street the air was cooler, and Solana closed her eyes in delight as a summer breeze caressed her cheeks and blew through her hair, the long curls appearing dark mahogany in the early half-light. She walked along the avenues of her neighborhood, deserted this time of the morning, and she appreciated having it to herself to think, to just be.

Along the next few blocks she passed multiple coffee houses, enjoying the heartening smell of their wares as they geared up for the Friday morning onslaught. She smiled to herself, realizing she'd never been out so early that *they* didn't yet have their doors open.

The next block down became solely residential again, and as she approached the intersection her attention was drawn to the black Bentley Continental Flying Spur parked in the street just ahead of her. The streetlights cast a fiery orange glow along its dark, smooth lines, while the grey of morning created pools of icy blue upon its gleaming black surfaces. Silent and unattended, it reminded her of a lone panther stalking its prey in the rain, concentrating so intently it was oblivious to the raindrops sliding off its coat.

Solana slowed her pace, curiosity piqued. Something about this Bentley wasn't right. Not that it didn't have good company here in the Upper East Side, where luxury cars were the norm rather than the anomaly. But even in this part of the City, a car like this would spend its evenings in a secured garage, not left to chance on the street. So it must have arrived recently. It was possible that the owner had an early appointment or flight and had ordered the car around. But if that were the case, there would be a driver or a valet, and it would be running. Instead, there was no one in its vicinity.

Nearing the sleek vehicle, she found no activity in the doorways of the nearby buildings...

But when she glanced down the alley she passed on her right, she did a double-take, her breath catching in her throat.

Instantly, Solana's reporter instincts took over. Disappearing into the deep shadow of the two buildings that towered over both sides of the alley, she closed her eyes for a moment, took a deep breath. Had she really seen what she thought she'd seen? Safe in the dark, she looked again.

Yes. A full block's length down the narrow concrete corridor, at its end where some of the weak daylight managed to streak its way through the darkness, she could just make out a group of well-dressed men in earnest conversation. Even at this distance she could read their body language - this was business.

The journalist's mind kicked into overdrive.

A clandestine meeting at dawn. In the Upper East Side. Following a two-day spree of unresolved mob-related shootings. The day after Kane's ball.

Her pulse pounded in her ears, her blood spiked with the potent liquor of ambition. If these men were in any way involved in the recent murders, and if they could be tied in any way to Mathison or Kane, overhearing their exchange could present the opportunity of a lifetime.

But how? countered the voice of prudence.

Solana assessed her surroundings. The dark tunnel of alley separating her from them stretched uninterrupted until approximately thirty feet towards its end, where one single yellow lamp struggled to cast its meager light onto a sizable dumpster. A yard or two beyond that, the tall rectangular shape of a giant backup generator jutted into the alley. *That could work.* It would land her within twenty feet of the group but still keep her safely hidden from view...

For a moment she hesitated, caution warring with ambition, but it didn't take long for the former to lose miserably to the latter. She had the chance to acquire exclusive access to privileged information that could break her investigation wide open, and she wouldn't pass it up.

Keeping close against the concrete wall of a building, Solana crept the distance down the long black alley, thankful she'd chosen her trusty old sneakers for the walk. Every silent step seemed to take an eternity, each one a calculated decision as she surveyed the asphalt beneath her feet for obstacles that could betray her presence.

She tiptoed between aluminum cans strewn among nests of foil wrappers and newspapers. She stretched over stagnant shallow puddles that never dried, perpetually deprived of direct sunlight. As she approached the dumpster decorated with its prerequisite litany of graffiti, she wasn't concerned so much with the industrial-strength stench coming from its contents as she was the dim lamp shining down upon it. She carefully skirted a wide circle around the pool of feeble golden light, crouching down to make sure she didn't make a shadow against the alley's opening far behind her.

Almost there, she thought, and she didn't dare breathe as she patiently traipsed the last few feet.

At last she achieved her vantage point, successfully concealed behind the silent generator, and she couldn't be more pleased with the spot as she focused on the scene unfolding before her.

Peeking around the unit, she counted a total of six men, and it appeared to be four versus two in the intense discussion. Of the four, one in particular commanded her attention. Silhouetted against the gathering light, this one was taller than the others, strong, finely shaped, and while he stood in ominous silence, the air hung about him differently. This man, Solana understood, was the authority, and the two men before him were in his immediate debt.

The man who seemed to be the second-in-command was speaking. "...when it became clear we weren't dealing with one mole, but two. How remarkably disappointing to discover it's the pair of you." At this close range, Solana could hear the obvious contempt in the timbre of his voice. "You two were the only ones fed that information, which leaves only one reasonable explanation as to how DiStephano happened to intercept it. Unless, of course, you have some other explanation to offer."

"Occam's Razor." The leader's voice sliced into the exchange with unsettling precision and clarity. Deep, resonant, powerful, but restrained with seemless effort. "The principle that the simplest explanation tends to be the right one. Don't you agree?"

"*Che palle!*" spat one of the two men on trial. "You're honestly buying this bullshit? For fuck's sake, Mathison, we've worked for you for years!"

Solana's blood froze in her veins. Her head snapped back to the commander of the group and the grey light of morning revealed Raine Mathison himself, who no longer stood in the shadows as he crossed the short distance to the two men standing before him.

"Oh no," she breathed. She gripped the edge of the generator as a growing apprehension plagued her where she stood, transfixed, staring at the frighteningly handsome mob leader who controlled the situation, so elegant in his element. This was more than she'd bargained for. It was one thing to cross paths with him in her world, but quite another to do so in his.

"You speak of honesty?" The chill in Mathison's voice made her shiver. "Clearly you betrayed my trust, otherwise the whole fucking City wouldn't have expected me to be in Italy last night!"

"We're being set up, Raine," the other defendant said, and the way he said it, the naked simplicity of it, made Solana want to believe him. "It's the truth, and it's all we can offer you."

"Truth," Mathison sneered. "The currency of partnership, while you tender your debts in counterfeit."

He was silent a moment, and Solana felt his deliberate words crystallize in the air between them. Not a man stirred, but a coldness, hard and absolute, moved among them, waiting to be shattered, waiting for the order...

"I could almost regret this, gentlemen."

Gunshots, muffled by silencers, fired so rapidly Solana barely managed to suppress the scream in her throat. Gripped by terror, she dropped to her knees while her mind took snapshot after snapshot of the two men falling to the concrete, the images burning themselves into her memory. She blinked, only to find the inky pools of blood growing deeper, darker, larger with impossible quickness around the bodies. And suddenly she could smell it, the thick, meaty, metallic scent of blood. She knew it was fucking impossible, but somehow, somehow the sickening smell reached her from twenty feet away –

No, she realized. *No. It's closer.* Some part of Solana's brain attempted to control the panic and forced her to drop her hand to her lap and stare at it. She hadn't remembered biting her palm to squelch the scream, but the evidence was there, bloody teethmarks on the pad beneath her thumb. The blood she smelled was her own, and it was enough to break the spell.

She leapt to her feet as if struck by lightening, paralysis giving way to instinct, and ran –

Straight into the side of the dumpster she'd forgotten was there.

The hollow, metallic crash ricocheted off the walls of the buildings surrounding her and Solana felt a rock take a nauseating plunge to the bottom of her stomach. The golden light of that single lamp no longer seemed puny; it felt like the sun itself burned down upon her, exposing her presence to the world. She flung away the curls that had fallen into her face, looked up to get her bearings –

To meet Raine Mathison's icy stare. His intense eyes analyzed her, piercing through her soul where she stood in the lamplight, and her heart stopped beating when she saw the light of recognition cross his striking features.

The others in Mathison's company caught sight of her in that split second, and in the next she was running, running like she never had before, adrenaline making her fast and agile, her feet slapping the pavement as she tore up the darkened alley. She heard voices but not words, footsteps chased her, and just as she reached the end of the alley she heard it.

The sound of the muted gunshot reverberated deep inside her, then the wind and whine of the bullet as it whizzed past her right ear.

She didn't stop, didn't scream as she turned the corner of the building, bolted up the sidewalk, took her first left down the next cross street, then tore up the avenue parallel to hers. Knowing better than to take the obvious, more direct route where she could be spotted, she zig-zagged her way up the blocks toward home and safety, her heart thundering in her chest.

At last she reached her building and she dashed into the side stairwell, taking the steps two at a time, all the way up to the 21st floor, where she ran down the hallway to her apartment, flung open the door, then locked and bolted it shut behind her.

She slammed her back against the door, shaking like a leaf, gasping for air as her mind continued to race for her life. Her eyes flew to her iPhone on the coffee table and she sprang towards it, acting on her first instinct to call the police.

But then she remembered what she saw transpire the night before between Mathison and Police Commissioner Andalus, and she stopped cold.

No. She couldn't trust the cops. If they were in league with Mathison, they'd cover up her story.

Or worse, they'd bring her right to him.

Solana buried her face in her hands. Even if by some slim chance the police weren't in his camp, she'd seen the other, more powerful alliances Mathison had made. The attorneys, the judges, the DA's office –

He'd turned *Alistair Prince*, for Chrissake, the one person she thought would never...

And then she remembered Al's words to her at the ball last night, and she felt the sudden, sharp sting of betrayal.

What she'd taken as professional *esprit de corps* was mockery delivered under the guise of intimate friendship.

If you find anything you can't *print, Solana,* he'd said, *I trust you'll keep me posted?*

"Right, Al," she choked back a sob. "So you can tell him it's time to send his dogs after me? What the fuck happened to you?"

She had nowhere to go, no one to turn to. Even if she did, even if she came forward, she knew Mathison would beat the charges in court, just like DiStephano had. After two back-to-back acquittals, her career, her reputation, would be ruined.

Donato. She thought of her editor and her closest friend, but she knew he wasn't an option either. Telling him would only endanger his life, and that was a risk she wasn't willing to take. No one she knew would die on account of her gross error in judgment. No one.

She was alone.

But that's okay, Alessandra, she reminded herself. *You're used to it.*

Solana raised her head from her shaking hands. Standing in the center of her wide-windowed apartment, with the rising sun casting its powerful glow over her, she closed her eyes. She focused on letting the light fill her, gathering its burgeoning strength, drawing upon its intensifying energy. She inhaled deeply, breathing the warming air of life itself, and she squared her shoulders, lifted her chin. When she finally opened her eyes they sparkled with the bright green fire of determination, reborn with the vitality of the star she was named after.

Now was not the time to wallow. She had to move, and there wasn't a second to spare.

ℰℬ ℰℬ ℰℬ

Raine Mathison saw her before anyone else did.

In the low light of the alley stood a beautiful female, young, with long shining tresses of dark auburn hair, a magnificent, nubile figure, and flashing green eyes that met his stare - and his alone. Taken aback by her presence in more ways than one, he knew he only had a second before –

Jesus H. Christ.

It was *her.*

The stunner he'd seen with Kane last night.

A. Solana Trent.

As if she'd heard him think her name, the girl took off at full sprint –

And Mathison let her go, confident in the knowledge he was watching a dead woman.

His eyes stalked her as she flew up the alley, knowing there was nowhere she could turn, no one she could approach for help in this City without it getting right back to him. With the kind of friendships he had in this town and along the entire Eastern Seaboard, she was as good as his. He could afford to let the journalist who'd done him an unintended favor get a running start, and he would gladly pay her the courtesy she deserved.

Because if the rumors were true, if she was as quick and resourceful as reputed, she would be a difficult one to catch up with, and the spoils of that pursuit would be worth every moment of the aggravation.

"A worthy adversary," Mathison mused, a strange electricity warming him.

His companions gave chase after her, guns drawn for their second kill of the morning.

"Stop," he ordered, "she's not important right now," and at the sound of his voice they halted, their confusion plain as they looked back and forth between him and the girl rapidly approaching the alley's end.

"But until then," he murmured, "a parting gift," and he raised his stainless Kimber Custom II TLE, aimed and fired, and the warning shot delivered precisely where he'd intended, just grazing her right ear before she disappeared.

Dumbfounded, his associates regarded him with shock as they regrouped before him. Their boss was an excellent marksman; the missed shot was not something they expected from a man on a first-name basis with the Kimber factory in Yonkers. Had it been his intention to hit her, they knew he damn well would have.

Ricci, a young freshly-made man on his staff, was beside himself. "Holy shit, she's getting away!"

"Not at all," Mathison replied, not the least bit fazed as he reholstered the Kimber under his jacket. "I know who she is and I'll catch up with her later."

"Wait," blustered Stocchero, a veteran in the ranks. "You know her?"

Mathison flashed a smile, perfect white teeth gleaming. "Not yet."

The men exchanged knowing glances. "You'll be handling this personally?"

"Oh yes."

"I expect she'll be a challenge, Raine," noted Hunter Cavenastri, Mathison's right hand and consigliere. "Solana Trent, the journalist from the Times, if I'm not mistaken?"

"Mind like a steel trap, Cavi."

"You have a plan?"

Mathison's eyes glimmered. "Always." He turned towards the two men dead on the pavement and glanced up to the sky, lightening at a rapid pace. "Right now, we need to *move*. Ricci, Stocchero, go ahead with the plan for handling these two. Cavi, I want that girl. Get Anesini on the phone and bring me everything you two can find on her. And I do mean everything. Addresses, telephone numbers, email addresses. Friends, schedules, hobbies. Social networking pages, usernames, passwords. Public records, medical records, transcripts. Credit reports, bank accounts, phone logs. All of it. Cover every avenue to get it. Pull the connections, anything, everything, I want her found. Meet me in two hours with info."

After accepting their orders, all three of them watched him stride up the alley with the same thought on their minds. The girl wasn't the first to be caught in the wrong place at the wrong time, and if his plans for her were anything like the others, she'd pay for it dearly. Someone in her position had only one chance to escape falling into Raine Mathison's hands.

Running like hell.

CHAPTER FOUR

7:07 A.M.

The sun had fully risen to a bright, beautiful, hot summer morning, but Solana felt none of its warmth. Staring out her office window, she watched Midtown bustle below her, teeming with people going about their daily lives. They were completely oblivious to the change she could feel in the air, while every nerve in her body sensed the oppressing, prowling presence.

The phone rang but she ignored it. Yesterday she would have snatched up the call in eager pursuit of her investigation, but today? Whoever was on the other end of that line couldn't help her now, no one could, and she had more important things to do with her time.

Like remembering to breathe.

Solana shivered in the sunlight. *Breathing.* A task not so easily accomplished with the constant memory of Mathison's frigid stare in the alley making icicles trace down her spine.

He's already got people after me, I know it.

Meaning she couldn't go home again. She'd spent those precious minutes back at her apartment packing a suitcase quickly and carefully, taking only what she'd need to survive. Bare essentials, clothing, valuables, cash to last her a while. Credit cards, anything traceable, would be of no use to her.

Then she got ready for work.

Sure, once Mathison's thugs struck out at her apartment they'd try to find her here, but the Times was the safest place for her right now. Fully secured, with lots of people, many keeping late hours, somewhere she could stay until she figured out what to do. It was also the perfect place to hide a little insurance.

Rushed as she was, she'd dressed with care for the office, figuring if she meant to pretend nothing was wrong, she'd better look like it. She'd chosen an elegant made-to-measure ivory ensemble by Bluesuits, pairing a sleek pencil skirt and fitted jacket over a sumptuous gold chemise accented with small turquoise peacock feathers and tiny clear glass beads. After slipping on a smart, comfy pair of four-inch Louboutin heels, she'd grabbed her belongings and was out the door, possibly never to return.

She'd fought a valiant battle against the tears that threatened to break free as she locked the door behind her, but the second she'd stepped into the empty elevator she lost that war. She'd allowed herself that one moment of weakness on the descent to the parking garage below her building, knowing she wouldn't be able to afford any more if she wanted to live. By the time the elevator doors opened to the garage, she'd regained her composure. Getting emotional would get her killed, and there was no room for any more mistakes.

Turning away from the window, Solana returned to her desk to reread the words on her laptop's bright screen. She'd drafted her document with critical, painstaking care, making sure to convey every single detail of the double homicide in the alley. It was an unbiased record, a statement of what she'd witnessed. *The insurance policy*, she thought as she saved the document and encrypted it with a password.

"You're here early."

Solana jumped three feet in the air and looked up to see Donato standing in the doorway of her office, grinning. Forcing a weak smile, she snapped the laptop shut as he approached her desk carrying two cups of coffee, and she did her best to keep her hands from shaking when she stood to accept the cup he offered.

"I bet you're needing this today," he said as he handed it to her, and she could sense an air of gloating about him.

"Why?" she stood up straighter. "What's happened?"

"Don't you know?" he asked, fully expecting his star journalist to already have the information he was just now privy to.

Her patience was growing thin. "What, Will?"

Donato's eyebrows disappeared into his graying hairline. "I can't believe you don't know this. Well, my dear, while you were getting your beauty sleep this morning or contorting about on that yoga mat of yours, two more mobsters turned up dead, practically on your doorstep."

Solana choked on her coffee.

"Okay, Lana, it's not *that* bad to have the story of the decade happening right under your nose – "

"How the hell was I supposed to know?" she snapped. "Last time I checked, clairvoyant was not listed in my job description!"

"Whoa. Easy. I'm kidding," Donato tempered. "Jesus, I didn't think you'd take it that hard. Don't worry, you'll get the story."

She stared at him like he'd lost his mind.

"What?" he demanded. "Are you, or are you not, covering the latest rash of mob killings in this fair City?"

"Not anymore," she retorted.

Will was incredulous. "Since when?"

"Since now."

"Too close to home?"

"You ask too many questions, Will."

"It's what we *do here*, Lana."

"Well, I've got some other articles I need to finish up for today's deadline, and then I'll look into it."

"This is not a backburner story!"

"Then give it to someone else! Steinberg's been chomping at the bit for a juicy one!"

Donato stared at her in disbelief. "What the hell is wrong with you?"

Solana sighed. This was going to end in a stalemate if she didn't try another tack. "Listen. You know what I discovered at the ball last night. Kane and Mathison are obviously plotting some racket directly related to the outcome of this election, so what's more important, Will? High-profile scandal or a couple mob peons snuffed in some alley?"

Donato opened his mouth to say something and then closed it, his expression changing to one of confusion. "I never mentioned the part about the alley."

Furious, Solana couldn't believe her slip. "They don't do this shit in broad goddamn daylight, Will! Where the fuck else would it have happened? In the street, Old West shoot-out style?"

For several seconds he could only blink at her in shock; he'd never seen her so out of character. "Educated guess, I suppose," he mused, pondering his next words. "All right, Lana, you have a point. Go ahead and start investigating what you observed at the ball, especially the Mathison-Kane partnership."

"Thank you," she breathed, relieved he was finally seeing it her way.

"You'll notice, however," Donato warned, "that the emphasis was on the word 'start.' This is a monumental undertaking. You won't find your answers overnight and I'm still going to need you to cover other mob stories. I want something from you on this double homicide by day's end, so plan accordingly."

Frustrated, Solana set her coffee down on her desk and put her hands on her hips. "I'll try, Will, and that's the most I can promise."

"Try? Solana Trent, you'd better pull your head out of your ass and get with the fucking program, kid," Donato barked, storming out the door. "These guys move fast; they don't work around your schedule!"

Asshole, she fumed, sinking into her chair. She'd come here to think, to formulate some kind of plan, but a cursory scan of her desk told her that wouldn't be so easily done. Her email inbox brimmed with correspondence regarding the articles she was writing. The voicemail light on her telephone blinked rapidly, indicating multiple messages. File folders stacked on the opposite side of her desk had become so numerous they were taking on the architectural structure of a makeshift fort. She knew she had a million things she should be doing, and if she stayed there all day with nothing to show for it, people would be asking questions.

Pulling up the agenda she'd compiled before leaving last night, Solana dived into her inbox and got started, for once grateful for the distraction of the ever-abundant workload.

❧ ❧ ❧

1 2:45 P.M.

Although the ristorante in Little Italy swelled to capacity with its daily throng of lunch hour patrons, Raine arrived to find Hunter Cavenastri and Gennato Anesini sitting in the favored corner booth in the back room. The trattoria had been one of Loiacono's favorite spots; it was a noisy, boisterous hole-in-the-wall on Mulberry Street, but it was the best Italian on the island. The intoxicating smell of the cuisine permeated the air as he strode down the length of the restaurant to the table, where the freshly baked bread and olive oil had just arrived along with three Nastro Azzuros.

"When you called me this morning to say you needed more time, Cavi," Raine said, taking his seat across from them, "I didn't think you meant half the damn day."

"Neither did we," Cavi replied, portioning off a piece of bread. "There's more to her than we anticipated."

"First, tell me the most important thing. Where is she now?"

"She's at the Times," Anesini reported. "After my research on her came back with an address in the Upper East Side, I hacked into her building's parking garage cameras. She left a little before 5:30 this morning in an Audi R8, which is registered to her in the DMV's records. I put in a few calls to some friends in traffic surveillance and they confirmed she went straight to the office on 8th. She hasn't left."

"Are we sure she was the one in the car?"

Grey eyes shining, Anesini pulled an iPhone from the pocket of his leather jacket, flipped through a few screens and passed it across the table to the boss.

A still from the parking garage video glowed on the display, showing the lusciously beautiful Solana Trent getting into her car at 05:26:12 that morning. When Raine advanced to the next image he discovered that apparently Anesini had also hacked into the cameras outside the Times, because this screenshot caught the same Audi, the same captivating driver, entering her office's garage at 05:31:44.

"Well done," he said, lifting his eyes to his hacker. "Any phone calls?"

"Nothing external and no activity on her cell phone, either," Anesini said while he returned the phone to his jacket. "I'm also tracking outgoing emails, social networking sites, bank account activity, credit card charges, and transactions online. So far, not a blip."

Raine's brow furrowed. "So what revelation monopolized the rest of the morning, then?"

His consigliere and his blackhat exchanged glances.

"The 'A.' in Solana Trent's byline," Cavi explained.

The mob leader patiently poured some olive oil on his plate and tore off a few hearty pieces of the soft homemade bread. "What about it?"

"Her full legal name is Alessandra Solana Trent."

Something about the way Cavi said the word "legal" gave him pause. "What's her *real* name?" he demanded, his chunk of bread suspended motionless over the pool of olive oil.

"Solana Taranto... Alessandra."

Raine stared at him. "As in *Damian and Isadora* Alessandra?"

"Based on our findings," Anesini said solemnly, "yes."

Further elaboration wasn't necessary. The story of the Alessandras was decades old, but the name was still said with reverence, even here on the other side of the world.

Nearly fifty years ago, Damian Alessandra assumed leadership of the Roman Mafia and built it to such power that it practically ruled the Italian capital for over twenty years. Parallels were often drawn between him and Julius Caesar: whoever commands the Roman army commands Rome. His influence extended well beyond the city into the far reaches of the Lazian province, but when it began to encroach upon the turf of the rival Campagnian syndicates, bitter resentment flared into an all-out vendetta. Allegedly, it was the Neopolitan boss who'd put the hit out on the entire Alessandra family, and that he alone was responsible for the summary execution of every last one of them.

Except for perhaps one.

It was a fact that five years before they were killed, Damian and Isadora Alessandra had given birth to a daughter.

It was a fact that when the murders hit the presses, there was no mention of a child among the victims.

Most believed it was an oversight, figuring the little girl was assassinated along with the rest of the family but it simply wasn't reported.

But there were those who believed the rumor that Damian and Isadora Alessandra had spent their last night on earth attempting to spirit their only child to the States before it was too late.

According to the story, the Alessandras were warned of their immediate peril merely hours before they were killed, and there was no question between them as to what needed to be done. Refusing to run for the rest of their lives and raise their daughter in the shadows, they chose to sacrifice themselves in order to secure her lifelong safety. But no shred of evidence, save for the anecdotal, existed to support the twenty-one-year-old tale.

However, Raine considered, struck by the irony of the situation, *what mafioso can't make someone disappear at a moment's notice?*

"All right, gentlemen," he said, "lay it out for me. What gives you cause to believe she's their daughter?"

"We found out about her first name when I ran the DMV search on her," Anesini explained. "We didn't really think much of it at the time; it just explained the detached initial in her byline. Then we started data mining for her background information, and everything we found on her seemed to make sense. Pulitzer Nominee halfway through her second year at the Times. Accelerated masters and doctorate from Columbia's Graduate School of Journalism. Undergrad at UPenn Philadelphia, *summa cum laude* from the Annenberg School of Communication. But when we went back farther to find out where she came from, suddenly we were getting no results on her. She was a vacuum, like she didn't exist before UPenn."

"It took us a while," Cavi jumped in, "but getting access to her matriculation records was the next logical step. After graduating early from high school at the top of her class, she came to UPenn at the age of sixteen. Nowhere in all that documentation did she identify an emergency contact or a close relative, but we found her home address in southwestern Montana. Bingo. Anesini cross-referenced the address in the property records of the county while I pulled a few strings with the courthouse, and this led to several key pieces of information."

"I'd wager one of them," Raine ventured, "is that she changed her name to Alessandra Solana Trent."

Cavi smiled. "Bet it all. She changed it just before she went to college. Prior to that, the world knew her simply as Lana Trent."

"And then the land records gave you the names of her adoptive parents?"

"Exactly," Anesini leaned forward in his seat. "However, it's parent, singular, and he sure as hell ain't a Trent. The 191-acre tract of land was an equine farm sanctuary founded and owned by her guardian - Nico Salvatore."

The name rang a bell, but Raine couldn't quite place it. "Who's Nico Salvatore?"

"That's what we wanted to know," Cavi said. "His deed for the farmland dates back about thirty years, and it recites him as being a widower as well as a resident of the county at the time he bought the property. The only other thing the county records had on him was his death certificate, which told us he died of cancer in August of the same year she started college - and that his birthplace was Rome, Italy."

Suddenly, Raine placed Salvatore's name, and Anesini saw the change in his expression. "I know," the hacker said. "That's when we started putting it together, too. Cavi went after the immigration logs and I dug deeper into her financials. Sure as hell, she's made periodic draws on an account held in a Roman bank, which turns out to be quite an impressive trust fund - with Solana Taranto Alessandra being the named beneficiary. That's why we didn't find it at first: it's not listed under her current legal name.

"The Alessandras pulled this together amazingly well under such pressure and with so little notice," Anesini went on, his admiration evident. "The two fund rules were simple. One, she gets control of the trust at the age of eighteen or when she matriculates, whichever occurs earlier - which meant no one could take advantage of the situation while she was still a child. And two, the only way the account can be accessed is by her fingerprint. Period. It not only safeguarded the funds, but it also guaranteed she'd be able to get to them, no matter what name she'd been naturalized under in order to conceal her true identity."

"So after they set all this up," Raine conjectured, "they called on Salvatore. I remember him now; Alessandra's former underboss who'd taken an early retirement and moved to some remote part of the States. He was loyal, trustworthy, raising two young sons of his own, and across the damn globe on his beloved horse farm - no one would ever think of it. He accepted, they sent a nurse with the girl and all her paperwork, and she was immigrated into this country under the name of Lana Trent."

Cavi nodded. "She grew up knowing she was adopted but never had any idea why. Salvatore must have divulged everything at some point before he died, otherwise she'd never know her real name, never find out about the trust fund, never understand where she came from. That's why she changed her name at sixteen - she just found out who she really is."

Raine took a long, thoughtful draught of his Peroni. "She didn't change it back to her full, true name, either. While eleven years allowed plenty of time for the danger to pass, she prudently chose not to advertise the fact she's still alive."

"That right there is the point of it, *Padrino*," Anesini said. "She's smart. There's a reason we haven't traced any phone calls, any emails, any transactions, anything. She knows better."

Unflustered, Raine smiled slowly. "I do believe she'll be the hardest one yet."

CHAPTER FIVE

8:39 P.M.

Solana looked up to find the shadows in her office had grown long by the time she emailed her last article to the pressroom. Her fingers lingering over the keyboard, she was surprised to see the timestamp on her message was 8:40 p.m. Despite the late hour, the fading pinks and reds of a fantastic summer sunset still warmed the walls, and she leaned back in her chair to hear... nothing.

Most of the staff had already left for the night, including Will. Thankfully. The belated delivery of her report could be blamed almost entirely on his constant interruptions, infuriated at her steadfast refusal to chase down the story on the alley hits.

If he only knew, she thought, watching her fingers type a string of digits they'd already grown accustomed to entering, calling up the file she'd uploaded into the system this morning. She didn't read the words this time, but stared through them, felt them, a coldness seizing her as she saw the bodies again, smelled the blood, heard the sound of the bullet flying through her hair.

She'd formulated a plan, and while it was a good one, there were no guarantees it would work. If Mathison's people got a hold of her, this document would be her only collateral. She saved it, burying it deep inside the fortress that was the document management system of the Times, and the password she entrusted to one other person.

Her email to Will was only one word.

TAXEIA.

He would have no idea what it was for, what it meant, or why she'd sent it.

But if she had to, one phone call with the document identification number would give him both pieces to the puzzle, and the world would know what happened in that alley.

Just as she clicked the send icon there was a knock on her doorjamb, and when she looked up to see Geri, the late-shift receptionist, Solana found comfort in her presence. She was a sharp Southern lady and a good friend, always ready to share her sage advice over a tall glass of homemade sweet tea.

"Why are you still here, Geri?" Solana asked. "Knowing you, I'm damn sure you've got better things planned for your Friday night."

"You were very lucky, Lana. I was literally locking up to head out when a delivery came for you," Geri smiled suggestively, a merry twinkle in her warm brown eyes. "You've captured yourself yet another admirer, I see."

"Come again?"

"You'll just have to see for yourself, dear - I had him put it in the Book Room for you. Now have a great weekend and I'll see you Monday." With a wink, she was gone.

"What delivery?" Solana rose from her chair and hurried to the library that served as a reception area, a relaxing space outfitted with black leather furniture and glass tables, the walls covered with antique books and framed newspapers. She barged into the converted study only to find it empty - but on the center table stood a tall crystal vase of two dozen, long-stemmed, blood-red roses.

Her brows knit together in confusion. *I'm not seeing anyone. I don't have any admirers. I haven't gotten flowers since Al sent me a dozen in March. Before that, it was the lavender and lilies from my brothers in January for my birthday. Will wouldn't send me something like this, no matter how much of a dick he was today. So who —*

She stopped.

You know who.

"But why?" she mused aloud. "Why would his goons do this?"

You know that, too.

"Jesus," Solana turned on her heel and rushed from the room. "Thank God you didn't handle them yourself, Geri."

She ran down the hallway to the kitchenette and snagged two rubber gloves and a face mask from the first-aid kit. Then, once she'd protected herself as best she could, she marched the vase back to her office. She might not be the only staffer working late on a Friday night, and the last thing she needed was some nosy reporter to find her in the Book Room surgically examining a bouquet of flowers.

And a damn impressive one at that. As Solana leaned over the roses to study them, she nearly lost herself in their beauty and scent. The dark scarlet blossoms opened luxe and perfect, each one big enough to fill the palm of her hand. They towered on stems that reached clear up to eye-level, and even through the mask she could smell their powerful fragrance.

Keep your head in the game, Alessandra, she warned, and she got down to business.

But a thorough inspection of the flowers yielded no significant findings. The velvety petals looked smooth and unblemished, with no visual evidence of poisonous dusts or powders. The water in the vase gleamed clear and unclouded, and she threw out the little pouch of flower food without even bothering to open it. She found no strange objects embedded within the blooms, just the clean white envelope standing proud on its tall plastic fork. She heard no sounds except the rustling of leaves, and detected no smells save for the intoxicating scent of red, red rose.

"Shit." Feeling foolish, Solana tore off her mask and gloves with an irritated snap. "The only dangerous thing about these are the damned thorns!"

So why send them?

She snatched the little card from their midst, ripped it open, and there was no misreading the sharp black strokes on the expanse of white linen paper.

> *For the beautiful girl in the alley.*
> *Will be seeing you soon.*
> R.

The hairs on the back of Solana's neck stood on end as she read and reread his words, crisp and clear on the heavy piece of fine cardstock she held between her fingers.

Mathison wasn't sending his henchmen after her. He was handling the situation personally, and the innocence of his message coupled with the romantic implication of the roses scared her more than any overt threat ever would have. It was patient, understated, absolute, and there would be no reasoning with him if he caught up with her.

"He's coming for me," Solana whispered in horror. "Christ, he might be here already... Son of a *bitch!*"

She dashed to her desk, locked down her computer, grabbed her handbag, and flew down the hall towards the emergency exit. The escape plan she'd hatched today was solid enough; all she had to do now was make it to her car alive.

Here goes, she prayed, and the second she flung open the door the alarm sounded, echoing loud and shrill down the bare stairwell. She waited through several excruciating heartbeats, resisting the urge to bolt too soon –

Until the doors above and below her burst open and people started streaming out.

Solana smiled at the sight. *Score one for me.*

ↀ ↀ ↀ

"Clever girl," Raine muttered, half in frustration, half in admiration. Barely ten minutes had passed since he'd had the flowers delivered to Ms. Trent when he saw her enter the parking garage, just as he'd predicted.

Only she wasn't alone.

Sitting in his metallic graphite Fisker Tramonto, hidden from view behind black tinted windows, he couldn't help but smile at her ingenuity. Dozens of people continued to file out of the building in response to the emergency alarm she'd thrown, even though it was damn near nine on a Friday night.

"Well done indeed, little one," he said as he watched her walk safely amongst the crowd. He'd parked in the same row as her car, two spaces removed from her impressive ice-white R8, and he waited patiently while she approached. Listening to the hot, sultry tension of Massive Attack's "Inertia Creeps" flow through his speakers, he studied her, missing not a movement her fantastic little figure made in that expensive suit.

She is absolutely exquisite, he thought, taking in the view of her, all dark hair, short skirt, and sexy heels. Long, wild auburn curls. Flawless, sunkissed skin. Finely shaped eyes of the brightest green. Full lips, pretty cheekbones, a graceful neck. Perfect proportions: ample breasts, a tiny waist, nice legs and ass, a delicious swing in her hips.

With that one, Kane had said, *anything is possible.*

Raine grinned. "Oh I do hope so, Chandler."

She was every bit as breathtaking as when he'd first laid eyes on her at the ball, only now she was business. Now he had a reason to get his hands on her, the possible had happened, and he burned for the moment when he'd take possession of her.

Unfortunately, that moment would have to wait. He'd planned to box her in beside her car and let his Kimber do the talking; then, after she'd been thus persuaded into the passenger seat of his Fisker, he'd drive her somewhere to finish off their spot of unfinished business.

But she'd altered that plan with a fox's artfulness, and the excitement of the challenge already dancing like wildfire in his veins only sparked higher now that she'd upped the ante.

Christ, he would enjoy this.

There had been others before her who'd fallen prey to him as a consequence of their own curiosity, and catching up with them had never presented the slightest difficulty. Within hours, they always made one mistake that led him right to them, and once he found them, it was over. Quick and easy killings, snuffed out like candles with no trace left behind. They became missing persons, unsolved mysteries, gone without so much as a whisper on the wind.

But Ms. Trent... *she* was proving to be a conquest of a different order, and he found himself wanting more from her than just her death.

He wouldn't stop until he owned her, body and soul.

And before he was done, he'd have her begging him to do it.

Watching her leave the thinning crowd and click a keyfob to the Audi, he had to congratulate her for outwitting him. But as soon as she stepped into the car, he fired the Tramonto's engine to life. The game was now afoot.

⁊ ⁊ ⁊

Solana resumed breathing as she listened to the gentle purr of the R8's fine-tuned engine.

"It worked," she said out loud, almost disbelieving it.

But there it was. Her plan had worked.

Bright energy surged through her. She felt like she was going to explode, the force of it bigger than her body could handle, and the rush came with only one instruction: *Go.*

While she waited for the last of the crowd to pass her car, Solana dropped the windows and cranked the volume on her stereo. She impatiently tapped her fingers to the heartbeat of Cookie Monsta's "Contract with the Devil" until the coast was clear, then peeled out of her parking spot, through the garage, and out into the electric summer evening air.

Speeding down the left lane of West 41st, the lights of Times Square lit up the sky brighter than daylight in her rearview mirror, and the sight strengthened her adrenaline burst. She loved the ebb and flow of energy in this City, the hub of the world, and the thrill of life hummed through her, the soul-shaking sound of dubstep rocking from her speakers.

I won't be gone long, she promised. *Just long enough.*

Reluctantly, she stopped for the light at 41st and 9th, Lincoln Tunnel-bound, and while she sat there rapping out the beat again on her gear shift in anticipation, a gorgeous charcoal grey Fisker Tramonto glided smoothly to the head of the lane next to her.

Nice wreck, Solana thought, watching its ground-hugging carbon-fiber body inch closer to the stop line. *Only fifteen of those were ever built.*

But then her pulse quickened when she heard a familiar, provocative taunt; the Tramonto's engine revved its throaty, supercharged V8 - an unmistakable challenge to the comparatively meager Audi idling beside it.

No way. Despite the dark tint of the windows, she'd be willing to bet she knew the identity of the Fisker's pilot, and she raised an eyebrow at him, accepting his summons to a duel.

Go ahead, buddy, she warned him. *I dare you.*

Not only was her six-speed R8 nicely equipped with its flagship 5.2 V10, she'd grown up in rural Montana with two race-fanatic older brothers. Long before she even had her driver's license, they were teaching her everything they knew about cars and pushing them to their limits - and that winning was all about the driver.

"Sure, the car helps," Steve had told her many times. "But cars don't win races, Lana - drivers do."

"Well, drivers who know all the dirty little tricks," Josh had added with a mischievous smile, and thanks to years of white-knuckled lessons with those two die-hard thrill-seekers, Solana *did*.

It didn't matter how fast his fancy car was, he wouldn't be able to touch her out here. Traffic going out of the City into New Jersey should be relatively sparse this time of the evening, too late for rush hour, too early for the night clubbers; there couldn't be a better time to give the man a run for his money.

"Come on," she muttered, willing the lights to run their circuit, and when her signal turned green, she didn't waste so much as a second glance on the Tramonto - she just floored it.

Hugging the inside of the two left lanes, Solana had the advantage, pulling ahead of the Fisker as they ran down 9th to the Lincoln Tunnel. Seconds later she sped through the entrance, the Tramonto not far behind, and the confined space roared with the sound of two perfectly engineered machines running at full throttle.

"Keep him back there, Alessandra," she said, and her voice was lost in the noise, her heart thundering as hard as the bass and beats reverberating through her car.

She burst from the confines of the tunnel back into the open evening air, piloting the Audi like a Blue Angel streaking for I-95. The few cars on the road that noticed the two vehicles rushing at breakneck speed behind them yielded the right-of-way, taking refuge in the middle lanes. As for the oblivious drivers, she passed around them on the left while the Fisker did the same on the right; when they cleared the pocket of traffic, she and the Tramonto were separated three lanes apart for the upcoming toll.

Solana kept a steady course, knowing the EasyPass was incapable of registering information over 80 mph. Despite the cramped space between the concrete dividers, she didn't once let off the accelerator, and she grit her teeth as she blew through the narrow toll at three-digit speed.

She emerged just ahead of the Tramonto, straining all ten cylinders as she staked her claim on the wide four-lane highway stretching before them. Her car flew at such velocity that the air ripping through the open windows took her breath away, whipping her long hair in all directions, and the exhilaration of holding the lead was indescribable, unlike anything she'd ever experienced.

But the Fisker wasn't having it. Vastly outmuscling her R8, he drew on his deep reserves of power to tie the race, bringing them head to head, and Solana could hear their engines' promiscuous growls rising to climactic screams. She gripped the leather-wrapped steering wheel tighter as he inched the length of his pristine silver chassis closer to hers, too close for comfort.

"The son of a bitch is toying with me," she hissed, and as if he'd heard her, the Tramonto stole another inch of her Audi's personal space. Solana gunned it into the left lane only to have the Fisker follow, keeping nose to nose, pressing in even closer, and she realized he was gradually forcing her into the Jersey barriers.

"Nice try, asshole," she fumed. "We both know if you take me out like that, you'll come with me." Because at this speed, the smallest divot, crack, or pebble in the road could wrench these feather-weight rockets from their control and transform them into pricy, carbon-fiber tombs. But still he kept encroaching, he took a leering swerve towards her, testing her, trying to see if she'd sideswipe the concrete barrier, and Solana's fury spiked.

In highway speed-racing, there are no finish lines or checkered flags. There's only cunning one-upmanship, where brains outclass brawn. A driver must be mentally present at every moment, plotting, scheming, and thwarting her opponent, looking for ways to shatter his confidence - which is exactly why her eyes left the road to lock on to him, tinted windows be damned.

She shook her head at him. "You wanna play? Fine."

Josh and Steve had called this particularly dirty little trick Shock and Awe, while law enforcement, she later learned, referred to it as the PIT Maneuver. By either name, it was used to disable vehicles in high-speed chases, and she and her brothers had practiced and perfected it, spending countless days both employing it and recovering from it on the miles of speed-limitless country road where they'd grown up. Of all the vehicular stunts in her arsenal, this one was the most promising choice, and if she managed to pull it off successfully, it would leave the Fisker with damn little chance for a timely recovery.

She only prayed he didn't have a clue what she was doing, otherwise he might decide to try his luck for real and just crush her right into that concrete divider.

It was an exercise in iron-fisted control, but Solana didn't evade him this time as he came dangerously closer. Instead, she let him come within inches of her, hoping he was under the false impression he was only seconds away from taking his final lunge to victory. She started to edge away from him, feigning imminent panic -

Then threw him another look, this time in triumph.

"Let's dance," she said, and she went both feet in.

The nose of her R8 dipped slightly, flexing the rigid Audi racetrack suspension as the weight of the car lurched forward under the extreme braking. The Fisker continued onward while she fell back into position, and she made her finishing move.

When her bumper dropped back behind his rear axle, Solana tapped him, just grazing his immaculately polished rear quarter-panel. Her touch ever so gentle, her timing absolutely precise, the hit made his rear wheels break traction on contact, sending him into a spin across her nose. The Tramonto's tires squealed in protest, the acrid smell of burning rubber scorching her nostrils, and she watched it happen in slow motion, her attention riveted to the flash of silver and chrome that went whipping past her front end. Those milliseconds seemed to last lifetimes, but the moment he was no longer an obstruction, time shifted back into high gear just as quickly as she did.

While the boost of power shot her off like a cannon, it was the music, the night air, the speed, the freedom, the thrill of being alive that electrified her, and Solana took advantage of his incapacitation to win this game for good. She redlined the R8 to the exit ramp on her right, knowing that even if he managed to recover from the PIT like a pro, he wouldn't make it to the exit in time to pursue her off the highway.

But even as she made her grand escape, she couldn't resist stealing a look behind her. Her eyes flicked to the rearview mirror to see the Fisker spinning out of control, sparks flying as his nose just scratched the Jersey barrier, and she watched in silent amazement as he skidded to a screaming stop in the breakdown lane, so far behind her now his headlights were pinpricks in the gathering dusk.

"I can't believe that just fucking happened!" Solana yelled in heart-pounding pride. She couldn't be positive, but somehow, she had the extraordinarily strong suspicion she had just earned score two on the boss himself.

CL CL CL

"Unfuckingbelievable."

Furious, Raine drummed his fingers on the Fisker's steering wheel. It was the only sound in the car as he sat, stalled, in the breakdown lane on the southbound side of the New Jersey Turnpike, attempting to regain his composure.

She'd bested him. *Again.* This time nearly killing him in the process.

And whoever taught her how to do that, he thought wryly, *I have to get on the goddamn payroll.*

His iPhone rang in its cradle on the console. "What?" he snapped.

"Having trouble with the lady, Raine?" asked Hunter Cavenastri, laughter in his voice.

"Fuck you, Cavi. Why didn't you tell me she'd taken driving lessons from Mario Andretti?"

"I wasn't aware that she had. What happened?"

"Nothing. The kitten just scratched my nose."

"Which means she made you crash the Fisker," Cavi corrected. "Do you need the McLaren? Tell me where you are and I'll get it to you."

"Not necessary," Raine growled. "You gonna tell me what the fuck is so bloody important?"

"Your dance card is full. We've got calls coming in from all the echelons; you just need to meet with some of these people to secure the strongholds before you head off to Rome on Tuesday."

"And the attorneys want a meeting, too, I suppose."

"Meticulous bunch of assholes, of course. But, you have to admit, they have their work cut out for them."

"That's why I picked them, Cavi. Flesh-eating lawyers of their caliber are hard to come by."

"Point is, we have work to do when you get your ass back here. How much longer are you going to be?"

"That all depends on where she's going."

"Anesini and I wager D.C."

"Nope. Philly."

"No way, Raine. It's not far enough."

"Bet you a hundred grand on it."

"Sure, I'll take your money."

"Good thing I pay you so well, Cavi."

"We'll see. Godspeed."

As Raine killed the connection, he looked back at the bright screen of the GPS built into his dash to watch a small red triangle speeding down the blue line of I-95. The girl may have escaped him via the exit, but the tracer continued to transmit faultlessly, safe and undetected where he'd planted it, wrapped in a neat little package amongst her belongings in the trunk of her Audi.

"Somehow I knew I'd need a contingency plan for you, little Alessandra," he smiled, and the steel blue of his eyes glinted like the sharp edge of a long sword as he fired up the Tramonto to give chase.

CHAPTER SIX

11:11 P.M.

The skyline of Philadelphia stood tall and strong, welcoming Solana with thousands of small beacons against the velvet darkness as she ripped down I-676. Exhausted, she already felt the safety and serenity she knew she'd find back in her college town; she'd driven this road so many times during her years at UPenn she could navigate it blindfolded. Philly was her second home, and although it wasn't all that far from New York, it was far enough - for now.

Until tomorrow, she sighed, exiting onto the Avenue of the Arts. *Then on to Chicago.*

Solana took in the familiar beauty of the buildings surrounding her as she arrived at her hotel, which was also known for its unique architecture. A renovated 19th century bank, the Ritz-Carlton Philadelphia more closely resembled a Roman temple with its stately Corinthian columns and graceful rotunda. The imposing edifice gave off the aura of a fortress, a giant block of impenetrable white marble designed to instill an awed sense of trust in the beholder. It made perfect sense given the building's former function, and where safety was precisely what she sought tonight, she'd known exactly where to pilot her car once she'd decided on Philly.

She pulled to a stop in front of the five-star hotel and quickly twisted her snarled, windblown hair into a make-shift updo, thankful she kept spare hair elastics around her gear shift at all times. She'd expertly evaded a wreck this evening; she didn't need to look like one to boot. It was imperative that she keep a low profile over the next couple days, and the more ordinary she looked, the less noteworthy her details, the better.

Solana nodded respectfully to the valet who opened her door, then at the bellhop who politely requested she open her trunk. An easy thing, but the second she stepped out of the Audi, agoraphobia seemed to set in. Even though she knew she'd lost her pursuer on the highway, she couldn't shake the feeling that she needed to get inside as soon as possible, out of plain sight.

She didn't want her rather conspicuous R8 exposed much longer, either.

Solana turned to the valet, already rifling through her wallet. "Would you please see that my car is parked for the evening ASAP?" she asked, passing him a large bill for the trouble.

"I'll see to it at once, Miss," he said with alacrity, and she gratefully passed the keys off to him. He might not be able to help her in the way that she needed it most, but every little bit mattered.

Trusting her car was in good hands, she followed her bellhop through an enormous pair of double doors into a palatial lobby. *Please hurry,* she begged, more than ready to secure her home for the evening, but then she forced herself to calm down.

Take a deep breath, Alessandra, she snapped. *Get a grip. Look at the nifty architecture. Be normal.*

Solana observed her surroundings. Reminiscent of the pre-Depression golden age, the impressive, opulent space respectfully preserved pieces of the building's financial history. Even the antique teller station beneath the domed ceiling fit into the hotel's neo-art-deco ambiance, and it distracted her enough to keep her from making a scene and running at full speed through the grand room to reception.

"Good evening, Miss," the concierge smiled as she reached the long desk. "How can I help you tonight?"

"I need a room for the evening, please," she replied, all swift business. "King-size, top floor, if you have it."

He nodded. "One night only?"

"Yes, sir."

"And the name, please?"

Solana didn't even blink. "Isadora Taranto," she said, using her mother's maiden name.

The concierge raised an eyebrow, studying her across the desk. "Would you kindly spell that for me?"

Swallowing her impatience, Solana obliged, and he thanked her as he entered it into the system.

"And what credit card will you be using this evening, Miss Taranto?"

"How much is it going to be?" she countered.

The gentleman discreetly scribbled a figure on a piece of paper and slid it across the desk to her. She glanced at it, nodded her approval, and withdrew triple the required funds from the cash reserves in her wallet.

"I trust this will cover it," she stated, "along with any security deposit you may require for lack of a credit card."

"Of course, Miss." While he drew up the receipt, he gave her the particulars on check out, the amenities of the hotel and the location of her room, and then passed the paper to her for her signature - and Solana paid careful attention not to sign the wrong name. He furnished her with a copy along with the swipe key for her room, and at last she was set to go. She thanked him, grateful this day was nearly over, and she let the bellhop lead the way.

ᎯᎦ ᎯᎦ ᎯᎦ

As soon as their newest guest was out of earshot, the concierge picked up the phone. Not thirty seconds before Miss Taranto had approached his desk, he'd gotten a rather unusual call from the owner. He'd insisted on being notified immediately if a woman who fit Miss Taranto's description checked into the hotel this evening, and to be ready with the particulars of her registration information.

"We've got her," he reported. "Without a doubt."

ᎯᎦ ᎯᎦ ᎯᎦ

Once upstairs in the large corner suite on the top floor, Solana kicked off her Louboutins and let her toes dig into the plush, cream-colored carpet.

"It's perfect," she sighed. Fresh ivory and gold orchids stood gracefully on black cherry tables placed next to sumptuous pieces of dark brown leather furniture. The city lights shining brightly, silently, through the many windows reminded her of Manhattan. Through a wide doorway at the back of the room, she saw her suitcase had been placed on a low wooden chest at the foot of a giant, welcoming bed. Thoughts of a well-deserved bath led her to a luxe modern bathroom outfitted in sandstone and glass, with candles and plants surrounding the wide tub and a small closet housing a thick bathrobe.

As Solana drew the steaming bathwater, she lit the candles, combed out her rat's nest of hair, and undressed, retiring her suit for the evening in the wardrobe closet. Although the tub seemed to take forever to fill while she prepared, it was worth every second of the wait when she stepped into it.

The water was so hot it was uncomfortable, but she wanted it that way. She wanted to forget the events of the day, forget why she was even here, force her muscles to release the tension that had seized them since dawn that morning. Stretching out the length of the tub, she rested her head against the porcelain rim and closed her eyes, enjoying the smell of the candles and the bath soap, and tried not to think about the fact her world had changed in an instant.

While hunting down a story, she had become the hunted, and she knew Mathison would stop at nothing until he found her. She remembered the way he'd looked at her in the alley, and despite the heat of the water surrounding her, chills swept her flesh. How different it was now from that first sight at the ball, when he'd compiled a mental blueprint of her, his stare so intense she'd flushed with warmth...

Solana squeezed her eyes shut tighter. "There's no way in hell he knows I'm here," she said, needing to hear it out loud. From the moment she'd gotten herself into this mess, she'd been extraordinarily careful, remembering every single instruction Uncle Nico had ever given her should something like this happen. She'd told no one where she was going, used an alias, paid for everything in cash from her sizable emergency fund. She was sitting on twice her annual salary, per her Uncle's orders, and she was glad she'd listened to him - even though she'd never understood why he'd insisted on such an outrageous sum of money.

She understood now. Because of his advice, she'd initiated no traceable monetary transactions, sent no communications online, made no phone calls. She'd even hidden her EasyPass transponder in her glove compartment and turned off the GPS on her iPhone. She knew what Mathison would look for and how he'd look for it, and she'd left no breadcrumbs for him to follow.

I'm safe here. I'm safe. Completely and totally safe.

Solana let this sink in for a long moment, and at last she began to feel her body unclench, relaxing into the warm embrace of the comforting bathwater.

She breathed deeply of the soothing steam scented by the lavender candles, and she opened her eyes to the ceiling, wishing she could see the sky. Somewhere up there, people were watching over her. People who had tried their damnedest to keep her out of this kind of danger and deliver her from the life they knew so well.

Solana thought about the little cedar box she kept in her safe deposit drawer at the bank, mentally rifling through every piece of paper it contained. Her father had made the box for her, even carving her birth date on its bottom, and she'd spent many an afternoon as a child studying the documents in it until she'd committed them to memory.

Included among her immigration and adoption papers was the only photograph she had of her parents, snapped while they walked hand-in-hand on a beach on the Amalfi Coast. It wasn't until she'd turned sixteen, after Uncle Nico told her everything, that the rest of the documents her parents had sent with her to the States made their way back into the little box. Her original Italian birth certificate. The trust fund formation papers. The document signed by her parents that substituted Nico, in place of themselves, as the trustee on her account.

After learning the truth, she'd made two contributions of her own into the box.

One was the document from the Roman bank that transferred control of the trust fund over to her.

The transaction had required her presence at the bank, to match her grown fingerprint with the tiny one they had on file. Uncle Nico was too sick by then to travel, and with her brothers in boot camp in San Diego, she'd had to go alone. Having just learned who she was, she remembered the fear she'd felt over those two days, realizing she could be stepping into hostile territory on native soil. But she did it, and the trip was not without its highpoint. She'd never forget the look on the bank president's face when she told him her name and her business there, laying the evidence of her matriculation into UPenn on the desk in front of him.

The other document was a copy of the form she'd filed in Montana, when she changed her name to formally recognize the Alessandra in her.

From that day forth, she'd known what she wanted to do with her life. The murder of her parents fueled the fire behind her career, centered on finding and exposing the powerhouses of organized crime. Until the day he died, Uncle Nico honestly and thoroughly answered every question she ever asked, sparing no detail as he provided her with first-hand accounts on the inner dynamics of a highly successful crime family.

But if he'd known what she'd do with that information, if he'd thought for a second it would eventually land her on the hit list of the most powerful don on the Eastern Seaboard - arguably the country - he would have reconsidered.

Or maybe he *did* know, and that's why he'd taught her how to protect herself in an emergency, long after the threat to her as an Alessandra had waned. His pointers had gotten her to Philadelphia, a familiar place to rest and regroup, before she would make a break for the Midwest at first light. Once she reached Chicago, she'd be out of Mathison's immediate sphere of influence, where she could afford to trust the local government agencies with her story and start to get her life back.

Thank you, Uncle Nico, she smiled, *for your advice, and for your two daredevil sons who taught me how to drive.*

Relaxed at last, she shampooed her hair and remained in the bath until the heat became unbearable, at which point she rose from the tub, rinsed, and wrapped one of the fluffy towels around her. The relative coolness of the ambient air and the stone floor beneath her feet refreshed her as she towel-dried her hair and brushed her teeth, letting her warm body air-dry. She combed out her long, damp curls, and they bounced back in thick heavy locks, tumbling over her back and shoulders. Her reflection in the mirror was proof that the bath had been a great idea; her skin rejuvenated, she glowed warmly, her cheeks regaining their color, bright green eyes sparkling.

Her feet delighted again in the deep, thick carpet on the trip to the bedroom, where she opened her suitcase - and gasped.

The small paper box nestled in the midst of her belongings looked innocent enough, but its very presence meant they'd broken into her car to put it there.

Cool fingers of trepidation traced along her skin as she stared at it, conjuring limitless possibilities as to what the package could be. Some kind of Trojan Horse? A bomb? Poison?

Securing the towel tightly around her, she leaned over the box and listened. It didn't make a sound. Not a beep, not a click, nothing. No strange smells came from the little parcel, and its white surfaces appeared to be of even, glossy texture. She poked it softly with her index finger and it moved easily, offering no resistance. Still no sounds, no smells. Lifting it gingerly, she held the weightless package between her two hands for a moment, then shook it. Whatever was in it wasn't hard; it sounded mostly like tissue paper. Intrigued, Solana lifted the lid and parted the neat sheets of dark tissue inside, and she gasped again when she discovered the box's contents.

The ivory silk of the lingerie shimmered in the low light of the room, bright against its nest of black tissue paper. She lifted out the two delicate pieces of Sambalina with trembling fingers, the cool, smooth material warming in her hands on contact. The matched demi bra and panties were tastefully simple in design and tied on with long, slim ribbons of champagne-colored silk - they were like nothing she'd ever seen.

Solana felt the tempo of her pulse take on a more interesting rhythm as she stood there, curiosity getting the better of her with each passing second. Fingering the soft, sturdy silk, she wondered just how accurate Mathison's visual assessment of her might actually be...

Why not? The roses were safe enough, weren't they?

As if possessed by another being, Solana let the towel slide down her body to the floor. *I can't believe I'm even considering this*, she thought incredulously, even though she'd already begun dressing herself in the delicate pieces.

When she finished and looked in the mirror, she stared in astonishment at the stunning fit. They were masterfully made, designed to flatter the curves of an hourglass. The low-cut panties tied at the swell of her hips, well below her small waistline, while the demi bra accented her full breasts to perfection. The ivory shined against her sun-bronzed skin and drew attention to her flat abdomen, long slim legs, and toned arms. The ensemble didn't leave much to the imagination, but the sophistication of the cut, the richness of the material... she felt strangely powerful in it.

"Christ, I need a drink," Solana murmured, leaving the mirror behind and walking to the wet bar housed in a handsome Roaring Twenties-inspired cabinet in the main room of the suite. She killed the overhead chandelier and tugged on the chain to the Tiffany lamp on top of the bar, and a warm, calming amber glow filled the room. Finding the bottle of Jameson's, she watched the light play with the rich aureate liquid as she poured two generous fingers' worth into a short rocks glass, then drew the rind of a lemon around the rim.

She carried her nerve-soothing drink to the sitting area, taking a deep draught from it before sinking into an impossibly large brown leather chaise lounge, and found the simultaneous sensations of hot and cold delightful. The slow burn of the sweet Irish whiskey ran through her, flaming her limbs from the inside out, while the cool smoothness of the soft leather against her skin brought on goosebumps. The only sound in the room was the gentle whoosh of the chaise as it settled underneath her, and she sat in silence, staring across the space to her suitcase at the foot of the bed.

She studied it, not understanding why there hadn't been something else buried in there. *Why would he go through the effort and expense?* she pondered, draining the last of the Jameson's. It just didn't make sense... unless it was something else entirely.

Her thoughts reverted to her initial suspicion as she put the empty rocks glass down on the table beside the chaise.

A decoy...

A Trojan Horse...

"Oh God," she whispered, and her head snapped back to the suitcase - to find Raine Mathison leaning casually against the bedroom's doorjamb, his glacial eyes alight with victory.

Icy fingers gripped her heart and stomach at the sight of him. His large, fine frame monopolized the doorway like a breathtaking piece of classical statuary, commanding the room by just being present within it. He stood there like he owned the place, dressed to the nines in grey Ralph Lauren slacks, a white Thom Browne broadcloth left unbuttoned at the top, and that pervasive silent power he possessed. His handsome features betrayed none of his thoughts, but something about that stone-faced expression made her cheeks burn acutely, and a cold sweat washed over her nearly naked body before him.

"My dear Ms. Trent," he purred, his deep masculine voice filling the room, "so pleased to finally make your acquaintance."

Solana's muscles tensed to run and he sprang into movement, crossing the room in several long, powerful, stalking strides. Grabbing her by the waist he slammed her back down onto the chaise and straddled it, holding her still as he stood over her hips. She dug her heels into the soft leather and pushed back from him but she hit the back of the chaise so hard her feet slipped off, her knees hooking over either side of the wide armless lounge.

He sat down in the open space between her legs, the backs of his hard-muscled thighs weighing down on top of hers, pinning them underneath him. Trapped, Solana's heart fluttered like a caged bird in her chest, frightened by the closeness of him, the overwhelming strength of his legs over hers, the rich smoothness of his grey slacks against her flesh. The sexy, strong, virile scent of him terrified her; it was hard, dark, redolent of power and permanence. She watched his face as he placed his hands on his knees and studied her before him, his noble features even more magnificent up close and personal, and when his cool eyes met hers, her breath caught in her throat.

At last, Raine had her exactly where he wanted her. Although she held her beautiful face high in defiance, her painfully perfect body trembled visibly, her fingers gripping the edges of the chaise on either side of her full hips. The lingerie detailed every luscious curve of her figure, more so than he'd imagined, and her soft, radiant skin glowed in contrast to the dark brown leather. Volumes of thick auburn curls ran wild and free around her, and he could smell the delicate fragrance of her, all spicy and sensuous. She was now his for the taking, and he was getting harder by the second with the anticipation of it.

All he had to do was control it, just long enough to get what he needed from her.

Her permission.

He leaned forward slowly, bringing his face inches

from hers, and he moved his large hands from his knees to wrap them tightly around her wrists. His palms covered her slim fingers; he could feel her rapid heartbeat against his thumbs.

"You understand what I must do to you now, don't you?" he said, his voice dead calm.

Solana refrained from telling him the first phrase that came to mind. Instead, she boldly raised her chin higher, refusing to dignify the question with a response.

But Raine wasn't one who took to being stonewalled. The ice in his eyes hardened as he patiently ran his hands up the length of her arms, over her smooth shoulders to her neck and closed his fingers firmly around her throat.

"Come now, Solana," he urged, "I have yet to hear the sound of your voice." He allowed her a few more seconds to reconsider her choice of obstinate silence, his thumb caressing the hollow of her throat, and when she still didn't answer him he pushed down in it. "You do understand, yes?"

Pain from the pressure of his thumb registered through Solana's body and she closed her eyes, gritting her teeth against the angry tears that threatened to manifest themselves. He may have won, but she wouldn't give him the satisfaction of seeing her break. When she locked her gaze with his again, she made damn sure there was no trace of weakness whatsoever in it.

"Yes," she hissed, her jaw set in a firm line.

"Good," he said. "Because you certainly should... *Alessandra*."

Livid green fire flashed in her eyes. *He knows. Everything.* And she could only imagine what he must be feeling, being seconds away from the bragging rights he'd be entitled to as the one who finished off the Last Alessandra.

But she had a legacy to defend. Her parents hadn't gone down without a fight, and neither would she.

"Likewise," Solana seethed, "you should know I won't be murdered so easily."

A slow grin tugged at the corner of the boss's sexy lips. "Now I never said anything about making this easy," Raine said, his fingers gently stroking her throat. "Matter of fact, I may be the hardest thing you ever experience."

A strange glint struck like lightning in the unfathomable blue sky of his eyes, and Solana understood. She understood the signal he'd sent her, and cold panic gripped her mercilessly.

It's not just my life that he wants.

He'll be taking something else from me first.

Solana fought against him, trying to push him away with every ounce of strength she had. Her legs squirmed under the weight of his in futile efforts to free them, and he pressed his thighs down harder on hers until she could no longer move beneath him. His hands left her throat to grab her wrists, and she gasped as he squeezed them in his fists and slammed them high over her head against the back of the chaise.

"I see you've caught my drift," Raine said so softly, so seductively, her hair stood on end. Numb with fear, she felt him cross her wrists and transfer possession of them to just one of his large hands. His thumb and middle finger circled the crux of the X they made, locking them together, and he buried them into the leather upholstery above her head.

"But out of respect for your ancestry," he murmured, his intense eyes never leaving hers, "things may not go so unpleasantly for you."

The enigmatic comment brought her little solace as he

moved his free hand from her ensnared wrists - until his fingertips began a maddeningly slow, torturous journey down the length of her forearm. Barely touching her, they traced a soft, precise line along her skin, leaving a trail of warmth behind them. They followed her elbow, the lean muscle of her tricep, and she inhaled sharply when he made contact with the sensitive spot underneath her arm.

His discovery expedition pressed boldly forward, and her teeth clenched as he let his thumb just barely graze the globe of her breast on the way to her torso. He traveled gently down her side... to her waist... over the swell of her hip... and stopped when he reached her thigh, where his fingers took hold of the ends of the panties' silk ribbons.

Solana could barely breathe, acutely aware he'd pinned her in a position that rendered her defenseless, unable to protect her core from him. He had complete power over her and she waited for him to unleash it, knowing full-well from the stories she'd heard what nightmares this man was capable of making into reality.

But there wasn't so much as a flicker of change in the glowing embers of his eyes. Unwavering, constant, the blue-white furnaces burned with the brilliant light of desire, not malice, and they held her still as she felt the gentle tug on the bow at her hip.

What he'd told her was beginning to make sense.

Things may not go so unpleasantly for you, he'd said.

He'll take what he wants, she realized, *but he so much as promised not to hurt me in the process - provided I yield to him.* Her heart pounded hard as his dexterous fingers loosened the silk ties, the ends of the thin ribbons tickling her thigh where they brushed against her skin. He then drew one of his fingers across her stomach to her other hip, and she shuddered against him, his soft touch stimulating the hypersensitive reflexes of her abdomen. With two deft movements he untied the second bow, and the smooth silk glided down into an ivory pool in the space between her legs. His hand took firm hold of her bared hip, squeezed it gently, feeling the curve of it, and then his fingertips began to carefully draw it forward.

"Lift," Raine ordered, his voice stern yet soft. He pressed down harder on her wrists over her head, and Solana realized he was giving her the leverage she needed to raise her hips. She pushed her wrists upwards, meeting the downward force from the heel of his hand, and she did as he asked, her flat abs tensing as she strained to lift her hips despite the weight of his thighs on hers.

Solana knew she couldn't fight him - wasn't sure any-more she even wanted to fight him - as he pulled the panties away from her shaking body. She never would have thought he'd take her like this, touching her so softly, his hypnotic eyes holding her steady, keeping her panic at bay. The smell of him, the magnificence of him consumed her, and that initial attraction she'd felt for him at the ball inexplicably ignited from a curious spark to a dangerous, encompassing flame.

Raine laid his hand flat on the soft plain of her belly, where he pushed down gently to nestle her hips back into the cushion of the chaise. The heat from his palm radiated all through her as he let it linger there for a long moment, rising and falling with her uneven breathing... and then he started to move downward. "*Oh, Christ,*" she whispered, and he felt her muscles go taut as his fingers ran through her downy merlot-hued curls. Her back arched from the back of the chaise when he touched the heart of her, where to his utter delight, he found her warm, soft, moist. *She wanted him.*

He watched her close her eyes as he stroked her sweet, wet softness, her lashes thick and dark against cheeks that suddenly flushed hot, and the tightness between his legs hit the breaking point. He brought his face next to hers, his lips to her ear. "Consider it a contract with the devil," he murmured, his voice ragged with naked desire.

Contract with the Devil... Solana's jaw dropped. "The Tramonto," she breathed, understanding exactly what he'd just told her. "It was you. I fucking knew it was you."

She gasped for him, sharp and piercing, as he sent one of his deft fingers questing into her deep, lush warmth. "Mmm-hmm," he hummed against her ear, just before he bit down on the tender flesh of her earlobe.

He heard her smile. "You know, if you hadn't wrecked your car in the middle of the highway, you'd have – "

Raine silenced her with a kiss, knowing he could have finished the rest of the sentence for her, and Solana could no longer maintain the pretense of denying him. The second his mouth possessed hers she parted her lips, his intense demand lighting her on fire. She felt him squeeze her wrists in mounting passion as she yielded to him -

And when her tongue met his with equal fervor, teasing him in return, when she released her inhibitions and let her hips begin to move against his incredible ministrations inside her, he finally let go of her hands.

Blood rushed back into her fingers, making them tingle as she lowered her stiff arms to touch him for the first time. Her palms went to his broad shoulders cautiously, as if she were about to lay them on a hot stove, and his white broadcloth shirt felt crisp and smooth beneath her prickling fingers. Their kiss deepened, growing more urgent, and she gripped the lean, powerful muscles of his shoulders, feeling them flex as he continued the sweet torment of exploring her center. She moved her hands down to his chest and grabbed hold of his shirt, gathering the fine fabric in her fingers, and she felt him smile against her lips as she tore it open, buttons flying across the room. His fingers left her core to find the strings to the silk bra, which he swiftly loosened and sent to join the panties on the floor next to the chaise. She then felt his hands wrap themselves around her waistline and slide up her sides until the heels of his palms brushed against the soft globes of her full breasts.

Raine pulled back from her to drink in the vision of her naked body, and Solana felt her cheeks redden again, keenly aware of him fully clothed while his eyes roved her bare, vulnerable flesh. He'd annihilated every last defense with his masterful game of seduction. He'd made her want him. She'd taken him at his word, trusted him because she'd had no other choice. *I'll be damned if you humiliate me now, after all this.*

As if he'd read her mind he raised his eyes to hers, and she understood the look he gave her better than if he had spoken aloud. *You think you're ready?* he lifted an eyebrow. *Be careful what you wish for, little Alessandra; you just might get it.* He watched her as he discarded the broadcloth, confidently tossed it to the floor, and then followed with the skin-tight CK undershirt.

Solana sucked in her breath. There was nothing soft about Raine Mathison. He was a masterpiece, chiseled, hard, flawless. His magnificent body tapered at the middle; her eyes traveled the span of his sculpted shoulders, over his broad chest, down his perfectly cut abs, and she could imagine the feel of her legs wrapped around his slim waist. Her gaze traced down the exquisite definition of his arms, and a sexy platinum Bulova ID bracelet flashed cold in the low light, the chunky figaro links glinting bright white against his suntanned left wrist. She watched the strong muscles move while he reached over the side of the chaise and loosened the laces of one of his shoes... took it off... lost the sock... repeated the same on the other side. When he finished he looked back at her, his smoldering stare holding her motionless, and she didn't dare breathe when he stood up before her.

Warm tingles shot down her legs as he loosened his belt, and when he dropped the Ralph Laurens he wore nothing else. She swallowed hard at the sight of him, and he paused for a moment, still straddling the chaise, the grey slacks catching over his sizable thighs. He wanted her to see him, to take in every well-endowed inch of him as he stood over her. Powerful, beautiful, capable, he was thick and hard, and Solana wasn't prepared for the swell of intimidation that seized her, nor the towering inferno of desire that blazed through her, making her palms sweat.

Raine drew his leg to his other one, took off his pants and threw them aside with a quick flick of his wrist. Robed solely in his sultry elegance, he came back down onto the chaise to kneel naked before her, the *come hither* look in his eyes as he reached for her hips. At the touch of his fingertips she moved down the chaise, towards him, bridging the gap between them with her body, and he advanced as she lay back apprehensively onto the warmed leather.

Solana trembled as he brought himself over her, feeling the taut, strong quads of his thighs take their place against the backs of hers. He rested his forearms on the leather on either side of her face and buried his hands in the mass of russet curls around her, his thumbs caressing her jawline. His handsome face was inches above hers, his blue eyes filling her vision, probing her soul, watching her, waiting, savoring the moment, enjoying it while she burned beneath him. The flames of lust licked her relentlessly, the painful tightness gripping her body begged for release, clutching her harder, scorching her deeper with every second he waited.

"Do it, Raine," she whispered up to him, unable to stand another moment of his torture, and she heard the urgent, unmistakable desperation in her own voice.

The corners of his mouth curved in a grin that made her insides twist with longing. "Lesson one," he said, his eyes sparkling with barely restrained desire, "is patience. In all things. The power to keep at bay the slow burn for what you want. For what is yours."

And he didn't need to say anything further, or fit the comment into context.

Solana knew what she'd just done. She'd just given him the permission he wanted.

She was his. And it was time.

Raine turned serious, dead serious, and Solana bit down on her bottom lip as he lowered his hips slowly, oh God so slowly, into the cradle between her thighs, forcing them to part farther to receive him. The dark golden curls on his chest teased the rosy tips of her breasts as they brushed against him. She could feel the blistering heat radiating from the flat plain of his sheetrock abs where they hovered over hers, holding his weight above her. She bit down harder when she felt the tip of his rigid shaft touch the gates of her warm core, and she watched his eyes flash as his willpower shattered. He couldn't hold back any longer, and she gasped when he finally entered her. He was hard, insistent, and maddeningly patient as he filled her inch... by inch... by glorious inch.

Raine felt the siren underneath him shiver as he began to thrust into her hot, smooth softness, and the sound she made when she moved to meet him boiled his blood. He crushed the curls in his hands as he took her, and his face descended to hers to capture her lips in an ardent, soul-binding kiss. She drew her knees up beside him, wrapped her slim, shapely legs around his waist, and when she rose her hips against his, drawing him deeper, harder inside her, it left him breathless. Their bodies were perfectly matched, the one half designed for the other, flawless.

Solana ran her hands down the length of him, reveling in the movements of his muscles beneath her quaking fingers. She pressed her palms into the small of his back, where she learned his powerful rhythm and matched it, meeting him hit for hit as she rolled her burning body in time with his. The more he demanded, the more she gave, rising to the challenge. She returned his intense kiss, tasting him, exploring him, fire consuming her, rushing through her bloodstream with a vibrance and speed never known to her before.

Suddenly, Raine's mouth took possession of her throat and he pulled his hands from her blanket of shining hair. He reached down and roughly ran his palms up the backs of her thighs, then grabbed hold of them firmly, gripping her hamstrings so tightly the hard metal of his ID bracelet bit into her tender skin under the heel of his hand. He spread her legs wider beneath him, wanting to devour her, tear her apart, and his triceps bulged as he fiercely wrenched her body against him, guiding her as he drove harder and faster into her.

Solana cried out in pleasure, her heartbeat pounding against his lips on her throat, and he smiled, feeling the muscles deep inside her body tighten around him. She was so close... so very close... he could feel it all through her. "Come for me, Solana," he commanded softly in her ear, and it sent her over the edge.

The delightful, delirious sinking feeling deep within her was like electricity gathering just before a lightning strike. Seconds later the bolt hit, searing white-hot through her core, and Solana clung to him as he obliterated the tension that held her prisoner with three violent thrusts. She called out his name with each one, loud and clear, once in terror, again in rapture, and then in joy, not caring who heard her as sweet release conquered her, filling her with golden light.

Raine was undone. The priceless sound of her voice crying his name, the exquisite writhing of her hot body underneath him, and the tight contraction of her muscles when she climaxed had a cataclysmic effect on him. His eyes turned a dark sapphire and he came hard, letting loose a moan of deep, complete, primitive pleasure as he exploded into her beneath him. He shuddered as the force of it shook him like the aftershocks of an earthquake, and when the tremors subsided he found his forehead resting on the leather of the chaise, his cheek next to hers, his hands once again seeking the softness of her rich hair.

Satiated beyond her wildest dreams, Solana felt a languid smile grace her lips as he eased the weight of his beautiful, sweat-slickened body down on top of hers. His intoxicating scent pervaded the air she breathed and she closed her eyes in delight, inhaling deeply. She let her legs slacken alongside his, her heels finding the comfortable nooks in the backs of his knees. She buried one of her trembling hands in his thicket of hair, and the dark blond curls wrapped themselves around her fingers as if they were alive.

Time seemed to stand still. She'd never know just how long they lay there in silence, each listening to the other breathe as they basked in the enervating aftermath. Lulled by the rhythm of his strong heartbeat against hers, she nearly drifted off to sleep, spellbound.

My first impression of you was wrong, her mind whispered blissfully from a cloudy distance, her fingertips idly tracing the muscles of his shoulder. *You* are *Apollo...*

...The golden God of the Sun...

...The light bearer...

...Lucifer...

Her thoughts stopped wandering.

And then slowly, as if waking from a dream, Solana came back to herself.

Her eyes fluttered open as the fog lifted.

Oh Jesus Christ.

What the fuck just happened!

Wide awake, she didn't move. She concentrated on keeping her breathing smooth and even, praying he hadn't detected the palpable change in her body as she came to grips with the gravity of the situation. She didn't know whether to laugh, cry, or panic, and her clear, bright eyes focused on the ceiling as if the answers she sought would be written there.

She knew he'd chased her down tonight to kill her. At some point, however, he'd added an extra item to that agenda –

And promptly realized it had probably been there all

along, from the very second he'd recognized her in that alley.

She'd studied this man at length for years; she couldn't believe it hadn't occurred to her before. He was a renowned marksman: his expertly placed bullet through her hair was only a warning. He'd *meant* to miss her, with the sole intention of catching her later... alone. Someplace where he could spend some quality time with her before silencing her permanently.

But *this*... She was sure this glowing, rapturous closeness had not been part of the plan.

There were no words to describe what he'd done to her. Allegedly, out of respect for her family, she had been spared whatever it should have been. Where she'd expected brutality, she'd received tantalizing gentleness. In place of apathy, she'd discovered passion. Instead of awkwardness, a confident, tacit understanding... He'd read her like a book.

But what shocked her more was *her* response to *him*. His touch lit her up like a Roman torch. At first he'd terrified her, but then he'd soothed her, and because she'd let him, he'd thoroughly pleasured her. Mathison had proved to be a man of his word; he'd done anything but harm her, even at his roughest...

Mathison.

Solana hovered over that word like it was a relic from another time. *That's not his name anymore*, she thought, feeling the flames of embarrassment lick her as she thought back to the blinding finale. Now he was Raine.

None of it made any sense. She was the liability he'd come to eliminate, and Solana couldn't fathom his next step - even though everything she'd ever learned about him told her what it should be.

The summation of her musings slipped from the depths of her thoughts to float in the smooth air above them. "What happens now?"

Raine remained silent for a long moment, and she sensed he was caught off-guard by her calm, matter-of-fact question.

"We have much to discuss, Ms. Trent," he said after a while, his lips next to her ear, "but now is not the time."

His answer offered no comfort, but portended no harm, and when he lifted his head to bring his face over hers again, his expression was undecipherable. He placed his hands beside her face, pushed himself up off of her and waited patiently, expectantly, his impassive eyes penetrating hers. The light shining from the Tiffany lamp behind him made his halo of hair glow golden, and she stared up at him, remembering the last words of Mary, Queen of Scots.

In manus tuas, Domine, commendabo spiritum meum.
Into thy hands, O Lord, I commend my spirit...

Trapped between his strong, muscle-carved arms, she understood his silent request, and she'd just have to trust her instincts that, for now, she was safe with him.

Solana rolled to her side on the long chaise, and in one smooth motion he lay down behind her. He pulled her possessively to him and wrapped one of his thick, heavy legs around both of hers, pressing her back to his warm, hard torso and drawing her buttocks against his swollen maleness. He kept his arm around her, with his forearm placed between her breasts and his hand splayed flat across her upper chest, just underneath her throat. The tip of his index finger traced along the hollow there, drawing a slow, smooth lullaby of circles in time with her breathing... He enveloped her. Completely. Even her head lay cradled in his neck, and when he rested his chin on her crown, she suddenly felt protected from the world - including him.

Along with the feeling of sanctuary came an overwhelming exhaustion that eclipsed the light of reason, eradicating the ability to think and replacing it with the imperative to rest. Within moments, the quick blackness of sleep overtook her, and she rested uneasily beside him.

C/3 C/3 C/3

Raine listened to Solana's slow breathing beside him, and he welcomed it, needing the time to think.

He was floored.

It had been a long two-hour drive to Philadelphia, spent entirely in thoughts of her. She was unlike anyone he'd ever encountered, and it fascinated him. He knew she was smart, but the way she outwitted him time and again was a sign of genius.

He'd gained access to her apartment early that evening, but she never made that fatal mistake of coming home from work. From Anesini's report he'd known she'd been back to her place after the alley, and he spent his brief time there reading the clues she'd left behind in her tasteful, uncluttered high-rise. Dresser drawers left open. All the toiletries missing. A pile of laundry in the middle of her bedroom floor - the clothing she'd worn so early that morning. She'd packed to leave town, and in one hell of a hurry.

All reports still confirmed no outgoing phone calls, no credit card charges, no emails outside of the ordinary. No airline or hotel reservations. No cash withdrawals from any of her accounts. Salvatore must have taught her well.

He'd had to come to the Times and scare her into leaving her office, but when she left she'd outsmarted him again, pulling the alarm and escaping in the crowd.

When he'd pulled up beside her on 41st he knew they were in for one hell of a ride. Few people shared his eclectic taste in music, but she'd nailed one of his favorites as she blasted down the streets of Manhattan, suitably inspiring him to skip tracks to Cookie Monsta's "Riot!" on his own playlist. The rush of the chase flamed him, but again she'd emerged the victor with the stunt she pulled on the highway, wiping him out. In fact, if it hadn't been for the tracer he'd buried in the tissue paper of the lingerie box, and the fact that the owner of the Ritz-Carlton Philadelphia happened to owe him a favor, he never would have caught up with her tonight.

Her quick shrewdness had more than earned his respect. It was the kind of prescient, tactical intelligence he recruited into his own syndicate.

Not only was she smart, she had balls. Not only was she ready to race him, she was ready to stake her life on the line and call his bluff, knowing damn well he wouldn't hit her at such high speed and take himself out with her. Not only was she proud of the fact she'd sent his Fisker spinning in a shower of sparks into the breakdown lane, she had the guts to call him on it, making the crack to his face, knowing she'd bested him.

His fingers traced along the soft skin of her arm, this woman who dared to sleep so softly next to him. "You know, if you hadn't wrecked your car in the middle of the highway, you'd have *been here sooner*," he murmured, finishing the sentence she'd started.

That was the kicker that sent him reeling. Alessandra Solana Trent, his quarry, had wanted him as completely as he'd wanted her. That smoldering moment between them at the ball had burst into roaring flames here on the chaise, burning hot enough to transcend this fucked up situation and transform it into something else entirely. The fact that he was already warring with himself over his imminent conquest of her was only compounded by this unforeseen element. He certainly hadn't needed her permission - what shocked him was that he'd found himself *wanting* it. Her raw, brave, unabashed passion had nearly burned him with its heat, and he would never let her know that it had been the final thing to tip the scales, causing him to permanently alter his plans for her.

Raine looked at her beautiful face as she slept beside him, let his eyes travel the length of her impossibly perfect figure, and his attraction to her continued to consume him. Fate had given her to him, the one who'd kept him spellbound from the moment he saw her at the ball, and there was a reason.

Keep your friends close; keep your enemies closer.

He could use someone of her position on his side of the court.

An intelligent, courageous, passionate journalist - with mob in her blood.

He knew of the story she was writing and the investigations she was making into his newly contracted alliances, and at this critical point, those alliances didn't need to be jeopardized by the prodding of a renowned journalist from the world's flagship paper. Now that she was indebted to him, not only would she cease working on the story, but she would clear it. And clear *him*. And continue to clear him throughout his career.

Raine lifted a heavy lock of her hair in his hand. He felt the heft of it, enjoyed its subtle perfume, watched the light shimmer along the dark browns, deep reds, and warm golds. At his attentions, the thick barrel curls wove obediently through his fingers like a grapevine, and he grinned.

She had been recruited. She just didn't know it yet.

CHAPTER SEVEN

Solana was only aware of the bright morning sunshine falling onto her, warming her all over where she lay naked on top of a sinfully soft bed. With her eyes still closed against the dazzling light, she stretched languorously over the luxurious sheets, like a cat sleeping in the sun. No matter how far she reached, she couldn't find the edges of the bed in any direction; it seemed to go on endlessly. She could smell the hotness of the white linens glowing in the brilliant sunlight, and she breathed in the life-giving heat with relish.

Suddenly there was a wash of coolness over her skin, a momentary reprieve from the scorching radiance as a cloud passed swiftly over the sun, and then the light was back, brighter than –

Gentle lips touched down on the sensitive flatland far below her navel and moved smoothly downward, downward, as warm fingers slid under the backs of her knees and firmly parted her thighs...

All at once, Solana remembered.

Her eyes flew open, only to be blinded by the brightness of the sunlight.

"Raine, stop!" she cried hoarsely, her face flushing with color as she yanked her legs from his strong grip. She pushed away from him but not fast enough, and she felt his hands grab hold of her calves, preventing her from retreating any farther from him. Caught, she sat up on her elbows and pulled, hard, but the more she fought him, the more viselike his fingers became.

When her eyes finally adjusted to the blinding light, she found him standing fully dressed before her in sharp Jil Sander, clean-shaven, his curling waves of dark blond hair shining like spun gold in the sun.

"Good morning," Raine said, laughter in his deep voice as he raised an eyebrow at her. "A little late for modesty, isn't it?" and he watched her cheeks burn deeper as she entered the next ring of hell.

She'd melt the ice of the ninth circle, Dante, he thought as he let his glittering eyes rove her nude body. Her thick dark auburn hair flamed its true fiery color in the blazing sunlight, flowing behind and around her like lava where she lay propped up on her elbows. He followed the curves of her breasts to her lean abdomen, and he gripped her calves tighter when his gaze traveled lower, lower, to the heart of her, to the crevice of soft hair that burned just as warmly as the sexy tendrils tumbling down her arms...

Yes. He'd decided last night when he carried her to bed just how he was going to wake her, and the thought of tasting her, the thought of making her writhe under his mouth would not be so easily dismissed. After the way she'd responded to him last night, her current reaction made little sense - until he realized the problem. For her, this kind of intimacy was nothing less than sacrosanct, something she relinquished only to someone she trusted... and she wasn't ready to share it with him.

He grinned. *Even better.*

Solana gasped when Raine forcibly pulled her to him. He didn't stop until he brought her ass right up against his thick thighs, to the very edge of the bed where he stood, and his fingertips stroked the backs of her knees where he held her legs wide open on either side of him. The skin on her back burned from being dragged across the sheets, but it was nothing compared to the feeling of his eyes on her body as he lowered to his knees on the floor in front of her.

"Raine, no!" She struggled against him, but she was no match for his strength as he decisively shoved her thighs outward and pinned the backs of them down on the bed. His bright eyes flashed a severe warning when she reached down to push him away from her, and he dug his elbows into the hollows behind her knees, cocking them out to furiously part her legs farther. He grabbed her hands, threatening to crush them in his fingers as he flipped them over, and she cried out plaintively when he bit them hard on the heels in punishment, nearly drawing blood.

Solana shook like a leaf as she watched him turn her hands back over and lay them palms-down on the insides of her own thighs. He placed his large hands on top of hers, holding them still, and when he looked at her again she saw a vehemence that was no longer attributable to anger. It was the confident triumph of conquest, and the heady joy of partaking in the spoils.

"Lesson Two," he said carefully, his fingers stroking hers where he held them to her opened legs, "is acceptance. You are beholden to me, and I will do with you as I wish."

Solana's eyes stung with tears and she squeezed them shut, swallowing the whimper she felt rise in her throat as he closed in. "Don't," she whispered desperately, "please don't... "

"Shhhh, Solana," Raine murmured, and at last his mouth met the sweetest part of her. He heard her inhale sharply when he parted his lips against her, and he thought she'd lift off the bed when he touched her with a quick, smooth curl of his tongue.

He moved slowly, inquisitively, letting his sensuous mouth survey the rich, soft landscape, like a conqueror traversing his new country for the first time. He savored her, drew out every line, discovered every ridge, navigated every valley, but he saved the expedition into her treasure cove for last. Making his way into that uncharted territory, he started low and traced higher, higher, gently probing and dividing until he reached the pearl nestled in the tender folds.

Raine felt her whole body shudder, and he knew the warmth that suddenly flooded her wasn't from the hot summer sun beating down on her bare skin. He teased her with the tip of his tongue, quick, firm, and tight, and his heartbeat spiked when he heard her soft, piercing cry of pleasure, felt her small, graceful hands ball into fists beneath his palms. Slipping his hands under hers, he gently pried her fingers apart to take her hands in his, and he held them securely, safely, his thumbs stroking the backs of her quaking fingers.

Solana gripped his hands, taking the solace he wanted

her to find there as she collapsed under the erotic motions of his heart-stopping mouth. Shockwaves burst from the center of her body and traveled outward, peaking over the tightening tips of her breasts and wreaking decadent havoc along her wakened limbs. Never again would naked mean the simple absence of clothing; it was an emotion, elating and frightening as she lay open to him, to the sun, to the air that caressed the expanses of her feverish skin. She surrendered her sacristy to the celebrant on his knees, spreading her legs wider for him, and she could feel his clear, crisp eyes on her as she began to rock her hips gently against his silvered tongue.

The way she tentatively, gingerly gave herself up to him made Raine want to eat her alive. The sacrificial lamb he'd thrown down on the altar no longer resisted him, but now rose willingly against the cutting edge of his sharp tongue to receive the fatal slash. Raw with desire and pride, he nearly perfected the rite, and it took an act of sheer will to rein himself in and slow to a painstaking pace. He'd broken her after she'd tried to deny him, and now he would make it last as long as he wanted, until he brought her to the limits of frustration and she begged him to finish her.

Wordlessly, Solana demanded more from him, rolling her hips harder under his long, forceful, deliberate strokes, but he thwarted her, not yet giving her more than he wanted her to have. "Raine, please," she whispered, barely breathing it, like the sound of snow floating on the winter wind, and he watched her perspiring body glisten in the sunlight as her back curved beautifully off the bed. He started to give it to her, and he felt her hands tighten their grip on his fingers, heard her breaths draw quick and shallow, growing sharper as he brought her closer, closer...

When she suddenly turned to hot, rich silk under his mouth he knew he had her, and he paused, holding her suspended between heaven and hell.

"Your body belongs to me," he declared softly, letting his lips and tongue just graze her with the words, and he heard her say it. The confession.

"Yes," she whispered, the single word that made him give her everything.

Releasing her hands, Raine cupped the soft, smooth cheeks of her firm rear in his hands and lifted her up to him, guiding her hips in a swift rhythm that drew her strongly, deeply against his plundering mouth. She threw her head back and screamed his name in pure ecstasy as the blade of his tongue finally cut her to the blissful quick, and he drank deeply of the nectar that flowed rich and sweet from her hallowed chalice.

Solana drowned under the breathtaking swells that washed over her, feeling the heavy rolling waves crush out the last of the fire that had ripped through her body. By the time Raine let her go, she couldn't move. Her extinguished muscles ached, smoldering deep inside her like the hot embers of a bonfire doused by a sudden deluge of rain. With her eyes still closed to the powerful morning sun, she saw only the luminous red-orange glow that filtered through her eyelids, and it felt like the same glow that warmed its way through every last quivering inch of her.

Slowly she rose up on her elbows, letting her head fall back listlessly under the weight of her hair cascading behind her. She drew her legs back toward her and dug her heels into the edge of the mattress to push herself to the safe center of the bed. When she rolled up carefully to a sitting position, tucking her legs underneath her, she felt the coolness of shadow soothe her sun-warmed skin. No longer in danger of going blind, she opened her eyes, and the world was a surreal watercolor of cold green-blue, an afterimage from lying in the intense sunlight for so long.

It got colder when she discovered she was alone in the bedroom.

Mortified, Solana grabbed hold of the huge white sheet and pulled it around her stark-naked body. Whatever sense of shame she'd felt the night before was of little consequence compared to the magnitude of what she now experienced. He'd laid siege to her temple until she let it fall to him, but the white flag hadn't been enough. She'd entreated him to take possession of it. And she had answered him honestly when she'd admitted to him that he had acquired sole right and title to her person.

Because he had.

She looked down at her hands where they lay in the soft hammock of bedsheet spanning her lap. Slowly she flipped them over, and she felt a tingle run along the deep red marks that showed livid on the heels where he'd bitten her.

But then she remembered how he'd held them so protectively afterwards, giving her the comfort she'd wanted and needed once she'd succumbed to him. It further confirmed the unspoken, unwritten lesson she'd come to understand from him: *If I don't fight him, he won't hurt me.*

It also proved the existence of an unexpected, undeniable corollary to Lesson Zero.

Not only will he not hurt me, he'll bring me to heaven and hold me there...

But what reason did she have to trust him? What if the precept was only a temporary amnesty and everything changed the second they left this room?

Solana sensed his footsteps approaching from the master bath, and she folded another layer of the sheet tightly around her. Mustering every shred of dignity she had left, she raised her head proudly and willed a coolness into her eyes just as Raine strode into the bedroom.

You smug, arrogant ass, she fumed icily, noting the added swagger in his step and his self-satisfied half-smile, but what made her angrier was the fact that she herself had given him reason to be so pleased with himself.

He grinned wickedly as he studied her sitting tall and queenly in the center of the massive bed.

"Now what happened to that becoming color in your cheeks, Ms. Trent?" he inquired, and Solana knew when he approached the bed that he had every intention of making the flush return to her face.

"Don't even think about it, Mathison," she said, holding the sheet fisted against her chest as she watched him reach down and take the edge of the white fabric in his fingers. He merely gave it a puckish tug, but she seized a wad of the soft cotton and yanked on the slack, ripping it right out of his hand.

"So there," Solana declared haughtily, but alas it was a Pyrrhic victory. Although she'd successfully won the bed linen from him, she couldn't stop the damned stain of red from coursing along her cheekbones.

Raine's smile broadened. "So *there*," he countered, and his soft, sexy purr made her body clench mutinously. "Now, it's time for us to go. You have fifteen minutes to get ready, so I'd hop to it if I were you." And his eyes lingered on her for a second longer before he turned and left the bedroom for the main chamber of the suite.

"What?" She tore the sheet off the bed and wrapped it around herself to chase after him, her moves less than graceful with every sore, overexerted muscle screaming in protest. "What do you mean fifteen minutes?"

He stood at the sidebar where he was stirring cream into a cup of coffee. "What, is that not long enough? You take much longer and we'll miss our flight window."

"No, where exactly do you think – ?"

His eyes lifted up to hers, all sense of levity gone from them, and the look quelled her.

"Downstairs," Raine said shortly. "In fifteen." He held her gaze for a long moment, leaving no room for misunderstanding before he strode across the room and left the suite, shutting the door hard behind him.

Fuck. Solana's pulse raced. Where the hell was he taking her? More importantly, why?

"Looks like that theory on Lesson Zero is about to be put to the test," she muttered, and got moving.

She quickly showered and gathered up her belongings, and when she opened her suitcase, she found that Raine had tucked the small lingerie box back into place amongst her things.

Nice, she frowned, stuffing it down to the bottom of her bag... and paused. She thought back to the realization she'd had last night, and grabbed the little parcel again.

Solana pawed through the black tissue paper, this time looking beyond the distractingly lovely ivory silk inside. She tipped the box, shaking it as she searched, until she heard the barely audible tap she now knew to listen for.

"Gotcha," she said, and she slipped her fingers into the corner of the package to find a tiny button of metal no bigger than a watch battery.

She flipped the silent little circle over in the palm of her hand, but there were no identifying details, no part numbers, nothing on its blank surfaces of brushed silver.

No sounds, no signs of activity... she was about to give it up for dead - when light glowed around its circumference.

"Fucking clever," she whispered. It wasn't a rapid blink; that would run too great a risk of discovery. And the light's color wasn't garish, like a red or electric blue. Every twenty seconds, the LED simply warmed to a deep amber then faded back into darkness, all the while not making a single sound as the tracer relayed its position.

Resisting the urge to throw it out, Solana returned the tiny transmitter to its nest of tissue paper and shoved the little package in with everything else in her suitcase.

Better to know where it is, she thought, *and smarter to let him think I haven't found it.*

Time was flying. She tossed the bathtowel to the floor and threw on a pair of white linen pants and a long pale pink tank cami of the smoothest silk. She pulled her damp curls together into a ponytail at the nape of her neck with a thin white ribbon, stepped into a pair of dress sandals, grabbed her suitcase, and flew out the door.

Across the bustling lobby under the rotunda Solana spotted Raine immediately, easy to find with that golden hair, those sharp clothes, that magnetic presence. He was having an amicable conversation with a finely dressed older gentleman, and her heart pounded hard when they both turned to look at her as she crossed the distance between them. Raine nodded in her direction while he said something to the other man, and the gent smiled easily, almost as if he were relieved. The respect between them was evident as they shook hands over a few more words, and then the dapper stranger disappeared into an office behind the reception desk.

When Solana reached him she didn't even slow her steps. "Fourteen minutes, forty-five seconds," she hissed, blowing right past him and out the double doors into the hot, bright July morning.

She saw that he'd called up the Fisker. The vehicle purred in front of the hotel like a predatory cat, and when the valet took her suitcase from her to place it in the trunk, a queasiness attacked her with such intensity it brought on vertigo. Stars danced in her vision, cold sweat washed over her skin as breathing became more difficult –

"Miss Taranto, are you all right?"

The voice seemed to come from underwater, but the words themselves had a medicinal effect. While the dizziness passed as quickly as it had come, the sickness in her stomach held ruthlessly on, and she was so intent on keeping her insides on the inside that she never sensed the presence behind her.

"She's fine." Solana jumped when she felt Raine's hand on the small of her back, propelling her gently yet firmly toward the Tramonto. "Aren't you, my dear?"

Her distress must have shown on her face because he took one look at her and his smug expression transformed into one of concern. The hand at her back pressed harder, and he skipped taking her elbow and went right for her hand to escort her down the steps to his car.

"That's right - we had an eventful ride last night on the way here, didn't we?" he said, just loud enough for the valet to hear. "I'm sorry, sweetheart; I promise I'll try not to scare you behind the wheel today."

Raine opened the passenger door for her himself rather than cede the privilege to the valet, and Solana glared green icicles at him as she stepped into the low car, still trying to quiet the riot in her guts. She listened to the sultry strings of Bond's "Space" flow from the fine-tuned speakers while she watched him slip the valet a generous tip and a clever word, and when he slid into the driver's seat next to her, she knew she'd have to choose her words damn carefully if she wanted to get any clues out of him.

"Are you all right?" he demanded, his keen blue eyes searching her face.

She ignored him. "I'm assuming you've taken care of everything, Mr. Mathison," she began formally, "so pray tell, what about the matter of my car?"

"The owner of the hotel has made the gracious offer to hold it for you," he retorted, then he threw the car into gear and burned rubber onto the streets of downtown Philadelphia.

Her mind raced. Not just hold it, but hold it *for her*. Last time she checked, dead people didn't need cars. So wherever he was taking her, he planned on returning her. That, at least, was promising.

So were his words from the previous evening. *We have much to discuss, Ms. Trent, but now is not the time...*

It didn't set her mind at ease, but at least the wave of near-blinding nausea relented as she watched him merge onto I-95, relatively trafficless on this Saturday morning.

Raine reached back behind her seat and Solana heard the distinct sound of paper rustling. "Here," he said, producing an apple and placing it in her hand.

"What's this?" she asked, realizing she hadn't eaten in over twenty-four hours.

He laughed out loud and glanced at her. "Food."

Bullshit, she thought, staring at the shining red orb in her palm as if it were about to explode. *From the Iliad, to the Bible, to Snow White, apples have never been innocent.*

When Raine saw her still hesitating, he softened. "Look, I'll show you," he offered, holding out his hand, and when she gave him the apple he took a bite from it himself, without the slightest reservation. "See?" he said, passing it back to her, and Solana couldn't help but share his grin.

"So," she ventured, gratefully munching the fruit, "what kind of favor does the owner of the Ritz Carlton owe you, anyway?"

His eyebrows shot up in surprise. Naturally, she'd pieced it together already. "Always on the job, aren't you?"

"Like you're not," she fired back. "It's the only thing that makes any sense. You wouldn't have gotten to me otherwise."

It was like she'd channeled his thoughts from the night before. "A big one, dear, a big one," he said, answering her question. "He granted me access to you on the express condition that you would not be harmed on his property."

Solana stopped chewing her bite of apple. *That's* why she'd felt so safe with him last night. She hadn't been able to put her finger on it, but somehow she'd known his hands were tied.

Then, as he took the exit for Essington Avenue, another realization followed fast on the heels of the first, and she whirled on him when he came to a stop at the light, in the lane for Philadelphia International Airport.

"And now this?" she asked, incredulous. "You think you're taking me on some airplane, to who knows where?"

Raine killed the music, and the silence in the car was deafening as he dropped his piercing eyes from the traffic signal to hers. "You'll be back in your office on Monday morning if you want to be, Solana."

They were the words she wanted to hear, but as they sped into PHL, toward the private jets, they only increased her sense of apprehension.

CHAPTER EIGHT

The vast expanse of the Atlantic Ocean stretched as far as Solana could see, the view unobstructed save for the few white clouds scattered like cotton balls far below her. From her vantage point on the private jet, she could see the limb of the earth curving in the distance, the waves sparkling in the summer sunlight all the way to the edge of the world.

She turned her head sharply at the sound of a glass being placed on the mahogany table in front of her.

"Jameson's, neat, with a twist - if I recall correctly," Raine said, sliding smoothly into the leather seat across from her.

Solana stared dubiously into the short glass of fine Irish whiskey where it sat glowing golden in the sunlight, appearing perfectly clear, unclouded by potentially fatal powders or liquids.

Another peace offering, she noted, knowing full-well if

he'd wanted to kill her by poisoning he'd have accomplished that quite easily with the apple. Or the roses. Or the lingerie. For motives still unclear, he wanted her to trust him and for now she really had no other option.

Fuck it, she ceded, taking the drink in her fingers and lifting it so she could peer through the rich fluid. *I've waited for years to get this man in front of me for an interview; I might as well take full advantage of this opportunity.*

She shifted her calculating green eyes from the drink to his expectant blue ones, holding him there before she brought the Jameson's to her lips. *Let's hope it's not my last,* she concluded as she took a long sip from the glass, and she watched him smile with genuine pleasure at hospitality being accepted.

"Good," he said. "Now we can move on to item number three on this day's agenda."

"Which is?" she asked, enjoying the burn of the whiskey on its way down, already untying the Gordian knot in her stomach.

He slid her iPhone across the table to her, and Solana frowned. She hadn't even noticed he'd taken it from her.

"How long have you had that?" she demanded.

"Long enough to know someone wants you pretty badly," he replied. "I'm making the assumption you're expected at the office today, so you have to call Donato."

Solana's thoughts warred. Should she tell her captor about the eyewitness account she'd written and hidden back at the Times so she could use it as leverage? But by doing so, would that jeopardize whatever the hell this truce was between them?

Assuming she didn't put the document on the table as a bargaining chip and just made the call as requested, if she tried to insinuate to Donato that she was in danger -

even attempting some kind of code - Mathison would figure it out. There was no way she could tell Donato about her insurance policy and not forfeit her life the second she hung up.

Furthermore, that would put her boss, her friend, in a very dangerous position. All Mathison would have to do is make a phone call and her editor would be a dead man by day's end.

"Fine," she scowled, snatching up her phone to make the call - and then her eyes widened when the screen came to life and she saw the missed item notifications.

"Four missed calls?" Solana cried. "I don't know who's going to kill me first, you or Will!"

He smiled. "Put him on speaker."

"Son of a bitch," she cursed, shaking her head as she navigated to Donato's number on her Favorites list.

"What, you're not going to listen to the voicemails first?" Raine asked, laughter lightening his deep baritone.

"No. Glad you're enjoying this, by the way."

"Oh, immensely."

Solana placed the call, activated the speaker, and laid the phone on the table to wait, but the first ring didn't even fully complete before the line picked up.

"This better be good," her editor seethed over the line.

Jesus H. Christ, here we go already. "Well, hello, Will, how was your Friday evening? Good, mine too, thanks for asking."

"Where the hell have you been all morning?" he stormed on. "I've been calling you for hours!"

Raine consulted his imaginary watch. "All morning?" he mouthed to her, eyebrows lifted. "Hours? Really?"

Solana's eyes narrowed. "You don't know Donato," she mouthed back, then returned her attention to the phone.

"It's barely nine, Will," she reminded him. "And I'm sorry I wasn't available - I'm driving so I've been recording some voice memos. I divert my calls while I take them."

"You still driving? Is that why I'm on speaker?"

"Yes. So if you hear any background noise or if I seem distracted, that's why."

"Whatever. All I know is there's nothing on my desk regarding the alley murders yesterday," he barked. "I just got this one word email. TAXEIA. What the fuck is *that?* Some tax evasion thing you're working on now?"

Solana broke into a cold sweat. "You're pronouncing it wrong. The x is hard, like a k," she said slowly, racking her brain for some kind of explanation to the email she'd sent him. "It means quick in Ancient Greek; it's where the word tachometer comes from."

"Thanks for the history lesson, Lana, but what's your goddamn point."

Solana settled on an excuse - it was actually a good opportunity. "I thought about what you said yesterday and you're right. These mob guys move quickly; they don't wait around for an opening in my schedule. I should be covering Mathison in more depth – "

She faltered in mid-sentence as Raine reached under the table and lightly stroked his fingers behind her knee.

"Step lightly here," he murmured, his threat clear.

"Good," Donato bowled on, oblivious to her stumble. "Glad you've come to your senses about it. Got any leads tying him to the hits?"

She worked to quell the shaking in her voice, amazed at how successful she was with Raine's hand on her. "No. Nobody saw it, so nobody's talking. But I'll see what I can do. I'll be out in the field all weekend researching it, so don't expect me in the office."

"That's fine, Lana. Good to have you back on the case. Keep me posted."

And the line that tied her to safety and civilization went dead as he hung up.

Frustrated, Solana flung the phone back at Raine and he removed his hand from her leg to catch it in midair.

"Well done," he said, regarding her with a look of respect. "Sounds like you planted something to protect yourself somewhere in that office, and I bet it took every ounce of willpower not to expose that to him."

"I wouldn't put him in that kind of position," she snapped, irritated he'd figured out what she'd done and what she'd been thinking. "Let's start talking about something of substance. You're not telling me what your plans are for me, so I want in on something else. Since I already know too much, you might as well indulge me. Tell me about the murders I witnessed."

Again, his eyebrows shot up at her boldness. She would most definitely be the perfect complement to his syndicate's roster of unique talent.

"You need to go a wee bit farther back, Ms. Trent," he said. "Start with Catello, Mastriani, and Santaglio."

She sat up a little straighter in her seat. *Why the hell is he offering this information to me unsolicited?* "You're behind those murders as well?"

"I suppose indirectly I'm the catalyst, yes." He settled back in his chair, the leather giving a soft whoosh. "As I'm sure you realize, DiStephano is falling out of favor. What you may *not* know is that his three top men decided to make a wise career change."

Solana's mouth dropped open. "Are you saying the men who stood to inherit DiStephano's empire defected into the rank and file of your organization?"

"What can I say?" Raine answered, a slow, seductive smile expressing his admiration of her intellect. "The market has spoken in favor of the competition."

"Tell me," she demanded, breathless with anticipation for the rest of the story.

"All right, newsie," he said. "Two weeks ago, Catello, Mastriani, and Santaglio approached me with a creative solution to a mutual problem. All three had union clients loyal to them personally, but also interested in joining forces with my organization. Of course I wanted the new business, but their fealty to them was their roadblock to pursuing a partnership with me."

Solana nodded. "Their close ties to these DiStephano contacts made them wary of switching service providers, so to speak, without the protection of these same people."

"Exactly," Raine nodded. "So when these three men proposed joining my group, naturally I put them through the wringer, but truly it's their clients that vouched for them. You have to be of a certain character if your customers won't trade up without you agreeing to go along for the ride.

"Evidently," he continued, "DiStephano got wind of this arrangement and decided to take appropriate disciplinary action. The question is, who tipped him off?"

Solana pondered his question. The consequent power vacuum left in the wake of this loss would wreak havoc in DiStephano's organization. It would be a great opportunity for someone in that family to step up, to find some way to stand out amongst the crowd and get the aging don's attention, thereby positioning himself as a potential successor. One possible way to do that? Ferret out informants privy to the details on how the hell this act of treason happened in the first place.

"But why would someone in your group offer any information to soldiers in the opposing camp?" she asked.

"Unclear, in all honesty," Raine replied, and his candor surprised her. "DiStephano would have paid a very handsome nut to whomever brought that kind of information to him, and although I pay my people very well, it had to be someone in my group. The news was simply too new, the meetings too clandestine. We had our suspicions but weren't exactly sure – "

"By 'we' you mean Hunter Cavenastri and Gennato Anesini, your two underbosses," she ventured.

"Well done again," he grinned. "Exactly. We narrowed it down to two suspects and planted a bogus rumor with the two of them: that I was heading overseas on business a week ahead of schedule. So, when it was all over the City within a matter of hours that I was in Italy, it left no doubt as to who leaked it to DiStephano. Simple as that."

Solana thought back to the last words of the men in the alley. People will say anything to spare their lives, but something about their earnest pleas haunted her. Maybe it *was* that simple, but something gnawed at her synapses about this particular case. It didn't sit easily. Not fully.

What if all this was a load of horse shit? What if Mathison didn't trust these defectors? If these men would leave their own boss after years of faithful service, what insurance did Mathison have that they would stay loyal to *him?* These guys had jumped DiStephano's sinking ship in favor of the healthy balance sheet and dynamic leadership Imbrialis offered, but suppose the financial tides turned someday? Would they abscond again? What if that was a risk Mathison wasn't willing to take? What if he simply killed them after he had the allegiance of the new unions?

She realized the subject of her study was watching her

intently from across the table. Bereft of her customary pencil, she'd been hammering her fingernails on the table-top during her musings and she promptly clasped her hands in her lap.

"Sorry," she frowned. "It may be as simple as you say, but something still nags me about this."

He nodded. "It's the journalist in you. I expect you think I killed them for the sake of simplicity, and some would argue that would have been the best course of action once the union deals were finalized. But speaking as a successful businessman, these guys made the same decision all the other unions who'd come over to me had already made. Their clients saw the trend - who can't right now? - so they just persuaded their former contacts to come along. And I have to say, while it was a hard call for those three men to make, they chose the right one. A good accountant always knows when it's time to leave a failing business."

Solana considered this, keeping her sharp green eyes trained on him. Why the hell would he offer all this information to her if it weren't the truth? She'd already witnessed two murders; if he'd killed Distephano's men, what would her knowledge of three more murders matter? And goddammit, his logic was sound. It was a solid theory; Uncle Nico had certainly shared similar stories with her regarding shit he'd seen in his time serving under her father. And although she knew a lot about the mob, Mathison lived it every day. Successfully. Wildly successfully.

She sighed. Mathison most likely didn't kill them, leaving DiStephano as the culprit - one possessed with plenty of motive and opportunity.

"Occam's Razor," she concluded aloud, and Raine smiled as he rose to pour refills on their drinks.

かわ かわ かわ

Solana closed her eyes and basked in the fresh, warm tropical breeze, grateful for the deliverance from the cold, sterile air of the private jet. After reaching the bottom of the plane's stairs and touching earth for the first time in hours, she stretched out her arms and breathed deeply, inhaling the hot, fragrant perfume of the island. It must be the intoxicating Caribbean air that instilled the inexplicable sense of ease she now felt - that and the Jameson's she'd had during the flight.

She watched as Raine and the pilot tossed their things into the back of a Jeep waiting on the small strip of dirt that served as a runway, and after the items were secured, Raine turned and unexpectedly tossed the keys to her.

"You drive," he said, jumping into the passenger seat.

"But, wait, I don't even know where we're going," she protested as she approached the driver's side door.

"This island is something you should experience to its fullest, and for *you* that would mean behind the wheel. Especially since I've seen firsthand how much you love to drive." He reached his hand out to her across the seat, his light eyes sparkling. "Come on, let's go."

Slowly, she returned his smile, took his hand, and climbed into the seat. She tried to keep her fingers from trembling - this time from a strange sense of excitement - as the engine rumbled to life. The Jeep's clutch and transmission were easy to master, and she was off like a shot, "Minor Thing" by the Red Hot Chili Peppers blaring from the stereo.

"Where are we?" she asked, raising her voice over the roar of the wind and the music as she piloted the Jeep down the long access road, already at 55 mph.

"St. John."

She turned to look at him. "St. John doesn't have an airport," she said pointedly.

"Yes, I know," he replied, but soon it was too loud for much talking. Bombing around the island with the top down and the tunes up was pure exhilaration. Speeding along the S-curves, navigating the switchbacks, testing the limits of the hairpin turns along the inclines and valleys of the island... Solana was in heart-pounding heaven. With the Jeep under her command, she drank in vistas of long sandy beaches, lush green mountains, cozy, nestled villages. Raine called out spots of interest and local culture, leaning so close that the golden waves of his hair would graze her cheek or her shoulder as he pointed out the highest peak on the island *here*... the first settlers landed *there*... the oldest running basket shop in the USVI started *here*.

At one point, he stopped her in front of a very small store in a very small island town, where they picked out the makings of a picnic lunch. They stashed the basket in the back, but when she ran over a bump in the road at 70, the basket flew cartoon-like off the rear of the Jeep.

"Shit!" Raine yelled. "Stop the car!"

Solana threw the Jeep in neutral. "What?"

"We just lost lunch," he grumbled, half irked, half amused, and when she turned in her seat to find the basket sitting there marooned in the road, she started to smile, but something about the sight of Raine Mathison chasing down oranges had her disguising giggles as a mysterious coughing fit.

Once they'd rescued their sandwiches from the tropical underbrush, he had her guide the Jeep to a quiet, deserted stretch of beautiful beach flanked by rocky cliffs. She killed the engine at his instruction, and her ears rang in the immediate silence that followed. After the noise of the car, the music, and the wind, they suddenly found themselves engulfed by the peaceful sounds of the crashing ocean, the gentle sea breeze, and tropical birds nesting nearby.

"I thought we'd stop here," Raine said into the ensuing quiet, "so we can have our hard-earned lunch beneath the shade of a palm tree by the water. Yes?"

"Yes," Solana replied, unable to climb out of the Jeep fast enough. As a city dweller who'd grown up in a land-locked state, pristine beaches like this were the stuff of dreams and "someday." For her, the place was paradise on earth.

She threw her sandals into the back of the Jeep, so ready to feel the pale powdery sand fluff through her toes. It didn't disappoint; following Raine down to the water's edge was like walking through soft, sunbaked flour. She watched the ebb and flow of the seawater coming onto shore, noting how gentle, how quiet it was. The surrounding rock faces bordering the beach were constantly battered by incoming waves, but here the water lazily lapped in, stretching its way up the sand with soft, bubbly hisses.

Raine led her to a particularly expansive palm tree, and while they settled down to eat, Solana continued to watch the ocean's hypnotic inhales and exhales. The clear blue water beckoned to her, promising respite from the hot, hot sun torching the air she breathed and sending sweat dripping in rivulets down the small of her back. For hundreds of yards she could see through the transparent water all the way down to the bottom, and she wanted nothing more than to immerse herself in it, feel the soft sand under her feet, the cooling water over her body, and the deep sky over her head.

"I think I'd sell my soul for a swimsuit right about now," Solana mused aloud.

Raine laughed softly as he handed her one of the warm foil-wrapped sandwiches. "We might be able to arrange that."

The Caribbean cuisine only added to her sense of nirvana. The succulent aroma of grilled chicken seasoned with cilantro, mango, and the signature spiciness of the islands mingled with the potent perfume of salty sea and hibiscus flower. One bite, and the perfect beach was nearly forgotten while she devoured the bit of heaven in her hands.

"Who taught you to drive like that?" Raine asked, lounging back against the trunk of the palm tree.

Solana grinned wistfully, memories of reckless teenage antics replaying in her mind. "Josh and Steve, my brothers. In Montana."

"Nico's sons."

"Yes." She traced her finger through the hot white sand baking in the sun before them, swiftly drawing out a makeshift map of her home state. "I grew up here," she said, marking an X in the southwestern part of the state. "Thirty miles outside of Bozeman, not too far from Helena. I don't know if you've ever been there, but it's goddamn gorgeous - beautiful pastureland seated amongst the Gallatin and Bridger Mountains. Big air, big sky - it's so open, just begging to be conquered. In a number of places the roads are speed limitless, and tearing it up on the open road is what we did for fun." She smiled again, softer now.

"Josh and Steve are older than I am by four and five years, and they taught me everything I know about racing cars."

"You miss them," Raine said pointedly.

"Yes." She toyed with the powdery white sand that clung to the cold, condensing bottle of San Pellegrino she held. "They're both career-status military. They're never apart - the Corps realized they work best as an unbroken team, so they move as a unit, assigned to the same stations and operations. After they finished their second Special Ops tour in Afghanistan, they PCS'd to Japan and they've been there ever since."

"So the only family you have is all the way across the world?"

"Yes. Something of a loner, but I bet you understand that all too clearly?"

He nodded to her in respect. "Indeed."

Their words hung suspended before being spirited off on the breeze that rustled the palm fronds above them, making zebra-striped shadows dance on the sand.

Full and content, Solana sat back on her palms and let her gaze wander the idyllic vista before them. Her eyes followed along the beach and up the ridge of the promontory that framed one side of the cay, jutting far into the sea a half-mile down the shoreline. She traveled up over the brush and bushes clinging to the high crown of the cliff all the way to its edge - where something interesting caught her attention.

"Holy shit, there's a house up there," she thought out loud, spotting the small structure that sat proudly on the rocky top, its whitewashed walls bright against the perfect spotless blue of the sky. "Rugged little place, it must have roots in the cliff rock. You'd think it would have blown off into the ocean as soon as it was built."

Raine's eyes lifted to the top of the promontory, following her gaze to the bright house at its tip. "It nearly did. You should have seen it when I bought it."

Her head snapped back to him. "That's *your* house."

"Mmm-hmm, and it was a labor of love, let me tell you."

"I don't believe it." Solana leapt to her feet. "Prove it. Let's go, right now."

"Keep that up and you'll be walking your way up that crag."

"Oh, really? I think you're forgetting the fact that you gave me the keys." She proudly dangled the chrome carabiner from her index finger.

He raised an eyebrow, a slow grin overtaking his face. "Well, now, that can be easily rectified."

Solana screamed as Raine grabbed her around the waist and began to tickle her, starting with the soft, sensitive skin of her belly. Laughing, gasping for breath, she reached her hand higher, which only ended up giving him more access to her body for his fingers to find. He gained the advantage and pulled her down to his lap, trying to pry the keys from her fingers, but she managed to use her weight to roll free of him. With a triumphant cry, she sprang again to her feet - only to have him tackle her into the sunwarmed waters of the ocean.

"Okay, I give, I give!" she cried breathlessly, offering the keys up to him in her cupped palms. Victorious, he reached down to pluck them from her, at which point she grabbed his wrist and pulled with every intention of bringing him down into the water with her. She took him by surprise, knocking him off his balance, and Solana dodged to the side when Raine took the faceplant into the ocean beside her.

"I'm sorry!" she gasped automatically, rolling him onto his back. "Are you okay?" She hadn't meant to drown him; she'd just wanted to beat him, but one look into his sparkling blue eyes told her he was just fine.

For a second Raine gazed up at the sea nymph who stared down at him, and the sight of her seared itself into his memory. Her wild dark hair burned red against the deep blue of the summer sky, and the star she was named after shined brilliantly over her head. Her pale green eyes searched his, concern written across her beautiful features, and when he smiled the worry began to lift from her lovely face.

"Don't be sorry, Solana," he said. "I'd have done the same thing."

"You *did*," she reminded him as she watched him sit up. "Are you all right?"

"I'm fine," he answered. "But at least I was dry on one side before you rolled me."

Solana took in the vision of him sitting beside her, drenched, and even though she tried her damnedest, she couldn't contain the laughter that bubbled free. He couldn't resist either, and that's how they found themselves sitting in the ocean laughing like friends, both of them forgetting for the moment who and what they were to each other.

Raine rose and pulled her out of the water, and soon they were on their way, rushing up the road to the promontory. As the ultimate victor, Solana had maintained her position at the wheel, so it didn't take long for their clothing to dry as they sped onward.

CHAPTER NINE

Solana pulled the Jeep to a stop in front of the small cottage that sat across the top of the cliff bordering their beach. The walls were blinding white in the sunshine, a canvas for the red limeberries, yellow casha, and green sage bushes exploding like firecrackers where they grew alongside the house. She could just make out a flagstone patio and its surrounding rock wall through a thick stand of incredible beach maho trees bursting with white blossoms. The only sounds that reached her all the way up here were the susurrus of the breeze through the starfruit trees lining the short, gated drive and the distant crash of the waves far, far below.

"You have the keys there," Raine reminded her, hopping out of the Jeep to pick up their bags from the back. "Go ahead and unlock the door for us."

More than ready to explore the charming little house high above the world, Solana pulled the keyring from the ignition and flipped to the only other key on the small carabiner. She jumped from the Jeep and paused to smell the exotic fragrance of the beach maho flowers, delighting in them before making her way up to the little covered porch. She slipped the key home in the wooden door, heard the click of the lock as it released, and then opened it wide for Raine to go in ahead of her with their stuff.

"How thoughtful," he observed.

"I stand corrected," she explained humbly. "It's your house, after all; you should go first. But I want the tour."

He smiled. "There's not much to show you, but come on."

Every cozy room effected a mood of privacy and peace. First was the luxurious sitting room done in teak-wood, cream, and sage green, complete with a mesmerizing painting of the Piazzale Michelangelo in Florence at sunset, the Duomo rose red against the dark mountains in the distance. The honey-hued hardwood floors glowed in the sunlight that streamed in from the patio, which opened off of this intimate space. The house formed an L purposefully situated around the flagstone semicircle, with the sitting room at the crux, giving the main room an infinite view of blue sky over stone wall unlike anything Solana had ever seen.

Heading up the top of the letter-shaped house, toward the ocean, was a small yet well-equipped kitchen, and then an open-air breakfast nook at the very capital, commanding an incredible panorama of the ocean beyond.

Back through the house, along the bottom of the L and off the sitting room, was the bedroom. *The only bedroom*, Solana noted, flushing at the thought of what that probably meant, and when she walked in she knew she'd hit the inner sanctum of the house.

A sumptuous ebony four-post bed monopolized the space, imperious yet inviting with piles of fluffy white pillows, a high, thick mattress, and a soft-looking white coverlet. A luxe canopy of sheer white curtains surrounded the bed, draping all the way from the high black posts above to the shaggy white area rug beneath. The coordinating nightstands and a wide, thick dresser stood proud in the same dark wood, smoldering in contrast to all the cool white accents. Half of the far wall didn't exist; it opened entirely to the patio to let the tropical air breathe freely through the room, setting the diaphanous material wrapping the bed aflutter in the breeze.

Off the bedroom, at the southern end of the L, was the minimalist-designed bathroom, with a stone-and-glass shower enclosure making excellent use of the small footprint without sacrificing aesthetics or luxury. Since the bathroom was the very last room of the house, the shower wall on that side was one giant etched window, letting all the glorious sunlight flow freely into the sparkling, clean-lined space.

The whole cottage, all five rooms of it, had encapsulated its own paradise on the planet.

"Thoughts?" Raine asked her at the short tour's end.

"It's incredible here," Solana answered, sweeping her arms in a gesture that encompassed the whole place. "I honestly don't know why you bother with New York."

He sighed. "This is my home away from home, and I come here as often as I can." Then his expression turned from wistful to impish as he grinned down to her. "Now, about that request of yours for a bathing suit."

"You know, I don't think I'm your size, Raine," she said as she followed him back into his bedroom.

"Nobody's perfect," he replied as he opened one of the doors to his closet, then the top drawer of his dresser. He stepped back, and Solana found herself staring at hangers of women's clothes, all in her size, tags dangling, while the drawer brimmed with swimsuits, lingerie, whatever she could possibly need, again all her size, tags still on them.

There's no way in hell he got all of this stuff just for me, Solana thought, and she felt something odd flutter in her stomach. "That's quite the collection, Raine," she observed as casually as she could. "You often have women here, do you?"

"No," Raine answered, watching her with an intensity she could feel in her chest. "I've never brought anyone here before."

Solana didn't know what to say.

"Here," he said, reaching down and producing a pair of hiking shoes from the floor of the closet. "You can go though the dresser and find a bathing suit that works for you, but you'll need these as well."

She looked at the size six Timberlands he'd handed to her. "We're going hiking?"

He nodded, grin returning. "See you in ten minutes."

Rummaging through the drawer, Solana quickly discovered he'd spared no expense. Lingerie by Cosabella, Carine Gilson, I.D. Sarierri, Myla, Ritratti. Swimsuits from Maaji, Aqua Doce, Badgley Mischka, Moontide, Eres. After trying on several options ranging from modest to all-out risqué, she settled on a red bikini fashioned by La Perla, with a simple bandeau top and crazy-sexy boy shorts.

Next, she pored through the packed closet, finding the hiking gear at the back, where she was met with another array of options. Columbia, North Face, Patagonia, REI, Athleta, L.L. Bean, Lulu Lemon, Mountain Hardware... she was like a kid in a candy store. It didn't take long for her to find something her speed - khaki cargo shorts, a sinfully soft and breathable white tee shirt, and lavender Smartwool ankle socks for the sporty, low-top hiking shoes.

Getting dressed, Solana got as far as the bikini before she realized she was short a crucial element from her wardrobe. Quickly, she threw on the tee and shorts over the suit and cracked the bedroom door.

"Raine?" she called. "Do you have any sunblock?"

"Name your SPF," he called back from the kitchen.

"You got fifteen?"

Less than a minute later he was at the door with the requested bottle of SPF15.

"Live dangerously, do you?" he asked, eyebrow lifted.

"Hey. It's just enough to block the burn, leaving nothing but tan behind. Besides, you're clearly no stranger to sunlight," she said, noting his own suntanned skin. "Being of Mediterranean stock does have its advantages, no?"

"Most definitely," he agreed. Looking her over, Raine could tell which swimsuit she'd picked, and it pleased him to know she'd opted for his first choice. The blazing red of the Perla bikini peeked sexily through the thin fabric of the fitted white tee. The lightness of the shirt looked amazing against her dark hair and tanned skin, and the short shorts showed off her lovely legs.

Solana blushed under his scrutiny and the oddness of the situation. She wasn't sure whether she should shut him out now or invite him in, or if she should take the sunblock with her and put it on later...

Thankfully, Raine bailed her out of her thorny quandary.

"Anything else you find yourself needing?" he asked.

She was about to say no, when she considered the sheer expanse of skin that would be exposed to the sunlight today once the tee shirt and shorts were off. She had no interest in bikini burn, and under this hot sun and in that clear water, it would probably happen within minutes. She couldn't very well pick another suit now that he'd seen the one she'd chosen, just because she was too shy to ask him if he'd...

"Actually, yes..." she began.

"With that suit," he smiled, "you're going to need some help with this."

She nodded, glad he'd saved her from the awkwardness of asking, and she stepped aside to let him enter his own sunlit bedroom. While he dispensed a generous dollop of sunscreen into his hands, she quickly took the ribbon from her hair, wove it through and retied the mass so that it was up on top of her head, getting it out of the way. She turned her back to him, pulled her arms out of the sleeves of her tee shirt so he could lift it up –

"Just take it off, Solana," he said softly from behind her.

Her cheeks were pinker, her palms suddenly sweaty as she took the tee by the hem and slowly pulled it over her head. She surreptitiously watched him in the mirror over the dresser, saw him step up to her. He rubbed the sunscreen in his capable hands, warming it a bit before he touched her with the cool white lotion. Despite the effort, she inhaled sharply when the chilly cream made contact, but it wasn't cold for long. His eyes lifted to meet hers in the mirror, and she found them smoldering as he spread the thick balm over her shoulders, down her arms, up again. Then his eyes dropped while he paid attention to her neck, her back, her waist above the hip-hugging shorts, plying her with ample coverage over every inch she couldn't reach. She closed her eyes in delight as he massaged the sunscreen into her skin, his hands strong yet gentle, moving like a lover's. And he was very thorough; he didn't stop until the last trace of white disappeared.

Her eyes opened when she felt him step even closer to her, the soft, warm cotton of his own T-shirt brushing the skin of her back now glowing with moisture. His hands moved down her arms, kneading the muscles on the way down, until his fingers touched hers. His luminous eyes caught hers in the mirror again, and she shuddered when he brought his lips to her neck in a soft kiss. He traveled up her earlobe, took it gently in his teeth for just a second before he whispered, "You're ready now?"

Solana shook her head, just the slightest movement back and forth. "Legs," she could only whisper back, heart pounding like a butterfly trapped in a jar.

Raine laughed deeply. "How could I forget?"

He turned her to face him and wrapped his large hands around her small waist. Like she weighed nothing, he lifted her to sit on top of the ebony dresser, and she watched in anticipation as he prepared another quarter-sized drop of lotion for her. He massaged her legs, starting with her feet and going as high as he dared into her shorts, making her gasp when his fingertips brushed the edge of the bathing suit between her legs. He repeated the delightful service on her other leg, and then took it upon himself to apply plenty more to her abs and chest, his face mere inches from hers.

Raine finished, bringing his warm hands to rest on hers again, and when he lifted his glittering eyes to meet her simmering gaze, his lips hovered over hers.

"Now are you ready?" he asked lowly.

When Solana shook her head a second time, he kissed her.

His mouth captured hers thoroughly and deeply, and she parted her lips for him at once, craving more from him. His lips and tongue teased hers with artful skill, making her moan with need for him -

And then he ended it.

Curtailing his own desire to nail her right there on the dresser, he forced himself to pull back from her, purposefully cutting the kiss short.

Because next time, he wanted *her* to bed *him*. He wanted to leave her burning for him, until she wanted him so badly she trembled. Until she could taste it.

Raine grabbed her waist again and lifted her from the dresser, setting her down to stand before him. "Shirt and shoes, my dear, and I'll meet you outside," he said, and then he was gone.

Alone, Solana grabbed the edge of the dresser for support, her heart hammering, her breath coming fast.

What the hell was that? she demanded of her reflection in the mirror. She thirsted for him after the firestorm of need he'd sent torching through her, but then he'd just sped off, leaving her unquenched and shaking in his wake.

Jesus Christ, she thought as the full realization of her reaction to him settled in. She knew now that she'd expected him - *wanted* him - to take her right there on his blackwood dresser.

And she wondered why he hadn't.

Where are we going that he didn't have time or interest in... Solana cut the thought off at once, remembering his attentive caresses, his lips on her neck, his kiss still warm on her mouth.

He was plenty interested. He was just biding his time. *But why?*

Drawing in a deep, calming lungful of air, she threw

on the white shirt, tied on the Timberlands, and rushed out to meet him under the blazing Caribbean sun.

❧ ❧ ❧

"Tell me about Nico."

Solana followed Raine through the thick vegetation on the trail, ducking the tree limbs he held aside for her once he'd passed under them. They were so deep into the tropical forest that the canopy of lush greenery blocked out the sun and the sky. Even without the bright sunshine, though, it was close and humid in the trees, making her crave the beach they'd lunched on not so long ago.

At Raine's question, she thought about the man who'd been like a father to her. "What do you want to know?"

"What was he like? If I recall, his reputation colored him as a rather reserved character."

"He was, with most people," she replied. "Very quiet, very patient. But he was also a great storyteller - he could paint pictures with words alone, remembering every last detail of an event until you felt like you'd been there yourself. His jokes were the best, built up to perfection and finished with expert delivery. He was fun but he was also devoted; we kids knew he loved two things in his life more than anything. Us, and his horses."

"No women in your life?"

Solana shook her head before she realized he couldn't see it. "No. I never knew for certain what happened to Archangela, the girl who brought me over from Italy. From what I gather, though, she developed feelings for Uncle Nico that he couldn't return. There would never be anyone else for him after Mary died, and I think Angie left as soon as she could. That must have been when I was about six, because she stopped showing up in our photo albums around then."

Solana sidestepped a wayward branch that threatened to lash her across the face. "So I grew up with the boys, and it didn't seem strange to me, all that testosterone. I just didn't know any differently. No one ever told me girls shouldn't be learning all about cars, horses, cards, sports, guns... whatever, you name it, the list goes on.

"It wasn't until I hit middle and high school that I really started bonding with girls my age. Lucky for Nico, my friends were the ones who schooled me in menstruating, makeup, and Marchesa."

She laughed. "You should have seen the look on the boys' faces when I came down the stairs dressed for prom. They didn't know what to do when their tomboy turned Cinderella, but I noticed three shotguns stayed by the front door from that night on."

Raine smiled at the thought of Cavi or Anesini tasked with raising a little girl. He wouldn't lay odds on the poor thing surviving childhood, and he honestly had to hand it to Nico for taking the matter so securely in hand as his last service to the doomed Alessandras.

"When you were little, what did he say happened to your parents?" he ventured.

"Nothing more than I already knew," she said tightly. "He didn't want to give me any more nightmares."

"Nightmares?"

"Yes. Before I even got to him I was told they'd died in a house fire, and it tortured me for the better part of ten years. I spent a decade of my life wondering why my parents were able to get me out but not themselves. Why I survived and not them.

"When Nico told me the truth," she continued, her

voice hardening, "when I found out they were murdered, I suddenly had an outlet for all that anger. I knew how to make my life matter, so that they didn't die for nothing."

Vexed, Raine's face darkened and he was glad she couldn't see it. "You decided to go after the mob to avenge them," he deduced, trying very hard not to make it sound like an accusation. Because it wasn't, not exactly.

"Yes."

He fell silent. For a long while, the only sound was the crunching of the underbrush beneath their feet, and the swishing of the branches back into place once they'd passed through them.

"Do you remember anything about them?" he asked.

"Uncle Nico knew them intimately, and because of his gift for telling stories I feel like I knew my parents myself. I used to love to have him tell me the story of how they met." She smiled in remembrance. "Nico matched them, actually. They were both friends of his, and he'd been trying for years to get them to meet, but they blew him off, thinking it was another waste of time. So, one night he took matters into his own hands. He invited them both over for dinner, unbeknownst to the two of them, and he ended up ignored at the table while they talked the whole night long. From that day on, they were inseparable."

Solana gave a heavy sigh. "I wish I remembered more about them, but I was just so young..."

And then, all at once, memories she hadn't touched in ages opened like treasure chests in the dark recesses of her mind.

"My mother," she said in soft wonder, digging deep into the mental lockbox. "I remember her voice. She'd sing to me, always, and it was beautiful. Clear and strong. Her favorites were Nina Simone and Ella Fitzgerald, and she loved *La Traviata*. And I remember the sweet scent of her lavender. She grew it herself. God, it was everywhere! We literally bathed in it nightly during our bedtime bath.

"As for my father..." Solana paused, unsure whether she should go on. "I could never explain this successfully to anyone, so I stopped trying long ago. People just didn't get it; they thought it was too bizarre. But to this day, I find the smell of cigarette smoke in the ice cold of winter comforting."

When Raine didn't make any comment, she continued warily. "I was born in January, one of the coldest months of the year. Winter had come round again when they were killed in December... ironically, on the Solstice, the darkest day of them all. So my first and last experiences with my parents fell in the chilly seasons.

"My father smoked, so when he came in at night to tuck me into bed, or if he got in late and I happened to wake up when he came in to check on me, the scent of his last cigarette still lingered on him, his cheeks still cool to the touch when I kissed him goodnight. So I've always associated that smell with love. And safety. Every bit as much as my mother's lavender."

Raine slowed to a stop and turned to face her. He saw her steel herself for the ridicule, but he only reached out to take her hand in his.

For him, it was very much the same, only his mother's signature scent was jasmine, and his father favored black cherry pipe tobacco. Music had carried such weight in his household that Billie Holiday and Louis Armstrong were practically members of the family. He knew their album covers on sight long before he could read, and as soon as he was able to walk, he was setting the vinyls to spin on the player for his parents.

"Come on," he said, giving her hand a soft squeeze. "We're here."

Raine turned off the trail and led her fifty yards into the rough jungle until they reached a rock nearly twice his height. He scaled it easily, then reached down for her, helping her up beside him. Once she was settled, he gave her a long look before he parted the hanging greenery to reveal their destination.

The natural pool and the forty-foot-high waterfall feeding it was a tropical Eden. The sun poured into the sacred hole, making the water run the gradient of pale green to impossible black from the surface to its immeasurable depths. Bordered on every side by towering rock faces, there was no beach, just the pristine hole itself. From their perch some thirty feet above the surface, they could see the faint rainbows that shifted and reappeared in the mist from the waterfall as the light caught the scattering droplets in midair.

"It's beautiful," Solana breathed.

Raine smiled. "For now, it's ours. Let's go."

He stripped off his clothes until he stood almost gloriously naked in a pair of form-fitting swim boxers. The blue square fit him like he was a professional athlete, and Solana tried not to stare, but not for the reason one might think.

Rather than getting undressed, she stood rooted to the solid ground.

He looked over at her, watching her stand there like a statue. "What?" he asked.

She colored. "I can't swim."

"*What?*"

"I grew up in Montana, Raine," she explained, feeling her shame intensify as he stared at her in disbelief. "I went to college in Philadelphia, I live and work in the concrete jungle, water just really hasn't been a major source of recreation in my life."

"On the beach you were all about going swimming!"

"I was all about getting a bathing suit so I could go into the *ocean*," she clarified. "Where my feet stay firmly planted in the sand!"

"You have no idea how amazing this will feel, Solana," he said. "You have to come."

She began to sweat, and not on account of the heat this time. "How deep is it?"

"Over a hundred feet, easily," Raine said, wanting no lies between them. "But you'll only see the first fifteen."

"Sharks?"

He smiled. "No, Solana. This pool is waterfall fed; no sharks are getting up here from the ocean downstream."

She trembled visibly, out of objections.

"You're scared," he said softly.

She nodded.

His expression darkened. "That I'll drown you down there."

She shook her head, surprised. That actually hadn't occurred to her in the slightest.

Well, that's good, he thought. "So you're scared of jumping into depths unknown."

She nodded.

He softened measurably. "Come on," he said. "We'll go together."

She stood there.

"Clothes off, my dear, let's go. It'll be fine. Trust me."

Solana thought back to every time he'd asked her to trust him, and every time she *had* trusted him, things had turned out rather well for her.

Her mouth moved before she had time to stop the thought. "Okay."

Before she changed her mind, Raine reached for her tee shirt and lifted it over her head. She followed his lead like an automaton and shimmied out of her shoes and shorts, a difficult task given how sweaty she was from the hike.

Raine really wasn't prepared for the full sight of her in that hot little red Perla number, and he was grateful he still held her tiny white tee fisted in his hands in front of him.

"You go first," she said, her voice shaking.

"You want to watch what happens?"

"Yes."

Her white shirt hadn't even landed on the pile of their clothes before he was gone. She watched him take his confident dive with envy, his godlike body launching in an arc over the azure pool, barely making a splash as he sliced into the water.

For a second, she panicked. *He's obviously an accomplished swimmer*, the reasonable part of her mind noted from a distance. *He won't die and leave you here alone.*

Seconds later he resurfaced, smiling, his eyes the same color as they sky above them.

While that brought her solace, she now had a frame of reference. He might as well have been thirty miles below her instead of thirty feet, and all of her muscles locked down in fear.

"Come on, Solana, jump," he called up to her. "You'll come up, I promise."

She hesitated.

"Just hold your breath, and you'll be fine. I'll be here to catch you."

Solana let it gather. Her terror, her energy, her sheer desire to escape the heat of the day and be part of that beautiful blue water...

And, goddammit, her pride refused to let him have one over on her. She knew she'd kick herself for the rest of her life if she wimped out, especially in front of *him*.

Do it!, screamed mind, body and soul.

She sucked in her breath, held her nose, and leapt.

Falling, falling, sickening falling, and then cool bliss, the silence and the softness of dark water swallowing her, bubbles dancing around her as she plummeted. And then she felt the change, the ascent, the air in her lungs bringing her up, and she broke free of the surface, the hot sun shining on her face once again.

Find him! The frenzied thought no sooner crossed her mind when she felt him, the touch of his fingertips on her arm as she dashed the thick tendrils of her hair from her face. The fingers tightened when she exhaled, and that hand on her was the only thing that kept her afloat when she started to sink. She gasped, grabbing for him frantically lest she go under again, airless.

"I've got you, Solana," Raine soothed, pulling her to him. "Just breathe."

She felt his arm circle her waist and she resisted the urge to wrap herself around him as he swam to the edge of the hole. He found a rock ledge close enough to the surface for him to sit on and still keep his head above water, and then he brought her in close to him so she could sit on his lap. She threw her arms around his shoulders, buried her face in the wet hair curling at his neck, and just focused on letting the air fill and leave her lungs.

You did it. You're safe. Calm down. While his hands stroked her arms, her legs, her back, reassuring her, Solana gave herself over to the beauty of their surroundings, delighted in the coolness of the water. She was safe here in his arms, in this magical place, and she couldn't really imagine wanting to be anywhere else.

Raine planted a kiss on her temple. "You okay?" he asked after a moment.

"Oh yes," she answered.

He laughed, the sound echoing off the rock faces around them. "*Che brava, bella.*"

Solana felt her heart swell with pride.

"Here, let me show you something," he said, pulling her away from him and holding her at arm's length. "I want you to take a deep breath and hold it."

She did.

"Now just lie back, lift your hips and your legs, and you'll float."

He kept his hand between her shoulder blades as she followed his instructions, and he saw her smile when her toes broke the satin surface of the water. She closed her eyes in rapture, and he was thankful for the opportunity to look her over at his leisure. Her hair was a spill of rich burgundy in the clear blue, her nipples taut against her red suit, and water droplets sparkled like diamonds all over her smooth skin.

"Just breathe normally, Solana," he coached, "and you'll keep floating. Good. Now I'm going to let go."

He did, and she smiled again. "This is incredible," she said, stretching her arms out to her sides and slowly moving them, propelling herself into the middle of the deep hole.

Solana couldn't hear anything with the water in her ears, just the silence of the pool and the sound of her breath going in and out in relaxing, rhythmic time. After a while, she could identify the low thrum of the waterfall hitting the surface farther down. She could sense without seeing the impossible blue of the sky above her. She could feel the hot sun beating down on her body, and the cool of the spring buoying her from beneath. Then she could hear Raine swimming toward her in the water, knew he was nearby now; she must have traveled rather far from him in order for him to come out to her.

"How do I get out of this without drowning myself?" she asked, her voice sounding full yet hollow to her water-filled ears.

Seconds later she felt his hands on her again, and she let her legs fall, trusting he'd keep her above the surface. When she opened her eyes, she found him smiling at her proudly.

"Just kick your legs and move your arms slowly, like this, and you'll tread water."

She picked up on it quickly and he released his hold on her, gradually, until he held her by only a finger.

"Got it?" he asked.

She nodded. "I think so."

"You sure?"

"Uh huh."

He let go, and she did it.

"Excellent job, *cara*," he grinned. "Excellent."

She grinned back. "So that's your secret," she said. "You're a swimmer. That's how you're so fit and tan."

"That's right, yogi. Now let's go explore."

Raine led her over to the waterfall, approaching it carefully from the side. He guided her through the curtain of falling water, where a collection of large rocks provided plenty of places to sit in the cool misting shade, out of the sun's fiery reach. He pulled himself up effortlessly onto one of the bigger boulders, water streaming in rivulets down his sexy body, and then he reached down and pulled her up to sit beside him, with plenty of room to spare on the rock.

They sat in comfortable silence as they watched the hypnotic fall of the water, veiling Vs cascading into the blue-green below.

"Would they have wanted that?" Raine asked.

"Would who have wanted what?"

"Your parents," he clarified, turning his face to hers. "Would they have wanted you going after the mob?"

It was her turn for incredulity. "*What?*"

"This is how they lived, Solana," he explained. "This was their life, how they chose to live it. And they did it remarkably well. So well, in fact, that it drew the attention of the rest of the country. Another ten years, Alessandra would have owned the entire boot of Italy. They chose to die rather than flee that life and live in the shadows. They chose to give you the spoils - where do you think the millions in your cushy trust fund came from, Solana? What if they respected the life and didn't want you targeting it?"

Solana couldn't formulate a thought, much less speak.

She'd never thought of it that way before. Surely her parents hadn't chosen death over spending life with her undercover.

Even if they'd wanted to run away, the three of them, it would have been too dangerous for them to travel with her. They'd be spotted so easily; the enemy *mafiosi* would have found them in no time. Surely they must have resented that, and regretted the life they'd built. Right?

But what did she know about living like this? She knew nothing, whereas Raine knew absolutely everything about it. What if he was right? What if her parents were proud of what they'd accomplished, even though they couldn't stop the tragedy that befell them because of it? What if everything she'd worked for wouldn't matter to them?

Or worse, disappointed them?

"What does it matter if it's not what they wanted?" she snapped. "They're dead."

"By the same token, then," he said pointedly, "what does it matter if you avenge them, Solana? They'll never know. They're dead."

Solana blew up. "I did it for *me*, Raine!" she exploded as the answer came to her, crystal clear in its sudden obviousness. "I needed to take the mob down for what it did to my family! For what it cost me! It's *my* revenge! But I wouldn't expect you to get it. You can't understand the anger, the loss – "

She stopped short when she saw a flash of pain tear across his features, but he buried it so fast she wondered if she'd really seen it. It tempered her anger, and she hauled it back under her control.

"Why are you asking me all these questions, Raine," she demanded.

"I want to know what makes you tick, Solana," he shot back. "What fuels the fire behind the sun you're named for."

Solana softened further. That look she'd seen... he understood more than he was willing to let on. She considered him, wanting to know more about his past, what had hurt him so intensely for that look to flit across his face. But she'd never find out by interrogating him outright, not yet.

"Why did they name you Raine?" she asked instead.

"Look around you, Solana," he answered, gesturing to

encompass the lush world they couldn't see on account of the waterfall blocking their view. "The sun gives life to the earth, the energy it needs to flush fertile and green. Oxygen is the byproduct of photosynthesis; we're only able to breathe because plants harnessed the power of sunlight. But too much of that intense light scorches the plains, burns off the crops. It kills."

He continued on, more quietly, his gaze holding hers. "Then the storms come, bringing nourishing water that quenches the thirst of the world, purifying it, shaping it. Everything alive on this planet, from the soil, to the plants and the animals, they all soak it up, and then they wait for the sun to come out and activate it. But here, too, lies danger. Just as an overabundance of sun will char the earth, neverending storms will drown it. The world needs both, in equal force and measure, to make it.

"Thus, fire and water are intimately entwined, and life is only possible when they act in congress. They are not truly opposites, Solana," he said softly, taking her hand in his. "They are partners. They are lovers."

Spellbound, Solana looked up into the impossibly blue eyes that held her motionless. If she had any doubt before about his interest in her, he'd just blasted it to bits.

The sun and the rain, she thought, her heart beginning to race as his face lowered to hers. *Lovers intertwined, not enemies across the field.*

"So to answer your question," he murmured, those eyes filling her vision, his mouth over hers, "we humans give the sun all the glory, from our religions down to our weekly weather forecasts. But the reality is that nothing, absolutely nothing, survives without the rain."

When Raine's lips touched hers, making just the slightest brush of contact, Solana felt the need for him explode in every cell of her body. She reached her fingers into the curling wet hair at his neck to bring him closer, and he responded with an ardent passion that took her breath away. Her desire for him that he'd left unfinished on the dresser now rose to towering heights inside her, and Solana wanted more from him this time than just his tantalizing kiss.

Sitting beside him with their legs dangling over the edge of the rock, however, made for less than optimal access to him, and she shifted her weight to change position. He must have felt her move, because she'd no sooner started the transition when she felt his hands close around her waist. He lifted her wet body like she weighed nothing more than a feather, turning her in midair to face him, and when he brought her down to sit on him Solana straddled his hips. She couldn't care less about the pain of her knees pressing into the hard rock; what she cared about was the rock hardness she could feel pressing into the softness between her legs through both of their swimsuits.

Raine's hands swept over her wet thighs, slick with water and melting sunscreen, and she moaned against his lips at the overwhelming sensations that danced through her. He cupped her firm rear in his hands, squeezed her cheeks, and then let his fingertips just graze the warm, wet heart of her. She nearly burst into flames, her fingers burying into his thick, wet hair, keeping his face turned up to hers while she drank in his kiss. She felt his hands travel up her hourglass-shaped torso, felt his fingers take firm hold of the bandeau top to take it off —

The violent blast of thunder overhead startled them so hard they nearly fell off the rock, leaving them clinging to each other in heart-rattling alarm.

"Shit," Raine said, his expression unsettlingly sober. "We have to go, Solana. *Now*."

He moved her beside him and he was off the rock and back in the water in less than a second. He waited there for her, and she jumped in without reservation this time, unnerved by his urgency. He lifted her to the surface and led her out from under the waterfall, to discover a world so dark it was like someone had turned off the sunlight. Menacing purple clouds raced low and angry, and the falling pressure crushed down on them, threatening one of the tropic's signature whoppers.

They didn't have much time.

"Hold on to me," Raine ordered, and he swam them with impossible speed to the other side of the wine-dark swimming hole, right up to one of the sheer rock faces. Solana was about to question his sanity when she saw the divots in the facade, making shallow foot and hand holds to climb out.

"Go," he urged, and Solana was proud to have an equal if not an upper hand in this case, her yoga strength shining with skill as she pulled herself swiftly up the height of the rock. He followed right behind her, and they raced back through the short stretch of jungle to the ledge where they'd left their dry clothing.

It was suddenly obvious they'd left something rather helpful back at the cottage.

"Did you forget the towels?" she asked, watching him struggle into his T-shirt.

"I was... rather distracted before we left, Solana," he smiled despite the next peal of thunder pounding ominously over their heads.

Solana moved like lightning. She pulled on her tee shirt and shorts over her dripping bathing suit as quickly as her streaming body would allow, then fought her wet feet into her dry socks and shoes, tying the laces with quaking fingers. Raine reached down for her and in the next second they were running, flying hand-in-hand through the jungle, back over the two miles they'd covered on the trail, dodging the face-slapping greenery as best they could.

At last, they reached the head of the trail and burst from the jungle onto the road that led up to his house. Now that they were free of the canopy of trees, they could see the entire supercell spanning the Atlantic like a giant black anvil, the storm clouds towering into the atmosphere like an omen of doom. Ubiquitous lightning leapt from cloud to swirling cloud, leaving behind eerie hues of pink and continuous riots of rumbling. As if to acknowledge their presence, an angry, jagged bolt seared into the ocean about a mile to the north, flashing deadly white.

"Holy – !"

The roaring thunder drowned out the rest of Solana's sentence.

"Run," Raine commanded, squeezing her hand in his, and they tore ass up the steep road toward home. They covered that better part of a mile like a pair of Olympic sprinters, reaching the cottage in less than four minutes. Another violent volley blasted over them as he unlocked the door with a calm, precise flick of his wrist, and he no sooner shut the door behind them when the deluge began.

Lungs burning, body trembling, Solana dropped to the floor. Too spent to even take her shoes off, she just sat there, grateful to be safely indoors while the storm went off like mortars outside. The black tempest blocked the light of day, making the house as dark as twilight on the inside, such a sinister change from the brilliant, beautiful day they'd left behind.

"How did it sneak up on us like that?" she wondered, still breathing hard.

Raine, who'd been leaning up against the door while he caught his own breath, kicked off his shoes. "I have no idea," he answered, and made for the kitchen. "I've seen some storms up here in my time," he called back to her, "but nothing like this one."

He returned minutes later with two glasses of orange juice, and he handed one down to her. "The only thing I can think of," he said, walking over to the edge of the room to watch the rain pelt the patio, "is that the water-fall drowned out the sound of its approach. It wasn't until the storm was practically banging on the door of our cave that we could hear it over the rush of the water."

Lightning struck nearby, and Solana braced herself against the fist of thunder that shook the cliff itself, not just the house. She could barely breathe from the pressure of the storm and the close heat of the afternoon weighing down on her. Although she was still soaked from their swim, the mad dash through the jungle and up the road to the house had left her hot and sweaty all over again. Her clothes clung to her as if she were sitting fully dressed in a sauna, sweat rolling along her temples and down the valley of her spine. The oppressive rainstorm, bringing more humidity and stickiness to the mix, didn't help.

She pulled off her shoes, lost her clinging socks. She sipped the chilled juice in the glass Raine had handed her, and discovered there was another flavor in there, along with some effervescence that distinctly made this a differ-ent class of orange juice.

"What's in this?" she asked.

"Raw orange juice and limeade, with a splash of seltzer water."

She took another nourishing swallow. "It's fantastic."

"You feel better?"

"Yes."

"Exactly."

Together they listened to the storm rage overhead, Raine standing watch at the patio while Solana kept her seat on the floor. Thunderstorms were not her favorite; she'd be perfectly happy to stay away from the windows for the duration of this hellish event.

"Jesus," he whispered after a minute. "Quick, Solana, come look at this."

She pulled herself up off the floor, discovering new muscles in her body as she did so, and cautiously went to join him at the edge of the room. He put his hand on her shoulder and pointed out to the roiling ocean, and she followed his line out to sea.

Even through the thick curtain of rain she could see it, and every hair on her body stood on end.

"That's a fucking *tornado*," she said, unable to tear her eyes from the waterspout tracing a line in the ocean like a divine white finger.

"Amazing, isn't it?" he whispered, watching the funnel twist and swerve unpredictably across the water. As they watched, another waterspout spawned beside the first, and the pair weaved a drunken path together while lightning crackled in the black clouds above them.

"Twisted sisters," Solana murmured, remembering her Nebraskan friends from college talk about the storms they'd seen regularly back home. "Are we safe here?"

Raine didn't know the answer to that question; he just pulled her closer to him. "Guess we'll find out, won't we?"

"Live dangerously, do you?" she asked, and he only smiled.

The waterspouts undulated like snakes over the water, dancing around each other, making chaos of the white-capped waves underneath them. When they took a collision course and pleated themselves together, they disappeared just as quickly as they'd formed. Like a wayward child, the storm sent lightning forking across the sky in a thunderous tantrum, furious that it lost its destructive playthings. Solana jumped three feet in the air at the blast, and Raine held her tightly to his side, his hand stroking down her arm before he took her fingers securely in his.

"Nothing survives without the rain," she whispered, feeling the spray from the drops that showered in bucket-loads from the sky.

"Well, I don't know if the beach mahos will make it so well through this one," he said.

She grinned at his joke, and then wider when she realized they'd forgotten something else of relatively major import.

"The Jeep is totally fucked, you know."

He blinked down at her, and then chuckled when he understood what she meant. "It'll dry out," he sighed. "Eventually."

Solana mentally counted the seconds between the blinding lightning and its answering cannonade of thunder, and eventually her counts began to lengthen. Soon the blasts were coming after three seconds from the flash... then after five... then ten. Full minutes began to pass before any forks split the clouds at all. The sky seemed to lighten a bit, starting to take on the electric pink that followed strong storms, which meant only one thing.

The worst was over; the front was moving out to sea.

The drenching rain, however, pounded on, showing no sign of letting up.

After a long while, once it became clear that nature had ended her impressive show, Raine released her fingers, giving her arm a dismissing squeeze before he pulled away from her. He left his guard post at the wall's edge, turning his back on the patio and on her, setting his empty glass down with finality on the nearest endtable.

"Now that things are a little quieter," he said, "I'm off for a shower. Help yourself to anything you may need in the meantime."

He disappeared into the heart of the house, and Solana stood there, acutely aware of how very alone she suddenly was, with only the rain pummeling the patio as her companion.

CHAPTER TEN

Raine stood under the pounding water, letting the cleansing warmth pour over him for a minute while he pressed the heels of his hands into his eyes.

I'm Raine Mathison, he thought crossly, wiping the water from his face. *I'm the boss of the most powerful crime organization in the goddamn country. Why the fuck is she affecting me this way?*

The answer came swiftly, startling in its simplicity.

Because she's unlike anything you'd ever expected.

He was thoroughly enjoying this delicious day with her, much more than he'd anticipated. Slowly he recalled each part, unwrapping it in his mind and savoring it like a multi-layered candy on his tongue.

First, he thought of how he'd woken her this morning, the electrifying challenge of getting her to yield to him, to fully understand that she was under his complete control. The spoils of that absolute victory, her cries of pleasure, still warmed him to the core.

Solana had learned by then to take him at his word,

but next there were the peace offerings, the apple and the Jameson's, to make her feel comfortable and deepen her trust in him.

She'd been the one to make the first forays into real conversation in the Tramonto and on the plane, and both times she went straight to the point. Fuck pleasantries and idle chit-chat; she took the bull by the horns and fearlessly asked him anything, from her deductions regarding the owner of the Ritz, to the murders themselves. She pieced things together with an efficient sharpness that astonished him - whether he wanted her to figure them out or not.

He'd purposefully dumped syndicate business on her to see how she'd take it, and he'd been delighted with the response. She'd talked with him about the murders of DiStephano's underbosses and his own two moles with objective journalistic curiosity, for the moment seeing past the fact she'd seen his two hits first hand. Her ambition, her innate desire for truth, could very well overcome any fear she felt in the face of an uncertain future.

The open candor they'd discovered with each other had carried over into the Jeep and onto the beach, and he thought of their laughter and the fun of the white-knuckled drive on the island. She couldn't wait to see his cottage - a space he'd never shared with anyone before, and she loved it as much as he did, this magical place where time stopped.

Just touching on the memory of the sunscreen episode on the dresser made him stand tall and hard against his body. He could still feel his lotioned hands on her soft skin, see the look in her eyes when he'd cut off their kiss. It was still there when she'd come out to him for their hike, telling him just how much it bothered her that he hadn't taken what they both wanted.

Raine recognized the honor she'd paid him by discussing her past so freely with him during their trek through the jungle. Even though she'd been wary of sharing the deepest, rawest memories of her parents, she'd pressed on anyway, and not only did he understand those powerful sensory recollections she'd described, he identified with them. He wanted to know her - he had to if he was going to recruit her - and rather than clam up on him, she'd answered every single thing he'd asked. It was further proof of how far she'd come in trusting him, but nothing cemented that fact like her crisis on the precipice over the swimming hole.

He honestly had no idea she couldn't swim, otherwise he'd have picked a different spot for them. On the other hand, though, it had worked out better than he ever could have planned. If they'd gone somewhere else on the island, she'd have never seen the place most sacred to him on earth. He'd have never borne witness to the depth of her trust in him when she leapt from that rock, knowing that bottomless hole of water would have swallowed her whole without him. Nor would they have shared that intimate conversation under the waterfall, making it clear he was looking to foster peace with her, not enmity.

Maybe he was looking to foster more than that.

Raine rested his forehead against the cold stone of the shower wall. This trip with her had not been on his schedule for this weekend; there were shit-tons of things he should be tending to right now before he left for Rome on Tuesday.

But all he could think about was spending as much time as possible with this incredible girl between now and then.

Loiacono had his reasons for swearing off women, he

thought harshly. *They made a mess of things. He was definitely on to something with that.*

But you know better than anyone that Loiacono had loved once, and deeply, countered the other half of his mind. *It's only because he lost that love that he refused to re-enter the bloodiest arena of them all.*

"No women," Nobile Loiacono had instructed him on countless occasions, and every time they discussed it his black eyes would glow like coals. "No girlfriends, no wives, no mistresses. The other soldiers, fine. Let them dally at their peril. But the boss? Never. He needs to have his wits about him. Nothing can cloud his judgment. He can reveal no vulnerabilities to the world. Listen carefully when I tell you there is no weapon on earth more destructive to a man than a woman. Take them to your bed for pleasure, but let them take nothing else from you."

Loiacono had said that last line so many times it should be carved on his headstone.

"But if my mother hadn't chosen my father over you, Nobile," Raine said out loud, his voice echoing back to him from the stone and the glass, "would your philosophy have changed?"

He lifted his forehead from the wall to let the water cascade down his body once again.

Surely no harm could come from the decision to keep Solana as his lover once he'd recruited her.

They'd have to keep it on the DL, of course, probably even from Cavi and Anesini, but he could manage that easily enough.

Honestly, who was there to stop him? How much power did he truly wield if he couldn't keep the most beautiful, courageous, intelligent woman he'd ever met in his bed? Who made the rules around here? He did. If he wanted something, he went after it, and he'd gotten it every time.

He wanted Alessandra Solana Trent.

And he wanted her to want him in return.

He'd been so close under the waterfall. He'd only teased her with the promise of a kiss, and she'd pulled him down to her with a need so great it set his pulse to pounding. If it weren't for the goddamn thunderstorm, he was positive she'd have ridden him right there in the swirling mist of their secluded cave.

Raine punched the wall in frustration as he remembered her strong thighs straddling him, her hot core burning against his rigid shaft clear through their bathing suits. How she'd moaned against his lips... how she'd kissed him more desperately when he'd been about to take that little bikini top from her breasts... Fuck, it was maddening. Even now his cock stood at attention, still ready for her.

He didn't know why it mattered to him so much, but he needed her to come full circle. He needed her to come to him, and he didn't know how long he'd have to wait –

The sound of the shower door closing behind him obliterated his thoughts.

Raine didn't think. He whirled on her and grabbed her to him like he needed her in order to breathe. Solana gasped his name, but there was no time for any other words before he reached down to take the backs of her thighs in his hands and lift her clear off the stone floor, spreading her legs around him. He could feel her scorching softness begging for him as he pressed her back against the glass of the enclosure, water pouring over them, but still he leveled his hard blue eyes to her flashing green ones, searching them to their depths.

"Here?" he demanded, his voice rough.

"Anywhere," she answered, unable to stop the trembling that took over her entire body. "Anywhere, Raine, so long as it's *right now.*"

Raine smiled down at her, and her moan of pleasure echoed through the entire bathroom when he filled her as far as her tight little body could take him.

She took all of him. She was so ready for him, so hot, deep and perfect, that she took every last thick, hard inch of him.

"Fucking Christ, Solana," Raine gasped, and his hands holding her thighs gripped harder as he pounded her against the unyielding wall of the shower. Solana wrapped herself around him as tightly as she could, using her arms around his neck and her legs around his waist to rock her hips in ferocious time with his. Her smooth, impossibly soft skin turned slick as the water washed off the remaining sunscreen from her hot body, making it even easier for them to move together. She took his earlobe between her teeth and he shuddered when she suckled it, teasing him while he took her harder, until he was fit to burst inside her. He swelled with his need for her, and she felt her own body tighten around him in response, her insides crushing with the climax that already threatened to strike quick and violent.

"Raine," she breathed to him, her voice shaking in his ear. "Raine, now. Please, *now.*"

His rock hard discipline crashed to the earth. He needed her, urgently, and he couldn't stand to wait another second. He slammed into her until he felt her go, releasing her to the sun, and then let loose himself, taking his own pleasure from her while she rolled her hips in bliss against him. Her cheek dropped to his shoulder and she called out for him, holding on with quaking muscles while the quenching waves of his deliverance washed through her.

"Solana, look at me," he said, his deep voice reverberating from his chest into hers like they were one single echo chamber. Her face lifted up to his, her head resting back against the glass, and when he searched her expression he found that she practically glowed, her eyes smiling languidly up at him.

She'd come to him. Of her own accord, on her own terms, she'd come to him.

Raine used his hips to pin her against the shower wall, freeing his hands so he could cup her jaws in them. "Solana," he whispered, his thumbs caressing her wet cheeks, and then he claimed her mouth with his.

Solana felt warmth course through her, one that had nothing to do with maddening desire. It was a fullness that started in her heart and radiated its way outward, tickling into her stomach, prickling along her limbs, tingling into her fingers where she touched him, pouring from her lips where she kissed him.

She hadn't been able to stand it, being out there in the sitting room alone after he'd held her so closely through the storm. The thought of him standing naked beneath a heavenly shower tormented her, bringing her back to their interrupted tryst under the waterfall.

As the minutes passed, she'd known what she wanted to do.

She'd wandered to the bedroom, heard the shower running in the bathroom just beyond. She'd stood there, trembling, acutely aware that each second she hesitated meant she might miss her opportunity. Guys didn't take long showers; if she wanted to surprise him, she had to swallow her nervousness and get on with it. She'd dropped her wet clothes to the floor and paused, naked and anxious, with her hand on the doorknob. Would he take this as an invasion of privacy? If he wanted her in the shower with him, wouldn't he have invited her to come along?

While the seconds ticked, Solana felt her window closing.

Swallowing hard, she'd entered the steamy bathroom as quietly as she could.

Her breath had caught in her throat when she saw him. He stood with his back to her, his palms resting against the brown stone tiles while the water spilled down his neck and back in wide streams. She took in the view of his tapered body, his broad, finely shaped shoulders, the muscles of his strong back, his slim waist, his firm rear. She followed down the length of his thick, muscular thighs, beautiful calves, and then back up to his toned arms when he straightened and ran his hands through his full head of dark blond hair. The Bulova on his wrist flashed in the low bathroom light, and her body tightened with breath-stealing ardor for him.

Solana's feet had padded softly across the stone floor, praying he wouldn't turn around within the next five seconds. When her hand closed on the handle to the glass shower door, her heart beat so hard she thought it would break through her chest.

Wait, she panicked. *Was it really a smart idea to sneak up on a mob boss for any reason whatsoever? Even if it was a good one?*

But she'd come too far to abort the mission now. She buried her fear, pulled the door open, and entered his inner sanctum.

The steam brought the sweat to the surface of her skin before the door even closed behind her. She'd no sooner reached out to touch him when she saw it, the split-second warning that told her he'd heard her. The muscles in his back and his arms flinched and flexed, and the next thing she knew he had her pinned up against the shower wall, her legs spreadeagled around him, his hard eyes boring into hers while the water ran like a river over them.

"*Here?*"

The way he'd said it brought goosebumps along her arms, even now after it was all over. He'd asked her permission. With that one word, he'd asked her if she really wanted him to take her right there against the wall, making sure he made no erroneous assumptions, took no undue license.

He'd been rough but she'd been ready, more than ready, and kissing him now, in the glowing aftermath, she knew she'd made the right decision to come to him. Her heart burned with a fulfillment she hadn't expected to find here in his arms, but she didn't question it. Wouldn't question it, not now.

It could all wait until later.

Much later.

Solana felt Raine's hands move from her face to her hips, and then he broke the kiss to press her gently against the shower wall while he withdrew his own hips and thighs that had been holding her up. She let her legs slacken, and she sucked in her breath at the soreness in her muscles from wrapping herself around him so tightly. Despite the overexertion, she stretched her shaking legs toward the floor until her feet touched the warm stone, but he kept his grip on her until she stood securely on her own once again.

Solana looked up at him, his broad back shielding her face from the deluge of water pouring down from the showerhead behind him. His eyes glowed beatifically down to hers, his full lips turning up sexily at the corners, and she smiled in self-conscious pride, color coursing her chevron cheekbones.

Raine kissed her forehead before he pulled her to him, keeping her head pressed to his chest while he reached for something above him. He protected her from the onslaught of water as he adjusted the angle of the showerhead to something more appropriate for someone of her petite stature, and when he stepped aside she no longer was in danger of drowning underneath the warm, refreshing stream.

Solana gasped as the massaging water soaked her, cleansing her hot, sweaty body from the exertions of the day. She moved in closer, turning her face up to the showering spray, and let the flow pour down her thick mane of hair. She sensed Raine move to stand behind her, confirmed when she felt his large hands on her hips, just holding her.

She stepped back, dashed the water from her eyes. "That's amazing," she said, letting out the breath she'd been holding.

Raine's chest moved against her back as he chuckled softly. "Hand me the soap, will you?"

She passed the bar back to him, and seconds later felt his large, soapy hands run down the length of her arms. She smiled rapturously at his slick touch, reveling in the soap's deliciously manly mixture of bergamot, mint, cedar, and suede. He moved up to her shoulders, and she pulled her wet, unruly mass of hair into a pile on top of her head and held it there for him, keeping it out of his way while he soaped her shoulders and her back, massaging her carefully and attentively.

"Don't move," he said as he moved onward, enjoying the look of her standing there like a classical nude statue, holding her hair up for him. He lathered her rear and her legs, kneading the muscles that had gotten more than their share of a workout over the course of this day. He was very careful with her feet, not wanting to tickle her, and when he was done he ran his hands all the way up to her hips and turned her to face him.

Solana watched him gather another layer of soap into his hands, and then he started on her throat, her chest, taking his time with her full, perfect breasts. He slicked down the flat plain of her abdomen, then let his lathered hand go lower, and she cried out to him as he washed the softest, most sensitive part of her body, his eyes holding hers the entire time he did so.

Afterwards, he let his hands travel up the sides of her torso, and she laughed out loud when he soaped up her ticklish underarms. Then he ran along her arms again, reaching up to her hands where she held her hair, and he pulled them down to her sides, letting her wet auburn curls tumble back down along her body.

He turned her again to face the water, and while she rinsed he took hold of the bottle of shampoo. He dispensed a huge pile into his palm, not exactly sure how much he'd need to sufficiently soap that volume of hair. It ended up being way too much, but he didn't hear anything that even resembled complaining as he thoroughly massaged her scalp, then repeated the process for the conditioner.

Raine turned a very clean, and very happy Solana around to face him one last time. "Feel better?" he asked, his eyes sparkling.

"Light years," she smiled up at him. "Thank you."

He grinned back down to her, and then reached for the knobs of the faucet.

"Hold it right there," Solana ordered, putting her hands over his to stop him. "I don't care if you showered before I got here; you're about to get another lathering."

Raine held up his fingertips to show her they were already pruning. "I think I've been in the water long enough for one day, don't you?"

Solana rolled her eyes. "You'll dry out," she retorted, and his answering laughter filled the small bathroom to its farthest corner.

She started on his back like he had for her, and she relished the feel of his firm muscles beneath her soapy palms and fingers. She massaged every inch of him, planting kisses on each area before she lathered it with her exploring hands. When she turned him to face her, she felt her body flush when she saw he was nearly ready for her again.

"You have no idea of the effect you have on me, little Alessandra," he murmured, planting a soft kiss on her torching cheek.

Solana blushed hotter in response, pressing on to soap his neck and powerful shoulders. She smiled at his sharp intake of breath when she kissed both of his nipples before lathering his strong chest and washboard abs. She ran her slickened hands over his hips, and it was her turn to watch his face when she took him in her hands and cleansed the most sensitive parts of his body.

Raine did *not* giggle like a girl when she washed his underarms; his eyes just burned like banked coals while he watched her finish her ministrations on his left side, reveling in the muscles and sinews of his arm, his hand, his fingertips.

Solana moved over to his right, and she hissed in her breath when she saw the four livid scratches that showed red against the smooth, tanned skin of his bicep.

"What the... ?" She ran a soapy finger over them, carefully, and he didn't flinch from her touch. "How did this happen?" she asked, her eyes flicking up to his. "They weren't there last...

"*Oh,*" she cried when she realized where he'd probably gotten them. "Was that me?" she asked shyly. "Did I do that when you came for me after I jumped in the swimming hole?"

He nodded. "But it's fine, Solana."

"Doubtful," she returned. "I'm sorry."

"Well now," he said lightly "That's two apologies from you in one day."

"Three's your maximum. After that, suck it up, cupcake."

His answering laughter made that radiating fullness move through her once again.

She turned him to rinse, and then had a much easier time shampooing and conditioning his hair than he'd had with hers. To make up for it, she made sure she gave him extra attention, taking time to massage his scalp, wash his handsome face, and finish him with a soft kiss on his lips.

When the water finally stopped, they were definitely the cleanest people on the island of St. John.

Raine opened the shower door for her, and Solana stepped out into a steam bath. He came out behind her, produced two thick, fluffy towels from the linen closet and handed one to her. They both dried off with a vengeance, ready to get out of the oppressively humid little room, and then left the bathroom hand-in-hand, dressed in only their towels.

The bedroom was a cool haven of bliss by comparison. The rain still barraged the patio outside the open wall, but the wind left behind by the storm blew through the room, chilling it down considerably from the summer inferno it had been.

Solana thought the bed was the most inviting thing she'd ever seen. After the day they'd had, a late afternoon nap was not only deserved, but required.

Raine seemed to read her mind. Wordlessly, he squeezed her hand and led her to the huge piece of furniture in the center of the room, parted the sheer curtains for her, and Solana climbed in on top of the soft coverlet, keeping her damp towel wrapped around her. He came in right behind her, closing them in a cozy white cocoon of fluttering sheers, luxurious cotton, and down feathers.

Raine pulled Solana to him, and they barely sank back into the nest of soft pillows before sleep swallowed them both under, serenaded by the sound of the pattering rain.

CHAPTER ELEVEN

8:49 P.M.

First were the delectable smells. The warm scent of cinnamon coupled with the seductive aroma of chocolate. The airy brightness of lemon soaring over the dense earthiness of almonds. Some sweet, fragrant thing had proclaimed its tempting presence, and Solana breathed deeply through her nose to get her fill of it.

Next came the soporific sounds. Over the soft rush of the seabreeze and the distant crash of ocean waves floated the voice of Billie Holiday crooning "The Very Thought of You." From somewhere in the distance, Billie's smoky, somnolent vocals smoothed their way over a tinkling jazz piano, and then the muted brass's lazy solos drawled on like a hot summer afternoon.

Then there was tactile heaven. Rising through the layers of sleep, Solana stretched over the opulent bed, her limbs sweeping over the lavish coverlet. Her reaching fingertips sank into plush down pillows, her pointing toes brushed against smooth sheer curtains, and her arching body lay wrapped in some soft, fluffy, slightly moist thickness.

Towel, her sleepy mind wondered, and then her subconscious released her into real time.

Solana rolled up to sit on the bed she already knew was empty, her still-wet curls tumbling into her face. Brushing her damp mane away, she opened her eyes expecting to see lingering daylight, but instead found the bedroom remarkably dark through the translucent nest of white surrounding her. Puzzled, she held the towel close around her as she crawled the length of the huge bed and parted the veiling canopy for an unobstructed view.

Through the open wall of the bedroom, over the lip of the patio's rock wall, wisps of grey clouds raced across a clearing sky, now a deep purple since it was well past twilight. She turned to the analog clock on the nightstand to discover it was nearly nine; she'd slept the better part of three hours. And in the Caribbean so much farther south, the sun set earlier here during the summer than in the northern latitudes she called home.

Solana shifted to sit crosslegged in lotus, her hand over her heart where she held the towel pinned to her chest.

Home?

Manhattan and Philadelphia seemed worlds away from where she sat alone on the curtained king bed like a pearl in a giant oyster. Watching the thinning clouds tear across the indigo sky, listening to the music in the house carry over to her on the summer wind, she felt relaxed, fulfilled, lulled into a stupor that could only be described as inconceivable. It just didn't seem possible, this day, this place, this moment.

Not after what she'd witnessed yesterday.

Not in light of what she knew with a career devoted to the study of the modern mob.

By some sick twist of fate, the milestones and accomplishments of her life had somehow landed her in this situation, in Raine Mathison's hands, with no clue as to what would happen next. Here, in this beautiful, sensual place, the world seemed to hold its breath along with her, during this time where time itself ceased to exist. Seduced by the island's otherworldly magic, she had to savor this evening for what it was and wait for whatever would come afterward.

Night was falling fast. As the seconds passed, the pool of light thrown from the kitchen window onto the patio grew brighter in the gathering dusk, and it was high time she got up to find out what this night held for her.

Solana secured her towel and crawled out from the canopied bed like a butterfly emerging from her cocoon. Her muscles protested sorely from their many over-exertions; just standing there in the center of the room made her body ache. But the breeze that tickled along her bared limbs made it well worth the effort as it caressed her sleep-warmed skin.

While the scents and the light from the kitchen window made Raine's location in the house rather obvious, she preferred he remain unaware of the fact she'd woken from her nap. Full dark hadn't yet fallen; she still had plenty of dwindling twilight to suit her purposes and she kept the bedroom lights off.

Eschewing her own suitcase full of clothes, she crossed over to the closet and began poring through the hangers upon hangers of things Raine had somehow arranged to procure for her for this trip. If looking beautiful was somehow a weapon in this game they were playing, she'd dress it up to her best advantage in clothing he'd personally picked out for her.

As soon as her fingers made contact with the silk of the little black dress by Zac Posen, her search came to its decisive end. Rifling through the overflowing underwear drawer yielded a similar absolute resolution; once she discovered the Parah strapless balconette bra and panties in the netherworld of the drawer, she knew she had a winner. "Leave it to the Italians," she breathed, fingering the delicate white French Chantilly lace that draped impalpable and transparent over her fingers.

"The Very Thought of You" ended as Solana dropped her towel to the floor, and she found herself anticipating the next installment on Raine's mix. Her dreams during the latter half of her nap had been soundtracked by the likes of Frank Sinatra, Jerry Vale, June Christy, and Rosemary Clooney, and now that she knew the source, she wondered who would follow the illustrious Billie on his playlist.

Provided with no advance warning, Solana had nothing to defend herself against the first hopeful notes of Nina Simone's "July Tree." She didn't listen to her mother's favorite by choice, and the sound of that singular voice wrapping itself around her again opened a hole in her chest, powering through layers upon layers of long-buried emotion. Nina cast her soulful spell, and while Solana stood powerless against it, the music coupled with the smell of the goodies coming from the kitchen unlocked another memory.

She was home. Home in Italia, carried on her father's hip as they made their way across a kitchen that smelled of baking anisette cookies and echoed with her mother's pretty singing.

Clear as day, Solana could hear her hitting the notes of the same song she now listened to from deeper within the cottage, the one about love's seed sown in autumn to nest snugly through the seasons, then blossom as a tree in summer. Now that she was older, she recognized the poetic allegory to motherhood, and her face warmed with the tears that pricked the corners of her eyes.

"True love deep in the winter white snow," Solana whispered along, remembering how her mother had sung the lyrics in greeting to her January-born daughter. How she'd stroked her child's nose with her fingertip before planting a tender kiss on the end. "How long will it take to grow?"

Thankfully, July Tree was one of the shorter songs in Nina's repertoire, but Solana wasn't released from the clutches of her reverie before the heartening point of the lyrical poem rose to its crescendo. *True love blooms for the world to see... True love blooms for the world to see...*

She closed her eyes and sang the last line from her heart. "Blooms high upon..." she belted, holding every single syllable, "...the July Tree."

But it wasn't her voice that resonated through the bedroom during the last uplifting notes of the flute. Instead, it was Isadora Taranto Alessandra's rich, deep contralto, and bittersweet tears rolled hot and fast down Solana's cheeks.

"I have her voice," she choked, overcome. "Mamma, I have it, too."

The suave French lyrics of Pink Martini's "Sympathique" thrust her rudely back into reality. Sucking in a shuddering breath, Solana dashed the tears from her face with the backs of her fingers, snatched up the clothing she'd picked out and locked herself in the bathroom, wanting someplace safe to dress and freshen up. If Raine had happened to hear her - and chances were good on that one - she didn't want him to find her in tears. He would ask questions, and she didn't want to have to explain this precious thing to anyone, not when she'd barely had a chance to deal with the revelation herself.

She took one look at her hot, tear-streaked face in the mirror and scowled. "Great. Nice job forgetting to bring one single goddamn bit of makeup with you, Alessandra."

With a resigned sigh, she washed her face with deliciously cool water, then paused while she dried off to take several calming breaths through the soft towel. She didn't even bother trying to comb through her voluminous mass of bedheaded curls flying wild and thick around her; the endeavor was pointless. She just ran her fingers through the long unruly tumble of chocolate brown and flaming red, tossed it, and let it fall where it would. Next came a good brushing and flossing, and after the soothing effect of such routine ministrations she almost felt normal again. Her sunkissed skin brightened and glowed in the Caribbean humidity, her pale green eyes sparkled, and her lips flushed red in the island's heat.

Solana took her time getting dressed, and when she finished her only regret was not having a pair of towering black heels to finish off the drop-dead gorgeous Posen. The strapless black silk dress hugged every curve of her hourglass while displaying a liberal amount of her tanned olive skin, drawing attention to her shimmering shoulders, generous cleavage, and making her legs look longer due to the hem stopping several dangerous inches above her knees.

She studied her reflection critically. She might be overdressed for the modest cottage, but if sexy was her weapon of choice against Raine, well... In her own humble opinion, she stood a good chance of killing him with it tonight.

Not that I want him dead, she thought hastily, searching her own eyes in the mirror.

Which only begged the next question.

What do you want from him, then?

Solana shook her head to clear it. *Later,* she repeated her mantra again, the one she'd adopted in the shower with him that afternoon. *I'll deal with all this much, much later.*

She left the bathroom, as ready as she'd ever be for this night, but upon reentering the bedroom she heard something of definite interest coming all the way from the kitchen. Ears pricking, she darted noiselessly through the cottage, grateful now to be lacking a pair of noisy heels, and held back just outside the entryway of the kitchen to listen.

He can sing, Solana marveled, warming as she heard Raine rock the bass harmonies with the backup gents on the second half of Ella Fitzgerald's "Solid as a Rock." Another one of her mother's favorites, this tune was a bright, jaunty, hip-swinging toe-tapper, and she'd sung it well.

And so can I, she thought as she took a hesitant step into the small, warmly lit kitchen, feeling the bold soul of Ella take possession of her.

"*Solid as a rock,*" she sang, channeling Ella pitch-perfectly as a sister contralto. "*Solid as a rock... Love is as solid as the Rock of Gibraltar, so come to the altar with me.*"

Raine seemed to forget all about his lines when he looked up to see her standing there in the doorway of his kitchen, and Solana smiled around her lyrics when she saw him almost drop the mixing bowl of icing he was preparing into the sink. He managed to recover himself quickly enough, and he rejoined his voice with hers in the song as their disparate parts complemented and flowed around each other's, different lines in different times.

Just like Ella and her guys, Solana took the lead while Raine picked up phrases and harmonized them, and singing the words to life with him felt so good, so goddamn good, she couldn't hold back when the tapping of her toes traveled upward to become a swing in her hips.

Icing forgotten, Raine stepped over to her just as his part in the song ended, leaving Solana to sing Ella's sultry, coquettish croons solo over the rest of the jazzy, finger-snapping tune. He took her hands in his and led her in a swing dance that made her smile through her singing again, and then he brought her in against his body for the end, her cheek alongside his for the very last line. Ella's lovingly simple, sweetly soulful command: *"Come to the altar with me."*

Raine's body tickled as Solana's breathy vibrato filled his ears on that last high note, and she cut it short with a giggle when he nuzzled his lips into the sweet-scented softness below her ear. He held her close for several seconds, his hands on the succulent swell of her silk-covered hips, before Louis Armstrong's "A Kiss to Build a Dream On" stole over the airwaves and broke the moment.

Solana shook her head in delighted wonder. "Your taste in music, Raine," she told him, her voice throaty and rich from her singing. "Really, it's just spot on."

He pulled her from him and looked down into her glowing face. "I'd say the same for you," he said, releasing her. "Not many know Cookie Monsta, who the hell Bond is, or some of the Chili Peppers' more minor works."

"Minor." Solana rolled her eyes at his punny reference

to "Minor Thing" from their drive in the Jeep. "Nicely done."

He laughed softly. "You may not be the only word-smith in the house tonight, you know."

"Evidently not," she conceded, and poked her head around him to check out the mixing bowl by the sink. "So, what's going on in here, anyway? This kitchen smells like a gourmet pastry shop."

"Cassatine," Raine answered, leaving her to give his icing another stir. "Otherwise known as nucatuli. By either name, though, they smell as sweet. They're Sicilian almond cookies, handmade from scratch."

Solana blinked in amazement. "You *bake?*"

His face lifted to hers. "You got a problem with that?" he demanded, only half in jest.

"No," she said, taken aback. "No, I'm just surprised. I mean, everybody has his own way to de-stress; I just wasn't expecting yours to involve confectioner's sugar."

His strong jaw flexed as his teeth clenched in a hard line.

"Not that there's anything wrong with that," she added hastily, beginning to babble under the intensity of his skin-flaying stare. "Even my brothers made brownies on occasion, so trust me, I'm not calling your masculinity into question or anything."

Raine's icy gaze never wavered. "In light of recent events, my dear," he said, his deep voice rumbling like distant thunder, "I should hope not."

Solana felt the hole she'd dug for herself reach China, but by some merciful twist of fate she was saved by the bell. Literally. The oven timer chose that precise moment to announce that the fragrant contents within required someone's immediate attention.

She cleared her throat. "Can I help you with any-thing?" she asked, watching him take out several sheets' worth of little half-moon shaped, ravioli-esque cookies.

"I'm all set," he answered coolly, snapping off the range. "These just need to be brushed with this frosting and then put back into the oven long enough for it to melt."

His clipped tone hadn't softened in the slightest, and Solana looked down at her fingers as she toyed with them.

"Really, Raine," she insisted, wholeheartedly contrite. "There must be something I can do."

Raine looked over at her and realized she earnestly wanted to help, wanted to prove she hadn't been mocking him. A chastened smile touched the corner of his lips, and he crossed to the corner of the kitchen to slide a stool over to the counter, closer to where he was working. He moved his pre-supper snack of red grapes and cheeses between the two spots so she could share it with him, along with the cool bottle of Gewurtztraminer still well over two-thirds full. He poured her a chilled glass, and then, last but certainly not least, he stepped to her, picked her up by the waist, and set her down gently on the stool.

"If you insist upon helping," he said, his intense eyes searching her face, "then you can sit here, *cara mia*, and talk with me." With that, he brushed his lips against her cheek, then turned from her to begin rifling through a drawer for a pastry brush.

Solana thought she'd fall off the stool with the next breath of breeze that passed through the open window. After receiving that sweet kiss from him, she was now watching the ruthless mobster that pulled the strings of New York City brush lemon-infused icing on piping hot, fresh-from-the-oven almond cookies.

Seriously? Standing right in front of her was the man she'd studied in depth for so long, whose raw ambition bought people off, blackmailed them, made them disappear without a trace when necessary. But clearly he had a story she didn't know yet. He guarded himself under layers upon layers of ironclad shields requisite for his position in life, yet he'd let her in far enough to show some of his true self to her.

She took a piece of the savory Fontina cheese and relished its pairing with the sweet white German wine while she watched him. Deep in her heart, she knew this trip hadn't been planned. Something had happened on that chaise in Philadelphia, the culmination of a unique chain of events neither one of them had anticipated. He'd brought her here to his paradise on St. John when he'd never shared it with anyone else before; she had a feeling the place was nothing short of sacred to him.

Why? Why would he bring her here? Why would he let her see the side of him she was damn sure no one else ever saw? The side that sang Ella Fitzgerald? The side that baked cookies on a Saturday afternoon? The side that taught a sworn adversary how to survive in a swimming hole? The side that lathered up a girl in the shower until she felt like a worshipped goddess?

How the hell did someone like this end up ruling one of the greatest cities in the world from the underground?

While she knew those other, deeper questions would go unanswered if she asked them, that last one might be a good start. He respected her journalistic instincts; he would honor that question as fair. He'd proven himself to be more than willing to divulge syndicate business to her, and while that alone was confusing, she knew she'd at least get somewhere with it.

Solana took another sip of the bright, fruity wine, matching it with a creamy wedge of Muenster this time, before she took her first swing.

"How did you do it?" she asked.

"Do what?"

"I saw what happened at the ball," she said. "All those acknowledgments you received that night. So how did you do it? How is the Big Apple just sitting there in the palm of your hand?"

Raine's eyes flicked to hers. "You always start with the big guns, don't you?"

"Would you expect anything less?"

He smiled in surprised pleasure. "No."

But then his demeanor changed, and when he started to answer her query Solana felt like a student under a veteran master's tutelage, tasked with the expectation that she never forget the knowledge now being passed down to her.

"Information," Raine began, "is quite possibly the most dangerous, yet by far the most profitable, of all commodities traded. This is not a novel market strategy; the same stock's been exchanged in the courts of complex empires for millennia. Upon first consideration it doesn't seem to fit the risk-versus-reward model, but what makes the investment so lucrative is the sheer number of interested shareholders.

"See, everyone has dirty secrets, Solana. Everyone. From nefarious crimes and taboo fetishes, to simple embarrassments and things best left unsaid. For example, I think you would agree that your interests are better served if your identity as Solana Taranto Alessandra remains a secret from William Donato, correct?"

Solana's insides stilled. "Is that a threat?" she asked.

"No," Raine replied. "I have no interest whatsoever in outing you to the Times. I've drawn that parallel solely to illustrate my point. But I'll offer another example to you - this time a gambit that I actually have in play. Let's take Alistair Prince, New York City's gifted Assistant DA."

"Al?" Solana sat up straighter. She would very much like to know how he'd managed to secure an alliance with the man who'd fought so hard beside her in the attempt to convict DiStephano. "What the hell do you have on Al?"

Raine's face darkened. "It's not *what* I have on Prince," he clarified, "but *whom*."

Unease put her on the edge of her seat. "Who is it?" she demanded. "What's he done?"

His lips formed a tight line as he studied her.

"Come now, that should be an easy one, Solana," he said after a long moment. "It's you."

Solana felt like she'd been punched in the stomach. "Me?"

"Yes, you," he repeated. "You think he wants his darling fiancée to catch wind of his torrid one-night tryst with a certain journalist in the wake of the DiStephano verdict?"

"You know about that?" she whispered, blushing from the visible spectrum clear through to infrared. It wasn't that she was ashamed of her night with Al; it was... she didn't know what it was that made her suddenly so uncomfortable under Raine's unflinching gaze. Something about him knowing the identity of other men she'd had before him didn't sit well, and when she saw a minatory darkness creep into those ice blue eyes, her feeling intensified.

Oh, he knows all right, she realized. *And now that he's had me himself, he's not thrilled about it one bit.*

"There's not much I don't know in this town, Solana," he answered.

She swallowed hard as guilt began its slithering sneak into her soul. After everything she and Al had been through together, she'd felt betrayed to discover his fealty to Raine, but now to find out she was the source of his defection...

Wait, she thought crossly, anger hijacking the guilt train before it had a chance to leave the station.

First of all, did Al blame her for his current predicament? Was that why he'd asked her for any information she couldn't print? Was that the reason he'd take anything she entrusted to him and forward it directly to Raine?

Secondly, taking it back a step, why did it even matter that they'd slept together? Since when is a one-night-stand an offense worthy of blackmail? How did that have any bearing whatsoever on Al's current relationship with his fiancée?

"Fine, so you know," Solana said hotly. "But so what? How is that significant enough for you to hold over him? We weren't even a couple, for Chrissake, and it was well before he even met Sarah Adriaan – "

"You sure about that?" Raine asked, and her answering silence was all the confirmation he needed. "Your question is a good one, Solana, because you're right. Your rendezvous doesn't seem so heinous a crime on the surface, now does it? But what you don't understand, my dear, are the *circumstances behind it*.

"What you don't know is that he was already seeing Sarah when the State filed suit against DiStephano. He was courting both of you at the same time, and he settled for silver when the gold told him to get lost. Yes, technically he didn't make it exclusive with her until after you'd rebuffed him. But she's a smart lass, Solana, and a vain one. When she finds out there's more to that touching front-page Post photo than meets the eye, she can do the math. It would be enough to throw a monkey wrench into his nuptials, don't you think?"

"That's reason enough to risk his career?" she cried. "His integrity? Enough for him to essentially have me killed if I were ever stupid enough to trust him with something I uncovered regarding your affairs?"

"Who are you to make those judgment calls for him?" Raine retorted. "Alistair Prince is a motivated, ambitious man whose values obviously differ from your own. Clearly you don't know him as well as you think you do."

He stopped short. "Incidentally, as an aside, I evidently don't either. Because if he's decided to put a bounty on your head by brokering your investigation information to me, he's acting outside the scope of our agreement. Now why would he do that, given what I know to be true about him?"

He gave a thoughtful pause, his shrewd eyes searching her face. "What exactly did he tell you to do?"

"He didn't *tell* me to do anything," Solana snapped, his dissecting tone putting her on the defensive. "We were discussing my articles on DiStephano's underbosses, and he specifically asked if I'd keep him posted on anything I couldn't print. I told him I would - until I saw what he did at Kane's ball. I saw him give you the proof that he's in your camp, and it didn't take me long to figure out he'd take my reports right back to you and pull the trigger on me by proxy."

Raine watched her while he considered the matter, and the heavy silence in the small kitchen gained weight as the seconds ticked off.

Finally, he shook his head.

"No," he declared. "You've misread that one, Solana. If he asked you for information unsafe for you to put in the presses, it means he's looking for you to get him out of this. The consummate idealist, he's hoping you'll find something catastrophic on me so you two can take another crack at putting organized crime on trial. That should settle your mind regarding his motives concerning *you*, but makes me rather inclined to think he may need some further convincing from *us*."

Solana didn't like the sound of that in the least. Yes, she was glad to have some semblance of Al's character restored, especially since it cleared him from wanting her dead.

But she'd been so preoccupied with him selling her out to Raine that she hadn't realized she'd done exactly that to him.

Solana's body turned to ice.

She'd just insinuated to Raine Mathison that Al was seeking a back door out of their arrangement, and double-crossing the boss, dealing behind his back, was a very, very bad idea.

"No!" Her hand shot out and grabbed his wrist so hard it dug the Bulova into his skin. "No, Raine, don't go after him. Don't hurt him, please!"

"That depends entirely upon you and what you tell me," he answered, prying her fingers loose from his wrist and holding them in his. "When, precisely, did he ask you this?"

Solana sang like a nightingale. "Early. He was the first person I ran into at Kane's ball, not two minutes after I walked in the door."

"Well before I arrived, then."

"Yes," she answered, perceiving where he was headed with this. "I don't think he realized at the time just how well-connected you are across the board. I know I didn't. Until you walked into that ballroom I had no idea the breadth of influence you had over the City, and I honestly wouldn't have believed it myself if I hadn't seen it with my own two eyes.

"So if your supposition is correct," she finished, "if Al asked me to feed him whatever I couldn't print because he wanted help getting out from under you, he only dared because he didn't know we don't stand a fucking chance."

Not right this second, anyway, she amended, but kept that part to herself.

Raine's eyes narrowed. "He should have known that already."

"Why? Because you've managed to turn everyone else around him?"

"Exactly. You asked why he'd risk his career and allow himself to be blackmailed for his upcoming marriage. It's because they're linked, Solana. He couldn't be the last man standing against me when I had the rest of his enclave tied in. Why? He's looking for his career to catapult. Could he have gone to another city to start over rather than accept my terms? Sure, but that's where Sarah Adriaan comes into play.

"As I alluded to before, her weakness is vanity. As far as she's concerned, nowhere else in the world compares to the city so nice they named it twice. She's very much looking forward to a successful, high-profile career in Kane's senatorial administration; that by itself was reason enough for her to follow suit with Kane and ally with us. She's marrying a rising star in New York City's justice system, and she fully expects that star to keep rising. She's planning an extravagant *haute couture* wedding and honeymoon, financed in part by a generous gift from yours truly, and she's eager to have every detail of the entire lavish event splashed across the celebration pages. The last thing she'd be able to handle, Solana, is the knowledge of who you are to her future husband."

"*Are?*" she blurted.

"Are," he confirmed. "Think back to what you asked me, why something so seemingly innocuous as your coupling constitutes grounds for blackmailing him. Think about the circumstances and the motivations I've just laid out for you. Then consider the real question of why he kept it from her in the first place, why the woman closest to him in the world doesn't already know about you, about something that should rate as ancient history.

"You know the answer to this one, Solana," he said, giving her fingers a soft squeeze. "Ultimately, there's no way I'd have anything on him, anything at all, if – "

"If he weren't still in love with me," she finished, and she tossed back the rest of her wine with rattled gusto.

Raine reached over and refilled her voided glass. "That's my clever journalist," he said, releasing his hold on her fingers, and when he turned his attention back to the cookies it put the matter of Alistair Prince to definite rest.

"My point in all this," he explained, "is the more ammunition I have, the better I can protect myself and the people under my banner. And I can tell you the syndicate has amassed quite the arsenal. This City's power elite covers the whole spectrum with drug habits, illegitimate children, contracted illnesses, mental disorders, gambling problems. They earn multiple salaries in kickbacks, bribery, and fraud. They profit off the black market, they patronize prostitutes, they deal in human trafficking. They hide abuses of power and acts of criminal negligence. They are exhibitionists, pedophiles, sado-masochists, philanderers, rapists, murderers, you name it, trickling all the way down to those whose crime was simply being complicit. The ones who knew and did nothing, finding themselves accomplices and accessories to illegal activities and unethical behaviors that would destroy their lives and careers if it were made public.

"Getting it down to the brass tacks, the entire infrastructure of New York City would fold like a house of cards if I laid my hand on the table. So we've all agreed to keep our mouths shut about each other, so we can all lead powerful, prosperous lives."

When Solana didn't say anything, Raine glanced over at her to find her riveted. "You're dying to ask who's who, aren't you?"

"Yes, and no," she admitted, wondering why she'd asked this question in the first place. She thought back to the room full of power players at Kane's ball and her conflict was classic. The journalist wanted to know, but as a human being who liked sleeping at night, she didn't want that kind of knowledge in her head.

"Orwell had it right," she mused, running her hands over her face. "The paradox of double-think. People know their governments are corrupt, but simultaneously expect their public servants to uphold justice and honor their promises. Then they're scandalized when they discover the politicians and officials they've put on pedestals are every bit as hypocritical and fallible as the rest of humanity."

She looked at him as a new thought occurred to her. "And you... you as the kind of white collar criminal they're always campaigning to bring down, you must find the irony positively staggering."

He lifted his wine glass to her in salute. "And highly lucrative."

But Solana caught his wry expression as she watched him take a draught.

"So what do they have on you?" she ventured in the quiet that followed.

Raine's glass landed a little harder than necessary on the countertop. "I'm not sure I follow you."

"Oh I think you do," she insisted, dropping her voice. "If you're holding information over their heads, you either need something from them or they've got something to bargain with in return." She cocked her head to the side and gave him a considering look. "I wonder if they've got as much on you as I suspect I do."

Raine only raised an eyebrow in silent, skeptical response.

"Here's one," she volleyed. "Not too long ago, in a rare show of corporate largesse, Imbrialis sold off a sizable interest in its extraordinarily profitable overseas bond market to a Swiss conglomerate at a discount. While that activity isn't illegal *per se*, I expect using the proceeds to finance the remaining months of Kane's campaign would constitute grossly unsanctioned activity."

He didn't move a muscle as he stared at her. "Very smart, Solana. How did you know?"

"Kane. He told me on Thursday night that you'd signed on as the campaign's financial advisor and that you'd made a generous donation to the cause. Imbrialis never sells off anything, so I always figured the funds must be earmarked for a purpose of some significance. After two frustrating months, I put it together not two minutes ago."

"Did I say something to tip you off?"

Solana shook her head. "Nope. It just came to me."

She had his full attention. "What else?"

"You killed John-Paul Marchesotto," she said, trying to keep it from sounding like the accusation it was. "His body was never found, but I bet the newly appointed CEO of SPQR Construction went missing last summer because he didn't want to continue his predecessor's imprudent partnership with La Cosa Nostra."

"He was standing in the way of progress," Raine admitted. "His successor proposed the idea, and was quite excited with his subsequent promotion. Business has boomed for SPQR and the syndicate ever since."

"I'm sure," she said sarcastically. "What about Vin Burtolo, Jeff Cantrell, and David Michael Walsh? Key witnesses in the racketeering case the FBI was starting to build against your organization two years ago? Three more men who just vanished without so much as a shoelace left behind?"

He sighed. "I'm sorry to say that there are more people on that list, Solana, than are dreamt of in your philosophy."

"*Are* you sorry over there, Hamlet?"

"Why the third degree, Alessandra?" Raine retorted. "You of all people know that a man of my position runs into problems that must be handled in a certain way."

"Like *Sofia* Marchesotto?" she countered, throwing the gauntlet, and watched his face cloud with exasperated consternation.

"John-Paul's lovely young widow wanted more than my condolences after her husband's untimely passing."

"Blackmail or your bed?" she pressed, none too gently. "Which version of the story is true?"

"Both," Raine snapped.

Solana held his sharpening gaze, her own eyes narrowing as she divined the rest. "You didn't just call the hit, either," she wondered. "You're the one who actually killed her."

"Yes."

"But she was your... "

"Girlfriend?" He supplied, incredulous. "No."

"But you slept with her," she accused.

"Multiple times, multiple occasions."

"So what happened?" Solana cried. "No, wait, let me guess. She wanted more than sex, but either you weren't interested or you wouldn't break Loiacono's cardinal rule for her. Once it became clear she'd never have any kind of official status with you, she got so pissed she tried to blackmail you for her husband's murder. She turned into a liability you couldn't afford."

Raine nodded sharply. "She became business instead of pleasure."

Solana's body prickled from head to toe, all the little hairs on her skin standing at attention while her mind drew the parallels. *Currently, I seem to be both for you*, she thought, her heart pulsing faster, and when she felt the question land on the tip of her tongue, she knew she couldn't stop it.

"What are we doing here, Raine," she demanded, her voice quiet in the kitchen.

He adroitly plucked a grape from the bowl beside her and brought it to her mouth. Out of reflex she opened and took the sweet little globe from him, but afterwards he kept his finger there, pressing it gently yet firmly against her closed lips.

When his cool eyes lifted up to hers, his implication was clear.

"We're baking cookies before dinner, Solana," was all he said, and after a long moment he removed his fingertip from her mouth.

No more questions, she understood as she chewed the grape that had warmed on her tongue.

And no more answers.

The silence fell awkward between them while Raine put the freshly iced cookies back in the oven to let the sugars melt. He straightened stiffly, and when he turned to her he kept his face carefully blank. "So tell me, Solana, how do you like your steak?"

She looked up at him, her heart weighing like a stone in her chest. "One more question before I answer yours."

He inclined his head, clearly open to the inquiry, but making no promise of an answer.

"Are you going to hurt Al?"

The heartbeat of silence that followed seemed to last minutes.

"No," he snipped. "With the caveat that I can't be held to that oath forever. As you know, relationships in this business are volatile at best; there's no telling what tomorrow might bring. But if you're asking me if I'm going to hurt him based on what you've told me tonight, the answer to that question is no. You have my word."

Solana closed her eyes for a moment, took a grateful breath through her nose. *Good enough*, she thought. It was an honest answer, and fair - one she could respect. More importantly, it was one she could trust. A man's word in the underground was the currency of his reputation, and to her knowledge Raine Mathison had never tendered in counterfeit.

"All right, then," she said, opening her eyes to his again. "On the few occasions that I have it, medium rare."

Raine nodded, the trace of a smile returning to his lips. "The only way, in my opinion," he agreed, pulling out a foil-covered square Pyrex from the fridge before he handed off the oven mitts to her. "You're officially in charge of the nucatuli; just keep an eye on them and you'll know when they're done. In the meantime, would you go out there, pick a starfruit from one of the trees and slice it up for me?"

Solana nodded, and he and his Pyrex disappeared to the patio. With a wary eye to the oven, she turned from the kitchen and padded barefoot through the sitting room towards the front door.

And froze with her hand on the doorknob when she saw the keys to the Jeep lying innocently in the woven basket on the entry table beside her.

CHAPTER TWELVE

Staring at the keys, Solana felt an icy coldness sweep through her, starting in her stomach.

She could do it.

Right now.

She could take that car and run, just go as far and as fast as humanly possible.

Solana let her finger run the length of the metal key, but as pretty as it was to entertain thoughts of a great escape, she knew all too well that she couldn't.

And for more reasons than one.

From a practicality standpoint, St. John didn't have an airport. She'd have to hop an inter-island ferry to St. Thomas or St. Croix and fly out from there, and who the hell knew what the boat schedules were like, or the flight itineraries out of Charlotte Amelie or Christiansted. Raine still had her iPhone; it wasn't like she could research that information ahead of time. If she ran now, blindly, she could find herself stuck on St. John overnight, and the last thing she wanted was Raine hunting her down on this tiny islet. He'd have her found by dawn.

Dawn? she chastised herself. *Fuck that, he'd have me inside of an hour.*

Which brought her to the issues on the tactical front. Let's say she got off this island tonight. Would he really just let her go? He'd turn over every grain of sand from here to the fucking moon until he caught up with her again. Even if she got away, even if she managed to reach D.C. or Chicago or L.A., even if she got someone in the field offices to listen to her story and that person had enough clout to get Raine arrested and indicted ASAFP, there were others.

There were other people Raine trusted to take care of his business for him.

If he found himself in a position where he couldn't come after her personally, he'd send someone else who most definitely would. And when they found her, she had a sneaking suspicion it wouldn't be nearly as pleasant as this weekend was turning out to be.

A realization that forced her to now assess her situation based on brutally honest reality.

She'd asked him for the truth in the kitchen, and he'd respectfully given it to her straight. No bullshit, no artifice. He'd risen to such power in the City by making deals with its criminal elite, and evidently everyone fell into that category some way or another. He'd even made it a point to show her that if she'd been a target on his list, she herself wouldn't have escaped assimilation, not if she'd wanted to keep her true identity safe. He'd given all of them a choice, and they'd all decided to throw in with him rather than let their dark secrets see the light of day.

As for his own crimes, he'd only confirmed everything she'd already suspected. To say his corroboration of her existing suppositions changed anything would border on hypocrisy. Moreover, if anything, the information he'd shared with her on the plane this morning had *exonerated* him from three murders she'd erroneously pinned on him. Since he wasn't the one who'd killed DiStephano's underbosses, technically he was three points to the positive on her scoreboard.

Four if she counted herself.

And that, *that right there*, was the biggest surprise of the weekend. The fact that there *was* a weekend, and one that was rapidly becoming the most incredible pair of days of her life.

She had to admit that to herself.

The last twenty-two hours she'd spent with him had been nothing short of extraordinary.

She traced the letters of the word "Jeep" with her fingertip, remembering with a little smile their wrestling match on the beach over the keys.

There was a reason he'd brought her here.

You'll be back in your office on Monday morning if you want to be, Solana. If his promise were true, they'd be going back to the City tomorrow. Why the riddle, then?

"If you want to be," she murmured aloud, repeating his words to her, the tone of them. As if she had a choice to make. But that didn't make any sense; he hadn't given her any choices.

Yet.

The man had something up his sleeve, she knew it.

And she wanted to know what it was, more than anything.

At the end of the day, the most important reason why she wouldn't leave was because she simply *couldn't*. The same goddamn journalistic curiosity that had gotten her into this mess in the first place was exactly what would keep her tangled up in it. If she left now, she didn't want to look back on her life - however long it might be - and wonder what would have happened if she'd stayed.

What did he have in store for her that he could promise she'd be home safe and sound by Monday? How much more could she learn about this man who'd just been a dossier on her desk for the past two years?

More importantly, how many more memories of her past would he help her unlock?

And the ultimate question: How much more passion would he awaken in her?

With one last caress Solana left those keys right where they were in their basket, turned the doorknob, and stepped out into the thick tropical night.

The beach mahos had taken a beating during the afternoon's storm. Their white heads lolled from the bullets of rain, and several branches lay strewn about the drive after the gusts that had ripped over the promontory that day. The Jeep was indeed quite waterlogged, but unlike the delicate blossoms of the mahos, it was better equipped to weather such calamities. The starfruit trees appeared to have fared rather well; leaves scattered the ground beneath them, but the tenacious fruits had managed to keep their hold on the nourishing branches. Solana plucked a rather luscious-looking specimen, then hightailed it back to the kitchen when she remembered the rest of her assignment.

Luckily, she made it to the cassatine in the nick of time. She was no baker, but after a thorough inspection she could find no fault with them. They looked perfect, golden brown on the edges, draped in blankets of lemony icing melting down their sides. After some digging she found the stackable cooling racks, and once she'd put the cookies out to cool, she set to work on the starfruit.

"Something of a misnomer," she mused, noticing as she washed the peculiar little fruit that it didn't resemble anything even remotely stellar. The waxy ovoid looked more like a grooved football or a spiky dirigible, leaving her puzzling over its astral name.

Light dawned, though, as she started slicing it across its width, and by the time she finished, she had a bright constellation of greenish-yellow stars arching across the white sky of her cutting board.

Solana stepped back to take in the view. *Sometimes,* she wondered, *things just aren't what they seem, are they?*

"Hey, Solana," Raine called from the patio, breaking into her thoughts.

"Yes?" She stopped mid-reach for a bowl in the cupboard so she could hear him.

"How's that starfruit coming?"

"Good; do you need me to bring it out there?"

"No need. Just put it in a bowl on the windowsill and I'll grab it in half a minute."

He must have had it timed; Solana no sooner placed the small relish bowl full of starry slices at their makeshift pass before it disappeared into the darkness of the patio.

"Thanks," he said. "Did the nucatuli come out as well as these?"

"They look good to me," she replied. "But then again, I've never had one."

"Quality control check," he announced. "Put one of those on the sill, too, would you?"

"Dessert before dinner?" she chided, placing one of the warm cookies on a napkin on the windowsill.

"What," he demanded, and then his handsome face appeared at the window, a grin pulling at his lips. "You've got a problem with that, too?"

His growing smile was infectious. "No," she answered, her own tease of a smile setting her cheeks to glowing.

"Good," Raine said, breaking the little cookie in half. As he chewed his own, he reached through the window with hers, and Solana leaned over the sink to take it from his fingers. He fed it to her, just like he had the grape, and his smile widened at the expression on her face as the flavors burst in her mouth.

"Oh. My. God." She covered her mouth in rapture as the warm, bite-sized morsel of divinity melted on her tongue. The perfect complement of sugar and almond, lifted by the lemon, seduced by the cocoa, spiced by the cinnamon, with a finishing glaze of smooth icing that had just the right ratio of crunch to goo. "Jesus, it's no wonder these woke me from my nap this afternoon."

"I take it you like them?"

"No. They're awful. In fact, you should give them all to me so you don't have to suffer through them."

"Right," he chuckled. "When I was a kid I used to plead the same case with my mother whenever she'd make these. Never worked, of course, but that didn't stop me from trying."

"Is this her recipe?"

"Yes," he answered, and his tone was curiously final. "Now, it looks like dinner's just about ready, so if you want to take a seat in the nook, I'll be in momentarily."

Solana accepted his invitation, and when stepped into the breakfast nook at the back of the house, she no longer felt overdressed in her little black number. Rather, she wished again for those high heels.

Night had given a completely different personality to the room with the greatest view of them all. Earlier, in the brilliant light of day, the nook had struck her as an open, bright place, perfect for reading a book, writing, sketching, or just watching sailboats race along the limb of the Atlantic. Tonight, though, with evening's darkness filling the open wall and low amber light filtering from the two wall sconces, it felt like a warm, intimate space floating in midair.

Raine had already set the small table in the center of the room, heightening the sense of close, soft ambiance. The tablescape didn't look like something she'd expected to find in a rustic Caribbean cottage; it rivaled settings she'd seen in posh five-star restaurants on Manhattan.

A full complement of silverware gleamed on red cloth napkins neatly folded beside red square chargers. A bottle of Malbec stood open to breathe beside two tall-stemmed, fat-bottomed red wine glasses. Tea lights flickered romantically in clear glass holders, scattered around a vase full of the white maho blossoms she found so enticing.

He'd thought of every detail... and more.

She couldn't pinpoint when exactly it had happened, but their sassy jazz was gone. The music now filling the house set a very different stage with intoxicating acoustic guitars, water drums, and darkly exotic island woodwinds, and the ambient soundtrack set her heart to pounding with its smoky promise of an unforgettable evening.

"This isn't a kidnapping," Solana murmured as she approached the decked table, her fingers tracing along the rich brown tablecloth. "It never was."

What this is... what it's been all along... is a date.

The drive... the lunch... the clothes... the hike... the swimming hole... the shower –

Solana halted. *To be fair, that was your own idea, Alessandra,* she admitted, feeling a flush of pink in her cheeks. *You can't pin that one on him. Any more than you can blame him for the sunblock affair. Or the fact that you can't swim. Or that you'd been the one to sneak up on him in the kitchen for an impromptu duet.*

But then the cookies... the homemade dinner... fresh flowers... candlelight... music that made her heart trip quicker...

The whole day felt like an elaborate, incredible, non-stop date.

She went ahead and poured the wine to give the bouquet a chance to release, then she sank into the seat opposite the doorway, on the far side of the table so she'd be able to see him when he entered. *Like Nico always said,* she thought, *if presented with the option, never take the chair that puts your back to the door.*

Solana waited for him, sitting very still as she tossed the date postulate around in her mind. Was that really his gameplan? Was that going to be his condition? That she agree to be his lover for the price of her life?

She shook her head. Ethical and emotional implications notwithstanding, it was too simple. Furthermore, as far as she understood the rules, Loiacono would have forbidden it –

The sound of Raine's footfalls on the hardwood floor sent her thoughts scattering, and Solana looked up just as he was walking in, carrying two square white plates of something that smelled positively divine.

Raine smiled at the sight of her. "You *are* a mobster's daughter," he said, noting her choice of seating at the table as he set the plates down on the chargers.

"Guilty as charged," she replied, watching him take his seat across from her.

He'd changed for dinner. Ever since they'd landed on the island he'd sported soft, form-fitting graphic tees and comfy cargo shorts just like any average guy on any given weekend. Now he rocked the debonair island look at its best in tailored brown slacks and a white linen shirt with the long sleeves rolled up to the elbows, displaying the muscles of his forearms and the sexy ID bracelet he wore every single second of every single day. The spine-tingling scent of him reached her from across the table, a scent she would forever associate now with power, privilege, and pleasure. She didn't think it was possible, but he looked even more handsome in this lowly lit room, his hair glowing golden and coppery in the amber throw from the wall sconces behind him and his light, light eyes glittering in the table's suffused candlelight.

Solana dropped her gaze, not wanting to be caught staring at him and instead focused on the mouth-watering dinner on the plates in front of them. A five-ounce char-grilled steak smothered in a rich brown sauce, with the slices of her starfruit topping it for show. Then long yellow, starchy vegetables that must be plantains, paired with some kind of fragrantly seasoned green bean she'd never seen before.

"This looks beautiful, Raine," she told him, impressed. "What is it?"

"The main dish is starfruit steak, and probably one of the easiest recipes on earth," he explained, dropping his napkin into his lap. "It's just sirloin marinated for a few hours in a blend of Worcestershire sauce, black pepper, sea salt, and starfruit slices. Then you grill it, garnish with some fresh starfruits, and you're done. Rounding it out, you have grilled plantains in a brown sugar glaze infused with orange juice, honey, and cilantro, and then sautéed bora beans with roasted coconut, lemon, and thyme."

Solana stared at him. "You're a *chef*, Raine."

He shrugged his shoulders. "Not really. I enjoy it when I have the time to devote to it, otherwise I leave it to the pros in my employ. My guilty pleasure of baking, however... I knock out a sheet or four of some tasty Sicilian morsel about once a month."

Solana nodded. "I've often heard that there are chefs and there are bakers; that every cook, when pressed, will favor one camp over the other. It's almost like they call for their own distinct personality types - one's an expressive, exploratory art, while the other's more of a methodical, chemical science."

"Which side would you be on?" he asked.

"If I had to pick, definitely the chefs," she answered. "I don't cook all that often, but when I do, it's dinner and not dessert."

Raine watched her for a second before he picked up his wine glass and held it out to her. "To opposites working in concert, then."

Solana felt her pulse quicken, thinking back to their close conversation in the cave. She lifted her own glass and brought it closer to his, but didn't quite let it make contact.

"I thought we weren't truly opposites, Raine," she said.

A rogue smile touched his lips as he chimed his glass against hers. "I'll drink to that."

Raine sipped his wine slowly, trying his damnedest to keep himself from staring openly at the knockout across the table from him. He'd had the lion's share of women in his time. But when she'd walked into his kitchen singing like a siren in that simple, yet so sexy black silk dress, with her hair flying thick and wild around her, barefoot, unadorned, without a single trace of unnecessary makeup, he thought he'd never seen anyone so beautiful in his life.

Until now.

That hair burned like a roaring wildfire, the reds and browns and golds catching the low amber light and sending it shining down the tumbling locks that danced like flames in the breeze. In sharp contrast were those shockingly pale green eyes that cut him to the quick, radiating over her high, pretty cheekbones, and then there was the very tip of her pink tongue that touched the rim of the wine glass just before her full lips did. Her tanned olive skin shimmered with a glow along her bared shoulders, her throat, and the generous exposure of her upper chest above black silk that fit her figure like a second skin.

But the most delicious part of all? Underneath the scent of his very masculine shower soap that he'd lathered her in this afternoon, he could still smell the feminine fragrance that was all Solana, so hot, spicy, and sweet.

Just like her name promised, she was the personification of the sun, a scintillating, vibrant force of fire and fight that challenged him in every arena like no other woman ever had.

If he weren't famished, he'd skip dinner altogether and get right to dessert.

And I don't mean the nucatuli, he thought, heat scorching through him as he watched her set down her glass.

"*Allora, cara, mangia*," he grinned. "*Non diventare freddo, si?*"

Solana smiled at the lovely sound of their native tongue spoken in his deep, full baritone. "Don't worry, Raine," she said, picking up her fork. "I doubt this will be around long enough for it to get cold."

She was right. The meat exploded with juicy flavor, spicy from the Worcestershire and sweet on account of the starfruit. The plantains smoothed rich and sugary on her tongue, while the beans lifted light, savory, and exotic with the respective contributions of lemon, thyme, and coconut.

"Jesus, Raine, this is incredible," she marveled, already more than halfway through her dinner.

"You're enjoying it, then?"

"Are you kidding? This is an orgasm on a plate."

"Well, then," he said with a sly smile. "There's more where that came from."

"Seconds, you mean?"

Raine's eyes lifted with significance to hers. "No."

Solana blushed as red as the Malbec in the glass she held. She'd walked right into that one, and the way he was staring at her made her core clench with torching need, her fingers beginning to tremble just that slightest bit.

"So explain something to me," he asked, turning his attention back to his plate. "Why didn't you leave?"

Solana ungraciously shoved the last forkful of plantains into her mouth so she'd have an excuse to keep quiet, buying herself some time to think.

"Because you could have, you know," Raine continued. "Matter of fact, you were thinking about it pretty hard for a few minutes, standing there by the door."

She swallowed with some difficulty, despite the fact she'd thoroughly chewed her mouthful of plantains to pulp. "What makes you so sure?" she asked evasively.

"Open walls, Solana."

Fucking A, she thought. He would have had totally unobstructed line of sight to the front door from the patio if he'd just taken a step or two to look –

She gasped. "You left the keys there on purpose," she accused. "You knew I'd see them when I went to pick the starfruit."

He nodded.

"Were you testing me?"

"Mmm-hmm."

"Have you been testing me *all day long?*"

"Absolutely."

She didn't dare ask why. "I'm assuming I passed them all, then, whatever these tests were."

Raine studied her over the rim of his wine glass. "I think you're stalling, *bella.*"

She was. Her time was up, and the only thing she could think to tell him was the truth.

"I didn't leave because it posed a logistical nightmare," she blurted. "I also recognized it as a gross tactical error. And I... " Solana fumbled for words, not wanting to divulge that last motive driving her choice, her *need*, to stay.

Finally, she sighed. "I thought it would have been... rude."

His eyebrows lifted. "*Rude?*"

"Sorry, I don't know how else to describe it."

"Rude," he repeated, shaking his head. "Is that the story you're going to stick with?"

"Were you expecting me to say something else?"

"The truth, Solana," he replied with unflapped, non-threatening evenness. "All I'm asking is what you were thinking. This question doesn't have right or wrong answers, just true or false ones. You were doing so well, too, up until that last surprising line of bullshit. Care to take another swing?"

Solana's heart palpitated. Confessing the deepest reasons behind her decision to stay was out of the question, but she couldn't very well admit to him that he'd correctly called her out on a lie, either.

"What's it to you?" she asked sharply, pushing him

back before he boxed her in. "Why do you want to know?"

Raine smiled like an ancient sage who had all the answers. "Do you trust me, Solana?"

Her heart thumped harder, like a rabbit sensing a snare. "Keeping it in context of the last twenty-three hours," she hedged, "yes."

"Can I trust *you?*"

The snare caught. Whatever she'd been expecting him to say, it wasn't those four complicated little words that trapped her so neatly. To answer yes to that question meant committing a blatant act of perjury, but to answer no...

At her silence, his enigmatic grin evaporated. "You see the crux of the problem now, don't you?"

Solana willed herself to keep breathing. "I just failed a test for the first time, didn't I?"

"Twice."

"So what happens now?" Déjà vu made her skin crawl as she realized she'd asked him that same question on the chaise less than one day ago. Somehow it didn't seem possible; it felt like they'd lived another whole life together since then.

"Often," Raine said casually, leaning back in his chair, "as in baseball, fairy tales, and a myriad other theaters, the magic number is usually three."

Solana watched him effect a calm, conversational demeanor, but the look in his eyes, the set of his jaw conveyed the true meaning behind his words. *The third time's a charm, Solana*, he warned her. *Don't fuck it up.*

"I can't," she surrendered.

"You can't... *what.*"

"I can't leave."

"As in there are insurmountable obstacles preventing a clean escape, there are wisely strategic reasons to not follow that course of action, or for some other reason you find yourself unwilling to do it?"

"All three," she admitted. "Practical, tactical... and personal."

Raine waited.

"You're not particularly interested in the first two, are you?"

He merely shook his head, perfectly aware of those factors just as much as she was.

He wanted the real reason, not the other two that were so convenient for her to blame.

Sitting there in front of him, the lone target of his steady stare, Solana felt a deep stillness take over her. Not the paralyzing grip of fear or the quiet finality of death, but the awed breathless silence that comes when an ordinary moment turns pivotal. He wanted the musings of her soul, and she had the feeling that whatever she told him now would shape everything to come afterward.

Whether she was ready to give it to him or not, this was the literal moment of truth.

"You've been a file on my desk for the past two years, Raine," she began softly. "I've learned more about you in the last twenty-four hours than I have in the past twenty-four months."

He kept waiting, his eyes never leaving hers.

"Somehow, I've felt closer to my parents today than I have in twenty years," she continued. "Memories just keep unlocking while I'm here with you, and I don't know why."

That one touched him; she saw it. But still, he waited for more from her.

"I need to see this through to the end, Raine," she said, her voice beginning to tremble as she took a steadying breath. "You've got something up your sleeve, and I have no idea what it is. If I left, I'd wonder what it was for the rest of my life - however long you'd let that last."

Raine continued his unwavering silence for several seconds, and Solana sent a prayer skyward. *Please let that be enough. Please don't press me for the last one, Raine. Please.*

Someone delivered on her petition, because much to her intense relief, he nodded.

"Good, Solana," he said solemnly. "Very good."

She took another calming breath, feeling like she'd just survived the Spanish Inquisition.

"But I think there's one more thing you've kept from me."

Solana's body froze, leaving her fingers stalled on the table on the way to her wine glass.

"Third strike?" she whispered.

Raine came forward again to close his hand over hers where it lay stranded on the table.

"I'll call it ball four," he warned, "but only if you finish it."

Solana's palm began to sweat where he pressed it into the tablecloth. How could she put this into words? How the fuck could she possibly explain this bizarre connection between them? This raw attraction that made her body bite with need for him? The way her heart had filled with golden light during their kiss in the shower? The sheer impossibility of whatever this was they were sharing across enemy lines –

Opposites working in concert.

She already had it.

She knew how to explain it to him, because he already had.

"I stayed because we are partners, Raine," she said carefully, her eyes searching his patient, piercing blue ones. "I stayed because we are lovers."

Raine made sure his face revealed nothing, keeping his personal feelings on this costly revelation to himself for the time being. She'd tell him anything he wanted now, and he moved in to collect, slow and deliberate. His larger hand on top of hers made it easy for his fingers to curl around her wrist, where the thump of her pulse fluttered under the pad of his thumb. He flipped their hands over, the palm of his cradling the back of hers, leaving her palm naked to the air.

When he spoke, his voice stroked over her like velvet. "Are you glad you stayed?"

She didn't hesitate. "Yes."

The index finger of his free hand traced an R in her open palm. "You're not sorry?"

She shivered. "No."

He traced an M. "Are you scared, Solana?"

"Should I be, Raine?"

He brought her palm to his lips and planted a kiss in it before rolling her fingers closed. "I would like to say no, but I'm sorry, *cara*. I can't answer that question for you."

"Try."

Raine laughed lowly. "By 'can't,' I don't mean 'won't,' Solana. Only you can answer it, because ultimately, the choice will be yours to make."

"What choice?" she breathed.

"Ask me again tomorrow morning," he said. "Not a moment sooner. Until then, in return, I promise I will ask nothing more of you."

Solana yanked her hand back, her palm tingling from his intimate attentions. While he still refused to give up any details as to what she was doing here with him, she at least had his word that the interrogation was over, and there was light at the end of the tunnel.

Tomorrow morning, the other shoe drops, she thought, and then his words from earlier that night came back to haunt her.

As you know, he'd said, *relationships in this business are volatile at best; there's no telling what tomorrow might bring.*

Solana's fingers began to fidget with the red napkin draped across her lap.

He wasn't really thinking about Al when he said that, she realized. *He was thinking about me. About us. And what's going to happen to us when he puts this... decision in front of me.*

That napkin became a twisted ball in her clenched fist.

Was she really sure she wanted tomorrow to come so quickly? Yes, she wanted her life back, but if tomorrow's answers to her burning questions also meant the end of whatever this had become...

Solana rose to her feet. "Would you find me a length of ribbon?" she asked, holding her hand out for the empty plate in front of him. "Or a rubber band?"

"What?"

She wasn't in the mood to indulge him. She needed to get her hands busy before she tore that napkin in two. She needed a project, something simple and uncomplicated where she could lose herself and get out of her own head, and right now taking on the dishes totally fit that bill.

"Anything will do," she offered by way of explanation, and she took off with a purpose to the kitchen, carrying the table's full panoply of plates, glasses, and flatware.

She was simultaneously pleased and disappointed to find the small kitchen in a respectable state of affairs. Raine obviously wasn't one of those chaotic chefs that destroyed a room when cooking and dirtied every piece of culinary artillery known to man in the process. The complete roll call of dirty dishes consisted of the Pyrex, a couple pans, a few bowls, some cutlery, a handful of utensils, their white wine glasses from before dinner, and then what she'd brought in from active duty on the table.

While she ran the water to get it up to temperature, she arranged her battlefield, mustering the dishes in like platoons so she could deploy them most efficiently into the compact sinks that would be the theater for this war. Then she recruited some more soldiers for herself by ferreting out a platter for the cassatine, thus freeing up the four cookie sheets for service in her reconnaissance mission to find some peace.

War and peace. She grimaced, crossing her arms over her chest as she waited for her sink to finish filling with steaming hot water. *Opposing forces that have no meaning without each other.*

Solana turned off the faucet - and gasped when she saw red. The crimson satin ribbon Raine pulled over her eyes was cool, silky, and smooth, and she started at the feel of the luxurious blindfold against her skin just as much as the surprise of having it appear there.

"It's for your hair, isn't it," he murmured in her ear, sending shivers down her spine.

"Yes, thank you," she replied, taking the length of sturdy, svelte stuff from his hands. She'd known before she touched a single dish that working with a sinkful of hot water in the tropical heat and humidity meant her hair had to go, and the yard of satin was exactly what she needed to prepare herself for this battle. She wove the ribbon through her hair and tied up the shining mass to get it off her neck, and she felt grateful for the seabreeze exhaling its cooling breath over her exposed shoulders and her back.

"You don't have to do this, you know," Raine said, toying with the fiddleheads of hair that curled at the nape of her neck. "We have a dishwasher."

"I actually like doing dishes," she confessed as she plunged the first of the cookie sheets into the soapy basin. "Dishes and laundry. I find them remarkably therapeutic, whereas everything else domestic I detest with a passion."

"A busy project you can see through start to finish, completely under your own direction, with positive, measurable results, accomplished within an extremely short period of time."

"Precisely. Now, since you know where everything goes, while I wash you get to dry."

"I'm guessing you hate that part."

"My dishwasher's main function is a drying rack," Solana confirmed, and then she immersed herself in the business at hand.

She started with the bigger, more challenging things to get them out of the way, which wasn't an easy task working in a pair of sinks the size of thimbles. But that was the kind of cathartic frustration she was looking for, and it wasn't long before she felt her angst begin to release. She and Raine made quick, efficient progress together, and soon she was humming along with the wordless music that moved slow and sultry through the house.

When she got down to the smaller, more pedestrian items, however, the project took on a more interesting aspect. Seconds after she handed Raine her sparkling clean starfruit bowl for drying, she felt his body brush up against hers while he reached into the cupboard beside her to put the dish away.

Solana's body went electric at the touch of him. She purposefully picked a similar bowl to wash next, thinking its permanent home might lie close beside her starfruit bowl, and she closed her eyes when he moved against her a second time for the same reason.

When she gave him the first of the fancy red wine glasses, though, it was no passing brush. These lived in prime real estate on the highest shelf of the cupboard, and Solana swallowed hard when she felt the full length of his hard body press along the line of hers. Her heart beat faster as she washed the second glass, knowing what was coming, and she sucked in her breath when she felt his hand grasp her hip for the next spooning reach into the lofty shelf.

Her eyes flicked over the items left to be washed. All that remained now was the silverware - and the two basic, everyday white wine glasses from before dinner.

Normally she'd go for the glasses to finish them off, but tonight she'd definitely save them for last.

She processed the flatware like the world was on fire, and then she took her time cleaning the first of the two plain glasses, looking forward to finding out where they lived. Surely these simple stems didn't sit with the swanky red wine goblets, did they?

Solana handed it to him, and a moment later was rewarded with the feel of him against her once more when he sent it home on the highest shelf.

The smile started in her heart before creeping its way upward to her face. "That's not where they normally go, is it?" she asked as she passed him the final dripping glass.

She heard a slow grin change the shape of his voice. "No," he admitted, just before he pressed himself against her one last time.

Solana reached into the sink and pulled the drain stop. "Anything else I can do?" she asked.

"You've done enough, Solana," he said, placing a fresh dry towel on her bare shoulder. "I'll take it from here."

"All right, then," she replied, and after washing her hands with his lavender hand soap - *lavender?* she noted - she gave the sinks a finishing rinse with the sprayer and turned to face him.

To find him gone.

Solana slowly slid the towel from her shoulder and dried her hands without really thinking about doing it. *He must be tidying the nook*, she thought.

And giving me some space.

She took it.

Killing the light in the kitchen, she traipsed her way through the dark sitting room and stepped onto the patio, the only part of Raine's home left for her to discover. Humbled by the view, she walked out to the center of the stone circle with reverence, like she was entering a sacred shrine devoted to the pagan gods of old.

The last of the clouds had pushed out to sea, and the waxing moon shined brightly over the small cottage, high on its peaceful promontory overlooking the calm ocean. She felt like she could command the water and the wind from the edge of this skyscraping rock wall; the whole blue world seemed to be at her feet.

But then she lifted her gaze to the infinite number of stars above her, amazed at how many more were visible here in the velvet darkness so far from the lights of civilization. Billions of worlds lay scattered out there over her head, reminding her just how small, how insignificant the illusion of power in this little world really was.

This place, where hubris meets humility... no wonder he'd chosen it for his retreat. Part mobster, part philosopher, he needed the balance. Part ruthless, part romantic, he needed somewhere to truly indulge both halves of himself without judgment from the rest of the world.

But here she stood, sharing it with him.

Even now, right this second. Silence... nourishing, humbling, enticing silence wrapped itself around her, punctuated only by the crush of the waves far below, the faint whistle of the seabreeze through the maho branches, and the soft music that reached her from the house. But even without the sound, she could feel him now, somehow knew he was there, watching over her.

Just then a meteor burned a fierce streak across the sky, white hot on impact, then arcing in flaming orange before winking with a flash into oblivion.

Solana took a deep breath. "Did you wish on that one?" she asked into the darkness.

"No," came the quiet response from somewhere in the black behind her. "I don't feel the need to."

She grinned. *Of course.* "For thine is the kingdom, the power, the glory, now and forever, right?"

She heard his soft laughter in the dark. "Something like that."

Solana sensed his approach on the flagstones just before she felt his hand on the small of her back, and she did not leap from his touch like she had this morning before leaving the Ritz on that other planet of Philadelphia. The far-off music drifting their way changed songs, and she recognized this one, beautiful in its heartlifting simplicity. Enigma, "Between Mind and Heart."

Raine reached down to take her hand in his, and he slowly, gently, turned her to face him. His eyes were warm silver in the moonlight as he drew her closer to him, as he lifted her hand to his chest and covered it with his own. His other hand went to the swell of her hip, and when he took a confident step forward, Solana placed her hand on his broad shoulder and countered his move in kind.

He was an excellent dancer, and he led her well. Her hand beneath his upon his chest was a tacit conduit of communication; she could feel his next step before he even took it, and they moved together in fluid harmony, barefoot over the moon-bright stone.

You ever dance with the devil in the pale moonlight?

Solana knew she could have told the Joker yes as she rested her head against Raine's chest. Closing her eyes, she breathed in his virile scent again, felt the heat of his skin through the richness of his white shirt soft on her cheek, and she surrendered herself to him.

Unpredictable, she questioned his motives, didn't know why he'd brought her here. Absolutely intoxicating, she didn't care, couldn't explain how completely she reveled in this moment, the music, the breeze, the warmth, the man who held her captivated.

Raine's hand left her hip to slide up her spine, and she shivered at his touch. He followed higher, along the line of her neck, eventually coming to cup her jawline, the heel of his palm against her chin, his fingertip grazing her earlobe. He raised her face up to his and kissed her with the firm urgency of someone who'd been holding back all night, and she returned it, stopping their seductive dance in its tracks. She gripped his powerful shoulder as their kiss deepened, harder as his fingers closed tightly around hers where he held them pressed over his heart.

Solana could feel his heartbeat quickening under her fingertips, inciting her own pulse to drum faster. His lips traveled to her cheek, to her ear, making a need for him spark sharp and deep –

"Come to bed with me, Solana," Raine said, and that burning inside her exploded into a full-on bonfire.

Even so, she pulled away from him, pressing her hand into his chest to push him back.

"You said you would ask nothing more of me tonight, Raine," she reminded him, and even though her voice was as soft as the night, it carried the smack of reproach.

He stiffened. "So I did."

Solana let his words speak for themselves. With a lingering look, she turned her back on him and walked away, leaving him alone while she entered the cottage's dark, doorless bedroom.

The second she was concealed in the inky shadows of the room, however, she ripped off her little black dress and tossed it back outside to the patio, and she beamed when she heard him mutter something colorful in Italian as it fluttered to his feet.

Moonlight shimmered along the gossamer canopy falling dramatically from the tall posts of the large bed, the sheer white panels swaying gently in the night breeze. Solana leapt for it, unhooking her bra and tossing it to the floor along the way, before she parted the thin curtains and crawled to the center of the bed. She sat crosslegged like a lotus flower on the soft coverlet, only her white panties remaining, in time to see Raine come striding into the room carrying her discarded dress in his hand.

"My turn," he purred, his tone almost a warning as he sent the retrieved Posen to join her bra on the floor.

Through the translucent sheers Solana watched him

undress, the moonlight playing over the cut of his chest, abs, and long, sculpted limbs, the cold glint of his Bulova bracelet winking with each deft movement. She felt the temperature in the room soar while he stripped, bordering on unbearable as he finished, and she swore she heard a thermometer burst when he passed through the veiling canopy and came to sit naked on the bed before her.

Raine reached back to pull the sheers closed behind him, and with that small movement, the outside world disappeared altogether. Because for a moment, the earth seemed to take a breath. The breeze stilled, the ocean hushed, even the music silenced as it changed tracks.

Time itself had stopped for them, and when Raine looked at her Solana felt herself flush at the promise she saw in his clear, silvered eyes. Nothing else existed except for the two of them sitting together in this scintillating nest of white, and whatever happened in this cocoon would be their secret to keep.

The deep registers of an acoustic guitar, haunting with soulful timelessness, reached them in their moonlit den. Slow and lush, the press of the frets echoed like they were strummed in the trees in an ancient rainforest. A soothing, somnolent voice sang quiet lyrics in a foreign African tongue that seemed older than time, sharing a tale that existed long before them and would for eras afterward. Muted whistling of a harmonizing tune carried so lonely, but so meditative and hopeful, it took every human's solo quest for redemption and put it to song.

The ageless yearning wove itself into the fabric of Solana's heart, tying her to its dark rhythm, rooting her in this ethereal place, seducing her into this time that was theirs. Raine felt the exotic spell twisting around them and he moved very carefully, honoring its presence, not wanting to spoil its powerful magic. He reached up to touch the red ribbon in her hair, rubbed the long silky tail between his thumb and forefinger before giving it a gentle tug, and her volume of curls flowed down like a black shining river in the diffuse silver light.

Raine fingered the slick scarlet satin that spilled like a bold stream of blood between them, smoothing out the kinks with an air of thoughtful consideration.

"You've said that you trust me," he began, his voice a low, intimate caress.

Heart in her throat, Solana nodded.

"Will you let me do this with you?"

She watched him pull that length of ribbon through his fingers while her logical mind vivisected his deliberate choice of words.

Not an imperative "I'm going to," but a solemn "will you let me."

Not "to" you. "With" you.

The air left her lungs as she found herself nodding again, and his answering flash of a smile turned her lace panties to liquid.

"Hold your hands up for me, then, Solana. Yes, just like that, with your wrists facing each other."

Solana pressed her palms together as if she were in prayer, then kept still as Raine slid the cool, smooth satin between her wrists. With delicate precision, he wrapped first one and then the other, binding them independently before tying them together with a figure eight in between. He finished with a neat bow, the ends of the ribbon tickling along her forearms, and she shivered at the light, free touch in contrast to the rigid, secure binding.

Raine covered her bound hands with his own and placed a soft kiss on her fingertips.

"Too tight?" he asked, his eyes searching her face.

Her heart pounded so hard she knew he must be able to see it. "No," she whispered.

"Good. Now stand up," he said, and he gave her a soft grin at her dubious expression.

"Don't worry," he urged. "I won't let you fall."

As gracefully as she could with her hands bound, Solana rose to her feet on the bed before him. True to his word, Raine held onto her until she had her balance... and then he focused his attention at eye-level, on the delicate French lace at her hips.

Sliding the backs of his hands up the front of her thighs, he invaded her panties from their southern border. He let his fingers slip under the fine fabric and keep climbing, bunching the material as he moved up her smooth loins, and once he cleared the waistband on the northern frontier, he curled his fingers over, took the lace down her legs, and held her steady while he helped her out of them.

"Come here," he commanded, wrapping his hands around her slim ankles to step her in closer to him. Jostled, Solana hooked her trussed wrists behind his neck to keep her balance, and he smiled at the feel of the ribbon's ends tickling down his back. He continued to move her feet closer to straddle him, spreading them apart, until her instep cupped the contours of his knees where he still sat crosslegged on the bed.

Raine felt her move to take another step, intending to put her feet beside his waist so she could sit down on him, but he tightened his grip on her ankles to stop her.

"Not so fast, Solana," he admonished.

"Why?" she asked, her breathing coming shallower and quicker.

"Because you have such amazing legs," he replied, and he leaned forward to touch his lips to one of her thighs just above the knee.

He planted soft lingering kisses there, gentle brushes of lips and quick flicks of tongue, while his hands wandered upward to knead the firm muscles of her calves. Solana sucked in her breath at his masterful touch; again when his questing fingertips grazed the sensitive softness behind her knees, making him smile against her skin.

But instead of moving up her thighs as she expected, he lifted his bright burning eyes to hers.

Raine grabbed her fine ass in his hands to hold her still while his mouth captured its plunder - the little jewel nestled high in the midst of her soft folds.

"Raine!" she gasped volubly, yanking on her bindings, and the piercing sound filled their small cocoon again as she tried to roll her hips against him and couldn't.

"Stop moving and feel it," he ordered, gripping her ass harder to keep her from thrusting. "Feel it take and trap you, Solana. Suffer it. Embrace it."

Overwhelmed, Solana squealed and squirmed against his restraining grip and ravishing tongue, making him squeeze still harder with the former and tease even quicker with the latter. She yelped prettily, helpless to stop him, and her legs began to shake when he traced an index finger down her rear and under her, into her, into that hot, sweet slickness just beyond his conquering mouth.

"Raine, please," she cried, her voice breaking in a sob. "Let me go."

"Ah, Solana, you must be a little more specific," he scolded, letting his lips, his tongue, his breath stroke her as he spoke. "Do you want me to let you go, or let you come?"

"*Yes!*"

"Oh I could do this to you all night," he cooed in delight against her, filling the words with threatening promise.

"Raine, no," she whimpered. "No, Raine, please."

"Mmmm, *cara*, how I love it when you beg me," he smiled, and he sent another finger inside her, made them curl in the smooth motion of *come here*, to come to him, and she screamed in skyrocketing, limb-shaking need.

When her trembling legs could no longer support her, Raine stopped his sweet torture and offered her his hand. Desperate, Solana grabbed him like a life raft, clasping his hand tightly between both of her bound ones, and again he had to stop her from acting on her basic instinct to sit down on him.

"No, Solana, not like that. Not this time," he said. "Turn around, get on your knees, and spread your legs. This time, I want you from behind."

Solana's heartbeat spiked so high she went lightheaded and nearly collapsed on him. "Don't let me fall."

"Never," he promised, and he kept his steadying hold on her while she followed his orders.

"That's it, beautiful," he coaxed. "Wider. Yes. Good." Then, once she was in place, he moved to sit on his knees behind her. He grasped her hips and pulled her down on him, bringing her to sit right on top of his hard thighs, and he felt her pulse trip when he rose up to meet her.

"Take me again," he murmured. "Take all of me." And in one skilled movement he filled her to the limits of her body, giving her every last thick, towering inch of him.

"Yes," she whispered, "God, Raine, yes," and her head fell back against his shoulder, her hair cascading in long tendrils over his arm as she called his name.

Raine made no attempt to constrain her when he began to thrust, and Solana took advantage of her freedom to move her hips strongly in time with his, meeting each rhythmic motion with perfectly matching force. It was so much deeper like this, and the feel of her smooth, firm ass against his tight loins made him even harder inside her.

He placed one of his hands between her breasts, directly over her pounding heart, to pull her back against his chest and pin her there. His other hand slid downward, below her navel, further, over her soft curls, and he smiled at her sharp intake of breath when he touched her, gently caressing her with his fingertips. Moaning, she threw her head back against his shoulder as she rose and fell on him, goosebumps rising all over her skin in response to his touch, and he buried a kiss in her hair.

"Cold?" he asked, beaming with pride.

"No," she said, and the sound of her voice made *his* hair stand on end. It came from deep within her, several octaves lower than usual, as if she were possessed.

Far from cold, Solana thought she would incinerate at any moment, consumed by the conflagration of desire sweeping through her. But the pride in his voice had set her blood to boiling, and for once she wanted nothing more than to bring him to heel.

She pitched forward, using the strength of her legs and the weight of her own body to tear herself free of his restraining arms. Tucking her bound wrists into her chest, she rolled clear of him and vaulted to the head of the bed, as far away from him as she could get. She rose up tall on her knees and spread them wide in a defensive stance this time, chest heaving, and when she flipped her hair out of her face with a violent toss, her hot green eyes dared him to follow.

Raine's confident gaze burned into hers as he slowly advanced on her, a predatory smile taking the corners of his lips as he crawled the length of the bed towards her. Solana held her ground and let him come so far into her trap before she lifted her wrists, took an end of the ribbon between her teeth, and tugged the bow loose.

"Oh fuck," he cursed, eyes glittering with the challenge, and he tried to jump her before she had time to yank free of her restraints. Still, he wasn't fast enough, and Solana used his momentum to her advantage, grabbing hold of his shoulders and flattening him on his back against the pile of pillows at the head of the bed.

"Who's the master now?" she demanded, and when she straddled his hips and brought him back inside her, when she made his thick hardness stretch and fill every tight slick inch of her, it was her turn to grin wickedly at the expression on his face as she moved above him.

Hers was not a gentle rhythm. It was demanding and hard; she wanted him, all of him. Raine thrusted up to her, his hands running over her thighs, up along her hips, around her waist where his fingers reached the small of her back, feeling the firmness of her muscles beneath her soft, soft skin. He held her tight while he drilled himself into her, trying to maintain some semblance of control over this before she wrested it from him, before he lost himself inside her.

"You feel so good," she moaned, and she leaned into his supporting hands, letting him hold her weight as she arched backwards, her head falling back, the ends of her long hair tickling his legs.

Raine could barely breathe, stunned by a magnificent view of her taut, spread thighs, curving hips, tiny waist, flat stomach, perfect tits, and her long, graceful throat.

Her entire moonlit body glowed with a dewy sweat that radiated like stardust, and he felt like he was in the presence of something divine, like he was being fucked by Artemis herself, a virgin Moon goddess finally let loose to feel the power of her prowess.

"Christ, you are exquisite, Solana," he whispered, spellbound, fighting the urge to release himself into her burning, lusciously flexible, incredibly talented body.

In response, Solana moved deliciously harder as she slid up and down the length of him, and she heard him inhale sharply between his teeth, felt him hold on tighter to her waist, gripping on for dear life. His thumbs dug deeply into the swell of her hips, his fingertips bit mercilessly into her lower back, cutting into her muscles as he met her rocking thrusts with equal hardness from below.

She knew exactly what effect her position was having on him; she knew that she was beautiful, heartbreakingly beautiful above him. She could feel his eyes roving her body, she could feel him thickening and hardening inside her with peaking desire. He was close, closer, holding himself back by sheer will alone...

In this moment she owned him, and the realization brought her immediately to the threshold of climax.

The impending force of it was more than she could handle and, shaking, screaming, Solana brought herself over him again. Her hands shot past his head to grip the lip of the headboard, and her bucking body tensed and tightened, the calm before the storm.

"Oh God, Raine, *don't move*," she ordered, and Raine felt her come as she shoved one last time against him, closing her eyes tightly against the flood of release that sent her quaking above him, singing his name over and over like a prayer into the dark.

It drove him crazy.

Reserve unleashed, Raine tore her hands from the headboard, pulled her down to his chest, and crushed her against him as he pinned her onto her back beneath him. Taking control again, he drove like a freight train into her hot, wet tightness, interlacing his fingers with hers, and then slammed their joined hands against the mattress when he hit with quick, violent vengeance.

"Solana - oh fuck... *fuck! Yes! Solana!*" and her name was a long, soul-wrenching moan into the pile of dark hair lying wild beside her face as he exploded inside her. He collapsed his weight on her, freed at last by the conquering, quenching warmth running the length of him, and the only thing he could say was a whisper - her name, once more in her ear as the sweet perfume of her tresses filled his world.

Solana closed her eyes, letting her senses savor every moment of this unexpected conquest. Completely spent, her overexerted muscles had reduced to quivering jello beneath him, but she wouldn't trade the intense soreness in her body for anything. It was a small price to pay for the thrilling reward of hearing his primal scream of pure pleasure, to have him belt out her name in desperate deliverance then murmur it again in grateful exhaustion. Watching the shimmering canopy undulate on the night breeze above her, she reveled in the weight of him, the scent of him, the sound of him simply breathing with her.

Slowly Solana turned her face towards him, careful not to pull on her hair which he still used as a pillow, and she met eyes of molten steel looking back into hers.

Oh yes, she thought, and a megawatt smile that rivaled the moon's light stole across her face. *He is well-pleased tonight.*

She brought one of his hands, still locked with hers, to her lips that curved in mischievous joy as she planted a tender kiss on the backs of his fingers. She let it linger, pressing her mouth against his skin as if she could permanently stamp it, her sparkling mint green eyes raising impishly to meet his over their knuckles.

Raine's eyes smoldered a hotter shade of blue as he placed a kiss on her forehead, and then he released their hands so he could lift himself off her searing body.

He lay down on his side facing her to draw her close to him, and Solana brought the full length of her body right alongside his, pressing her breasts, belly, hips, and legs flush against his scorching skin. He reached down to catch hold of her behind the knee, his fingertips gently yet insistently bending it up along his hip, and she drew a sharp breath when he slipped one of his strong, thick thighs between her slim ones, nestling it right up against her warm and very moist center.

Solana clung to him, fully enjoying this possessive, intimate position that opened her up to him while closing her off to the rest of the world. He protected her, he claimed her, and she smiled as he stroked the length of her leg from heel to calf... along the bend behind her knee at his waist... up her thigh and onward still, leaving her feeling like the sexiest woman alive.

Her cheek lay against his chest, and when she felt his chin come to rest on the crown of her head, she felt fully enveloped, just like she had the night before, and she heaved a blissful sigh. She closed her eyes in rapture as his hand continued its gentle course up the length of her spine, caressing her all the way to the nape of her neck and beyond, until his fingers lost themselves in her hair.

At last his hand slowed to stillness, cradling her skull

in his palm, and Solana barely had time to acknowledge how content she felt, just lying there entangled with him, before she found herself falling prey to a deep, consuming sleep, soothed by the sound of his slowing heartbeat and the distant music in the dark.

ↄ ↄ ↄ

Beside her, Raine's mind worked furiously.

By the rise and fall of her breathing he knew Solana slept softly in his arms, and at last he could take time to review the catalogue of his thoughts.

"Jesus, girl," he whispered, burying the words in the dark depths of her hair. His heart had finally stopped thundering from the tumultuous orgasm she'd brought him into... she'd taken him like some possessed goddess, and however he'd managed to lose control of that particular situation was just beyond him.

But - and he couldn't help but smile - he was strangely comfortable with it. *Give her a taste of power*, he thought, *and she'll perform beautifully.*

After all, that was ultimately the heart of the whole plan. He'd teach her to fully embrace the latent Alessandra within her and watch that potential take wondrous flight.

But could he trust her?

During their preprandial conversation over the cassatine regarding his affairs, she'd proven just how much of a threat she posed to him and his organization.

But during their intense dinner, the sexiest dishwashing experience on record, their provocative moonlit dance, and now this...

They'd proven to each other how deeply they connected, mind, body and soul.

He'd brought her here to make her a generous offer, but the more time he spent with her, the clearer it became that he'd need to add one more condition to the recruitment agreement he planned to put forth to her.

Should she accept his terms as he'd originally conceived them, she'd be released safely back into the world, with three key facets of her life vying for precedence.

First, the City. She'd be the young, successful, breathtakingly beautiful Manhattanite coveted by all the cliques in the social diaries, with a myriad of suitors like Alistair Prince attempting to court her.

Second, the Times. She'd be the high-profile Pulitzer Prize nominee expected to release another front-page blockbuster on organized crime, with an editor hellbent on having her deliver.

Third, the syndicate. She'd be the newest recruit beholden to him, yes, but for all intents and purposes her life could go back to normal. After a while, once she felt all safe and snug within her familiar circles once again, she may not give their agreement the full attention it would require.

Loyalty had a price.

As he ran a finger along the sensuous valley of her spine, a foreign, nameless emotion flickered within him. It would be a poor business decision to let her off that easily. With all those variables, things could get complicated - and very messy - right quick.

He realized with perfect clarity that he needed a stronger reason to trust her. He needed something to further ensure that his organization always remained her first, if not only, priority.

And there was only one way he could see to guarantee that.

CHAPTER THIRTEEN

SUNDAY, JULY 26
5:30 A.M.

When Solana woke early the next morning, she knew the definition of peace. The ocean waves crashed against the rocks far below, and the warm sea breeze caressed her skin as it breathed into the room, ruffling the sheer canopy surrounding the bed. For a moment she just lay there in tranquil comfort, snuggled in the soft, white cotton coverlet and the thick, quiet grey of dawn. She stretched languidly and reached her arm across the bed - only to find it empty next to her; Raine had already gone.

Solana frowned, her hand resting on his pillow. Three days ago, if someone had told her she'd wake up Sunday morning on St. John and in Raine Mathison's bed, she'd have had that person promptly committed. But here she was, and still clueless as to why. Part of her didn't want to question it, part of her still wanted to wait until much later to deal with this.

But tomorrow morning had come.

Meaning that trick card up his sleeve was about to make its appearance.

What the hell could he want from her that she hadn't already given him? After all this, she didn't think he was out to kill her, not anymore. She'd opened her past and her present to him, and if he didn't kill her, he'd certainly be a majority stakeholder in her future. He wanted her silence, of course, but what would he barter with to get it?

What if he'd lied to her yesterday? What if, just like all the others he'd brought under his dominion, he had every intention of using her true identity against her?

Or worse, what if he threatened to go after Al, or even Will, if she didn't keep quiet about what she'd seen?

Her unease grew stronger as the room grew brighter, as the harsh, practical reality of daylight permeated the sultry night's illusion of safety and wonder, and Solana tore out of bed.

The breeze felt even better after another hot, luxurious shower, cooling her moist, damp skin while she chose her next set of weapons for the day. After some deliberation, she opted for lovely snow-white underthings by Cosabella, sexy and soft with pretty eyelet details, before pulling on an alluring yet simple A-line Escada sundress in pale mint green. She towel-dried her long hair as best she could, then piled it up on top of her head, the wet locks curling in shining bunches along the nape of her neck.

"They'll dry nicely in the sun," she noted, looking out the open wall where bright young sunstreaks were already burning off the grey in the sky, the prelude to another hot day.

She left the bedroom, and after searching the patio, the sitting room, and then the kitchen, she finally found Raine in the breakfast nook at the other end of the house.

Where the room faced east and opened to the wide ocean, right on the promontory's rocky edge, it was like a square three-walled porch with the sea as the front yard, and it must have been perfect for watching the sunrise.

Already dressed in his smooth, sophisticate couture, he sat with his back to her in the same chair now as for dinner last night, reading the Times Sunday Edition in the morning light, his hand resting on a steaming mug of coffee. *He's a stone cold fox,* she thought, appreciating immensely the look of his fine broad shoulders in pale blue Prada, the long sleeves rolled up his tanned forearms, the Bulova bracelet shining powerfully in the sunlight. *He's a goddamn handsome stone cold fox.*

"Get yourself some coffee, Solana, and come sit. We have to talk."

Solana's heart stopped. He didn't look up, didn't turn around as he addressed her, but his deep voice easily filled the room, the tone of it seeming to echo off the walls and hang ominously in the air.

It was a voice that haunted her, one she'd heard before, in an alley seemingly years ago. It was the voice of a man who was the head of a powerful crime syndicate, and she swallowed hard. Foreboding filled her as she turned back to the kitchen, more to gather her thoughts than to pour herself a cup of the strong morning brew on the counter in front of her.

This can't be happening, she thought, gripping the edge of the counter. *Not after everything we've shared.*

Then, without warning, deep-seated anger roared to life inside her. *You will never, ever see me scared of you again,* she seethed. *If you think you can erase the last two days, and if you think I've forgotten who I am and where I come from, you've got another fucking thing coming.*

Taking her sweet time, she poured herself some of the deliciously fragrant coffee, making it the way she liked it, extra cream and extra sugar, then breezed into the nook, her head held high. She gracefully sat in the seat across from him, just as she had the night before, and looked him straight in the face, leaning her forearms on the table.

It took every ounce of determination she had to eradicate any shaking in her voice when his hard blue eyes looked up to hers, penetrating her through to her very soul, his face an expressionless mask.

"You have an offer for me, don't you," she said matter-of-factly, stealing the thunder of his checkmate.

"I do."

"And it's one I can't refuse."

"Naturally."

"So what's the deal you're offering."

Raine paused for a second, then lay the copy of the Times between them on the table.

"Let's review some of your accomplishments," he said. "You exposed Preston and DiStephano last fall."

"Yes."

"You've figured out a lot on your own regarding my affairs, while I've illuminated you further on my business and its... activities over the last few days."

Solana's pulse raced. *Here it comes. The reason behind the disclosures, the reason for drawing me even further into his dealings.* "Yes. Why did you decide to let me in on all that information? Why did you answer every question I asked you about the syndicate in such detail?"

For the first time, Raine smiled, but it was a cool, slow smile. "Because, my dear Ms. Trent, in order for you to hide the truth, you have to be privy to it."

"*Excuse me?*"

He sat back in his chair, keenly studying her from across the table. "While you happen to be in the most dangerous situation you could have possibly gotten yourself into, you are also in a unique position to help me. I could use someone of your many talents, and I believe you enjoy living your life. A fair and simple trade."

"How the *hell* am I supposed to help you?"

"You discontinue researching any stories concerning me or my interests, and you print the ones I feed you in the future. You'd be the syndicate's propagandist, my dear."

Propagandist. The weighty word barely registered before the two preceding it took priority.

The syndicate's propagandist.

Solana gasped. "You're *recruiting* me?"

"Yes. It's your legacy, Alessandra. Now you own it."

She let it sink in. He'd decided to let her live if she chose to help him by joining the ranks of his organization. By compromising her professional integrity and drafting whatever story he - *they* - came up with to cover his ass throughout his career.

"And what if I refuse?"

"You know you can't, Solana."

"What *if?*" She wanted to hear him say it. Actually say it.

Like Zeus on Olympus, Raine inclined his head in the direction of the vista behind her. "You have any idea how high over the water we are right now?"

Solana stared at him. "You wouldn't and you know it."

"Well now, that's quite the wager," he observed. "You sure you really want to place it on the table?"

Raising her eyebrow, she merely lifted her chin higher in response, daring him, calling his bluff.

"Fine," Raine nodded, and Solana jumped when he sprang from his chair and flipped the table between them with a horrific crash. He charged her, no emotion whatsoever crossing his features, and she yelped when he grabbed her hard enough to bruise. "Raine, no! No, Raine, don't!"

"Then fucking stop me," he growled. He ripped her from her chair with frightening ease, merciless as he lifted her roughly into his arms and pinned her tight against his chest. He didn't give her a second glance as he kicked her empty seat out of his way with another terrific smash and proceeded posthaste to the edge of the room, not a halt or falter in his step as he carried her full speed to her death.

It was the longest moment of Solana's life. Terrified by his violence, she fought him but her struggles were futile against the viselike strength of his arms. Ashamed beyond measure, she couldn't believe he was the same man who'd known her so intimately - even now his spellbinding scent mocked her as he brought her to the cliff's edge. Incensed, she was too proud to give in to him, even as she sensed the yawning void beneath her, heard the waves dashing the sharp rocks far, far below her.

But in her heart she knew it was a good offer, the only one he could really give her.

But it tore her in half to know that at the end of it all, after the conversations, the laughter, the intimacy shared, she was a business deal - no more, no less. She cracked, bursting into tears with the weight of the decision, the crushing emotions of fear, shame, and betrayal too much to bear.

"Fine, you fucking bastard, I'll do it! *Now put me down!*"

And like that, it was over. Without the slightest hesitation, as if the last fifteen seconds had never happened,

Raine stepped back into the safe boundary of the porch and set her down gently on her feet in front of him.

Shaking head to toe with the adrenaline flooding her veins, Solana shoved him away from her the second her feet touched the floor. She dashed the tears from her eyes and cheeks, struggling to catch her heaving breath and regain what little remained of her composure –

But when she looked up to find the glow of victory in his icy blue eyes, blind fury struck her.

"You son of a bitch." She didn't think twice about crossing the distance between them and slapping him as hard as she could across his confident face. His head snapped to the side with a sharp crack that echoed off the walls, and her fingers tingled painfully from the contact she'd made against the flat of his cheek.

"Well played," Raine nodded, granting her that one moment of satisfaction. His face burned where she'd hit him, a bold act of lèse-majesté no one else had ever dared before. "And you'd best not ever do it again," he warned, *sotto voce*, watching her green eyes flash fire at him, her auburn hair blazing in the early morning sunlight.

Solana had to bite her tongue as she could literally taste the words "or what?" wanting to make their grand, sarcastic escape.

And she knew he could tell.

"*Bene*," Raine smiled, and then he turned from her to right their overturned table and chairs.

"See, you've learned to trust me at my word, Solana," he said, "but I find I have very little basis on which to reciprocate that. Now, that's another problem we need to address." He indicated the chair she'd previously occupied, and after a moment of consideration she crossed the room and sat back down in her seat.

He pushed her chair in. "More coffee?"

She only glared at him, and as he left her momentarily to get himself another cup, she used the time to school her features into a blank mask.

Of course, she thought angrily. She'd been thinking of the document she still had buried in the system back at the Times, trying to devise a way to use it to regain some of the ground she'd lost.

Or, more accurately, she'd never had.

But after their conversation over dinner last night he knew better than to trust her, and the fact he'd read her thoughts so clearly - again - pissed her off even more.

"Trust is not granted, Raine, it's earned," she told him when he returned, her voice thick after the tumult of her tears. "You can't simply snap your fingers and conjure it into existence."

"I couldn't agree with you more," he said, resuming his seat across from her. "The strength of a syndicate rests solely in the strength of the bond each soldier has with his leader. It's a partnership, built on loyalty and honor. I need to be able to trust each one of them implicitly, and once they earn my respect, they can expect nothing less from me in return.

"You," and he leaned forward to rest his arms on the table, "are no exception from anyone else I've recruited in that aspect. The fact that I don't trust you jeopardizes the stability of our pending agreement. Until we breach that impasse, I need access to you at all times. Our bond is tenuous at best; it needs to be significantly strengthened. Your loyalty is questionable; I need it to be absolute. Therefore, there is one more condition left for you to agree upon before our contract will become binding."

"And what's that?"

"You, Ms. Trent, will agree to marry me."

Thunderstruck, Solana couldn't move, couldn't think, couldn't speak, nor could she hear a single goddamn thing except the words she was sure she'd misheard from him.

"Come again?" she managed, all traces of hot anger doused by ice cold terror.

"My assets become your assets, legitimate and not. Not only do you enlist in the syndicate, you legally join me in directly running it via Imbrialis, with a paper trail tying you to every single facet of its operation."

Mute, Solana could only stare at him. *If I take you down, I take myself with you.* It was genius, leaving her with no avenue for escape or retaliation. Her hands would be tied, forever, and it frightened her to the core.

"You're joking," she whispered, finding her voice once again.

She watched him take another casual sip of his coffee. "No, my dear lady, I do assure you I am in earnest."

You calculating, diabolical, beautiful son of a bitch. Solana's world began to swim, vertigo stealing her breath away while she moved past incredulous to shellshocked.

"But how... ?" she blurted, trying to focus on just one of the hundred thoughts and questions overloading her brain.

Raine understood what she was asking, despite her ineptitude at articulating it. "For many reasons, most prominently to protect our mutual interest in your career at the Times, this will be kept in the strictest confidence, known to the highest-ranking members of the syndicate only. Any detection of a conflict of interest on your part - by the Times or anyone at all - would preclude every word you write about us from being published. But," and he watched her intently, "you will wear the ring at all times."

Solana's blood returned to a boil. "And you won't?" she hollered, her sudden fury rebooting her knowledge of the English language. "I'm going to have to make up some fantastic excuse to explain a *wedding ring* manifesting itself out of thin air onto my finger, what about you? And while we're at it, how many times have you done this, Raine? Do you acquire women the way you acquire companies? How many wives do you have out there? What number in your collection am I? Three? Five?"

He fired her a warning look. "No one who has landed in your precarious position has ever been given any kind of choice, Ms. Trent. Much less what I'm offering you."

They stared at each other in electrified silence, the contract filling the air between them.

He was right, and they both knew it. All she had to do was say the word.

Solana rose from her chair and turned away from him, knowing she was trapped, literally, between the darkness and the light. Before her, the bright sunshine streaming in through the open wall kept growing in intensity, pulling her away from the darker power emanating in waves from the magnetic presence behind her.

Numb, she walked to the porch's edge, leaned her shoulder against the wall, and just watched the sunlight flash off the rolling ocean, like thousands of tiny mirrors scattered over a vast expanse of navy silk far beneath her feet. She knew she had precious little time to think, and she intended to hoard every single second of it.

As if she'd spoken her last thought aloud, Raine stood from the table. "We take off in an hour; you have until we land in New York to make your decision," he announced with finality, and she closed her eyes at the sound of his retreating footsteps.

"And if your answer is no, Solana," he added, pausing at the door to take in her slim silhouette, "take my advice and jump. You'll wish you had."

❧ ❧ ❧

Packing the Jeep, Raine prepared himself for the worst.

He had to give himself credit for his masterful performance back there.

He'd known when he woke up this morning, with her soft auburn hair spilling across his chest, her lashes dark against her flushed cheeks in sleep, that he'd have to put on the game face of his life. He'd spent all morning girding himself in layer upon layer of armor against her, but when he'd heard her getting ready for her day, heard her subconsciously humming the music from their blistering liaison in bed last night... The haunting sound of Geoffrey Oryema's "Makambo" in her soft, vibrating, pitch-perfect hum nearly tore off every scrap of well-placed iron, and he'd had to nail it down with a vengeance to hold it fast.

After that incredible day they'd shared together, it was imperative that she see only the cold, calculating side of the man who led the most powerful crime organization in the country. She had to truly believe - beyond the shadow of a doubt - that he would kill her without a second's hesitation.

Because he would have done it. That wasn't the issue. He absolutely would have dropped her to the waiting waves below; he simply didn't have any other choice.

But the truth was, the truth he could in no way let her see, was that the decision would have haunted him for the rest of his life.

And what if I refuse? she'd said, wanting to hear him actually say it.

You know you can't, Solana, he'd answered, somehow managing to deliver it with hard impatience rather than the softness, the angst, he'd truly felt. *Don't make me,* he'd wanted to say. *Please don't make me.*

But goddammit, she did.

He couldn't even look at her when he'd picked her up with the full intention of literally carrying out his threat. Not her face, not her toes, nothing in between - it would only have made it pointlessly, unbearably harder. He'd done his best to ignore the sweet scent of her incredible hair, the intoxicating feel of her body in his hands, her skin hot and soft under the thin fabric of her dress, that lovely light green sundress that complimented her mint eyes so perfectly.

He'd shut himself against the barrage of emotions he could sense running through her: the paralyzing fear, the impotent anger, and worst, the raw humiliation of sharing so much with him only to have it mean less than nothing. He'd had to close himself off from it, forcing his mind to withdraw to its quiet place whenever he faced a uniquely unpleasant killing, otherwise it would have been disastrous. He'd have stripped that thin linen dress from her body and taken her right there on the floor in the blazing sun to show her that no, it wasn't like that. Something had developed here between them over the last couple days - he couldn't deny it. He fucking *liked* her. Killing her was nothing personal; it simply needed to be done.

He'd pushed away his own emotions, locking down the frustration that she would push the envelope so far. The disappointment that he very well might have to waste such an invaluable asset. And the sense of loss –

He'd blocked it all, stuffing everything under a calming quiet so profound that by the time he made it to the cliff's edge she'd become an object to him, simply because he couldn't afford to think of her as anything else.

But thankfully she'd agreed. She'd capitulated at the last possible moment. And damned if he couldn't help but feel joy in that victory.

But then she saw that joy, not fully seeing it for what it was, and so when he saw her snap and knew down to his toes she was going to hit him, he decided not to block her strike and let her take her revenge. It was a ballsy move on her part... and fucking hell, seeing it from her perspective, he bloody well knew he deserved it.

Now his proposal lay on the table, and she had another decision to make. She'd be a fool not to take his offer, but if that should be her election, he'd kill her solely for rejecting him.

He was convinced there was no woman on earth more suited for him than the Last Alessandra.

She would be indispensable to him and his organization. She was the first, the one, the only he'd ever considered worthy of sharing his empire, the only one he'd ever encountered worth breaking Loiacono's rule. She had infinite potential; he wanted to teach her everything. He wanted her, period. And he refused to part with her.

But if *she* refused *him*...

"God help her," he said, throwing the remainder of their belongings in the car. He stalked out onto the patio, iPhone in hand and already dialing, and waited for his consigliere to pick up.

"Where in the *fucking hell* have you been?" Hunter Cavenastri came roaring over the line.

"Good morning to you, too, Cavi," he said shortly.

"I've been trying to reach you for *thirty-six hours,* Raine! What the fuck is going on?"

"I hope you took the time to rest, because we have work to do."

A heartbeat. "Uh-oh."

"First of all, you owe me a hundred grand."

There was silence before Cavi started to laugh. "Shit."

"Are all the meetings set for tomorrow?"

"Of course."

"Good. There's been an addition to the agenda."

"I figured as much. What do you need?"

And Raine gave him the details.

And then heard nothing on the other end of the line.

"I'm sorry, I had to switch the phone over to my good ear because I know I didn't hear that correctly," Cavi said.

"You certainly did."

"Are you *out of your fucking mind?*"

"Funny, that's what she said."

"You've lost it, Raine, haven't you?" he cried.

"No," came the stern, laconic reply.

Cavi knew better than to reason with the boss once he'd gone Spartan. "What makes you think she'll say yes?"

"She rather has to, don't you think?"

"It's one hell of an offer."

"It's the only way to recruit her and force loyalty out of her."

"I know. It's goddamn smart, you crazy fuck. I just hope you know what you're doing; we've come too far to jeopardize this now."

"Agreed. Have I let you down yet?"

"No," Cavi admitted. "You never cease to amaze me, Raine."

"All right, then. End of discussion."

"Hey, it's your empire; I'm satisfied if you are. You're coming back soon, I take it?"

"We're leaving the island shortly. She has until we land to make up her mind."

"Okay. Keep me posted. Meanwhile, I'll start making some phone calls. *Arrivederci,* Romeo."

CHAPTER FOURTEEN

Watching the curves of the Mid-Atlantic coastline pass by far beneath her, Solana sat by herself in some small closet of a room on the private jet and let her thoughts war against themselves.

The source of the conflict didn't lie in yes or no; she'd moved past that question long ago. *Please*, she thought ruefully. *As if I have any real choice in the matter.*

She should hate him for putting her in this position.

Problem was, she didn't.

Yes, she was pissed. She seethed at the thought of him claiming her like so much chattel property, the spoils of another successful business acquisition. She chafed under the pressure of perjuring her byline, knowing she'd be penning complete bullshit beneath her name in order to safeguard his - or rather, *their* - career.

But at the same time, she knew the offer he'd given her was borne of respect, otherwise she wouldn't be sitting where she was right now.

It was a favor in return for the Preston exposé and the subsequent windfall she'd inadvertently helped bring him. It was a nod to her ancestry, honoring her as Damian Alessandra's long lost daughter. It was an acknowledgment of her skills as a gifted detective and renowned journalist. It was an act of faith in *her*, that even though he didn't trust her, he believed she could successfully handle this assignment and live with her feet firmly planted in two very different worlds.

Furthermore, the proposal was also borne of something else, and Solana came to the frightening realization that she could no longer delay dealing with this.

She needed to recognize it for the mutual attraction it was.

In two days' time, an undeniable, inexplicable bond had grown between them. Their immediate connection at the ball. That shocking first night together. The conversations that felt like chess matches. The laughter, the stories, and the experiences of a perfect day in paradise. The way they often read each other's thoughts, and how they kept finding common ground, time and time again.

In many ways, he was a perfect match for her. Armed with the intelligence necessary to drive his ambition to unspeakable power, he'd taken the City by storm. Phenomenally successful, the respect he commanded was the stuff of legends. Soulfully philosophical, he'd kept her riveted with questions and answers the whole weekend long. Handsome beyond words, his mere presence often left her breathless.

It could be worse, she thought.

But would the real Raine Mathison please stand up? It was impossible to reconcile the cold, draconian businessman she'd met in the nook this morning with the man

who'd held her like a treasured lover merely hours before-
hand. Who the fuck would she be marrying? The soul-
mate who'd made her trust him, made her want him,
made her feel safe with him, or the mob boss who'd scared
her to death, who'd humiliated her to the point of rage
this morning?

Did he even *care* that he would be wed to her?

Why the hell should she even care if he cared?

No use trying to fool yourself with that one, Alessandra,
she chided herself. *You know damn well you care what he
thinks.*

And you know you're no Sofia Marchesotto to him, either.

Solana sighed and stared out the window. It wouldn't
be long now before they were on the ground in Manhattan.

She hated giving in to him - she could see the gloating
look on his face already - but she had no other choice but
to accept his proposal. She'd won many battles against
him, but ultimately she'd lost the war.

Alessandra Solana Trent, she sneered. *Presstitute to the
mob boss of New York.*

Overwhelmed by the task ahead of her, she thought
she was going to be sick as a vicious hit of nausea struck
her in the gut. Fuck him and his faith in her - she had no
clue how to pull off what he was asking her to do at the
Times.

And as much as the mob world had always intrigued
her, as much as it was part of her blood, the prospect of
being inextricably linked to the syndicate, to *him*, was
nothing short of terrifying. This was a world where people
disappeared without a trace, and throughout her career -
her very life - she'd managed to outrun it, expose it. Not
live it.

But she knew that so long as she protected him, he would protect her in kind.

She would be his wife, after all.

And there was the heart of it. As much as she wanted to deny it, as much as it scared her, she couldn't help but feel honored by his proposal.

Nobile Loiacono certainly would not have approved of this tactic. Raine's predecessor firmly believed that no wives belonged in a boss's business, and he would have thoroughly schooled his protégé in that psychology long before handing the syndicate down to him.

Before two days ago, she was sure Raine Mathison never had any intention of tying himself to anyone. Even though this was obviously a business decision for him - although yes, it came with its perqs - the fact that he'd offered this to her in the first place was a compliment of the highest order. To refuse him would be a gross insult, *period*, and she shuddered to think what would happen to her if she actually dared to turn him down.

He'd chosen her for a reason, and he wouldn't have done that lightly.

All she had to do was accept the honor. Two little words, *"I do,"* and she'd get some semblance of her life back.

She'd just have to learn to share some part of that life with him.

But how much? Where was this going to go?

She had no idea.

All she *did* know was that Manhattan Island was looming larger by the second.

ભ ભ ભ

1 2:39 P.M.

Two minutes before the descent into LaGuardia, Raine was surprised to hear Solana open the door to that blasted room she'd holed herself up in for the entire flight. Hidden from view in his office at the back of the plane, he threw down the pen he'd been twirling to distraction in his fingers and sat back in his chair.

It's good news then, he realized, and a lambent warmth unlike anything he'd ever felt coursed its way through him.

Solana held her breath as she emerged from her little room, half expecting to find Raine at the table they'd shared on the plane yesterday, but he was nowhere to be seen. She wanted him to know she was coming to *him* with her decision; she'd be damned if he came after her in that room like a recalcitrant child. So she stood at one of the windows, watching the New York City skyline grow taller in the distance, knowing it wouldn't be long before she felt his presence next to her.

"Jameson's, neat, with a twist," he said quietly, passing her a short glass of the sweet Irish whiskey when he came to stand beside her.

The return of the peace offering, she thought, and when she looked up at him it was her turn to be surprised.

There was no trace of the smug glow of victory she'd expected to see on his face. Instead there was a genuine softness, a quiet respect, that completely disarmed her.

"Your answer is yes, then?" he asked, his light eyes holding hers.

She nodded, and he raised his glass of The Dalmore to hers. "*Cin-cin*."

"*Cin-cin*," she repeated, and she drank deeply of the smooth whiskey, feeling the warmth begin its delicious, consuming journey. "So. When will this happen?"

"Tomorrow. I'll send the Bentley for you at noon."

"Married on my lunch hour. My, how times have changed," Solana said, and she downed the rest of the Jameson's in one swig.

"Come, we should sit." Raine took her hand and led her to a large leather couch as the jet cruised the final stretch before landing. He pulled her down onto his lap, gathering her in close to him, and she buried her cheek in the golden waves of hair curling at his ear.

"You will want for nothing, Solana," he pledged. "All of your debts and expenses will be paid. I will make sure you're protected, so long as you promise to protect me. It's that simple. Does that sound unreasonable?"

"No," she murmured. He made it sound so easy, so uncomplicated, she could almost find comfort in his words.

Raine pushed her back from him and searched her face with an intensity that melted away all traces of her apprehension. "It may not be so bad as you think," he whispered, and drew her into a deep, consuming kiss just as the plane made its touchdown on the runway below.

CHAPTER FIFTEEN

"Where'd you get the flowers?" Donato asked gruffly as he strode into her office for his daily briefing.

Solana glanced at the vase of impressive roses on the table across the room and felt her face flush scarlet. She'd had half a mind to trash them on sight this morning, but the other half...

"They're a gift from my brothers," she blurted. "It's their way of saying hello from across the miles."

"Oh, good," Donato said. "From how you're dressed I wasn't sure if somebody died or something."

In Shakespeare's parlance, she thought, her face losing none of its flush, *I died at least four times this weekend.*

But to be fair, her editor's observation wasn't at all off the mark. Even though the hot summer day outside couldn't be any more scintillating, Solana had suited herself entirely in bespoke black. She'd chosen a trim button-down cap-sleeved blouse by Tom James tucked into long wide-leg cuffed trousers by Moi-Même that nearly covered her smart, four-inch Dolce & Gabbana heels.

It was as antithetical to a white dress as she could possibly get.

After spending every waking moment of the weekend with Raine, her first night back home had felt... strange.

Once they'd landed yesterday, he'd simply let her go.

"Here," he'd said, placing the keys to her Audi in her open palm. She'd only stared at him in bewilderment, but sure as hell when they disembarked, two vehicles were waiting for them right there on the tarmac - his Tramonto and her R8, somehow extracted from Philadelphia.

"See you tomorrow," he'd said in solemn goodbye, and they both went their separate ways.

At first, Solana had been overjoyed with her newfound, newly appreciated freedom, speeding her way, with Cookie Monsta's "Riot!" blasting, to the Park Avenue apartment she'd once thought she might never see again. She'd thrown on her own clothes - holy jean shorts and a threadbare UPenn tee shirt - and cleaned her entire place top to bottom with the alacrity of a reunited lover. She then went to unpack her things, to put everything back to normal - and stared open-mouthed at Raine Mathison's newest plant amongst her belongings.

Two large plastic baggies full of nucatuli, tied together with a certain red ribbon.

Normal, she'd choked. His simple, thoughtful gesture had brought it home to her that, for better or for worse, nothing would ever be normal again.

And while she unpacked, did laundry, made dinner, checked her email, climbed into bed, curled up with a book, she half expected to find him next to her, appearing out of the shadows.

It never happened.

She'd woken up alone this morning, on the day that would be her wedding day.

As inconceivable as that was.

"Lana?"

Snapping back to the present, Solana refocused her gaze to find her boss staring at her from the doorway, and she faked her best smile. "I'm sorry, Will, what was that?"

"I'm looking forward to your findings from the weekend," he repeated, studying her with open curiosity.

"Of course. Let me compile what I have and I'll debrief you this afternoon."

Donato nodded. "Good. I'm looking forward to it."

Solana watched him leave, her eyes burning with the threat of tears. She wanted so much to confide in someone, just so she didn't feel so completely alone, isolated from any help, terrified by what she was about to do.

Dry it up, Alessandra, she scolded. *You made your bed, now lie in it.*

She turned her attention back to her laptop and called up the document she'd written seemingly decades ago Friday morning. She reread it slowly, feeling like someone who'd buried a time capsule as a child only to dig it up years later, smarter, more experienced, more cynical.

She highlighted the entire document, hit delete, and pressed save.

It was gone.

She marked the file for deletion, sat back in her chair and looked up at the clock on her wall.

7:45 a.m.

T-minus 4 hours, 15 minutes.

℘ ℘ ℘

11:45 A.M.

Hunter Cavenastri understood that Raine hadn't completely lost his mind as he watched Alessandra Solana Trent emerge from her office building and begin her approach to the Bentley.

Well well well, he thought. *If everything he says about this Mafia princess is true, if a sharp mind and quick wit comes wrapped in a hot little package like that, then he's the smartest - arguably the luckiest - sunovabitch on this planet.*

Cavi moved to get out of the car to open the back door for this beauty in black with fiery dark hair and glinting green eyes, but he stopped short when he saw her shake her head.

"Please don't," she mouthed, and when she reached the sleek black saloon she opened the front passenger door herself and slid nonchalantly into the seat next to him.

"Solana Trent," she said shortly, extending her hand to him. "You're Hunter Cavenastri."

He stared at her in disbelief. She sounded just like someone he happened to know very well, especially when he's giving orders on the other end of a mobile phone.

Yes, Raine was thinking perfectly clearly.

He had found *himself* in a female.

"Perceptive, Ms. Trent," he said as he shook her hand. "But many, especially Raine, call me Cavi."

"Very well, then. Likewise, it's Solana," she snipped. "And so far, you and Gennato Anesini are the only others who know I'm the syndicate's newest annexation?"

"Well, don't forget about the attorneys," he said. "The rest of us will know soon enough."

"Of course." *Naturally, that's where we're going,* Solana

thought wryly as he paused the Bentley for the right hand turn at the intersection of 8th and 46th.

"Raine wanted you to have this," Cavenastri said, and when he produced a tiny square box from the pocket of his leather jacket, she recognized the trademark turquoise color on sight. The familiar hue announced Tiffany & Co. just as clearly as the company's logo written elegantly across the top, and she stared at the little package sitting tall in her open palm.

The size, the shape, the store... it could only be one thing.

But why? Solana blamed her trembling fingers on the inordinate amount of coffee she'd had earlier that morning as she untied the white ribbon, lifted the pale blue top and opened the hinged leather box nestled within.

Free of its confines, the one-carat Lucida solitaire sparkled energetically, proud with its wide corners, high-step cut crown, and brilliant style pavilion. It flashed and fired in the sunlight beaming through the car's windows, burning with mighty attitude and great expectations, ready to leap from its plush prison.

Utterly speechless, Solana didn't know whether to sob, smile, or rage, each emotion vying for prevalence as she removed the ring from its pinch pillow. She slipped it on, and the platinum band hugged her warmly, circling her with a snug, comforting power, and she appreciated why the Romans believed a direct line traveled from that finger to one's heart.

Raine wanted you to have this. Fine, but she understood Raine well enough to know there was more to this gesture than mere appearances. From their heated debate on St. John she knew he expected her to wear a wedding band, but he'd said nothing about an engagement ring.

This was a gift, and she knew he'd done it to soften the impending blow.

She'd be willing to bet he hadn't divulged the shady circumstances behind their marriage to the lawyers. He'd simply tell them to draw up the papers, no further details forthcoming. His attorneys must be beside themselves wondering about the particulars behind this extraordinary event, and she already chafed under the hot spotlight she knew would be thrown down on her.

Raine wanted to make her feel as comfortable as possible when she stepped into that office. His personal code of honor dictated that she be given consideration for her acceptance of his contract - and if the lawyers even suspected the unsavory details precipitating their marriage, they would be looking for it. So he'd armed her with the universally recognized token that marked the dramatic interim status of engagement, and she could wear it like a talisman against the stares of whomever was marrying them.

But if he cared so much for her comfort, why hadn't he delivered it to her personally? Last night would have been the perfect opportunity, but he'd never so much as checked in on her.

And why wasn't he the one picking her up today? If her recruitment was so important, and this rite so crucial to securing it, why was he so glaringly absent?

Solana looked over at Cavenastri - *Cavi*, she reminded herself - and wondered how much information Raine's second-in-command would give her.

"Why didn't he give this to me himself?" she asked, already toying nervously with the ring on her finger.

"He didn't tell you?" Cavi glanced over at her as he turned onto Lexington Avenue.

Dread shot like an arrow through her heart. "Tell me *what*," she demanded.

Incredulous, the consigliere shot a longer, harder look in her direction. "That he's off to Rome tomorrow morning for at least two months, working on the acquisition of this small Italian bank with impressive amounts of growth potential. Outside of Kane, it's our top fucking priority. He really didn't mention it?"

She stiffened. "No."

"Well, I'm sure he has his reasons; he always does," Cavi shrugged. "I'll probably catch shit for dropping it on you, but that's life. Anyway, I can tell you it was damn near impossible to coordinate today's schedule of meetings for him. Believe me, every second of his time is accounted for, otherwise I'm sure he would have been here."

"I see," Solana said, and the sickening wave of disappointment she felt surprised her with its intensity. Once she was acquired, Raine's attention would rest with his next business deal halfway across the goddamn globe.

Like so much chattel property, she sulked, and she felt a numbing coldness coil protectively around her heart.

Maybe the diamond wasn't a token of respect. Maybe it was a brand, another physical reminder that she was claimed by him, and he wouldn't let her forget it.

Solana's eyes dropped to the ring that wrapped itself securely around her finger, glittering with glee in its new home.

Looks like we're in this together, friend, she thought bitterly. *Because we've both been purchased at a price today.*

By the time the Bentley glided to a stop in front of 405 Lexington Avenue, the Chrysler Building, Solana was glad for her choice of black clothing. She felt like she was attending her own funeral.

ﭏ ﭏ ﭏ

The law firm at the top of the Chrysler building literally reeked of omnipotence, smelling of rich leather, black coffee, expensive cologne, sharpened pencils, Scotch tape, and unspeakable power. Floor-to-ceiling windows commanded panoramic views of the Hudson River and the Atlantic Ocean beyond, where black clouds towered in the distance, lightning licking the surface of the water. At this height, the strengthening wind already buffeted the windows, promising a thunderous summer storm, which in this room could be watched in safety like a spectator sport, almost mocking the power of nature itself. Being here gave one a sense of owning the world, orchestrating its machinations, impervious to its dangers, while the hoi polloi chased their small lives in the streets far below.

"Right through these doors, Miss Trent."

Upon her arrival, the staid receptionist had briskly marched Solana through the office without delay, leading her directly to the corner boardroom where she'd been informed her presence was *"already expected."*

The snappy woman stopped short in front of an immense pair of closed double doors, rapped smartly with one sharp knock, and, without even waiting for any acknowledgment from within, promptly threw them wide open for her.

Solana only nodded her thanks, barely able to breathe through her apprehension as the portals of power opened before her. She set her jaw in resolution and strode confidently through the heavy wooden doors –

Yet found herself unprepared for the sinking in her stomach when the eyes of thirteen men fell upon her.

She'd wondered how many of them would be in there but she'd never expected to be so grossly outnumbered. All of them stood silent, smartly dressed in shades of black, white, and grey, as they watched her like a lamb brought to the lion's den.

And there, in the center of them all, stood Raine, tall, blond, and breathtaking, sharply suited in tailored Pierre of Paris, midnight black with razor-thin grey pinstripes.

Solana zeroed in on him as the doors slammed shut behind her, making him her channel marker in this sea of intimidation, and he nodded to her in respect as she took the boardroom by storm.

"Gentlemen," she said, astonished at the cool strength of her voice as she walked the length of the room to the leather chair Raine held out for her at the head of the long mahogany table. If any of them - including Raine - said anything to her in return, she didn't hear it due to the unrelenting pound of her pulse in her ears.

The leather gave a soft swoosh as she sat down and crossed her legs with controlled elegance, and the lawyers waited until then to fill their chairs down the length of the dark wood. Raine pushed in her chair, and when she felt his hands come to rest on her squared shoulders from where he stood behind her seat, the sinking squeezing in her stomach grew so intense she was afraid she was going to be ill.

On the table in front of her lay a neatly stapled stack of heavy legal bond paper, red Post-It flags with the imperative "Sign Here" poking like bloody daggers on the fine white sheets. Beside them lay a sleek black Cross pen, impatiently waiting to be picked up in her slim fingers. Painfully aware of the many pairs of eyes on her, she flipped the cover sheet to read the first page of paperwork, to find two names leading across the top of the opening paragraph.

Alessandra Solana Trent and Raine Sinagra Mathison.

Her heart faltered. *Sinagra*. Native to the Messina province of Sicily, the name meant "strange honor," from the pairing of two Greek words, *xenos* (stranger) and *geras* (honor). *It couldn't be more fitting.*

She then stared at her own last name, Trent, a truncation of the toponymic Taranto from when she'd naturalized as a child. The teeming port city of the same name was located in Puglia, tucked high on the inside of the boot's heel in southeastern Italy - not too long a trip from the infamous island Raine evidently hailed from.

She continued on with her perusal of the materials. The marriage license to join them legally as husband and wife. The equity interest paperwork to establish her sizable shareholder position within Imbrialis Acquisitions, making her an official owner in the corporation that was the front for the syndicate. The agreement to inextricably combine their assets, hers to become his, his to become hers, tying them to every facet of each other's financial and legal lives.

But there was no prenup, no mention of the real consequences should their marriage fail. Nowhere in these pages would it be committed to writing that should she welsh on her part of the bargain, there would be no divorce, no sale of her interest in Imbrialis, no separation of assets. Just a death sentence.

Solana moved on to review the last remaining pages - and blinked when she found a notarized copy of her birth certificate, which as far as she knew still lay safely locked away in her bank deposit box. There was also a likewise-validated photocopy of her Social Security card, followed by one of her driver's license, and still another with the first few pages of her passport.

Impossible, she thought as she finished her furious skimming. *It just isn't possible that he can do this.* It staggered her, the power, the depth and breadth of influence that had so seemlessly pulled this together in so little time.

But there was more to come.

With a shock, she realized that two of the twelve attorneys in attendance occupied other offices as they stood in their places at the table. One was the Clerk of the City of New York, whose presence was required to witness the signing of the marriage license, and the other was the Chief Justice of the U.S. Court of Appeals for the Second Circuit to officiate the marriage itself.

She nearly passed out when the latter started speaking, just as the first peal of thunder rolled in the distance.

"Raine Sinagra Mathison, you understand that with the signing of these documents you take Alessandra Solana Trent to you as your wife under the laws of the State of New York?"

"Yes, sir," came the sound of his deep, resonant voice behind her.

"Do you enter into this legally binding contract under any duress or coercion?"

"No, sir."

The Chief Justice's gaze dropped with significance to Solana.

"Alessandra Solana Trent, you understand that with the signing of these documents you take Raine Sinagra Mathison to you as your husband under the laws of the State of New York?"

"Yes, sir," she repeated Raine's solemn words in a voice she didn't recognize as her own.

"Do you enter into this legally binding contract under any duress or coercion?"

Solana felt Raine's fingers on her shoulders tighten ever so slightly, felt his thumbs trace the barest line along the curve of her upper spine, and the touch conveyed more than words ever could have.

Say yes, he promised, *and I will break you.*

"No, sir," she answered, goosebumps prickling down her arms.

The two men nodded silently, and Solana sat perfectly still as she felt Raine move behind her, watched him bend down over the table, his handsome, confident face coming within inches beside hers. His right hand moved from her right shoulder to lift the pen, and she saw the warm glow in his eyes as he flipped slowly through the pages and signed his name reverently in all places indicated. When he was done he turned his light eyes to hers, handing her the pen, and as they both held it together for a moment, with the nib hovering over the sheets of bond paper, she knew she was signing her life away to the devil himself.

But if the devil is this god of a man, she thought as she looked up into his heart-stopping, breath-stealing, logic-stripping face, *I'm sure as hell not interested in heaven.*

Tearing her eyes from his, Solana took the pen from his fingers and turned back to the contract on the table. She felt Raine's hand return to her shoulder as she found her empty, waiting signature lines beneath his long, black strokes on the white paper, underneath the words:

> *IN WITNESS WHEREOF, the parties to this agreement have caused this instrument to be executed in a manner so as to be binding, this the day and date hereinabove written.*

And she signed her name in every required place, hard and strong, with resolute flourish.

It was done. Within moments the documents were witnessed, notarized, and couriered away for same-day recording in the county's vital records, most likely to be misfiled so ingeniously they would never be discovered by anyone outside this room.

Oh God, it's done. Solana's world swam as the adrenaline rushed out of her system, leaving an empty void behind. *Now what?*

Raine must have heard her anxious thoughts, because she felt him squeeze her shoulders in a very different way this time as she heard him say above her, "Gentlemen, I believe that concludes our agenda for this day. Thank you most graciously for your assistance in these matters."

She didn't know whether it was his normal protocol with them or some kind of prearranged code, but Solana watched, numb, as the attorneys, the Chief Justice, and the City Clerk all took his parting words as their cue to rise from the table - without so much as a word of conversation. No banter, no post-meeting discussion, and certainly no congratulations; to a man, they simply nodded their regards before filing out of the boardroom.

When they were alone at last, Raine swiveled her chair around so that she faced him —

And an emotion replaced the numbness in Solana's chest when he got down on one knee before her.

He's going to ask me, she panicked. *But why now? After he left me alone all night? Without so much as a phone call? Now that it's all over and he's heading off to Rome to seal his next big deal?*

"Raine, what are you doing?" she asked in a breathless whisper.

"We only have a couple of minutes before I have to go," he answered with quiet urgency. He withdrew a small item from his suitcoat's inner pocket, another little package in trademark Tiffany blue, and Solana felt her heart break and burst in an explosion of light when she saw two platinum wedding bands appear between his thumb and forefinger.

The room was so silent she heard the soft *shing* of metal on metal as he palmed them with one dexterous movement of his hand, and just before his fingers closed over them, her photographic mind had time to snap a shot.

She'd always remember the image of the paired rings in his palm, the smaller one lying within the circumference of the larger, completely surrounded, with plenty of room to spare. His ring would eternally envelop hers, just like he himself did after taking her in his bed, keeping her safe and secure.

While they'd taken no vows today, the wedding bands were the promise she'd been seeking from him.

Raine lifted his clear gaze to hers. "Marry me, Solana," he murmured, simple and sincere. "Please."

"But I already did," she breathed.

"Wordsmith," he rolled his eyes. "Just answer me, will you?"

She laughed out loud. "Yes, Raine. Yes."

Raine felt his own smile flash like sunlight, and with gentle ceremony he took her left hand in his. He slipped off the engagement ring, and while it was a pretty thing, he considered it plain in comparison to the understated band that would now take its place.

Despite the time crunch he was under, he did it slowly, with reverence, savoring the moment of sliding the impossibly small, classically simple wedding ring in prime position on her finger. He replaced the diamond, now upstaged by its infinitely more significant partner, and as soon as both were seated, he felt a conclusive sense of peace fill him.

Unlike anything he'd ever experienced, it came out of nowhere, pervading every cell in his body, seeming to reach clear down to the atoms. She was now his, and he couldn't believe how right it felt. It was like she was the puzzle piece he'd never known was missing. Would she reciprocate that feeling? Would she understand this any better than he did?

Raine turned her hand over, and that completing calm he'd just discovered evaporated, leaving behind an anxiety that was also altogether unfamiliar.

And completely irrational, he scolded himself. He remembered from their conflict at the cottage how important this next part was to her. He'd planned to wear a wedding ring right along with her, for exactly the same reasons she'd pointed out.

But this gesture... she might not be ready to return the one he'd just made to her. Yes, she'd just accepted his official proposal, but could she really say anything else? *This* would be the acceptance of him and this situation he'd forced her into, this new phase of life they would both experience together as a couple.

He moved decisively lest she sense his hesitation. He lay the significantly larger wedding band in her open palm, and once it was delivered, he retreated, letting the tips of his fingers softly trace along her slim ones. When his fingertips touched hers, he rolled her fingers closed over the ring, then held his left hand suspended over hers.

Solana understood him, and for reasons she couldn't

fathom, she felt tears sting her eyes as she took the heavy ring from her palm and slid it home on his waiting finger.

She cleared her throat softly as she raised her eyes back up to his. "Sinagra?" she asked.

"My father's the Scot," Raine explained with a renewing smile. "My mother, on the other hand, *she* was the Sicilian."

Solana couldn't help but laugh again. "That must have been an interesting childhood."

"You have no idea."

They sat there together in the first few minutes of their marriage, laughter between them, and Solana felt an indescribable emotion surge through her. It flowed all the way to the fingertips Raine still held in his hands, then intensified when she realized she was seeing the same thing reflected back at her in the depths of his light, luminous eyes.

Overwhelmed by its simplicity, warmed by its truth, Solana leaned close to him, brought her face down to his, and captured his lips in a slow, firm, ardent kiss. Matching her passion, moved by it, Raine drew her closer, his hand on the back of her neck, his thumb caressing her behind her ear while he kissed his bright, beautiful bride.

After several delicious moments, thunder blasting in the distance brought them both back to reality and Raine reluctantly pulled away from her.

"I have to go," he said, wishing more than anything he could get stuck in the elevator with her for an hour or two, and he rose up, bringing her to her feet along with him.

"Cavi will bring you wherever you'd like," he told her as they strode out of the boardroom and out into the hall, heading for the elevator banks. "Incidentally, you'll be seeing a lot of Cavi. While I'm away, I've given him the prime directive of watching over you."

"And is that for your protection or for mine?" Solana asked pointedly.

"Both, actually," he grinned, and he escorted her into the waiting elevator.

The car dropped with dizzying speed to the ground floor of the Chrysler Building, and they walked out into the bustle of financiers, lawyers, politicians - corporate power players on the move. Solana spotted Cavi standing on the other side of the concourse and they crossed to him, Raine reaching him first. She watched him place a hand on Cavi's shoulder and say something lowly in his lieutenant's ear, to which the second-in-command gave a solemn nod. She caught up with them then, and Raine turned to her.

"I will see you," he said, fixing her with his warm gaze, and in the next second he was gone, out amongst the crowd on Lexington Avenue.

CHAPTER SIXTEEN

She's one of us now. Guard her with your life, as you would me.

As he watched Solana Trent walk back into the New York Times Building, Cavi remembered his boss's whispered words to him and smiled at the writing he already saw on the wall.

This new relationship was progressing entirely too well, burgeoning far beyond the realm of simply genius business.

Raine Mathison had developed a weakness, a soft spot for this woman, and she for him.

She would be his undoing.

Not that Cavi cast any aspersion on her in the slightest. He could see her potential as clearly as Mathison did; she would be an excellent asset, completely blameless in his downfall.

She was just the weapon against him that Cavi had been waiting for.

It would take time, of course, the sabotage of this new relationship that would create the distraction to get Mathison off his game.

But that was just as well. The syndicate's freshly-contracted alliances were too new, too unstable; they needed to foster before they would be ready to handle a change at the helm.

And once that happened, he'd seize for himself the throne of the empire he'd help build.

It was about goddamn time.

CHAPTER SEVENTEEN

3:31 P.M.

Solana stood watching the rain slash violently against her office windows while lightning bolts raced like light cycles overhead, thunder rolling angrily in hot pursuit. Just inches from her face, the second summer storm of the day was in full swing, unleashing its wrath on the metropolis and its ill-prepared inhabitants scurrying for cover on the streets below. The wind howled and the black clouds roiled, echoing the emotions tumbling wildly in her heart, and for the umpteenth time she turned her attention from the window to the rings glittering and glistening on her left hand.

They were exquisite. Just the right proportions for her small-sized hands, the one-carat Tiffany and its companion wedding band looked perfect on her. Not gaudy or ostentatious but proud and immodest, they burst with confident energy, announcing their presence to the world.

They would not escape notice.

Fuck.

Donato was due in here any minute for the - totally nonexistent - alley murder debrief, and she was hoping he wouldn't catch the fiery glimmer of the new gem from across her desk. She didn't know how he *wouldn't* see it - she felt like a walking lighthouse, for Chrissake.

She shook her head to clear it. This anxiety was ridiculous. Who would be looking at her hands, anyway?

Or Raine's?

She smiled in warm remembrance. He'd chosen to wear a wedding ring, too. It made her feel less alone, knowing that he himself was carrying a visible symbol of whatever this arrangement was between them, and it was nice to know that he'd have some explaining of his own to do on occasion. She wondered if this had always been part of his marriage plan, or if he'd done it out of deference to her in the wake of her outburst in the cottage.

But Raine Mathison didn't strike her as the kind of man who'd wear a wedding band if it didn't suit his interests. So he must find something special, something meaningful in this new union of theirs –

"Ready, Lana?"

Solana turned to find Donato at her door. "Sure, Will, come in," she said, and she instinctively folded her arms across her chest to hide her hands from view.

But rather than rise to sit at her desk, she suddenly felt paralyzed, glued to the window at her back. She wanted nothing more than to maintain that extra bit of distance between them, so she did her best to lean casually against the windowsill and appear perfectly at ease.

Donato took a seat in his chair opposite her desk, and then regarded her with a puzzled look when she didn't come sit down across from him. "Got a minute or what?" he asked.

She smiled sadly. *Just bite the bullet and get it over with.* "Yes, but that's all. See, I have plenty of time to give you, but no news on the alley murders."

He regarded her skeptically. "A weekend's worth of field work brought nothing to light on these?"

"Unfortunately, no."

"Whom did you consult about this?"

"The normal sources," she said. That was safe - as a rule she never disclosed the identity of her informants to anyone on her staff. But she could see Donato was about to go all Socratic on her miserably unprepared ass, and she knew she'd better preempt his strike before he backed her into a corner.

"I'm beginning to think you were right about what you said on Thursday, that I've been reading too much into these activities of late," she said, trying to move the topic from anything directly relating to Raine. "Maybe the murders of Catello, Mastriani, and Santaglio truly are cut-and-dried cases of mob business as usual, just like Kane's advisors suggested to me during my conversations with them at the ball."

"You're rarely wrong about these things, Lana, and you witnessed quite a few interesting acknowledgments to Mathison that night," he warned. "Trusting the judgment of anyone tied to Kane may not be in your best interest."

The irony of Donato's usage of the words "witness" and "Mathison" in the same sentence wasn't lost upon her.

"Fine," she said, "but it's not like I can go knock on DiStephano's door and ask him point blank if he killed his top men."

"You could."

"Sure, but it's not entirely advisable. I'm not the man's favorite person, remember?"

Donato sighed. "I see your point. However," he said, and the timbre of his voice took on an air of significance, "it may surprise you that I myself managed to garner some intel on the murder vics in the alley."

"Really?" Solana's stomach plummeted to the soles of her sexy high-heeled pumps. "What did you find out?"

Her editor smiled. "You're going to love this. Coincidentally enough, they have ties to Mathison's syndicate."

"They do?"

"Yes, but they're pretty low on the totem pole; the Bureau doesn't have much on 'em. Now riddle me this: why would a couple of Mathison's mob peons get offed with the same M.O. as the three big timers from DiStephano's family?"

My question exactly until the man himself explained it to me in an exclusive one-on-one interview on his posh Gulfstream 450. "I have no idea," she told him. "Like I said, Will, no one's talking."

He nodded. "For now. Your sources are probably tight-lipped with all these shifting allegiances. You'll get something eventually."

"Or maybe no one's talking because there's nothing to tell, Will."

Donato raised an eyebrow. "These are *murders*, Lana. No matter who committed them, there's a story to tell."

"True," she countered, "but that's what the police are paid good money to figure out for us. I'll keep tabs on my sources and see what comes up in the next few weeks."

Donato studied her hard. It wasn't like her to eschew the role of the bloodhound when there was an unsolved mystery reeking of her favorite scent. Something had changed with her over the past few days; he just couldn't put his finger on it. "What's going on with you, Lana?"

She gave a wan smile. "Not getting any answers is frustrating for me, too, Will. I mean, look at my phone," she said, pointing to her desk. "Silent, no blinking message lights, no calls being returned to me. I'm doing what I can but coming up empty."

Donato didn't buy it, not fully. But then again, he'd been there; he knew the feast or famine of story chasing.

"Be patient, Solana," he advised. "You'll find what you're looking for; you always do. In the meantime, until something breaks on this, I want you back on Kane's campaign trail with Steinberg. He's learning a lot from you and it'll keep you tied into any developments on the Mathison-Kane partnership. Also, I've got enough proofing to keep you busy dawn to dusk. Good?"

"Good," she grinned, relieved that the inquisition was over.

"Now what's with the Harry Winston?"

Her smile melted like a snowball in hell. "I'm sorry?"

Slowly, Donato rose from his chair, fixing her with a look that said "Really?" He came around her desk like a police officer approaching a pulled-over vehicle, and Solana held her breath as he came to stand in front of her.

"The diamond, Lana," he said, holding out his hand to her. "Have you been holding out on me? Is there something I need to know?"

Looking up into his grey eyes, Solana's mind raced. *Dammit, how did he know?*

And then she realized she must have gestured to her silent phone with her left hand; there was simply no other way he'd have had an opportunity to see the rings.

Internally cursing herself for her stupidity, she reluctantly uncrossed her arms and gave him her bejeweled hand.

"Sorry to disappoint you, Will, but it's not what you think," she said. *And boy isn't that the fucking truth.* "It's much easier to live life in this City if the creeps think you're taken. And furthermore, it's the hottest new trend, women buying their own bling for themselves. Why should we have to wait for Mr. Right?"

Donato turned her hand from side to side, studying the flash and fire of the Lucida from different angles. "You'll find him someday, Lana, but he might resent your stealing his thunder - that set is pretty damn convincing."

"That's the idea. Thank you for confirming it works."

Her editor laughed. "You never struck me as the type for retail therapy, but if it gives you the street cred you need to get the stories you seek, by all means, take all the shopping time you want." He released her hand and gave her a long look, but made no further comment before he turned to head for the door. "Now, come over to my desk so I can give you that stack of new assignments."

As she followed her boss out of her office, Solana lifted her eyes skyward in a silent prayer of thanks, stuffing her hands deep into her pockets.

So far, so good.

CHAPTER EIGHTEEN

9:05 P.M.

Imbrialis Acquisitions, headquartered on the 100th floor of the Empire State Building, boasted an absolutely enviable view of Midtown. Having finished reading the last page of the five-inch binder weighing like a brick in his lap, Raine sat back in his chair and kicked up his feet on his boardroom table to take in the soaring vista.

Skyscrapers of all shapes, heights, and sizes glittered against the night sky in every direction, and while each was an architectural marvel in its own right, it was the Chrysler Building with its glowing terraced crown that stole the show to the northeast. Raine shifted his feet over a couple inches until he framed the iconic art deco building between his polished Brunori's, enjoying the view of the world literally at his feet. Even from this distance he could pick out the offices of his attorneys, their lighted windows a ribbon of illuminated squares burning late into this lovely Monday evening.

Ah, he smiled, *no rest for the wicked.*

"Fine work, gentlemen," Raine said, dismissing the view and turning to address Anesini, Cavi, and his crack troop of financiers that made up part of his employ. He closed the giant binder, laid it on the table and nodded, signifying that finally, after countless hours of editing and review, the required paperwork for the UniBanca di Roma acquisition negotiations had passed muster.

The life stories of Imbrialis and UniBanca were now at his fingertips, told in the form of performance projections, historical trend analyses, investment prospecti, security portfolios, debt agreements, glossy annual reports, interim financials, press releases, board meeting minutes, key man rosters, policy reference guides, and various other bits of miscellaneous corporate minutiae. In mergers and acquisitions, nothing spelled success like the mastery of the details.

Perfectly prepared information was the currency of confidence, and Raine knew how to spend to his advantage. In a show of grand hospitality, each person expected at the negotiation table - specifically him, Anesini, the seven-member Imbrialis field team, and then the entire senior management roster and Board of Directors for UniBanca - would receive a complete set of these reference documents. And they'd receive them in two different languages, English and Italian, just to ensure every attendee's comfort during the weeks of meetings to come. Furthermore, he'd had Anesini deploy a custom fleet of iPads fully loaded with soft copies of every scrap of the information he'd prepared - perfect for financiers on the go. Throw in thirty pairs of VIP season tickets for the UniBanca CEO's favorite soccer team - A.C. Milan, of course, for the native of Sesto San Giovanni - and Imbrialis was in a fine position to make a lasting impression.

"Very nice work, indeed," Raine said, surveying the landscape of binders and iPad boxes spanning the entire length of the boardroom table. "And you've arranged to have everything shipped overnight to UniBanca for receipt tomorrow?"

"Everything's all set, Raine," Anesini confirmed. "The courier should be here within the next half hour to take delivery and get it to Rome in plenty of time."

"Good," he nodded. "Gentlemen, you're dismissed. Feel free to take the rest of the week off; you've earned it over these past three weeks. However," he cautioned, "do remember you're on call 24/7 while I'm in the field over the next months; I'm sure I'll need the occasional addendum and clarification clause."

And the very tired, yet very grateful, M&A subcommittee wished him luck before making a break for their well-earned freedom.

"Anesini, Cavi, a word." Raine motioned to his black-hat and consigliere as the room emptied, indicating the seats across from him at the table. While they took their chairs, he rose to the sidebar and poured out three rocks glasses of The Dalmore, bringing one to each of them before resuming his seat before them.

With a wry grin, the boss seemed to settle on a toast, and he tipped his glass in salute in their direction. "To one hell of a fucking week."

"Quite," Anesini chuckled, and Cavi laughed at the understatement.

Raine took a long draught of his eighteen-year Scotch and regarded them with a look of complete seriousness. "I wanted to take a moment to thank you, both of you, for your flexibility in light of... recent events. It's been one thing after another with our new alliances vis-à-vis Kane, the UniBanca deal, and the mole issue, and your professionalism in the face of unforeseen complications has not gone unappreciated."

His underbosses nodded in respect, gracefully accepting his thanks. They knew damn well what he meant by "unforeseen complications," and they waited on the edge of their seats, hoping he'd further address this wholly intriguing development within their organization.

Raine obliged. "On top of everything else, securing our newest recruit brought us into uncharted territory, and I especially wished to express my gratitude for your expert arrangement of last night's impromptu reconnaissance mission."

Cavi and Anesini nodded again. As soon as his jet had touched down in New York yesterday afternoon, Raine had set them to work on a special assignment, namely securing a suitable stake out location for Solana Trent's apartment. He'd given the express order that she was to be under constant surveillance ASAFP, and his reason had been twofold.

One, he'd needed to ensure she made no attempt to flee the City, possessed as she was of syndicate secrets. It was her first night on her own after he'd delivered her safely back into her world as promised, and while he was willing to lay odds that she would follow through on their agreement, he simply couldn't leave it to chance. If she failed her first critical test, it wouldn't be long before she took her last living breath.

Two, he'd needed to ensure her safety, because the second she'd accepted his proposal she'd become a target. If word of their imminent marriage fell into the wrong hands, Raine Mathison's intended bride would ransom a very pretty penny for someone crazy enough to cross him.

His agreement with Solana rested on mutual protection, and if there was ever to be a bond of trust between them, he absolutely could not risk failure from the getgo.

Within hours of his order, his two extremely talented underbosses had - somehow - managed to come up with a vacant apartment in the building across the street from hers, directly opposite her windows. From there, Anesini arranged a secure hack into her building's cameras, then mounted an array of flat screen monitors on the wall to display the feed, providing them with clear views of her apartment door, each of the stairwells, both entrances of her building, and the parking garage.

Meanwhile, Cavi had planted a permanent tracking device in the trunk of her Audi, and installed a motion sensor detector the size and shape of a straight pin on the floor outside her apartment door. Meaning if her R8 ever left the garage, they'd have a continuous live GPS feed of her location, and upon anyone entering or leaving her apartment, the detector would send out an audible alert through the speakers in the wall-mounted LCDs.

In short, the girl wouldn't get out - and, more importantly, the outside world wouldn't get in - without them knowing about it first.

Once all systems were go, Raine had handled the surveillance personally, unwilling to delegate the task of standing watch over her. All night long, Anesini and Cavi took turns serving as liaison between Imbrialis's CEO and his M&A team immersed in UniBanca, swapping their questions and discussion points for him with their next set of red-penned revisions as part of his critical review.

They were able to complete the whole panoply of acquisition materials in this manner. By the time they were done, all Raine required was the final examination of the finished package after his team assembled the full roster of polished documents during his very busy day.

Throughout the burning of the midnight oil, there hadn't been so much as a whisper of activity from the journalist's quarters. The lights of her apartment had gone out around 2:00 a.m., and the hot summer evening slumbered on thankfully without incident. Dawn had arrived to find all three of them standing at the window, enjoying potent espressos after a long night's worth of successful work, and they stopped in mid-discussion of the day's marching orders when the motion detector sounded its little alarm.

Cavi and Anesini wouldn't forget the look on their boss's face when he saw Solana Trent leave her building for work that morning. She'd been a breathtaking vision in sexy, figure-flattering black, walking with a purpose so intense it made the curls of her hair bounce in time with the smart strident strike of her tall heels. Watching him watch her, there was a reverent pride and an amused softness in his demeanor that neither one of them had ever seen before.

"She doesn't exactly look the part of the blushing bride, *Padrino*," Anesini had observed.

"She looks pretty pissed, Raine," Cavi had added. "If she could punch a hole through the pavement with her shoes, I think she'd do it."

He'd only glanced at them before returning his attention to the woman who'd be his wife in a matter of hours.

"She's scared of what she's about to do today," Raine had said. "She of all people knows exactly what she's getting into after spending her life trying to bring it down.

"But," and he'd smiled here, letting the appreciation he felt for her show plainly, "she's not scared enough to resist giving me her own subtle 'fuck you.' Look. She's picked an outfit that's about as antithetical to a white dress as humanly possible."

Far below them, the subject of their scrutiny suddenly halted in midstride. She turned to look behind her, slowly, cautiously, and then stood perfectly still as she observed the crowded path she'd just taken. With New Yorkers bustling past her on the busy Monday morning sidewalk, she didn't have the look of someone who'd forgotten something back in her apartment. It was more like she was waiting, watching, expecting someone to appear.

A long moment passed.

"What's she looking for?" Anesini had mused aloud.

Keeping his eyes trained on his girl in black, Raine's admiration seemed to intensify. "Us," he'd replied proudly. "She's looking for us, for the eyes she can feel on the back of her head. You can bet on it. Just watch."

Finding nothing behind her, she'd then turned her pretty head to survey the teeming concrete corridor ahead of her, but she came up empty there, too. When she'd turned her attention across the street, however, her shoulders straightened at once.

Something had crossed her radar.

"Are you fucking kidding me?" Cavi breathed, watching her keen gaze scan up the side of their building. He and Anesini stood there in disbelief as her eyes climbed higher, closer - she was actually going to find them.

"Shit!" Anesini whispered.

"Stand your ground, gentlemen," Raine advised in the second before she'd spotted them. "She won't recognize us from this distance, but any movement on our part is an admission of guilt."

She found her target at last, and from a distance of

nearly two dozen stories, she stared them down. While it was true she couldn't identify them, she made it abundantly clear that she'd found them out, and she wanted them to know it.

For seconds that seemed to last hours, neither party moved, deadlocked. Finally, the girl inclined her head, whirled on her heel in a swirl of auburn curls and stomped off just as purposefully as before, if not more so.

Cavi had smiled wickedly in Raine's direction. "Firebrand, hmm?"

"Let's just say you'll have your hands full while I'm gone, Cavi," he'd said with an equally wicked grin. "Better get some rest now, both of you, while you can."

They'd parted ways then to rest and recoup before their jam-packed day kicked into high gear. Each event and appointment that followed went according to plan, down to the last detail, much to the credit of his underbosses' indispensable ability to execute his orders - express and implied - perfectly.

Now, many long hours later, Raine wanted to further debrief his men on the next phase of what Anesini had affectionately come to call *Operazione Sposa*. First and foremost, though, he had to give credit where it was due.

"I realize it wasn't the evening either one of you had scheduled," he acknowledged, "but the amount of work we accomplished last night paid off handsomely today, and for that I thank you."

Anesini took a long sip of his Scotch. "I thought it was a pretty quiet night, Raine," he smiled. "And I have to say, I honestly expected more from your bachelor party."

Raine returned his blackhat's grin. "I'll make sure to spice up the derivative analyses for you next time."

"Throw in a few blondes for me and it's a plan. But I

suppose such debauchery will have to wait until we're back from Rome."

"Which may be longer than we think," Raine advised. "I'm getting the impression UniBanca will be a tougher nut to crack than I'd anticipated - they've got a strong balance sheet, a solid suite of products, and shrewd leaders who are very proud of what they've accomplished. They probably don't realize they're growing faster than they can handle, so they may not be willing to sell us the majority shareholder position just yet. I'd like to avoid a hostile takeover in this particular instance, but that depends entirely on them and how they receive our proposal."

"Your proposals," Cavi said pointedly, "seem to be well-received of late."

"They have, Cavi," Raine concurred, "and I'll be entrusting our stateside interests to you for the duration of our absence. I've devised a plan which will simultaneously enable you to keep Kane under Imbrialis's banner, while perfecting Ms. Trent's conscription into the syndicate."

And for the next several minutes, Raine gave his second the details.

When the boss finished, Cavi sat silent a moment. "That's one hell of an undertaking for her."

Anesini agreed. "But she's passed every other test with flying colors. If she's as sharp as Raine says she is, I'd expect nothing less on this next."

Raine nodded. "Cavi, you will be her advisor during this project. She'll need you to show her the ropes, get her access to our strongholds, introduce her to everyone on staff - from the MBAs at Imbrialis to the greenest soldier on the syndicate roster. When presented, she can identify herself as our newest recruit, but her official status must be kept in the strictest confidence - for her protection and for ours. Which brings me to my next question: How long do we have that apartment across the street from hers?"

Cavi saw where the boss was going with this. "As luck would have it, indefinitely. I can be moved in by tomorrow afternoon."

"Excellent. Since you will be tasked with protecting her at all times, the recon spot you secured last night will continue to serve perfectly well for the same purpose. Of course, in thanks for your flexibility, please avail yourself to whatever resources you need to appoint the apartment to your liking."

"My pleasure, Raine," he said gracefully. "While we're on the topic of resources, I'll also apprise the accountants so they can research her finances and settle any outstanding debts she has."

Raine nodded. "One last thing - and you can consider it a gift from me. I want her trained in firearms and ballistics, and for Chrissake, get the girl a gun."

"Oh yes," Cavi's face brightened in delight. "Let's hope she shoots as well as she drives."

"If she does," Raine couldn't suppress a smile, "you're in for a treat. Now, any questions?"

The two men across the table looked at each other before turning back to him.

"No, *Padrino*," Anesini said. "We're straight here."

"Good," Raine stood from his chair. "Then unless it's urgent, we are not to be disturbed."

Cavi gave him a quizzical look. "We?"

Raine flashed a roguish grin. "Now that this long day is finished, I'm going home to bed my wife."

❧ ❧ ❧

11:02 P.M.

Frustrated, Solana took the fiction novel she was pointlessly attempting to read and threw it across the room, pages flapping wildly before her missile hit the wall with a cathartic smack.

I will see you, he'd said.

She'd taken that as an earnest promise this afternoon, not a lame goodbye.

Raine left for Rome in the morning, presumably for months while he worked this Italian bank job. Would he really just take off without so much as a word to her?

Really?

Sitting crosslegged in the center of her sumptuous queen bed, Solana leaned back on her palms and glared at the paperback lying facedown in a crumpled heap across the floor. She'd thrown it just to hear the violent noise her impetuous action would make - anything to break the thick, pressing silence that suffocated her.

She surveyed her bedroom, a haven of peace hued in rich creams, earthy tans, sultry golds; textured by sturdy cotton, plush down, and smooth sateen; accented with lavish throw pillows, aromatic candles, and flourishing plants. Normally the room would weave her in its tapestry of opulent comfort, but now her retreat felt mockingly vacant.

Solana thought back to last night, when she'd first sensed the stirrings of this foreign emotion. How she'd been somewhat alarmed to find it still lingering this morning, when she'd woken up in an empty bed. But by now, tonight, the feeling was intensifying dramatically - and worsening with each passing hour.

It irritated her that she felt so bothered by his absence. This marriage was a business deal, no more.

But while she understood that fact, there was also that binding magnetism between them, resonating with a power she couldn't deny. Could he? Was it so easy for him to just move on to the next thing?

Evidently, Solana scowled. After everything they'd shared over the weekend, this vacuum of contact only underscored her initial suspicion that she meant nothing more to him than a pretty piece of property. She'd tied herself to him, irrevocably, and now he was off to Italy without giving her any concrete details about his plans for her within the syndicate.

She supposedly held the new office of propagandist. But what exactly did that mean? What was she expected to do? Just sit by and wait until some article he'd written showed up in her mailbox, then submit it to press like it was her own work?

It couldn't be that easy. There had to be some kind of recruitment test, an introductory hazing ritual that simply must occur at this juncture.

And she'd have to do it without him. Because this was it. This was his last night in the City for the foreseeable future.

Which was another facet to her unease.

This wasn't just his last night in New York. This was their wedding night. After a very private ring ceremony that had left them both glowing with a mutual tenderness they hadn't thought possible.

It wouldn't fit Raine's character to leave something so important... *unconsummated.*

She took a deep breath as nervous butterflies flit about her stomach.

He would come for her. She knew it. The question was, would she get the ruthless mobster, or –

The soft knock on her front door shattered the silence like a thunderclap, and Solana's head snapped toward the sound, her heart thumping in her chest.

He's here, she told her reflection. With her bedroom door closed, her eyes had fallen on the mirror mounted there, and she found a beautiful, confident woman staring back at her, with sunkissed skin and a thick mane of flaming auburn hair still slightly damp from her evening bath. She sat like an Indian princess atop an elegantly made bed with her legs crossed in lotus, leaning back on the heels of her hands, palms flat on the sinfully soft white duvet cover. She wore a floor-length, semi-fitted nightgown of whisper-thin gossamer silk, the light champagne color just translucent enough to show off the shape of her lissome body. It dropped very low in the back, with the thinnest spaghetti straps tracing the lines of her shoulders, then cut a deep V in the front, the tips of her nipples rising against the tease of the smooth material as it moved with her breathing. Her eyes glittered with a radiance that rivaled the palest peridot, and her cheeks were flushed a becoming pink on account of the summer night's heat.

She nodded in approval, and then the striking woman in the mirror was gone as Solana leapt from the bed.

She left the warmth of her bedroom and plunged into the cooler darkness of her apartment, and she paused to tug the chain on a table lamp before approaching the door. The quiet knock came again as she reached it –

And the sound gave her pause.

Slowing, Solana placed her hand flat against the door, resting her forehead down beside it while she mastered her breathing and her wits.

Wait a second. He was actually knocking on her door this time rather than sneaking his way in. That was certainly different from his usual M.O. He'd always appeared like a ghost out of the shadows, but not tonight. Why –

Respect.

She instantaneously recognized this chivalrous gesture as the significant show of respect he intended it to be. She was his wife, insomuch as she was a partner in a business arrangement they'd crafted to protect each other. Other than that, there were no rules of engagement - he'd never expressly stated that her body was part of the deal. She knew better than to think he'd let her have anyone else in her life, but she realized with perfect clarity that she could refuse him tonight if she wanted.

Her heart faltered. He *did* care what she thought of him. He needed to know, just as much as she did, what exactly was happening between them, and there was only one way to find out.

Solana lifted her head, took a steadying breath, and opened the door.

Raine stood there on the other side of her threshold, tall, suave, and handsome in that made-to-measure Pierre power suit, and when their eyes met she found the same warmth, the same angst, the same longing that she felt mirrored in the clear sharpness of his piercing blue gaze.

"Ms. Trent," he said reverently, bowing to her, and the sound of his rich baritone sent shivers along her limbs.

"Mr. Mathison," she managed, her unused voice taking on a sultry, gravelly tone as she pulled the door open wider for him to pass through. He straightened and stepped into her apartment, close enough to her that the smooth, rich fabric of his suit brushed her bare arm - and their eyes locked.

That touch was all it took. A breathless heartbeat passed as they watched the false pretense of aloof ambivalence they had both prepared themselves to affect for this meeting come crashing to the ground, laid waste by the firestorm of naked longing that raged just beneath the surface. After two days apart, that barest touch lit a match that ignited the banked coals of their smoldering desire, and he stepped closer to her, closing the gap between them as she lifted her face to take his life-altering kiss.

Solana pushed the door closed by feel and Raine swiftly moved them up against it, pressing her back into the hard wood without so much as a caesura in their kiss. She felt his hand searching out the locks beside her head, and when he found them he deftly pulled, twisted, and slid each one into place, not so much to lock them in, but to close the rest of the world *out*. This was their time, the last time, and damned if anything should jeopardize it.

Pulse pounding, Solana loosened the buttons of his double-breasted suit and felt her way up to his shoulders, ready to push the tailored jacket down his arms.

But then Raine took hold of her wrists to still them, to stop her, and hurt stabbed her in the heart as he broke the kiss and pulled back from her.

"Why?" she asked, unable to read his downcast eyes. She could only watch in growing confusion as he reached behind the neatly folded pocket square of his jacket, and she blinked when he withdrew, of all things, a flower.

A pristine, short-stemmed white rose, one day shy of full bloom, bursting with sweet, delicate fragrance.

Raine lifted his intense eyes to hers. "A rose for the bride," he murmured, and he carefully slipped the flower into her hair, tucking the dethorned stem along the curve of her ear. She looked up at him with lips parted in surprise, completely at a loss for words, and he smiled before he caught those soft, full lips in another binding kiss. Her mouth opened to his, eager for him, and their tongues rolled, played, and teased, bringing the burn of desire to a critical state of unbearable.

Solana reached her hands again to his broad shoulders, and this time Raine shrugged out of the custom cut jacket, catching it behind him and throwing it aside. She started untucking his shirt while he began undoing the buttons, and soon the smooth cotton broadcloth was also sliding down his toned arms and tossed to the floor.

Freed, Raine brought the palms of his hands flat against the door beside her head and deepened their kiss even further, and Solana could feel the heat radiating from the flat, muscled planes of his bared chest and abs. The need to touch him was primal, and she let her fingers explore his strong shoulders, trace the defined cuts of his biceps and forearms, play with the Bulova bracelet at his wrist, then travel back up his arms and over his shoulders to his beautiful, chiseled back. She kneaded the muscles there with her fingertips, following down the valley of his spine, until she reached the waistband of his pants.

Carefully she drew her fingers along his trim waistline until her hands found his belt buckle, and she deftly loosened it... unbuttoned his pants... dropped the zipper. She put her hands on his waist and pushed his pants downward, but given his wide stance they didn't move much past his hips. Undaunted, she smoothly swept her palms to his rear, shoved the fine fabric of his pants down a little farther, until they snagged again at the tops of his powerful quads. That was all she'd get for now, but it was good enough for her purposes as she brought her hands to the inside of his bared thighs and slowly drew them upward.

Raine inhaled sharply through his nose when she touched the solid, thick mast of his cock standing tall against his body. His mouth plundered hers with deeper desperation as she gently stroked the length of him, traced the sensitive edge of his head, played soft circles around the tip. He moaned against her lips, passion mounting, and she relished the feeling of control over him. She was enthralled by it, and she decided she wanted more.

Moving with graceful, catlike swiftness she grabbed his hips and dropped to her knees before him. "I want these gone," she ordered as she yanked his pants down his legs, and the sound he made when she took him into her mouth made her insides clench.

She stripped him of his remaining clothing while she let the length of him run along her tongue, and she heard the door rock on its hinges as he pressed his palms harder against the wood at her back. "Oh Solana, *yes*," he hissed, and his raw need made her bolder, driving her to take as much of him as she could. With skilled delicacy, she pulled back until she caressed only the very tip of him with her tongue, flicked it along the head of him, teasing him a delicious moment before taking him deep again.

"Holy *fuck*," Raine groaned, and Solana heard him pound his fist into the wood of her door. She let her eyes travel up the length of his body that suddenly glistened with a sheen of sweat, taking in the view of his loins... his washboard abs... his chest...

Then she saw his face as he stared down at her, and her heart nearly stopped. His eyes were molten pools of white-hot blue steel that watched every single motion she made, and she closed her eyes against the intensity of it, the corners of her mouth curving in a smile as she continued to blow his mind.

"God, Solana, you just don't understand," Raine cried through clenched teeth. "Just watching you do this is enough to make me come."

"Mmmm," she hummed in pleasure at the thought, and he gasped at the sensation that thrilled through him. She sucked him slowly, deliberately, feeling his muscles tighten beneath her palms resting on his thick thighs, and she teased him mercilessly, thoroughly enraptured by the power she wielded over him.

Solana felt him make a slight shift in his stance, and in the next second his hands came down to touch her hair with a gentleness that moved her. He ran his fingers through her heavy auburn tresses... gathered them in a loose bunch... lifted them off her neck for a moment before letting the magnificent mane tumble down her body. Then the backs of his fingers made soft contact with her cheeks, stroking them and caressing them in wordless gratitude for her exquisite ministrations, and she opened her eyes again to meet his. He was burning, his entire body rigid to the point of shattering, but he reverently cupped the muscles of her jawline, barely touching her, letting her continue to torture him as she wished.

And oh, did she wish.

Solana started to take him faster, and his muscles strained impossibly harder, approaching the breaking point in his primal need for release. She kept her gaze fixed on him, watching him, waiting, and then she saw him reach the point of surrender. She'd won. His face was a perfect study in abject torment as he let his guard down, succumbing to her, and he touched his hands to her jaws, praying she would finally liberate him from the hell she'd wrought upon him.

"Please, Solana," Raine whispered, baring the pain of

his longing need for her, and it touched her to the core. Here he stood before her, his palms softly holding her face, begging her to bring him, and her heart exploded. Flooding with joyful warmth and accomplished pride, she happily gave him his freedom, taking him with an intensity that brought him within seconds.

Raine threw his head back and belted out her name, crushing her curls in his clenched fists as he flowed thick and rich into her mouth. Solana's heart fluttered like the wings of a hummingbird as she drank him, and the ice fire of adrenaline racing through her veins made her tremble on her knees before him. Delighting in his pleasure, she drew every drop from him, taking everything he had to give before releasing him at last from her lips. She sat down on her heels, letting her hands run down the backs of his thighs and calves, and she had just enough time to lean back before he collapsed down on one knee, framing her body between his suddenly unsteady legs.

Solana lifted her face up to his, which was now only inches above hers where he knelt over her, and she found herself looking into the grateful face of a devilish angel. His eyes sparkled with marveled affection and respect, his lips curving in a sexy, languid smile that made her warm down to her toes. She returned his grin with one of her own, and Raine gently pulled her head back by her hair and kissed her with a completeness that left no room for doubt as to how thoroughly pleased he was with her.

"Thank you, my beautiful wife," he murmured with heartfelt sincerity against her lips.

"My pleasure," she whispered back.

"It is," he confirmed, and this time his smile outwatted hers. "Because it's your turn, my dear, and payback's a bitch."

"Oh no." Solana paled in excitement and dread. "No!"

Laughing deep in his throat, Raine grabbed hold of her hips and pulled her to him so swiftly she had to throw her arms around his neck for balance. He rose from his knee on the floor as if she weighed nothing in his arms, then stood her at arm's length from him so he could survey her luscious body wrapped in sheer champagne silk.

The pale, diaphanous material barely kept the secret of that perfect hourglass figure, one capable of making artists and sculptors weep to behold. But Raine was ready to see the rest of her, and all he had to do was bring his hands to her shoulders, place his fingertips beside the capellini straps and gently flick them outward, and the ethereal gown flowed in a swift, silent river to the floor at her feet.

Despite the night's heat, goosebumps raised all over Solana's bared flesh as the smooth silk raced softly down her body, and Raine chased the chill away, running his hot hands down her arms to warm her. He circled her wrists with his fingers, drew them around his neck, then slid his hands along her sides and onward to her hips. He cupped her delicious rear for a priceless second before he seized the backs of her thighs and lifted her up to him, spreading her legs and wrapping them around his waist. She buried her face in his neck to nuzzle him with her lips and tongue, sending electric tingles shooting along every nerve of his body, and he could feel her hot, moist core burning against his abs as he carried her through the apartment to her bedroom.

Solana paused in her delicious assault on his earlobe. "How do you know where the bedroom is?" she asked, her voice dark and low in his ear. "Lucky guess?"

Raine almost felt guilty. "Because I've been here before," he admitted solemnly, remembering his search of her apartment on that fateful day she'd fallen into his hands. But she still wasn't privy to that little detail, so when she lifted her head from his neck to give him a quizzical look, he knew he couldn't preempt her question.

"Before Philadelphia?" she guessed.

Preparing himself for her reaction, he nodded.

But she only flashed him a sly, sexy smile. "I know," she told him. "I just wanted to see if you'd admit it."

"You're making my revenge that much sweeter," he warned, but he couldn't stop his own smile. "Besides, even if I hadn't been here before, I'd know where to go. Your bedroom is the only other light on in the whole place, Solana. It's like a beacon guiding me home."

And she bit her lip shyly as he closed the door to her bedroom and locked them in again, creating a sanctuary for a man and his most definitely blushing bride.

Raine shoved the throw pillows from the bed, tore the duvet and sheet back in one strong rip, and set her down gently in the center of the wide white expanse. She wore only her wedding rings, and he stood at the edge of the bed, one knee perched on it, letting his eyes rove the beauty of her divine body on display before him.

Solana watched him watch her, knew he was cataloguing the list of sweet torments he'd exact upon her, and the air in the room became something solid. It pressed upon her chest like a lead weight, and she couldn't get enough oxygen to support her rapidly quickening breath. Her fingers itched to grab the sheet and wrap it around her, anything to stop his intense scrutiny that simultaneously pleased and frightened her.

Raine saw it, the infinitesimal motion of her hand sliding in the direction of the discarded covers, and instantly his hand covered hers.

"No, Solana," he said quietly, the bass of his voice clothing her in a protective reverence that eradicated all traces of her fear. "Let me see you. I need to remember every inch of you to keep me warm in Italy this winter."

Solana was speechless, staring into the depths of clear, fathomless blue eyes that promised her safety and understanding borne on the foundation of deep-seated respect. Respect for a worthy adversary met and conquered, for a woman who matched him in passion, ambition, and skill, for a future they could build together for themselves and for the syndicate if she just trusted him.

Rapt, she could only nod, and he squeezed her hand as he came to join her on the bed, as his lips captured hers in a soul-binding kiss, this last just as powerful as their very first.

"Now lie down, *cara mia*," Raine said, and his tone teased just this side of wicked. "I vowed retribution, and I still fully intend to take it."

He touched every inch of her body, his hands traversing irresistibly soft skin over firm, young muscles that flexed and strained under his discovery. He started with her hair, letting thick tresses of brown, gold, and red twist around his fingers and forearms. Then he stroked her face, her earlobes, her throat, his fingertip drawing a heart in the hollow there before moving on to her shoulders.

He caressed her breasts next, taking his time, bringing her nipples to pinpoints taut with unmitigated need, and he smiled in delight as she moaned and writhed for him. Brushing her ribs, he danced his fingers across the flat plain of her sensitive belly, squeezed her ample hips, and he thoroughly enjoyed her sharp intake of breath when he let only the barest tip of his finger trace along her loins, bypassing her core and heading straight for her thighs.

Raine knew Solana burned for him, wanted nothing more than for him to run his fingers along the heart of her, but he completely ignored it. Instead he moved right on, kneading his hands along her slim, smooth, maddeningly perfect legs that he constantly fantasized about having wrapped around him. Carefully, he touched her feet and then her toes, somehow managing to not tickle them in his complete worship of her physical inventory.

"Turn over, Solana," he ordered softly, and she did as he asked, much to her own delight as his hands began a thorough massage of her neck. He stretched her arms up over her head to rub along her firm biceps and triceps, then her forearms, all the way up to her hands.

And for a moment, Raine took in the vision of their two left hands clasped together, their wedding rings glinting and sparkling like stars in the low light of the room. It was a sight he never thought he'd see, but there it was, and it brought him more peace than he'd felt in years.

Releasing her hands, he continued his massage on the return trip down her arms and over her shoulders, and he stopped to spend several moments on her toned back. He followed his thumbs firmly down the valley of her spine, making her moan, and then he had the distinct pleasure of paying ample attention to her perfect ass. He traversed her legs again, devoting extra time to her shapely calves, and then he finally returned to her feet.

At the touch, Solana breathed a little more deeply. *At last, he's done*, she thought. *He's touched just about every —*

But then she felt his lips make contact with her ankle.

She gasped at the sensation of his hot mouth on her relatively cooler skin, his tongue drawing sensuous circles up her calf, behind her knee, his teeth biting her playfully along the backs of her thighs. She realized then that he fully planned on resurveying every inch of her body, this time with his lips, his tongue, his teeth...

Solana entered the next ring of fiery hell, praying he'd hurry or she'd fucking incinerate. By the time he reached the side of her neck, the curls of his hair tickling her earlobes and cheeks, she'd been reduced to a trembling mass of need that could only understand one word - *please*.

"Lie on your back," Raine murmured in her ear, and he smiled in pride at the searing look she gave him when she faced him once again. He brushed his lips over hers in just the slightest trace of a kiss before continuing his oral survey, moving along her chin, traveling down her throat, pausing over her pounding heart. She cried out sharply when he took the tip of one of her full breasts in his mouth, and he gently licked, sucked, and played with her mercilessly, just like she'd teased him not so long before. He kissed a line of burning warmth down her flat belly, her hips, again ignoring her center and passing straight on to the tops of her thighs –

Solana gave a lung-splitting gasp when he spread her legs with impossible swiftness and brought his lips to the inside of her knee. Her insides solidified into a hardened knot of painful, all-encompassing, mind-melting lust, and she thought her heart would stop beating as his teeth nipped all the way up her inner thigh, coming closer, closer, oh God, closer...

"Oh Christ, Raine, please," she whispered, trembling in anticipation. "Please release me. You have to, Raine, *please...*"

"Not yet, Solana," he returned, and her back lifted clear off the bed as his mouth came in contact with the heart of her. His tongue caressed the perfect pearl folded deep inside her, while he let a finger quest softly into her well of scorching wetness beyond, and the scream she let loose made every hair on his body stand on end. She couldn't take much more. She rocked her hips against him and he held her back, giving only what he wanted her to have, and the sounds she made drove him nearly berserk with the wanting of her. The drive to devour her bordered on manic, but he had to wait until he had her exactly where he wanted her. He needed her ready to receive him, and he kept restraining her until he heard her forsaken cry of absolute frustration.

Just when Solana thought she would combust under his conquering mouth and coaxing fingers, Raine rose up onto his knees between her legs and she lifted blistering eyes to his confident, *come hither* stare. His magnificent body poised over hers, like a proud lion about to pounce on his defenseless kill, and he was so hard and so long he was practically touching his navel. He placed his hands on her knees and pressed outward, flattening her legs against the mattress as he ran his hands along her thighs, opening her up to him. He gripped her waist, lowered himself over her, and when he kissed her Solana could taste herself on him, wet, clear, and salty, like fresh ocean water.

She opened her mouth to his just as she opened her body to receive him, and the second Raine touched his engorged tip to her slick, shivering core, she instinctively rammed her hips up to his, trying to force his entry.

"*Wait,*" Raine growled, tightening his viselike grip on her waist as it was the only thing stopping her from taking him from beneath.

"Raine, please," she sobbed.

"Wait," he said again, more gently, and he rolled their bodies in slow, erotic rhythm, showing her how to take it from him this time.

"Slow, Solana, slow," he whispered, and once she learned it, once she understood, he pulled his hips back and filled her in one crushing blow.

It was cataclysmic, his rock-hard thickness fighting its way to the hilt of her wetness that was so tight, so fucking tight, they both broke the kiss in a gasping cry of pleasure. He held them there for a second, savoring that first moment of being perfectly joined, before he began to lead them in the most mindblowing experience of their lives.

Raine took her slowly, maddeningly, heartwrenchingly slowly. He drew himself out, just the tip of him remaining in her hot softness, before he resheathed himself to the limit of her body, reaching for the very center of her. He wanted to make every delicious second of this last, and Solana took his lead, rolling her hips against his in a slow, seductive undulation that left him breathless.

"Lesson One," she breathed with a shy smile, and he thought he'd melt.

Patience, he'd said on that first night together. *In all things. The power to keep at bay the slow burn for what you want. For what is yours.*

"Well remembered, *carissima,*" he said, eyes glittering as he gave her hips a roguish squeeze. He moved his hands to hers and lifted them up over her head, interlacing their fingers before burying them into the plush mattress. She gripped him hard, their wedding rings biting into the bones of their fingers as they used their joined hands for leverage, letting their loins meet in a patient, torturous rhythm that was the epitome of excruciating. They moved in a tacit pact to rein each other in, depriving themselves of their basic urge to finish it with a brutal, frenzied pounding, both of them hellbent on this encounter taking as long as they could stand it.

Gradually their pace increased, their bodies rolling together harder, more demanding, and when Raine felt Solana's core shudder with the telltale stirrings of quickening climax, he bit down and pulled back, forcing himself to slow almost to stopping. She cried out for him, wild, burning from crown to toes for him to come back to her in full force. But he waited, waited for the critical moment to pass, before he started to lead them again through the steps of their delightfully arduous dance. He kept going with his tantalizing torture; he almost brought her again and again, denying her at the last second, until she couldn't breathe past the need holding her prisoner.

Raine pulled one of his hands from hers and ran his palm along her thigh beside his hip, gripping her behind the knee as he butterflied her wider beneath him. He let their slow rhythm gain momentum, their bodies moving together with breathtaking, single-minded precision, and he could feel the explosive climax again gathering within her. She got tighter around him inside her, tighter, primed by the tantric game of seduction he played with her, and he knew the force of it wouldn't be thwarted this time.

He'd brought her to the point of no return.

Solana felt the imminent flood approaching, the sinking feeling deep within her body so intense in its power she nearly convulsed. Raine plunged his thickening shaft into the depths of her, and her fingers gripped him like he was the last solid thing on earth, the only one who could keep her rooted while the impending storm surge threatened to drown her. She fought against the tidal wave of pleasure, sinking her teeth into his shoulder in desperation, wanting to make it last, wanting to come with him –

"Oh God, Raine," she cried, and he heard the urgent catch in her voice, "Raine, I can't hold it – "

"I know, Solana," he whispered with a smile in her ear, and he finally finished it, four hard, blinding thrusts that brought them both screaming together to an orgasm so perfect it was almost painful. The shivering walls of her core crushed around him as he released a torrent deep into the heart of her, claiming her as his, filling her with light and freedom that erased all darkness and doubt.

Solana thought she would die, ripped apart by the force of him, pulled under by the swelling waves of her pleasure, trembling from head to toe with the enormous potency of their passion. Her breathing came in shaking gasps but she didn't care; she turned her face to him and he kissed her, both of them breathing sharply through their noses as they nibbled and tasted each others' lips, the ruthless tsunami of ecstasy continuing to wash over them.

Raine released his grip on her leg at his waist and grabbed hold of her hand again, squeezing it tightly as he collapsed on top of her. He buried his face into her pile of sweet-smelling, sweat-dampened dark curls and let go of the remaining tension in his limbs, his heart pounding directly above hers. Likewise spent, Solana let her legs slacken alongside his, burrowing her head in the hollow of his neck, and inhaled deeply of the sweaty, masculine scent of him, her thumbs tracing his where he held her hands above her head.

They lay there for time immeasurable, bodies still joined, hands clasped, neither one of them able to move a muscle any further. The gentle sound of their heartbeats slowing, the soft rhythm of each other's breathing became hypnotic, drawing them into the depths of a blissful oblivion until they slept together, exhausted by their contract consummated.

CHAPTER NINETEEN

Some time later, Solana woke to moonlight falling brightly on her face.

Her eyelashes fluttered open to find the bedroom a stygian palette of blacks, silvers, greys and midnight blues, dark save for the lunar light streaming in through the open window. Sheer white curtains undulated to the sultry, soporific summer night's breeze that rolled seductively through the room, and for a cloudy, sleep-filled moment she thought she was back on St. John.

She lay nestled in an impossibly soft bed, wrapped in a luxurious cotton sheet, bathed in silvered moonlight, caressed by warm summer wind... but there was no crashing of ocean waves nor any smell of briny sea. Instead, she heard the faint whoosh of a car rushing down the street over twenty floors below, the sound carrying up to her apartment high in the concrete jungle, and her mind clarified, focusing with a sharp brilliance on the present.

She could feel Raine's presence in the bed behind her. For some reason, they weren't touching, but she knew he was there, his skin a furnace of radiating heat that burned her body even from a distance. She didn't hear a thing, couldn't tell if he was sleeping –

"Solana."

She swallowed hard. It was a voice she'd know anywhere now, wouldn't forget as long as she lived. It had spoken her sweetest dreams and her most terrifying nightmares. It had promised absolute protection and unspeakable danger. It had conveyed deep respect and soul-shattering apathy.

Solana lay frozen, unsure whom she would see when she turned to him. If he was that man she'd found on the breakfast nook on St. John, brutal after a night spent in passion, she didn't know if she could handle it. Not again, not after this night, not after everything...

"Solana," he said again, and she slowly rolled over to face him, steeling herself for the worst.

Raine lay next to her on his side, his head propped up on his elbow, the Bulova bracelet winking smartly in the moonlight. He was covered up to his waist in the soft cotton sheet, and his suntanned torso seemed so much darker in contrast to the white bed linens all around them. His dark blond waves looked almost brown in the color-robbing light of the moon, but his eyes sparkled unnaturally lighter, washed silver white instead of the ice blue that normally held her gaze. Despite the eeriness of the color, his eyes showed her exactly what she needed to know - he was not the harsh businessman she'd met the morning after on St. John.

He was a man glad to see his lover awake, because there were things still left unsaid.

Clearly he'd been watching her sleep for some time, and Solana smiled shyly at him.

"Why are you already turning pink?" Raine asked *sotto voce* into the dark, and the cool metal of his wedding band caught the lambent lunar glow as he brought his hand up to stroke her cheek with the backs of his fingers.

"For keeping you waiting," Solana answered, leaning her face into his caressing hand. "I expect we have some business to discuss."

Raine nodded as he pulled his hand away and rested his arm back alongside his body. "We do, unfortunately."

"I'm assuming it's my first assignment?" she said as easily as possible.

"Yes."

She held her breath, drawing on every ounce of resolve she could muster. This was it. The recruitment test, the hazing ritual she'd suspected was coming. "Tell me."

Raine regarded her with a look that told her just how much he admired her. "This is a project that will fully immerse you into the syndicate and Imbrialis," he began, "while also helping us fuel the Kane campaign, which as you know, is crucial to our interests.

"In order to accomplish this task successfully, though, there are rules you must understand absolutely perfectly," he cautioned. "One, for your safety and for ours, you'll introduce yourself to the other soldiers in the syndicate as our newest recruit, but you must not, under any circumstances, reveal your real status in the organization. Yes, they will know you work for the Times, and yes they will know you're on the make, but do not tell anyone about *us*. It will come out in time, but now is most certainly not that time.

"Two, as far as Imbrialis is concerned, I've informed

key members of the staff that you'll be serving on a consulting basis spearheading special events concerning our sponsorship of Kane. That's *all* they know. In the interest of plausible deniability, not every employee at Imbrialis knows what kind of organization he ultimately works for, so everything operates on a need-to-know basis. I'm sure Salvatore made this one abundantly clear when he discussed the Alessandra family history with you, but as a rule of thumb, you never, ever, breathe a word of business to anyone outside the syndicate. *Capisce?*"

At her nod, he studied her intently before he dropped the bomb.

"Your first assignment, Solana," he said, "is a charity ball hosted by Imbrialis in support of Kane's candidacy, and I want the article covering the event on the front page of the Times."

Solana couldn't breathe. "What?"

Raine raised an eyebrow. "I'm making the assumption you've already thrown Donato off the alley murder trail, so I'm expecting he'll have you focus on the Imbrialis-Kane partnership in the hopes of uncovering another scandal vis-à-vis Preston and DiStephano. This is a golden opportunity for you to sell him on a story that will get you closer to the action, and get that story front and center once complete. It's also the perfect chance for us to establish your position in the syndicate, and further promote our interest in Kane's successful election."

It was, she thought, numb with shock, *I have to hand it to him.*

"You won't be doing this without some assistance," Raine continued. "Cavi will be your resource throughout the entire assignment. He's your mentor, for lack of a better term, tasked with providing you anything you need to see this project through to completion. Furthermore, as I mentioned to you earlier today, you can think of Cavi as your personal guard - again, for your protection as well as for ours. Any questions?"

Other than how the fuck I'm going to pull this off? Solana shook her head.

"Bene."

They lay in silence for a moment, energy crackling between them, and Solana could only stare at him in awed respect. Every day it became increasingly evident to her why Loiacono had chosen to leave his organization in this tactical mastermind's hands upon his death. It was probably the smartest choice the boss ever made, despite its controversial nature, because the returns were paying off handsomely.

She thought about that conversation with Donato, millions of years ago in her office, about the syndicate and Raine's unique genealogy. As she'd explained to her editor, Raine was only half Italian, so the leadership of an Italian crime organization could only legitimately pass on to him with the boss's express blessing. It made her wonder how Raine himself had been recruited, what Loiacono had devised in order to make him, and how Raine had earned such respect to take the business over without so much as a peep from the rank and file.

And what was the connection? How would Raine have gotten involved with the mob in the first place? As she'd learned today, he was the son of a Scottish father and an Italian mother...

And she was a Sinagra, based out of Sicily...

And if Solana remembered correctly, Loiacono was also a Sicilian surname –

"Loiacono knew your mother," she mused aloud.

Raine's eyes snapped to hers in surprise, and she saw that they sparkled, glowing that eerie silver white in the moonlight. "You never cease to impress me, Solana."

"I'm right, though, aren't I," she demanded, the boldness of her journalist instincts taking over.

He laughed deeply in the dark. "Yes. The Loiaconos and the Sinagras share a history of friendship as old as the island itself, so our families have known each other for years. My mother put me in touch with Loiacono when I started college at NYU. She'd heard through the grapevine that he needed someone to run his books due to a recent... vacancy, and I'd been handling them for my parents since I was fourteen. Also, she wanted to make sure I was under some kind of familial protection while I was stateside, so calling in a favor via the age-old Loiacono-Sinagra connection was the most logical choice.

"I've been running the financials for the syndicate ever since. I graduated top of my class at the Stern School, rose through the ranks at the M&A firm I joined and ended up taking over, and then founded Imbrialis. As you know, my privately-held corporation specializes in financial institutions and industries heavily dependent upon labor unions: transportation and logistics, real estate, construction, law enforcement. Loiacono took notice; it wasn't long before he put me in charge of his union contract acquisitions, and the business flowing between Imbrialis and the syndicate became the ultimate symbiotic relationship.

"As you also know, Loiacono didn't have any heirs. Ironically enough, he didn't believe in having a family in the family business, so he couldn't pick a legatee by the book either. He wanted someone who could take his organization into the modern era, someone who could run it like a business, so when the time came for him to name a successor, he looked to the one who was making money for everyone hand over fist. By then, I'd certainly earned my stripes in the organization, so no one took umbrage - it just made sense that the honor should fall to me."

Solana nodded. "Your mother must be very proud," she said, unable to resist the cliché.

He smiled softly. "I'd expect so, but I'll never really know for certain."

"Why?"

"She died my senior year at NYU."

"I'm sorry," Solana said, immediately contrite. "What was her name?"

"Natalia."

She let that linger for a moment, gracefully giving a moment of respect for the dead. So his mother was gone and never knew about her son's groundbreaking accomplishments...

"What about your father, then?" she asked. "What did the Scottish gent think of the career path your Italian mother had nudged you into?"

Raine regarded her with a long look, and Solana knew she'd hit sacred ground. She'd inadvertently stumbled on something he'd probably only divulged to a select few, and he was deciding whether he trusted her enough to let her in or if he should shut her out.

He sighed. "It's what broke their marriage."

She blinked at him, stunned.

"You called it today on my interesting childhood, Solana, because Italian temper clashing against Scottish stubbornness truly is a sight to behold," he said ruefully. "Cailean Mathison did not want his son involved in the mob, but his wife could already tell it's where he would make an indelible impact. Da always expected me to return to Sicily to run our small winery, whereas *la mia mamma* knew I was better suited to a trade that ran a richer shade of red."

"Did you know they were fighting about it?"

"No idea," he said. "They agreed that nothing should interfere with my studies, including the battle royale raging back home between them. I didn't know there was a problem until I came home during the summer between sophomore and junior year. And even then, they didn't really tell me on their terms. Despite their best efforts to keep it from me, I could feel the tension in the house the second I walked through the door. At that point they didn't have any choice but to tell me they were getting a divorce."

Solana gasped. Even in this modern era, divorce was still a sin in the Roman Catholic Church and something you just *didn't do* over there.

"Oh yes, I can assure you they were the vanguards in their neighborhood on that one," he said with no small trace of bitterness. "Da kept the winery while *Mamma* moved to Firenze, where she pursued her dream of painting beautiful oils on canvas. She passed a year later, though, so the few pieces I have are what exists of her entire catalogue."

Solana remembered the absorbing painting of the Duomo gracing the wall of his sitting room on St. John and waves of chills swept down her arms. "How did she die, Raine?"

"Ovarian cancer. She was gone inside of three weeks."

Silence hung between them. "Where is your Da now?" she asked.

"Inverness. He sold the winery when she died, went home to Scotland, and hasn't looked back since."

"Because he can't."

"Yes," he said tightly.

"Do you guys talk?"

"No."

He blames you, doesn't he? she thought, but couldn't quite bring herself to say it.

Raine's silvered eyes bored into hers. "Yes, Solana, he does. The last time I saw him was the funeral, and it turns out our *deoch an doruis* really was the parting glass."

"You don't believe that, do you?" she asked softly. "That it was your fault?"

"No," he said with strident finality. "What *does* haunt me is that even if I'd known my vocation was behind their marital strife, I don't think I could have given up the job."

Raine managed a smile despite the regret he'd long since learned to bury. "Working for Loiacono beat the shit out of the work-study gigs my friends were schlepping through. I've never seen a Ramen noodle. None of my cars have ever had anything less than leather seats, panoramic sunroofs, and lethally fast engines. And my God, the girls... The point is, my freshman year in college, I was making double the average household income in America and building inroads into the most exciting job there is. I couldn't have given that up, even if I'd known what it cost my parents. So their divorce remains a demon that I deal with."

A look of naked pain crossed his face, and suddenly Solana was back with him behind the waterfall, in their cave on St. John, after she'd yelled at him for not understanding the loss of her parents, when in fact he absolutely did. The mob had torn his family apart just as surely as it had her own, but while she carried the torch to burn it, he lofted the flame to lead it.

But why? she wondered. Why would his mother want her son in this life so badly that it meant the ruin of her marriage? Why would she send a financial virtuoso with the world as his oyster to *Loiacono* instead of the tycoons ruling Wall Street? Yes, one could make the argument that Raine wielded more power than all of them combined, and the shady tactics they employed often overstepped the fine line of legality anyway. Regardless of whether he was better off in this nefarious position of authority, the point remained, why did it matter so much to her that she let it impact her life to such a devastating degree?

After a moment's debate, Solana pitched the only question that could answer them all.

"Raine," she said, "what aren't you telling me about Natalia Sinagra and Nobile Loiacono?"

Her husband took a deep breath through his nose and let it out very slowly. "Any particular reason you're choosing to use her maiden name to ask that question?"

"Call it a hunch."

Again, Raine resisted the ingrained impetus to put the iron wall up and shut his astute wife down. "I can see why Donato treasures you on his staff," he said, and the edge in his voice could split silk thread.

"It's why you recruited me, isn't it?"

He smiled in spite of himself. "How very strange, to have your own weapon used against you." And with a resigned sigh, he launched into the story he'd told only two other people in his entire life, those two people being Hunter Cavenastri and Gennato Anesini.

"Over the years, many Sicilians have come over from that little island to make their home here on this one. Almost immediately, the missives begin crossing the pond to the friends and family left behind, endless letters and phone calls inviting them to come visit the promised land of America.

"My mother was twenty when several families dear to the Sinagras left for New York, and they'd no sooner settled before the constant barrage began. She received notes and calls weekly from her friends pleading with her to make the move to Manhattan, or begging her to at least just come out for a visit. After months of their cajoling, she gave in, deciding to spend the holiday for which she was named in the City.

"Natalia and Nobile met at a mutual friend's dinner party on Christmas Eve, and to say the connection was instant would be an understatement. To hear people tell it, the meeting beneath the mistletoe between the boss of New York and the songstress of Sicily turned winter to summer in seconds. After they met, no one else in the room existed for them. The raven-haired, black eyed pair made a matched set, and they spent the entire time talking, laughing, drinking, dancing the night away. Long after the party was over, they were still together, taking their non-stop conversation to the streets so they could continue their talk beneath the trees that glowed with the holiday's lights.

"After that night, Nobile called on her daily, without regard to the hour. Painfully aware they were on borrowed time, they spent every moment they possibly could together during her two-week vacation. But as the end of her holiday drew unbearably closer, she suddenly decided to take her friends up on their long-standing offer to move in with them. 'There's so much life to live here in this city,' she'd said, 'and I need more time to experience it!' While her friends were thrilled to have their firebrand back in their fold, it came as no surprise that she'd mysteriously changed her tune about Manhattan. Anyone who'd ever had occasion to see Nobile and Natalia together knew at once that the striking couple were already passionate lovers.

"As Nobile Loiacono's girl, she didn't need to find work to finance her new life. In fact, he'd have preferred it if she didn't. But Natalia Sinagra was fiercely independent, and never one to sit idle. As a uniquely talented singer, she managed to land several regular acts at some of the most sought-after venues in New York. She made quite the name for herself on the stage; her finances flushed to the point that she was paying the rent for her friends in its entirety in thanks for their hospitality. But that kind of success wasn't what she was after.

"She quickly discovered she had a keen mind for business, and she wanted nothing more than to use it. After several months of exposure to Loiacono's dealings, she had enterprising ideas of her own for the syndicate. She wanted to be in the mob, to run it alongside Nobile rather than sit like a pretty thing on his arm or settle for the shadow of the sidelines.

"When she pitched the idea, rumor has it Loiacono actually laughed until he saw the look on her face and realized she was absolutely serious. Needless to say, he flat-out refused. A true dyed-in-the-wool patriarch, his world was a man's world, somewhere his woman would never rank. He put her in her place, beneath him rather than beside him, and the matter was not open to discussion of any kind.

"Natalia went *incazzata nera*, black with rage at the slight. If he was too much of a chauvinist to share the syndicate with her, then she would play the feminist card and refuse to share her life with him. He pulled all the stops, arguing it was too dangerous for her and that she'd never get the respect she deserved, whereas she understood he simply didn't love her enough to let her take some of his limelight. When he rebuffed her, she not only left him, she left New York entirely. The City wasn't big enough for both of them to occupy it and still maintain their own separate circles, and she couldn't stomach seeing him, not anymore.

"So she came home to Messina, looking to put Manhattan as far behind her as possible. Her first morning back, she answered an ad in the paper for a bookkeeper position at a local winery, eager to get her financial brain in the game. She took an instant shining to the work - and to the owner, the laconic, stubborn, handsome Scot running the place by himself. He quickly realized he'd opened his books to a beautiful, ball-busting iconoclast, while she rapidly discovered the man had no head for business whatsoever and "the way it's always been" was a mantra better left to the vines. For three tumultuous months they battled over the numbers, over the grapes, over logistics, but when he finally let her have her way, the financials proved her right."

A warm smile split Raine's face as he recalled one of his parents' favorite anecdotes. "They used to say that by that point, the only other thing left for them to argue about was who fell in love with whom first. They married after those three intense months, and I was born exactly nine months afterward, in June."

Solana returned his grin. "And thus the vintner and his wife named their son after the rain that meant everything to the livelihood they'd cultivated together. When you were older, did they explain your name to you the same way you explained it to me?"

Raine's smile turned impish. "Not the same way, no, but the agricultural allegory, yes."

"Such a lovely story..." Solana sighed. Opposites attracting had worked for the Scot and the Sicilian, creating a marriage right as rain, whereas the matched pair of Nobile and Natalia had gone down in flames.

"So while the Mathisons chase the dream of happily ever after," she wondered, "Loiacono grows more bitter by the day, realizing he made the biggest mistake of his life. Even though he really had no one to blame but himself, *she's* the reason why he never married, why he developed such a virulent wariness of women.

"But then, eighteen years later," she continued, sitting up a little straighter, "she drops in on him out of the clear blue sky. When you decided to attend a school in New York, your mother put a proposal in front of you, didn't she?"

Raine nodded. "Her exact words were, 'I know someone who'll have a job for you, and a good one, but there's a catch.' She had me from the getgo; who can resist something wrought with such dark mystery?"

"The catch being it's all illegitimate business, completely unlike the financials you were used to preparing for her and your father," Solana deduced. "After she gave you all the details of what you'd be walking into and found out you were up to the challenge, she called in a long-overdue favor to Loiacono. She wanted to send her son to the best there is, for a crack at the life she was denied.

"And I bet Loiacono was only too happy to do it," she went on. "Whether his motives rated for good or for ill, he'd refused her a place in his ranks and she'd left him because of it. He'd regretted the decision every day of his life since, and when she called him, the torch he still carried for her burned just as brightly then as it had before. Even if he had grounds to deny her son a place in the business, he wouldn't - he was the link to the woman he lost."

Raine nodded again, his contrite, wistful smile pulling at his lips once again. "He told me, more than once, that I was the son he wished he'd had with her."

His grin broadened as another memory lighted his face. "You know, I'll never forget Loiacono's parting words to me after our very first meeting. 'You may look like your Viking father, kid,' he'd said, 'but you are your mother's child, that's for goddamn certain.'"

"Your Viking father..." Solana mused. "I'm positive he knew exactly who Loiacono was to Natalia and what he'd meant to her. Not only was she sending you into a highly questionable vocation, she was reopening the communication lines to her old flame and placing you in an apprenticeship under his direct protection. Awkward doesn't quite seem to cover it."

"To put it mildly," he agreed. "Her intentions were platonic and purely maternal. As much as your parents sought to deliver you from the underground, my mother fought like hell to get me into it. She knew from firsthand experience the kind of power and influence that could be mine for the taking, and if I wanted that life for myself, she'd be damned if I would be denied access to it after she had been.

"But Da saw it much the way you described, Solana, and that's why the battles raged so bloody back home. He felt disrespected by her steadfast refusal to honor his valid concerns, while she felt he'd called her fidelity to him into question. They'd reached an impasse, and the divorce was a done deal by the time I left again for school in the fall.

"I came back to New York devastated, guilt-ridden, second-guessing everything I'd accomplished. Loiacono knew something was wrong when he picked me up at LaGuardia, and I told him what happened when he asked. While his primary concern was for me, he nearly rear-ended the car in front of him when he found out that his Natalia was a single woman of the world again.

"Thankfully, he managed to talk some sense into me on that ride to Mulberry Street. He made me realize that there was nothing I could have done to save my parents' marriage, and that it really wasn't about me at all. 'If you want reparations for this, Raine,' he'd advised, 'you just keep doing what you're doing. You stay on the path you're taking and you're going to own this fucking island some-day.' He taught me that the best way to make our pain worth the price was to take the opportunity she'd given me and run with it.

"A couple weeks later, though, it was my turn to pick up the pieces for him. Turns out he found my mother in Firenze, and he made the phone call he'd been waiting almost twenty years to make. He asked for her, and she turned him down with a handful of words that ruined him on women for the rest of his life. 'I love my husband, Nobile,' she told him. 'And I always will.' So even though happily ever after wasn't in the cards for my parents, she was always my father's wife, right through to the end."

Solana's heart went out to them all, and as she studied her own husband in the thick silence that followed, she began to realize that Raine might have more riding on this marriage to her than she'd ever expected. At the very least, she now knew she hadn't given him nearly enough credit when she was "considering" his proposal - this had been even harder for him than she'd thought.

And she wondered if that was part of the reason she was expected to keep it under wraps.

"How many people know about your parents, Raine?"

"About as many who know about *yours*, Solana."

She smiled despite herself. "Fair enough."

But regardless, he'd answered her question - the tragic dégringolade in the Mathison household wasn't the reason he was hiding her real status from the organization she now helped preside over.

Solana tried another tack. "Did the other members of the syndicate know you got in because of your Sinagran tie to Loiacono?"

"Interesting question, but no. *I soldati* didn't learn of that until well after I'd made my mark."

She nodded. "And that's why I can't tell anyone about our status," she said, finally understanding his cryptic rule.

"Explain that to me," he pressed.

"You and your tests," she smiled. "It makes perfect sense why the world at large can't know, but as far as the syndicate itself is concerned, I need to earn respect within the ranks on my own merits, just like you did. Telling people my true position would force them to accept me automatically out of deference to you, at the risk of instigating underlying dissension. It could also cause them to dismiss me as a useless figurehead, just talentless *tette e gnocca* with no real value to the organization, Alessandra bloodline be damned. But once I pass this recruitment test of yours and I'm made on my own, then the true nature of our agreement can be disclosed."

Raine flashed his perfectly white teeth in a smile of pure delight. "You, my dear wife, are a fucking genius," he said before taking her hand in his and kissing it lingeringly on the palm.

Solana sucked in her breath at the sensuous touch, her heart beginning to pound as he drew his tongue over his fading bitemarks from that infamous Saturday morning in Philadelphia. It wasn't long before his mouth found hers, before he pulled away the white sheet that separated them and slipped one of his strong, muscled thighs between hers. He pulled her beneath him and took her again, slowly and sweetly, until they came together in another blinding climax that rendered them both speechless.

Exhausted but satiated beyond measure, Solana lay by Raine's side. Her head rested comfortably on his chest while his hand played with the length of her hair, inky black in the moonlit dark, and she sighed in utter contentment. The warm breeze drifted over their entwined bodies, cool to their bare skin glowing with sweat, and sleep began its stealthy descent upon them as they watched the moon sink lower in the sky.

"You know something?" she murmured drowsily, on the verge of oblivion.

"Mmm?"

"You're not the total hardass you're reputed to be."

Slowly, Raine's finger traveled up her arm to her chin, and he lifted her face to his. She'd never forget the look on his face as he replied sweetly, in all earnestness, "A secret I trust you to keep, *carissima*, for the rest of our lives."

CHAPTER TWENTY

7:30 A.M.

This time, it was the sun that woke Solana from the most absorbing sleep of her life.

She stretched like a cat, reveling in the heat of the young day, and reached for Raine.

Only to find empty space.

Solana sat bolt upright in her vacant bed, wrapping the bedsheet tightly around her. A frantic look around confirmed her fear that yes, she was alone in the bedroom, and a sense of loss she hadn't expected to feel gripped her by the soul.

She whirled to check the time, but never saw the clock in lieu of what had been left on her nightstand.

She immediately recognized Raine's long, resolute strokes on the piece of paper lying on the oak table by her bed. And with it, the chunky figaro links of his Bulova bracelet flashed mightily in the morning sunlight, the smooth silky platinum curving a sinuous river beside the delicate rose he'd placed in her hair last night.

Solana felt tears prick the corners of her eyes as she grabbed for the note, and when she read it, one let fall.

> *I hold you as a thing enskied and sainted.*
> *Yours,*
> *R*

Shakespeare's *Measure for Measure*, a play wrought with offers that can't be refused, and the beautiful line was Lucio's to Isabella, a novice in a convent.

Gingerly she picked up his bracelet with reverence, feeling the heft of it in her palm for the first time. It was heavy, masculine, svelte, with an understated power and grace that so clearly reflected the man who wore it. She let the gleaming links drape over her fingers, stretching it to its full length so she could see it in detail. The brushed face of the curved ID bar announced to the world a stately, reserved 'RSM,' and when she flipped it over, she discovered another inscription on the underside of the bar, the part closest to his skin at all times.

Audentis Fortuna iuvat.

"Fortune favors the bold," she whispered. From Virgil's *Aeneid*.

Solana cupped the bracelet in her hand, drawing a deep breath. It was not lost upon her, the significance of this bequest, and she stared at the closing of his note. *Yours.* He'd given her a piece of himself last night, one he rarely shared with anyone, and now he'd given her another piece, a physical one, that was more precious to her than the Tiffany diamond sparkling on her left hand.

She then took up the fragile rose in her palm, now in full bloom, but looking remarkably battered for all their lovemaking last night.

Lovemaking.

The word appeared underscored in Solana's mind, indelible in bold, black, italicized type.

There really was no other word for what they'd shared on their wedding night.

She mentally stared at that l-word that carried so much weight, studying it, trying to find some way to discredit it, to chock it up to Stockholm Syndrome, or relegate it to some dumb, girlish, morning-after infatuation responsible for overdramatizing a uniquely stressful situation.

"No," she said out loud, pushing those suppositions away with a violence that surprised her.

She'd never been one to fall prey to unfounded obsessions in the arena of hopeless romanticism. There *was* something to this. To *them*. She wasn't imagining it - the evidence of it was lying right there in her hot little hands. Trying to ignore it, to deny what it was, would not change anything.

She could feel it stirring. A startling affection for the man who was now her husband.

And she now had proof that he was likewise... *affected.*

Did she dare believe it?

Solana could feel her heart beginning to pound, her breath coming in shallowing gasps.

This is too much right now, she thought swiftly, using her brain to interrupt the train wreck of an incoming panic attack.

Turning back to her nightstand, she caught that long overdue glimpse at her clock to check the time, realized she was late for work, but honestly couldn't give less of a shit. The last thing she needed to do was get to the office. What she needed to get - *right now* - was a grip.

She launched out of bed, found her handbag and dug for her iPhone. She dialed Donato's number and thankfully got voicemail. He'd just have to deal with her taking a personal day; Christ knows she hadn't taken one in two years.

After running herself through a lightning-fast shower, Solana ripped apart her dresser in search of her favorite set of clothes, one that always delivered results and armed her properly for a successful day. Charcoal grey cropped yoga pants with gold designs down the sides of her thighs, and a bright orange, impossibly soft Jois Yoga tank top that cheekily exhorted yogis to "Eat More Chapatis."

She realized it had been almost a week since she'd last gotten on her mat, after years of maintaining her commitment to her Ashtanga practice for at least five days a week. All she needed was ninety minutes of silence in the Mysore room, where the only thing she had to focus on was getting herself into the postures of Primary Series, and her head would clear.

Dressed, she grabbed her car keys to leave, then put them down. It was a great day for a long walk to her studio on Broome Street in SoHo, which would be open to students for guided self-practice for another four hours. If she was too tired after practice, there was always the 6 train from Spring. Or she could come partway back on the R train followed by a leisurely stroll through Central Park...

But hadn't she ridden enough of the R train lately?

"Get thee to the studio," she chastised herself for her lewdness, and she was out the door, the ancient chant of *vande gurunam caranaravinde* already on her lips.

CHAPTER TWENTY ONE

11:45 A.M.

Hunter Cavenastri leaned on the windowsill of his new digs in the Upper East Side, monitoring the streets below for a vivid orange tank top, the sign of Solana Trent coming back from her run.

He'd watched her leave her apartment building just before eight, fully appreciating the beauty of her sexy little body in her sexy little workout clothes. She'd cropped it like it's hot in a pair of skin-tight calf-length leggings, and while he didn't have any idea what a chapati was, he'd sure as fuck eat hers given the opportunity.

Unfortunately, though, he'd been deprived of the luxury of studying her any longer. She'd taken off at a sprint, like the devil himself was chasing her, and he knew exactly what she'd been running from.

He'd met with the devil this morning, too, just before his jet lifted off for Italy around 6:00 a.m.

Raine Sinagra Mathison, CEO of Imbrialis Acquisitions, boss of the front-running Mafia family in New York

City, head of the most powerful organized crime organization in the country, was glowing.

He was fucking *glowing*.

Like a schoolkid who'd landed his dream date for the prom, or a homeless schmuck who'd won the State Lotto.

But so much better than that, Cavi grinned.

Like a man who'd found his counterpart in a world where he'd never expected to find it, who'd filled a void in his life he'd never even realized was there.

Who was so dangerously close to falling in love that he'd do anything to protect his *inamorata*, but prudent enough - and *proud* enough - to never, ever tell her so.

It was perfect for his plan. Absolutely goddamn perfect.

"Well, good morning, sir," Cavi had said with a laughing smile.

"Good morning indeed, Cavi," Raine had replied with equal warmth.

"You seem... quite pleased with the events of the evening; I take it everything went well?"

Raine was almost sheepish. "I've come to realize just how lucky I really am, Cavi."

Cavi couldn't keep the shock off his face. He and Raine had always enjoyed a relationship of open candor, but this exceeded all precedent.

"You're all set to move in across the street from her apartment?" the boss inquired.

"Yes, that's being arranged as we speak."

"Good. She knows you'll be guarding her and assisting her with this project that I've assigned her, but she isn't yet privy to your location. You can disclose that to her at your discretion; the decision to keep it to yourself or let her know about it both have their strategic advantages."

"Understood. Anything else I need to know?"

Raine shook his head. "I don't foresee any compliance issues with her, so your biggest challenge will be keeping her protected. While I don't think our situation has existed long enough for our enemies to catch wind of it, once the certificate was filed yesterday in the Clerk's office, anything is possible. Even with the most clever misfilings, truth will out eventually; the question is when."

Cavi nodded.

But the beautifully ironic part of the whole thing was that DiStephano, Raine's nemesis, already knew.

After all, he and Cavi were partners now, and partners always kept each other informed of little developments such as your arch rival taking a bride.

For years, Cavi had been looking for a way to take Raine down; there was simply no way to do it without the evidence pointing directly to him.

Loiacono would have chosen Cavi, his own nephew, as his successor if Raine hadn't been ushered into the syndicate on a favor to a long lost lover.

And also, Cavi admitted grudgingly, *if Raine wasn't so goddamn good at what he does.*

No matter. He'd had been taking notes over the past years, and when the time came, he'd know exactly how to run Imbrialis and the organization - without the spendy MBA to back it up.

Only the opportunity for his victorious overthrow had forever eluded him.

Enter Catello, Mastriani, and Santaglio.

DiStephano's top underbosses leave him in a shocking *coup de grace* that would surely sink what's left of his dying empire. With no successors for DiStephano to name, there would be no DiStephano family - just a power vacuum leaving behind some very profitable strongholds in prostitution, drugs, and gambling. It would be a shame to let all that unclaimed money and power go to waste, but with Raine's white collar taste in crime, the syndicate would never get so much as a sliver of income from that unsavory sector.

Time for a new guard who didn't snub the old school, who recognized cash flow was cash flow, simple as that.

As for the three traitors from DiStephano's camp, they would surely present an eventual problem for the syndicate. From personal experience, Cavi knew firsthand what it felt like to go from first in line to inherit to a lesser status within the hierarchy. There was no way in hell those three would settle to work as peons under Raine after running the bloody show for DiStephano. It spelled a power struggle in the ranks down the road, and that was a contingency Cavi wasn't leaving to chance.

A plan was born.

Cavi had managed to arrange an audience with DiStephano, not only to tell him about his underbosses' treacherous walk-out, but also present himself as a potential successor to the aging don. Now they had a mutually beneficial reason to take Raine out, and if they succeeded, DiStephano and Cavi would rule the City of New York, equal partners in two administrations that would join in the ultimate merger and acquisition.

How?

They simply had to put contracts on Catello, Mastriani, and Santaglio, and then frame Raine for the murders.

Blind with rage, DiStephano had gladly ordered the hits on the men who'd walked out on the family, and as Cavi's first act of fealty, the don had given the assignment to Cavi himself to execute.

The question remained, how the hell would Cavi explain their deaths to Raine? These three bastards decide to defect and wind up dead two days later? Too coincidental.

Besides, Cavi and Anesini were the only others who knew about Raine's negotiations with them - it could only get to DiStephano through one of them. If Cavi planted it on Anesini, that would make Raine suspect him as well, and he couldn't risk being under that microscope.

So the only thing he could do is pin it on someone else. It ended up being two underlings he'd picked at random from the rank and file of the syndicate - a couple of package boys who worshipped the ground Raine walked on. He just said they'd somehow managed to intercept the intelligence and fed it to DiStephano for a handsome chunk of dough, and so they devised the Rome rumor to flush them out.

And wouldn't you know it? Somehow, within hours, it was all over town that Raine was across the pond on business almost a week ahead of schedule. Half the world saw the boss make his cameo at Kane's ball, blowing up that rumor - and his alibi for the contracted hits on Catello, Mastriani, and Santaglio right along with it. Add the orchestrated assassination on the "moles" made to mimic the ones for DiStephano's underbosses, and it wouldn't be long before the feds pinned all five murders on Raine.

That was the irritating part, though. It would have to be a federal matter because Raine had the legal eagles and the law enforcement agencies of the entire City wrapped around his little finger. It would take time for the higher powers to catch on, but it would happen, and DiStephano and Cavi would be the only ones left to gain.

And then, once DiStephano kicked it, Cavi alone would rule the Five Boroughs of New York, and beyond.

He'd have it all, real estate, unions, prostitution, logistics, drugs, waste management, gambling, financial institutions... *everything*.

Then, along came a spider.

At first sight, Cavi had been overjoyed by the presence of a witness in the alley. It would be exactly the thing to get an even swifter indictment against Raine - especially when that witness turned out to be the notorious Solana Trent.

The next second, however, brought the disappointing realization that the woman he stared at was as good as the ground. Dead witnesses can't talk, so he'd resigned himself to the fact he'd have to wait for the original plan to follow through, until the feds caught up with Raine.

But then the situation took a wholly unexpected turn.

Cavi and Anesini knew something was wrong when they didn't hear back from Raine on the night he'd chased the girl down. Or the next day. They could only find out he'd called in the jet for an unscheduled trip from LGA to PHL, and then tracked the flight to the USVI. They had no doubt he'd taken off for St. John, but there wasn't a word about coming to collect a body.

And then that call came in from Raine, and Cavi's life changed forever.

After hanging on every word of the boss's shocking disclosure regarding his plans for the lovely Ms. Trent, Cavi no sooner killed the connection before calling an immediate meeting with DiStephano. Raine's kryptonite had materialized in the form of a five-foot-four journalist with beautiful hair, flashing eyes, and a fire to match, and they needed a plan to capitalize on it.

DiStephano had taken the news with nothing short of glee. Needless to say, there was no love lost on his part for

Trent on account of the blow she'd dealt him with the Preston snafu. Not only would he get to take down the half-breed upstart who'd taken over his turf, he'd also be able to exact a bit of revenge on the little bitch who'd helped make it possible.

And the fact that she was the legendary Last Alessandra?

"Delicious," DiStephano had said. "I'll make a rug out of her hair and put it on the corner of my desk as a carpet for Mathison's skull."

Fuck the feds, it didn't matter now if they figured it out. This was infinitely better. And safer. If those pencil pushers pinned the murders on Raine, they'd start picking into matters too close to home and the cocksuckers might end up taking down the whole East Coast.

Oh yes, this was infinitely better.

When the time was right, once the syndicate's new alliances had some time to solidify, after Kane won the election, and Raine and Anesini secured UniBanca, Cavi and DiStephano would use the girl as a weapon against Raine.

All Cavi had to do was sabotage the fledgling relationship, get her to trust him instead of her own husband, and she'd fall right into his trap, let him lead her right into DiStephano's hands. Cavi knew Raine would hunt down anyone who so much as dared touch a hair on her head, but if all went well, Raine would end up trading himself for her as a hostage.

Of course, the poor man wouldn't know until it was too late that his darling little wife was already dead, well before he'd even arrived to take her place. And then, alas, no one would ever know what happened to him.

The perfect part of the whole thing?

DiStephano takes the blame for the kidnapping and killing of the new Mrs. Mathison and for Raine's subsequent disappearance, while Cavi gets off without a scratch on him. He'll get to play the part of the mourning consigliere, hellbent on avenging the murder of his boss and his pretty bride like the striking hammer of God.

Such was the state of affairs when Cavi watched Raine get on the plane for Rome this morning, knowing that the next time they met, it would be under very different circumstances.

Until then, it was time to do some damage... and Cavi smiled. He'd start with the ravishing woman who was just now bounding up the sidewalk to her building.

The devil she'd been running from this morning wasn't a man. Not anymore. It was her intensifying feelings for that man, and the implications they meant for her. They'd built a bridge together over the past few days, shared something incredible while doing so, and she found herself about to cross that bridge, not knowing for certain whether she'd find him waiting for her on the other side.

Standing, Cavi rose from his perch by the window. He was off to burn that bridge, more than happy to sabotage it until it crashed to the ground in a smoldering, acrid heap of unrecognizable black ash.

ABOUT THE AUTHOR

After earning three degrees, finishing a marathon, and blazing a unique career path, K. W. Keith has taken eighteen years to finish the story she hopes her readers devour in eighteen hours or less. Accountant by day, novelist by night, she lives in New Hampshire with her patient husband and their three hiss-and-vinegar cats. While they wait for her to close the MacBook and give them some attention, she's putting the finishing touches on the second suspenseful installment of the Alessandra Legacy Trilogy: *Equinox.*

www.kwkeith.com
www.pinterest.com/kwkeith/solstice
www.twitter.com@K_W_Keith
www.facebook.com/kwkeithsolstice

Made in the USA
Lexington, KY
10 July 2013